Sinuous Passages

by

D J Walker

Book Three of the Tek & Nika Series

D J Walker
P.O. Box 145
Sloansville, NY 12160
U.S.A.

paperback ISBN 979-8-9888573-0-3
ebook ISBN 979-8-9888573-1-0

January 2024

Tek & Nika Series ~ speaking of shapeshifters ~
Book 1 – Sliver Of Evil
Book 2 – Nika Rising
Book 3 – Sinuous Passages

Cover design credit: The design includes a modified iStock graphic by vinap.

Chapter 1

Book Three begins in colonial times, in the northeastern forests of what is now the United States of America.

The drenching rain, the crash and boom of the storm, made no difference to the spirit bear.

No storm ever touched him.

In the darkness he turned away from the old woman's hut with what he had come for, as well as something he had *not* come for.

He had come for the shapeshifter Tek, and left the hut with the old man, in his lynx shape, clutched to his chest.

But the girl shapeshifter, clinging to the lynx's collar in her owl shape — she came uninvited.

He shrugged off the urge to pluck her from the collar and toss her into the raging storm. Mindful of his own frayed collar, with its trailing lead, he decided to do nothing, for now.

He went three–legged down to the creek and crossed it, continuing up the far slope into the forested hills.

Some distance on, he set Tek down in a small clearing at the top of a hill. Raising himself on his hind legs, he sniffed the air for his bearings.

* * *

Tek settled down beside the spirit bear to wait, safe in its aura from the punishing storm. He owed his existence to this spirit bear: because of him, he was living outside the time and place he had been born into, never knowing why, or how much longer it would continue. But he supposed that since the bear had come for him, his existence was nearly over. *That is alright,* he thought. *I never expected to live forever.*

The brutal drag of age was in his bones. *I am ready for this to end.*

1

But Nika is another matter. She is young — barely fifteen, and the bear did not want her to come with us. The bear made that very clear, back at the hut.

She and I agreed to be inseparable family to each other. Me as grandfather; she as if a granddaughter. Even so . . .

Soon the bear will continue the journey. But it might not be too late for Nika to turn back.

Tek began a low growl, and worked the loose collar up his neck and over his ears and head. As soon as the pieces of flint in the collar were away from him, he was able to shapeshift into a man. It was difficult, aged as he was. It was always difficult for him to shapeshift now.

"Go back," he croaked to Nika as soon as he could speak. "Live out your life here, where you belong."

Nika's large dark owl eyes shone with defiance, as she clung with her talons to the collar on the ground. But the defiance faded to resigned acceptance. Tek's heart nearly broke for her.

At that moment the bear shifted away from them and the storm's howling, savage winds struck them. An enormous talon slashed out of the sky and snatched Tek's collar up and away, with Nika clinging to it.

Tek glimpsed the gigantic black bird and one of its blazing red eyes, as it disappeared into the dark sky. Truly, only a thunder bird could have hooked that collar with such precision and speed.

Abruptly the bear lowered himself and moved away on all fours, still heading toward the higher hills, but in a slightly different direction than before. Tek realized that the bear was not going to carry him any further, so he shapeshifted from man through to buck as quickly as possible, to be able to follow the bear more easily. The bear seemed to move slowly at first, giving him time to catch up. Even so the storm drenched and lashed him until he reached the becalmed area that trailed a short distance behind the bear.

I wonder how Nika is faring, in the full force of this storm, wherever she is.

The pace quickened. He was hard pressed to keep up as they

traveled through myriad stands of trees, thickets and brush in the darkness. The bear stopped now and again to sniff the air and adjust their course. They journeyed up slope and down, but always higher into the hills, until they reached a stand of ancient black spruce.

Leaving the storm behind, they entered a dense mist while going higher, ever more steeply. Before long an enormous wolf came up and kept one pace back along the bear's left side, and a huge panther came huffing through the mist along the right side, also a pace back.

Tek was faltering by then, falling behind. But something came up behind him, and when it reached him he could see that it was a fawn — scentless, as were the bear, wolf and panther. Also like them, it had a loop of old hide rope around its neck, trailing a length of frayed rope that might have once been longer, like a leash.

The fawn nudged Tek, and with that touch, strength returned to his limbs, and he kept pace beside the fawn as they both followed the bear, wolf and panther.

The mist cleared at about the same time that the full light of day came to the sky, and they reached a place where the land sloped upward more steeply than before. There the wolf and panther surged ahead and charged up the slope at a run; the bear lumbered up to it and just kept going, steadily upward, barely slowed by the steeper climb. Tek and the fawn were left to clamber up as best they could.

It was a strenuous climb for Tek, but it was hardest of all for the fawn. Tek in his buck shape could use his longer legs to get over the jumble of rocks and boulders. But the fawn's short, slender legs and small hooves were not made for this kind of climbing. It often picked its way more sideways than upward, searching for a route that it could manage.

Tek was keen to catch up with the bear. He wanted to shapeshift from buck back through man to lynx; as lynx he thought the climb would be easiest for him. *But I will not leave the fawn to do this difficult climb alone.* He shapeshifted to man, to help it as much as he could.

At first the fawn seemed too shy to accept his help, but then it allowed Tek to give it a steadying push up over boulders. Further on it let Tek take hold of the frayed rope around its neck, to help it over rocks that would otherwise have been too large for it to climb.

As they labored upward, Tek thought he knew where this journey was leading. *I suppose we're going to the longhouse of the Good Twin in the Sky World.*

In time immemorial, the Good Twin parlayed with the four wind spirits, and they allowed him to leash their strength, becalming the Below World so that it could be habited by the People. Ever afterward the four of them — the he–bear of the north, the she–wolf of the west, the he–panther of the east and the she–fawn of the south — went together every year or so to the longhouse of the Good Twin, in honor of their agreement.

On the steepest part of the climb, close to the end, Tek took the fawn onto his shoulders and carried it. He was wondering how the fawn ever accomplished the last part of the journey on its own, when he heard someone or something coming down the slope toward them. Soon a burly young man came into sight, but when he saw that Tek was bringing the fawn, with a smile and quick wave he turned and climbed back up ahead of them.

Tek wanted to ask the young man to come back and help him, but he had no breath to spare. At long last, he broke through some clouds, into a large sunlit clearing where a longhouse stood solitary, with its front door open — its hide cover pegged back. Tek set the fawn down and together they entered the longhouse.

It was a council house, built very large — large enough for the four wind spirits to have entered it. At the center, under the main smokehole, was a low fire with an old man seated beside it on a mound of pelts, smoking a long pipe. Beside his place at the fire sat the massive spirit bear, with the colossal wolf seated to his right, and the enormous panther to his left. The fawn took its place on the opposite side of the fire from the man and the bear, while Tek joined the bear.

4

The place was very quiet, except that once Tek was seated he thought he could hear muted voices and other sounds as if, right outside the walls of the council house, there was a large, busy knat that was full of the activities of daily life. He had not seen anything like that when he had arrived, but now he half-heard different sounds — a woman's voice asking a question, a man's shout, the pounding of maize, the clatter of a basket being emptied, the excited laughter of children. The sounds came and went, as if tossed by a fitful wind. The only sound that Tek could hear clearly was the old man quietly drawing on his pipe nearby, inside the council house.

The interior was dim, with harsh light coming in through the open doorway and the smokehole above the fire. The fire gave off a dull glow, modulating the shadows.

Once Tek's eyes adjusted, he did not presume to stare at the old man, but he stole glances at him. The old man gazed fixedly at the fire, and seemed lost in thought. Tek wondered if he was in a trance. The smoke from his pipe distorted what Tek could see of him. Sometimes, through eddying smoke, he seemed to be a much younger man; other times a much older one. Sometimes he seemed about the same size as Tek; other times he seemed as large or larger than the wind spirits. But in Tek's fleeting glimpses, despite the distortions, he thought the man looked quite ordinary. *He must be a lesser chief, and this council house must be a stopover on the journey to the longhouse of the Good Twin.*

Suddenly the light from the smokehole winked, and a moment later the light from the doorway disappeared. A large creature — too large to come inside and smelling strongly of storm ozone, thrust its head and long neck through the doorway. Tek could see, by its long hooked beak, its red flaring eyes, and the pitch black of its feathers, that it was one of the thunder birds.

The bird's fiery eyes snaked through the darkness, exuding a primal cruelty. Tek felt that it looked at him with a savage hunger.

But the bird simply dropped something small inside the council

5

house and withdrew.

The bear nudged Tek; Tek went over and picked up what the bird had dropped.

It was the hide collar that Nika had made for him, for carrying the two pieces of flint.

Once before when Tek had been in the Sky World, he flaked off the two pieces of flint and, not having anything to carry them in, he carried them in his mouth, between his lower jaw and cheek. He lost one of them before he fell from the Sky World, and had only found it recently in the Below World.

Nika had wrapped and knotted strips of hide around both pieces, binding them into the loose collar, so that he could easily carry them whether he was lynx, buck or man.

He had last seen the collar as it was swept into the raging sky with Nika, small and fragile, clinging to it in her owl shape. *And now the collar is here, but Nika isn't. She's been separated from it.* Tek was certain that this did not bode well for her.

Now both pieces of flint, knotted inside the collar, were back in the Sky World, where they had come from. Where they belonged.

He took the collar to the bear. The bear hooked it with one of his long claws and held it out to the old man. Now Tek felt he could look directly at the old man, to observe what would happen to the collar.

The old man set his pipe down and took the collar, examining it, tugging at the tight knots that held the collar together, and bound the flint inside it. He took his time, sometimes gazing off in the distance as his fingers flexed the collar and plied the knots.

The end came quickly. The old man's head came up and he looked eye–to–eye with Tek. Tek knew at once that there was nothing ordinary about him. *This is no lesser chief!*

The eyes of the Good Twin then 'spoke' to Tek. Breath left Tek for the last time, and his earthly existence ended. In his dying moment he prayed to the Good Twin, to go easy on Nika. *Because I cannot be family for her.* He had already guessed that this would be so, but had kept back a thin strand of hope, now snapped.

The snap flicked his last, sad thought away, into the Sky World's rarefied air.

His body fell to the ground, beside the fire pit. Some men of the knat came into the council house and bore his body away to the women, for it to be shrouded for its afterlife journey.

Chapter 2

The Good Twin continued to finger Tek's collar, staring at the fire. Occasionally he turned the collar toward the light to look closely at the knots. Once he smiled a little, but his expression soon grew grave again.

He had given the People life; therefore it was only fitting that they should honor him. But they also sent him supplications, for everything from prowess in their wars, to luck in their most foolish wagers. Most of them would never understand what he knew so well: it was best for them, in matters great and small, that he not meddle in their affairs.

A different kind of supplication, though, had arisen of late. It was a cry for their lost existence — their lost ways, their lost hunting and planting grounds, their lost sense of what they were intended for.

Left to themselves, their essence might die out. They would be absorbed into an amalgam with those of a foreign father — those who had come and taken over the People's lands — their lands in the Below.

The Good Twin had been thinking that perhaps this should be allowed to happen. Even in this matter that was so dire for his People, he was loath to interfere. They must find their own way. And yet . . . his People, thwarted at every turn . . . perhaps they could be given . . . an opportunity . . .

And then there was the matter of that speck of a girl, that owl shapeshifter who had come uninvited. In the World Below she gave honor to him, at times. But she also gave homage to the foreign heavenly father. She was still one of his children, but . . . should anything be done for her? His fingers continued to ply the knots in the collar she had made, for an answer.

No answer came, at least not yet. He twisted the collar into a loose double loop, and slipped it onto his wrist.

* * *

The Sky World never goes full dark, but as its twilight approached the knat prepared itself for the great feast of the four winds. This time it would include special chants and dancing, in honor of the Visitor who had come today with the four winds, from the Below. There would be no mourning rites for him — no one was ever mourned in the Sky World. But his shrouded body lay in a place of honor, beside the Good Twin at the knat's central outdoor fire, open to the upper sky. Tonight, his deeds and character would be extolled during part of the dancing.

That night the great wind dance proved to be exceptional in another way. Besides being heightened by the honor given to the shrouded Visitor, this time the Good Twin joined in the dancing at two critical times, and each time he could be heard chanting as he danced.

Normally the Good Twin did not dance at the feasts, and he rarely chanted. Instead he watched in contented silence with his ancient, knowing eyes.

The first time he danced that evening was near the beginning, while the four wind spirits reenacted their pledge to be guided by him, for the sake of the People of the Below. He grew large and joined them as they wove their winds in a great blur of loops and rolls around the fire, just above the heads of the knat's dancers. He began a whispery chanting.

Everyone kept dancing, but they went quiet in order to hear what they could of his windborne words.

He seemed to be speaking to the People of the Below. He seemed to be reminding them of all he had done for them, as if they no longer knew who he was. He seemed to be exhorting them to return to him, as if they had become lost and scattered. A wonderment passed through the people of the knat, and when the Good Twin resumed his seat, their dancing expressed their wonderment. They did not know why, but they felt that this dance was going to have some exceptional importance, and that they must contribute to its success by dancing their very best.

The second time the Good Twin danced was near the end, not long past the middle of the night, when the dance reached a climax. Usually it was *the* climax of the dance, but this time there was more. The Good Twin rose and seamlessly joined the dancing flow around the fire, and the other dancers responded with ecstatic joy. The beat of the log drums drove like thunder, and the rattles hissed like snakes. The steps quickened until in a blur of movement everyone was dancing as if a single being.

But at nearly the same moment that this idyll was reached, subtly but absolutely, the Good Twin went out of step.

The best dancers worked their way in close to him, absorbing the disparities of his beat and step with their skill and strength. They buffered him, and set a pace for the other dancers to follow.

By their unswerving loyalty, of limitless depth and breadth, the effect was as subtle as a slight waver in a spinning top. The Good Twin went out of time and place from them, without leaving the dance. In the swirl of the dance around him, his far–seeing eyes peered into distances that were normally shrouded.

The sight was never clear, and it often provided more jarring questions, than answers. But he looked very long and very far.

What he saw troubled him. His steps became hesitant. He chanted quietly to himself, often repeating phrases in odd, disjointed patterns.

At length he came to a decision, and though he did not seem to be certain of it, or pleased by it, he firmly chanted the 'It Will Be Done As I Have Decided'. Then he left the dance, and stood by his place at the fire. The dancers continued with steps in place, waiting for a sign from him.

10

The Good Twin gazed at the shrouded body of the Visitor lying beside his place at the fire. He then signaled to the bear spirit. No words were necessary. Though slightly surprised, the bear spirit did as he was bid. After a slight shrug he gave a nod, and a pallet of tightly woven wind slipped under the shrouded Visitor and lifted him into the air.

The Good Twin removed the Visitor's collar that he had earlier wrapped around his own wrist. With a touch of his finger the binding knots loosened around the two pieces of flint, and he removed the smaller one from the collar. With another touch the knots tightened around the larger piece. Then he placed the collar on the breast of the shrouded Visitor, and took a step back.

The knat's dancers had their sign, to resume the dance. A great, unexpected honor was about to be given to the Visitor. Instead of being consumed in a lesser fire on the morrow, his body was going to feed the Sky World's central fire, the most sacred of them all.

The bear spirit moved the levitated Visitor over the fire, where the flames reached hungrily for the body. But the pallet's winds frustrated them until the drumming changed and the dancers shifted flawlessly into the steps for a consummation dance.

The bear spirit dissipated the wind pallet, and the shrouded body descended into the flames.

Fire leapt to devour the corpse, but when it reached the piece of flint in the collar, a mighty battle of elements ensued.

The flint proved to be stronger than the fire. It drew the fire into itself until its strength became enormous and unwieldy. With a blindingly bright, powerful explosion the amalgam shot into the sky. Tek's rising ashes combined with the vaporizing flint, and together they began a formation that would, in a million years, provide a modicum of light and warmth in the vast firmament. A great honor to the Visitor, indeed!

Chapter 3

The cataclysmic explosion at the Central Fire was seen and felt throughout the Sky World. For Nika, far away and under siege in a poplar tree, it was a vivid pulse of brightness, and a seismic jolt in her hiding place. Then all went dark again.

In the following silence and darkness her spirit was lower than she had ever felt it to be. During the past day cycle she had been pummeled, nearly drowned, slashed at, and stalked. And she could expect no better of the coming day. Her nerves throbbed in the wake of terror. In her weakened state at the ebb of night, hope was slipping away like ashes in the wind.

She remembered the last moments of peace she had felt, when in the hut with Tek, Old Phoebe and Ruth, in the Below World. There, despite the storm raging outside, she felt safe with those three particular ones whom, in all the world, she loved, and who loved her. When the spirit bear came for Tek, she clung to Tek's collar in her owl shape, determined to stay with him. But Tek had removed the collar and exhorted her to go back.

She intended to, but before she could release her hold on the collar, it was swept high into the stormy sky by a great shadowy bird.

She instinctively tightened her grip on the collar. As a small owl she could not possibly fly in the violent storm, and if she shapeshifted back into a girl, she would fall from the sky to her death.

At first she did not understand how the gigantic bird was able to stay airborne in the lashing rain and powerful winds. But she came to understand that the bird was part of the storm, and reveled in its fury. Swooping and rolling in the sky, it whipped the storm into an ever greater frenzy.

Another huge dark bird joined the one that had the collar, and the sight of the second bird terrified her — its enormous shadowy form and blazing red eyes showed her the real size and power of the bird that was carrying her! And it wheeled in close, pecking to snatch the collar away from the first bird.

Nika did not know the old stories about the thunder birds. If her father had lived, he would have told her about them, eventually. But he and her mother and little brother had died of the smallpox when she was eight, and in the six years since then she had been a lowly servant — and the only Indian — on a white family's isolated farm. At most she had a vague recollection of her father saying, whenever there was a bad storm, to take cover because some big birds were at work, and bound to cause some trouble somewhere.

She had always imagined the birds as a throng of raucous blackbirds, fretting along the edges of a stormy sky. But *these* huge, malevolent birds — storm birds, as she named them — they were something else entirely.

They flew ever closer to each other in rapid, daring swoops. Their bodies never collided, except in a deliberate sparring with their beaks. Lightning jagged through the sky each time their beaks clashed, and thunder boomed off their great wings.

The second bird never got the collar away from the first one, but Nika was slung and jerked around, battered by the wind, blinded and nearly drowned by sheets of freezing rain. She locked her talons in the collar and somehow held on.

The sparring of the storm birds seemed to go on forever, but eventually the one carrying the collar wheeled upward. With powerful wing strokes it rose above the storm, until it was flying over a vast twilight land, with the second bird in close pursuit.

As an owl shapeshifter Nika had an unerring awareness of altitude. Her world was far, far below, and this place could not possibly be a part of it. She knew just enough, from her father's

13

stories and from what Tek had told her of his journeys, to guess that this might be the Sky World of the Good Twin.

With her superior night vision she could see an enormous forest stretching out below, with some crags in the distance. The two storm birds flew toward the crags and when the lead bird was over a massive slab of rock forming a high tableland, it released the collar. Suddenly Nika was tumbling through the air weighted by collar in her talons. She spread her battered wings to slow her fall, but closed them in the next instant, only too aware that she was an easy target for the second, following bird. Her erratic flap and fall spoiled its eager pass at her — it missed snagging her in its beak by little more than a down feather's breadth.

She fought an urge to spread her wings again, while the two giant birds made rapid swoops at her. She fluttered errantly, whenever one came at her, to make it harder for them to snatch her out of the air.

She never thought for a moment that if she let go of the collar, the two birds would go after it and leave her in peace. *Clearly they want the collar — for the flint in it, I suppose. But I can see all too clearly in their blazing red eyes, that they also want to destroy me.* Whether it was because she had come uninvited, or simply because her existence irked them, she could not know.

The rock slab seemed to rush toward her, but she could not flare out her wings — one of the storm birds was making another pass at her. She avoided its great open beak by somersaulting against the weight of the collar — or perhaps the huge bird had, in its hurry, misjudged the air sink above the cooling slab. She was bounced along the bird's upper beak, past its fiery eye — which singed some of her feathers. She was raked along its coarse neck feathers, scraped over its shoulder and tossed into the turbulence behind its wings.

The turbulence saved her. It spun her sideways, slowing her fall. She hit the slab in a slanting tumble, instead of a straight-down splat.

Dazed, she barely regained her senses before hearing a loud flapping, and feeling pressure in the air above her. The two storm

14

birds were landing close by.

They were like black mountains towering over her. Each cocked a flaming eye at her . . . and at a deep jagged crevice in the rock's surface that was not very far away.

She did not give them time to gauge whether she would make it to the crevice before they got her. She *ran* for it.

Small owls are not thought of as good runners, but they can outrun a mouse in a sprint, if they want it badly enough. And Nika was desperate to get into that crevice. A rush of fear and anger propelled her — fear for her life, and anger at the storm birds' kill lust.

She left the collar behind, knowing it would slow her down.

In her mad dash she fairly skimmed across the slab.

She made it, though not without some loss of feathers and a gouge into her back, from a talon that scrabbled into the crevice after her. Fortunately there was an undercut in the crevice wall, which protected her once she got herself tucked into it.

And there she stayed for the rest of her first twilit night in the Sky World — cold and aching, but safe from the storm birds which, she knew from the occasional rustle of their great noisy wings, did not leave.

Occasionally one of them brought an eye down to peer into the crevice. This was always presaged by a rustle of stiff feathers, and it caused a blaze of lurid red and intense heat in the crevice. Nika became used to it, dozing off and on in snatches, until a thin grey light began to filter down to her niche. She supposed the light meant that dawn had come.

Not long afterward, she heard the unmistakable sounds of both storm birds flying off.

She was wary, in case it was a trick to draw her out. But the storm birds were not built for stealth.

She eased herself out of the crevice.

An early morning sun was shining. Tek's collar was gone, of

15

course. *The storm birds must have taken it with them.*

She limped on her owl legs to the edge of the rock slab, where the breeze teased her bedraggled feathers. Below her, for as far as she could see, was a vast forest. A distant river running through it looked like a silver thread.

Surely, she thought, *I'll be safer from the storm birds if I can get down into that forest. And Tek might be down there, as well as some food and better shelter.* After taking a careful look and listen for danger, she gave her wings a cautious stretch and stepped off the rock edge.

And nearly died in a plummeting fall.

It was agony to keep her wings spread for a downward glide. They were so battered from the storm and from being wedged in the crevice.

She lost altitude more quickly as she got closer to the trees, and was soon falling more than gliding.

Somehow she steered enough to reach the top branches of a massive pine, which flexed as she scrabbled for a hold on their long thin needles. Then she slid, bounced and flapped a long way down through a myriad of boughs, until she landed on a blessedly thick layer of pine needles coating the forest floor.

And the first thing she saw there was . . . another crevice! It was a narrow vertical wedge in the trunk of the pine.

She skittered into it for protection, and found that it was filled with pine needles, and housed a small mouse family. All of the mice got away except one. She dined on it and then burrowed down into the needles for warmth. Feeling safe at last, she gave herself up to a rejuvenating rest.

* * *

She awoke from a dream in which the crevice in the pine was much larger, and she was living in it happily with Tek. But then in the dream the swooping storm birds came and set the pine tree ablaze with their fiery eyes. Scrambling out of the crevice and out of her dream, she was relieved to find that the pine was *not* on fire. But the

16

crevice was small again and Tek was not there with her.

There was the smell of cooking smoke though, wafting through the forest.

I'll follow the smoke. It might lead me to Tek, or to someone who could help me find him.

Her wings were too sore for flying, so she shapeshifted to her girl form to cover more distance walking. As a girl she hurt more though, and without her feathers her bare body was chilled. Shafts of sunlight were weak and few under the massive trees.

She heard the rustlings of small animals and forest birds, and saw a number of deer in the distance. As she travelled she kept watch for places to hide, either as a girl or an owl, in case a predator came after her.

Gradually she found that she was following a deer trail, which led to a small sunlit clearing. There she rested and absorbed some of the sun's warmth, while trying to decide which of two paths to take, that led off on the other side of the clearing. One was wider and looked more travelled; the other was barely visible.

She chose the wider path.

The scent of smoke grew stronger, and soon it was heavily laced with delicious fragrances of cooking food— venison, among other kinds of meat, and a number of different maize and root breads. Her mouth watered and her nose fairly quivered. Before long she saw a clearing up ahead, but remembering what Tek had told her of his experiences in the Sky World, she approached it with caution.

There was a bark shelter at the center of the clearing, with a lot of meat roasting on a large fire in front of it. *That meat is not being smoked or dried for storage,* Nika thought, *so whoever is cooking all that food must be expecting many dinner guests.* The area was quiet, but the thought of people streaming toward the clearing made her nervous. She shapeshifted to owl and hid herself in a laurel bush.

A young woman came out of the shelter and bent over the roasting meat, humming to herself as she expertly turned it. She was dressed for a feast but even if she had been in rags, she was still the most beautiful woman that Nika had ever seen. And she seemed to radiate a personality that was as beautiful as her looks. Nika felt a surge of eagerness to go right up to her and speak to her. *Surely she will be kind and help me,* Nika thought. *Then everything will be alright.*

But Nika did not quite trust the way those lovely thoughts nudged at her to hurry into the clearing.

The woman's humming filled the air; all other sounds receded. There was a numbing, lulling lure to it, and it nearly snared Nika. But her hearing was not only exceedingly sharp, it was also perceptive. She became aware of a slight falseness in the humming voice. Once that aroused her suspicions, she began to hear and see other jarring details. The woman's humming had a strange hollowness, and her tunic did not have a natural suppleness. Suddenly Nika was convinced that everything she was seeing and hearing was wrong, all wrong. Instead of wanting to approach the woman, she wanted to get away as fast as possible!

She also sensed trickery, and she guessed that the woman knew that she — or that someone— was close by. The woman was trying to get her to cross over an invisible threshold by entering the clearing. *And if I cross that threshold,* Nika thought, *I will be within her power and, at the very least, I'll have to do her biding.*

The woman seemed to realize that her humming was not going to draw Nika out. She stopped it abruptly and went back into the shelter. Nika felt sure that the woman was going to devise another trap for her, so she immediately left the bush and started back down the path as fast as she could go, on her little owl legs. *I'll stay in my owl shape to be less conspicuous, until I get further away.*

It wasn't long before she heard someone or something following her rapidly on the path — *It's the woman from the clearing, probably. And there's someone or something approaching on the path from the other direction — someone or something large and heavy, from the sound of it.*

She flitted off the path, and got herself hidden in the low

branches of a nearby spruce, just in time to see the woman reach the place where she had left the path. The woman paused there for a moment, and Nika got a glimpse of her. *She does not look nearly so young or beautiful as before, and now she's carrying a large wooden hoop.*

The woman continued down the path, and not much further along she stopped. Nika could not see her through the trees and bushes, but it sounded like she had met whoever or whatever was coming the other way on the path.

Nika then heard two voices raised in argument. The woman spoke in a true voice, which crackled with anger, age and spite. And the man — Nika could not see him but she supposed he was a very large man — he boomed back at the woman, snarling and grunting out loud, harsh words.

Nika did not recognize many of their words. But from those that she could understand, she gathered that the man was ordering the woman to get back to her work of preparing his meal.

The woman insisted that she had something to do first.

The man roared back that his meal was more important. He threatened her with something —something about darkness — *maybe a tunnel or cave*, Nika thought.

The woman spat back that what she wanted to do wouldn't take long, and that she'd tell him about it later.

He demanded that she tell him right away, or he would stop her from going.

She muttered something, and then said sourly that he had probably ruined everything anyway. And something about having likely missed the place.

The argument got more heated, less coherent. Past grudges were hurled back and forth. Burnt food. Undercooked food. Inept hunting. Lazy bones. Being held captive. A lot about filth. Slop.

The raging argument ended when, with a snort of disgust, the woman turned back, and Nika watched from where she was hidden, to see what she could of her and the man as they went by on the

19

path. She caught a glimpse of the woman's stormcloud face as she strode past — it matched the voice exactly. Harsh and unforgiving, taut with fury. And — a frisson of terror coursed through Nika — in its true form, the woman's visage was decidedly hawk–like!

When the man passed, Nika could not see much more than a massive shape with huge shiny whitish scales, as if the man was half–carrying, half–dragging the skin of a giant snake.

A stench came from the direction of the path. It was sour, off–putting — like meat going bad.

Nika waited for the forest to go quiet. Then she waited longer, just in case. At last she hopped off the spruce branch and cautiously made her way back toward the path.

It was more cumbersome to walk as an owl, but she stayed in her owl form to have her best possible sight and hearing.

That was why she saw the woman's hoop, floating in the air over the place where she had left the path. The hoop had looked dark and heavy when she glimpsed it earlier, in the woman's hands. Now it was nearly invisible — gossamer thin and translucent.

The woman must have left it there on her way back, Nika thought. *And if I step back onto the path there, could it fall on me, like a trap, and hold me prisoner for the woman?*

How could the woman have known to put the hoop in that spot? she wondered. *And if she knew where I left the path, then why didn't she find where I was hiding, so very close by?*

She thought back to the last clearing, before she had taken this path. *If it's a magical path, maybe it can 'tell' the woman things, but only about the path itself. If that's so, then the woman left the hoop where the path 'told' her that I had gone off it, in case I returned by the same route — as prey is likely to do. As I was, in fact, about to do!*

She backed away from the path, shapeshifted to girl and struck out in another direction, away from the path.

It was later, when she was in a marshy area picking some sour berries, that a snap in the breeze seemed to speak to her, of Tek's regret that he and she could not be family together. A dread settled upon her that Tek had died. *This was what I feared, when the spirit bear came for him.*

Nearly certain that she was now alone and friendless in the vast, inhospitable Sky World, she knelt and offered her prayers for the safe journey of Tek's spirit.

Chapter 4

For a while Nika continued her journey in the same direction as before. Then she began to look for a tree hollow to spend the night in.

She found several old pines with likely hollows, but remembering her recent dream about being in a pine that was on fire, she passed them by. She pressed on until she found a gnarled yellow poplar in a stand of hemlocks. Unlike the tall straight hemlocks that surrounded it, its trunk twisted upward in an uneven spiral. The lower half of the trunk had a number of hollows, from cavities that formed where branches had broken off. The upper half had some large branches spreading upward and outward. Overall the tree looked strong and healthy to Nika. She also remembered that, in wood lore, forest poplars were said to be slow to catch fire.

She shapeshifted to owl, and used her beak and talons to climb the long ropey ridges of bark, sometimes making short awkward flits with her sore wings. She rejected the first hollow she came to as too low. The second one had a feisty raccoon in it. The third housed a colony of bats that were beginning to stir for the evening. The next one, nearly half way up the tree, was vacant. She scrabbled and flapped her way into it. She would have felt safer if it was smaller, but it had a seam of punky wood at the top. She pecked at the spongy wood, and dug at it with her talons, until she had a niche carved out for herself above the hollow's opening.

The twilight of this world came. For a short while she rested.

Then came a vibration through the ground, and a crashing and rustling among the trees. The vibration grew more pronounced and the noise louder. Something was coming through the woods toward the poplar.

Her hollow faced the direction it was coming from. As it got closer its approach was marked by a creaking and moaning among the higher tree branches, and from lower down came the sound of branches snapping, and the crackle of underbrush being crushed.

A giant snake slid out from under the hemlocks, its whitish scales glinting in the twilight. A woman came out beside it, carrying a large hoop. It was the woman who had tried to ensnare Nika earlier that day! Nika guessed that she was now in her true form — no longer young, with a face that was sour and haggard, and distinctly hawk–like.

The snake circled the poplar and then its head rose until it was level with the lowest of the tree's hollows. Its tongue flicked inside, but finding nothing of interest there it wound its way up to the next hollow, which was on the same side of the tree as Nika's.

Nika heard the chittering of the raccoon ensconced there. Then as she watched, the snake's head pulled back and it spat into the hollow at the raccoon. The chittering stopped abruptly, and the snake deftly flicked the raccoon out of the hollow with its tongue. The raccoon's body was limp, but its eyes bulged with terror. It fell to the ground, where the woman caught it up in her hoop.

At the third hollow the snake ignored the colony of bats.

At the fourth it found Nika.

She had just scuttled into the niche she had made, in the top of the hollow, when the snake's tongue flicked into the hollow. It tickled the tips of her tail feathers, which protruded slightly from the niche.

She felt the tree creak and quiver, and guessed from the sound of scales rasping on bark that the snake continued up the tree to examine the rest of it.

Soon it was back.

The tongue came in and tickled her feather tips again. This time an array of images flooded her mind, of an extremely handsome,

23

virile man. He was richly dressed, and his soft, wooing 'voice' proclaimed his total, burning love for her.

He 'said', *I have the greatest possible fondness for women who can shapeshift into owls. You in particular are beautiful like no other woman could possibly be. Come out to me, and you will have a life of bliss. There will always be plenty for you — whatever and however much you want. I will make others do all of your work for you. You need only come out to me, for all of the joy and wonder of your life with me to begin.'*

Nika did not believe it one jot.

An ordinary girl or woman might have found it too beguiling to resist. But to Nika's owl sight, the conjured imagery was fissured with falseness, and her sharp owl ears heard off notes of cloying sweetness in the murmuring voice.

I'll stay put, she decided.

The air became charged with a potent silence that first held an element of surprise, and then danger.

The snake wound itself back down the tree.

But it did not go away.

Nika quietly backed out of her niche. There was an unpleasant fragrance in the air. *He's trying to hide that stench of soured meat,* she thought.

She peered cautiously outside. The snake was flattening the trees closest to the poplar, and looping itself around the tree's base. Its head was tilted to look up at her, which gave her a jolt of fear until she remembered that a snake's eyesight was not very good. *Probably,* she thought, *it can only see larger movements, that don't blend in.*

She returned to her niche and quietly clawed and pecked at the punky wood above her, to elongate it. *This is just what a mouse would feel, trying to be less conspicuous to its enemies . . . enemies like owls . . . enemies like me.*

When she had extended the niche to several times her own length, she broke through the bottom of a hollow above hers, which faced out on the opposite side of the tree.

She was still examining it when one of the storm birds arrived.

How did it know to come here? she wondered. *How could it find me —
one small owl in this huge forest?* But as a bird of prey herself, she
realized, *It probably follows the giant snake, to snatch away its prey, if it can..*

As the storm bird circled overhead, the snake uncoiled itself and
slithered away.

The storm bird's feet crashed down amongst the hemlocks, as if
the massive boughs were mere stalks of meadow grass. Its long neck
brushed along the tree tops and then its head plunged down to the
poplar where Nika was.

Nika backed herself halfway down the vertical tunnel she had
made. She then guessed, from the noise of the bird's movements, *It is
circling the tree to examine each of the tree's hollows, like the snake did.*

The hole in the floor of the upper hollow could not be seen from
outside it, but from her hiding place Nika saw a red glow when the
storm bird's eye was at the upper hollow. There was a surge of a hot
air and, to her horror, some of her tiny bedraggled head feathers
loosened and floated up into the hollow. The red glare intensified. *It
knows,* Nika thought. *It's sure now, that I'm inside the tree.*

The storm bird widened the circle of trampled hemlocks around
the poplar. Before long, the poplar stood alone in a broad circle of
shattered, strewn hemlocks.

Why doesn't it knock down the poplar, as it did the hemlocks? Nika
wondered. *It never actually touches the poplar.*

But that did not stop it from trying to set the poplar on fire with
its pyrolytic eyes.

It concentrated on her upper hollow, and on the thick branches
rising just above it. She backed further down her narrow tunnel from
searing heat, and she heard the snap and sizzle as leaves, bark and
wood scorched.

It's trying to panic me into flying from the tree. The owl part of her
nature was keen to flee. But her human part fought back. *If I leave the
tree I'll be an easy target. I'm safer where I am.*

25

The tree's leaves shriveled and some smaller branches took fire, but the tree as a whole did not ignite. Inside her tunnel, Nika soon realized why. The walls became moist; and she could hear water trickling up through the core of the tree, drawn to the warmth of the fire. The tree was a veritable water wick!

But, she wondered, *how much longer can it hold out against the storm bird's fire?*

There was a quickening in the heavy rattling noises that the bird's feathers made as it circled the tree. Nika heard more fire crackle, and felt a lot more heat.

The poplar groaned as the fire consumed its water. *The storm bird must know that the poplar is getting close to igniting. It's using its wings to fan the wood to flame.*

But that was when a shudder roared through the earth, and a brief, brilliant light strobed, leaving no darkness anywhere. Absolutely everything seemed to pause, shocked from the ordinary by the strange, potent phenomena.

In the moments afterward the storm bird remained still, and Nika stayed put. This was her low point when, wan and weary, she longed for the Below World, where she had last felt safe and secure.

But the past is swept away. Even if I could get back there, Tek would not be there with me.

Then came the distinctive sound of the storm bird's huge neck feathers shuffling as it craned its head up, as if trying to see or hear something far away.

The next thing Nika heard was the noise of the storm bird taking wing.

It is leaving! But what could have caused it to go? And . . . will it be back?

She cautiously peered out of her lower hollow. It was still the twilight of night here, but dawn could not be far off. Worriedly she hoped that neither the storm bird nor the giant snake would pursue her during the day.

The storm bird did not return.

But at dawn, Nika heard the giant snake coming long before she saw it. Then it poked its pale head out from between two hemlocks at the edge of the enlarged clearing around the poplar.

It began to enter the clearing but recoiled suddenly, darting its tongue and shifting its head, as if trying to get a better 'taste' of something beyond the poplar, on the other side of the clearing.

The woman with the hoop came up beside the snake's head, and looked up at Nika with malevolence. But she did not advance toward the poplar either.

Nika scrambled up through her tunnel to her upper hollow. Even before she looked out, a soft breeze caressed her disordered feathers like a touch of kindness — the first she had felt in the Sky World.

Chapter 5

Peeping cautiously over the bottom edge of the upper hollow, Nika saw a fawn at the far edge of the clearing. It was trailing a short frayed rope from a loop around its neck, and there was something folded and tucked under the loop.

Then, from the forest behind the fawn, came Tek's spirit, in his man shape.

Nika knew it was his spirit, rather than Tek himself, though she did not know why she could see his spirit. Later she learned that shapeshifters, when they are in their animal shape, can see the spirits of the People's dead, as they journey to their afterlife.

Tek's spirit took the folded bundle from the fawn's neck and clambered toward the poplar through the jumble of flattened hemlocks. He was old and bent in form, but he moved easily now. It seemed to Nika that he sometimes leapt through the shattered branches with the agility of a deer buck, or balanced on the fallen trunks with the grace of a lynx.

At the base of the poplar he unfolded the bundle, which was some kind of hide pouch. He opened it wide and held it up, beckoning for her to come down to it.

Unhesitatingly, she did.

Her wings were still strained. She plummeted in a barely controlled fall.

But the pouch seemed to reach up, and it enveloped her in a soft cushion of safety and protection.

* * *

On that day in another part of the Sky World, the Central Fire was allowed to burn out. Usually this only happened once a year, but

28

this time was an exception.

When the fire pit was cold, the Good Twin took a handful of the ashes and journeyed long and far, to one of the edges of the vast Sky World. There he released the ashes, invoking the wellbeing of the People of the Below, and exhorting them to save themselves from their own passing.

Most of the airborne particles fell hither and yon, to no appreciable effect. But one — just one — lodged itself in the earth of the Below, and eventually it nourished a fruiting plant that in time, provided an answer sought by a singular man, one Joseph Pigean, in the year 2069. Thus was another crucial pivot in the fate of the People.

* * *

Nika journeyed in the Sky World with Tek's spirit and the fawn for two full days. She slept through the first day and night while being carried in the pouch, which was soft and warm.

Early on the morning of the second day, Tek set the pouch down and the fawn touched its nose to Nika's owl head. Nika felt a wonderful rejuvenation — not completely well and healed, but very much better.

Tek's spirit beckoned to her; she shapeshifted to girl to follow him.

In the Below World — in Nika's world — a shapeshifter can only see a journeying death spirit when the shapeshifter is in an animal shape. But here in the Sky World, as a girl Nika could still see his spirit, as a wavery outline.

She longed to converse with Tek's spirit and the fawn, but they turned away whenever she tried to. Thus she realized that they could not, or would not, communicate with her, unless it had something to do with the journey, and for that they always used gestures.

They passed through a beautiful forest. Unlike the forest she traversed the preceding day, this one was dappled with sunlight, and filled with warm breezes and birdsong. It was home to many forest

29

creatures, though all of them kept a distance from the three travelers.

The fawn led; Nika kept pace behind it with Tek's spirit. They paused only for Nika to forage now and again.

Nika talked to Tek's spirit even though he could not — or would not — respond. Politely, she looked straight ahead as she spoke, or off into the forest, to indicate that a response was not necessary or expected.

She gave him an account of what had happened to her after they were separated in the Below World, soon after leaving Phoebe's hut with the spirit bear. She spoke slowly, with long careful pauses, choosing each word and phrase with painstaking care. At one point, she explained, "I've been thinking about how false the giant snake and his woman are. I do not want my account to have anything false about it."

The spirit and the fawn never showed any reaction — except once. When she described how the snake's tickling tongue had failed to entice her to come out to him, up ahead the fawn gave a sudden little leap and kick, and Tek's spirit fleetingly bent over with head down and hands on knees — almost as if they both thought it an excellent joke!

When the twilight came they stopped near a place where Nika could forage. Tek's spirit gestured for her to build a fire, and the three of them sat comfortably but silently around it. Nika felt completely safe. By now she understood that nothing in the forest was going to disturb *this* fawn, or anyone or anything travelling with it.

Weary from the day's journey Nika shapeshifted to owl, to sleep more warmly in fluffed feathers, rather than having naught but bare skin — scraped and singed skin, at that. She nestled down beside Tek's spirit, which sat quite still. But unlike the time in the Below World, when as a lynx he kept her warm with his body and fur, he could give her no warmth now, as a spirit.

In the morning they did not go far before reaching a path that led out of the forest. Before them a meadow sloped down to a stream, and near the center of the meadow stood a bark shelter with a few small trees nearby, and smoke rising from the shelter's smoke hole.

Tek's spirit pointed to Nika and then pointed to the bark shelter. And the fawn nudged her in that direction. Clearly, they wanted her to go down there, but they were not going with her.

"Let me stay with you!" she cried. But they gazed back at her blankly.

She peered at the meadow more closely. It seemed a pleasant sort of place — but so had the snake's lair, at first.

She turned back to the fawn and Tek's spirit, but they had already left and were far down the path they had come on, and nearly out of sight.

She hurried after them. *I'm sure they brought me here for a good reason, but I want to be with them. It hurts to lose Tek again, and I miss the fawn's protection, and nurture.*

Her steps slowed, and then stopped. *Even if I catch up with them, they will not — or cannot — accept me. My journey with them is over.*

But that doesn't mean I have to go down into that meadow. At least, not quite yet.

The forest was suddenly much colder than it had been. *I'll shapeshift to owl, for warmth and to try my wings. And perhaps I'll catch a mouse or shrew, if I can find one slow enough.*

She turned on the path, to look and listen for small rustling creatures in the brush, and found that there was an old woman standing on the path, close enough to touch her! *And close enough to grab me,* she thought with fear.

But the woman did not seem interested in getting any kind of hold over Nika. Instead she examined Nika minutely, from the top of her tousled head to her bare, dirty toes with their torn and broken nails. No detail seemed unworthy of her avid inspection.

Such an intense examination would have been off–putting, if the woman's gaze was not so intelligent, and generous. In fact, as Nika

31

watched the old woman's eyes travel all over her, she thought she had never seen such kind eyes before.

Nika thought that at some point the woman would look directly into her own eyes, but though she came close to it, she never did.

When at length the woman completed her study of Nika, she simply turned on the path and headed toward the meadow.

Immediately an icy wind buffeted Nika's bare back, and a few snowflakes came from nowhere to swirl past her nose.

At about a dozen paces the woman turned and faced Nika once more. "Come, Nika," she said, before continuing on her way to the meadow.

I wish it could be that simple, Nika thought, *to go with this woman who seems kind and somehow knows my name.* But a jumble of fears held her back — fear of this Sky World without the protection of the fawn and Tek's spirit, fear of falseness and trickery, fear of ever more painful losses.

As she stood shivering, uncertain, the woman dropped something on the path.

A vivid memory came to her, from six years past. Her mother had dropped her comb in just such a way. Nika remembered running to pick it up, and how her mother's face lit up when she gave it to her, so pleased, because she had not realized that she had dropped it. It was her favorite comb, nicely cut from fine-grained maple wood, though it was missing three teeth four over from one end — Nika's baby brother had broken them off when he had teethed on it.

The comb's loss and Nika's recovery of it happened on their first day in a river town of the white people, where Nika's father hoped to find some trail or river work. Losing a comb in such a place would have been a total loss. Nika's sharp eyes had kept that from happening.

But then it all came to naught. Within a few days they were all down with the smallpox, which only Nika survived, pocked with it for life.

When she recovered, she was a ward of the town until she was indentured. She owned only a plain coarse dress, given to her by the town. Her family's belongings were gone, taken to offset the costs of their illness and deaths.

Nika shook herself out of those memories, and ran to pick up what the woman had dropped.

It was a nicely made comb, with three teeth missing four over from one end. Nika's fingers trembled as she felt the wood around the gap, for the marks of her baby brother's teeth.

She caught up with the woman in the meadow, just beyond where the path left the forest, and gave her the comb she had dropped.

The old woman smiled, and thanked her for bringing the comb to her.

Nika then followed the woman to her shelter in the meadow, without fear, and relieved to leave the unnatural chill of the forest behind.

Chapter 6

Later Nika was not sure how long she stayed with the old woman in the meadow. She notched sticks to keep track of the days, but the sticks would disappear from where she left them. Sometimes she found them later on, other times she never saw them again. She tried notching a tree branch, but sometimes when she went to add a notch there were fewer notches than she remembered, or more.

She was certain she spent at least a year there, because she had memories from all four seasons. Though when she tried to trace her recollections from one season to the next, they slipped past each other like eels in a trap. She was never able to recall them in a definite order.

Eventually she concluded that time had no meaning in the Sky World. What was important was to live in harmony with the Meadow Woman, as Nika always thought of her — though when speaking with her, she called her 'Auntie'.

As Nika became accustomed to living with the Meadow Woman, she wished for nothing more than to stay with her, for always. She was at peace, willing to work for her place, and wanted nothing.

On her first day the woman took her around and with a few words indicated how the essential work of the place was done. She gave Nika a plain tunic made of softened deer hide, and showed her where she could wash up.

Over the next several days, the woman tended to Nika's injuries with salves and healing prayers. The gash in her back that had been paining her, no longer hurt. The sprains and tears in her muscles and ligaments were soothed and got noticeably better each day. The roughened skin where she had been singed became smooth again.

Meadow Woman used few words. Nika was not familiar with some of them, but before long she understood most of what the woman said, and not only used the words herself but also tried to speak them in the same way.

The woman was strong, spry and quite independent, but she accepted Nika's help and seemed to appreciate her efforts to work with her. Together they gathered foods from the meadow, streams and forest. They planted and tended edible and useful plants. Nika learned to cook and preserve the foods and medicines according to the Meadow Woman's ways, and to make many useful things, along with the proper prayers of thanks to offer for the bounty.

She also learned a number of simple chant–like tunes that the woman sang under her breath while she worked. Nika often sang along with her quietly, and also found herself singing them — or ones she made up for herself — when they were not working together. The words were repetitions of old prayer fragments, not making much sense, but lightening the tedium of the work, making it go faster.

Now and again a particular call would sound across the meadow, and they would go to the forest edge, where they would find a freshly slain deer that had been left for them. They prayed over it and, depending on the size of it, they either cut it up there or dragged it down to the shelter. They harvested every usable part of the deer. Under the woman's tutelage Nika became proficient at making soft hides from the pelts.

In most ways the Meadow Woman was the teacher and Nika the pupil. But in one way Nika felt that she contributed something that the woman did not already have.

The Meadow Woman often had difficulty settling down to her rest at night. She would fidget and toss and turn, quietly tsk–ing or sighing in frustration. Remembering a flute that she had watched father make when she was a child, Nika searched along the edges of the forest for a likely bush with soft pith — something like an elderberry. When she found one, she cut off several straight branch lengths and, after drying them by the fire, she reamed out the pith. She cut some holes along the lengths, testing the sounds until she had a few flutes that made pleasing sequences of notes.

It was difficult to get any sound from such simple flutes, especially the one she made for a range of lower notes. But the Meadow Woman seemed to hear the promise of soothing tonals in Nika's whispery, breathy efforts. She made no objection to Nika's playing, and it improved over time.

At evening after all else was done, Nika would sit on her bedding mat and play her flutes. As her playing got better, it pleased her to notice that, most of the time, the Meadow Woman's restless fidgeting would lessen. Her breathing would slow as the flute's cadences wove through the air.

Nika based many of her tunes on the chant sequences, but also came up with her own variations, suggested by the flute's frequent off–notes, which Nika caught up and worked into her tunes, or by the wind and the chirrum of animal calls and noises. She snatched them up into her music, or played against them for contrast.

There was one melody though — a particular series of low tonals — that Nika learned to never play around the Meadow Woman, and then to never play at all. Instead of soothing the Meadow Woman, the first — and only — time Nika played it for her, the Meadow Woman got up and paced restlessly, drawing so close to Nika that she crowded Nika's elbows as she circled in an odd little step and hop dance. It was a melody that Nika rather liked, especially when the notes were low pitched. It often ran through her mind. But, *I must only play it when out of the Meadow Woman's hearing,* she resolved.

For a long while she did not have a chance to do that. When she did go off on her own one afternoon, the melody reverberated and amplified itself, which at first intrigued Nika. But it put her into a trance–like state. She could see her fingers playing the flute and feel her breath feeding its voice. But it was as if someone else took control of her hands, and gave each note a weight and significance that she could not fathom.

She heard two distinct voices in the flute's music, and then two more, but all four voices clashed out of time with each other. The sky darkened and a storm brewed up. Winds came in from all directions and carried the four voices strongly and smoothly past each other in a swaying weave of flowing air. Rapidly the wind's force increased. The airy weaving tightened, and an urgent power built. Suddenly in place of a low quiet melody there was something with serious potential to aid or destroy, depending perhaps on something so slight as whether a swirl in one of the voices would be supported or crossed by the others.

Nika instinctively feared having anything to do with a power so arbitrary. She worked to regain control over her fingers and breath, by fixing her mind on it and then forcing her fingers and breath to segue into a different melody. Note by note she moved away from the potent melody toward a safer one. Note by note the wind calmed, the voices quieted, and the sky lightened.

When she stopped playing she sat listening to the sounds around her, for any traces of the wild music. Animals that had drawn near her wandered off, and everything seemed normal again.

She ran her fingers along the holes of her flute, and in the quiet she decided to never play that particular melody again. It raised something that she did not feel she should be involved in. *I will have to enjoy this particular melody only as something that runs through my mind,* she thought.

Her playing continued to improve, until now and again everything seemed to align to create something exceptionally fine. All would mesh — her skill, the night air, the interwoven sounds from outside, and the caress of the notes inside the shelter — so that the music seemed magical. It was then, in her fancy, as if she split into two, with one of her selves rising to look around and discover who was actually playing. But all that her floating self ever saw was her

37

other self below. Her floating self would try to remember the playing, so her other self would be able to use the recollection to improve her playing afterward. And these special trances often did actually improve her regular playing.

At times she imagined that while she was 'split in two', her floating self would go up and away until, in a dreamlike way, it was sitting in a large dark council house, across a low fire from an old man sitting on a mound of pelts. She played her flute, and he smoked his long pipe, staring into the fire. For some reason she could not explain she always felt compelled to look into the fire too — never at his face.

Nika always thought that the 'splitting into two' was completely imaginary — just two parts of her mind busily engaged at the same time. But then one evening, when her floating self was coming back down to rejoin her other self, she saw that the Meadow Woman's eyes were open and seemed to be thoughtfully following the slow, spiraling descent. Only when the two selves settled into one, did the Meadow Woman close her eyes and turn her head away.

*　*　*

The Meadow Woman was Nika's ideal of a companionable, motherly friend. Nika admired her, and copied many of her mannerisms and turns of phrase. And she tried very hard to please her.

There were only three things about the Meadow Woman that Nika thought were a little odd.

In all their time together, the Meadow Woman would never look directly at Nika, eye to eye.

And then sometimes in the evening at the fire, the smoke and heat would distort what Nika could see of the Meadow Woman, until she looked like a much younger woman, or a much older one. Or through the smoke Meadow Woman would seem much larger — far too large to be comfortably inside the shelter.

The third odd thing involved the Meadow Woman's 'not–

lessons' about the magic of the place.

She would gather some objects and herbs and say, with a quiet emphasis, "You must not watch, or listen. This *cannot* be taught to you." But then she signaled that she actually wanted Nika to pay close attention. And as soon as she was done, she placed the objects and herbs in front of Nika, and pretended to be occupied doing something else, all the while — as Nika learned — expecting Nika to take them up and repeat what she had seen and heard.

When Nika tried it, she would not always get it right the first time or two. Then the woman would engage in a series of tongue clicks and 'ah–ah–ah's' to guide Nika toward the correct result, or she would repeat the entire 'not–lesson' more slowly and with emphasis on the parts that Nika had trouble with. With the former, she would sound almost comical, like a chipmunk fussily chittering. But Nika never laughed, because Meadow Woman always took these 'not–lessons' very seriously.

None of the 'not–lessons' seemed particularly valuable to Nika — in fact at times she thought they were more trouble than doing things in the usual, unmagical way. And at times they were unsettling. There was for instance the matter of the hoop snare.

The Meadow Woman and Nika set a variety of normal snares for small animals and ground birds. Their drop snares and loop snares were easy to set and usually worked quite well. But Meadow Woman persisted in 'not teaching' Nika about the making of a *magical* hoop snare.

It was a small hoop left across a channel made in the leaf litter of the forest, or in the grass of the meadow, with some herbs crushed and sprinkled along the channel in a particular way while chanting. Nika did not understand how it could possibly snare any animal. And the words that the Meadow Woman crooned over the hoop and the herbs were not a prayer of thanksgiving for the sustenance — instead they sounded to Nika like a nonsensical jumble of lulling words and phrases.

39

But then the snare always worked beautifully, at least when the Meadow Woman set it. The first time, a fat hare was found the next morning where the Meadow Woman had set the snare. It sat there with the hoop hanging loose around its neck. Nika wondered, *Why doesn't it toss the hoop off and hop away?* But it seemed unable to move. The Meadow Woman picked it up, removed the hoop, and snapped its neck. She then tossed the hoop and a bag of herbs to Nika, and, after chanting a prayer of thanks for the hare, knelt on the ground a short distance away to gut and skin it.

Though the Meadow Woman's seemed to be concentrating on the hare, it was clear to Nika that she was expected to set the snare. She went through it, while the Meadow Woman tsked and 'ah–ah'd' correctives.

The hardest part for Nika was the crooning, because the words made so little sense. It was only when she thought that it might not be the words so much as the repetition of syrupy ululations and lulling cadences, that she got on with it better. Only then did the Meadow Woman's tongue clicking and sighs lessen, and eventually go quiet.

The next morning Nika found that her hoop snare had worked. But there was only a small shrew in it, and it had died of fright before she got to it.

Nika did not like those hoop snares. *They are so potent — too potent for fair hunting,* she thought. And, she learned to her dismay, that their potency was irreversible.

She once found a very young raccoon in the snare, and decided to let it go. But when she removed the hoop from its neck, it not only failed to run away, it shivered and followed Nika as if it did not want to, but could not help itself.

Its potency and the hoop shape also reminded Nika of the larger, heavier hoop that the snake's woman had used to try to entrap her. It was no wonder that Nika greatly preferred the ordinary, unmagical snares, to this one!

40

But in her indirect way the Meadow Woman was especially insistent that Nika master the hoop snare. To please her, Nika worked conscientiously to improve her hoop snares until the Meadow Woman seemed to be satisfied with them. Hers were never as good as the Meadow Woman's, but they sometimes caught a small animal that if not plump, was at least meaty enough, or useful in some other way.

Chapter 7

One day in the fall when the call sounded across the meadow —
which meant that a slain deer had been left for them at the forest
edge — the Meadow Woman's lap was overflowing with squash pulp
and seeds that she was sorting. Nika offered to go and get the deer.
The woman hesitated a moment, and then nodded.

About half way there, Nika felt a restless itch in her shoulders,
which could only be relieved by shapeshifting to owl and using her
wings. It had been a while since she had last gone to owl. She slipped
out of her tunic and leggings, and flew the rest of the way.

The day was fine and the air delightfully buoyant. She had no fear
of hawks here — she had never seen even the shadow of one over
this meadow. She indulged in some fanciful flight, pirouetting up into
the sky, diving in a tight twist, and then soaring sideways in a curling
spin.

All the while she was trending toward her destination. She
spotted the deer stretched out on the ground, and looped down
toward it in a fast roll.

When nearly there, she spied a grasshopper swinging on a tall
grass spike — a perfect, tasty morsel. With a quick angling of her
wing, it was hers.

She landed beside the deer and was still in her owl form, still
gulping down the grasshopper, when a pair of hands seized her from
behind!

How could anyone sneak up on me here?! she wondered, more
surprised than afraid. Despite the distraction of going after the
grasshopper, she *had* been alert for danger before landing beside the
deer. *That* was inborn caution. But even so, hands clasped her

loosely, but firmly.

The hands lifted her and flipped her over. The person attached to the hands — an old man who seemed vaguely familiar — looked her over. His face was deeply lined, and Nika thought it must normally be a very grave visage. But now his features were softened; he seemed to be amused about something. And Nika realized that she must have looked very silly — or just plain crazy — flitting and looping over the meadow. She guessed that might be part of his amusement . . . *but the rest of it,* she thought, *is that he's rather pleased with himself, for catching me unawares.*

She kept herself very still, hoping to lull him into relaxing his hold. But he shook his head slowly, as if to say, 'That will never work with me.'

With a fingernail, he flicked away the grasshopper femur that was sticking out from between her beak's upper and lower mandibles. Then after saying, "Tell my grandmother that I am coming," he tossed her into the sky, and bent down to pick up the deer.

Nika flew straight back to her clothes and then ran in her girl form to the Meadow Woman to deliver her grandson's message.

When the man arrived with the deer, Nika could see that, though grandmother and grandson barely greeted each other, both were pleased about his visit. And clearly, it was a special occasion. The woman took greater interest than usual in every detail of preparing the meal. She bustled about much more avidly. She asked Nika to bring out the best that she had for her grandson to sit on and to eat with. She herself chose the cuts of fresh venison and prepared them for cooking.

Nika adopted the woman's keenness as her own. She was her ready assistant, and she also undertook her separate work in the meal preparations with heightened care and attention.

While they worked together the man sat under a small fruit tree near the shelter, smoking his long pipe and looking off into the distance. He seemed relaxed and abstracted; he didn't seem to be paying any attention to his grandmother or Nika. All the same, Nika had a feeling that he wasn't missing much of what was going on around him.

When the meal was nearly ready, in the late afternoon, the woman sent Nika away to the far end of the meadow, to gather some anise hyssop blooms for a condiment. When she returned, the grandmother and grandson were sitting together under the tree, talking.

They stopped talking as soon as she arrived.

It seemed to her that both of them were watching her surreptitiously after that, as if they were trying to assess something about her, or — perhaps — come to a decision about her. But they gave no hint of what they were thinking until, near the end of the meal, the woman asked Nika to tell them about her other spirit father.

Nika had never mentioned her mother's Christian religion to the woman, but somehow she and her grandson knew about it.

"My only spirit father is the Good Twin of the Sky World," Nika told them. Both the Meadow Woman and her grandson nodded solemnly at that, but their gaze seemed doubting.

"When my mother was a child," Nika explained, "she was taught by one of the white sachems — ministers, they are called — and by his wife. They taught her their beliefs and the language of their people — including some of the markings for it, and they were also very kind to her, in times of trouble. They protected her. Later my mother taught me, as she had been taught."

Neither the woman nor her grandson spoke, so Nika continued. "It seemed for the best, to learn the white people's ways, because they were taking over everywhere. And it did help me to have their religion when my family died, and I was a servant among them.

"But then after being a servant for six years, three things happened at about the same time, that changed my thinking forever.

"I was badly injured when I tried to save the life of one of their

44

animals. Perhaps I should not have attempted it. But it caused me to see that . . . well, that nearly everything about my masters was wrong for me.

"That was also when I became able to change into an owl. When I am owl, my connection to everything else is so much clearer to me. And that stays with me when I am a person. Shapeshifting led me back to the ways of the People.

"But most important of all, I came to know Tek, and through him I began to understand things about myself and my people, that I had not understood before.

"Tek showed me what it could be like, to fully be one of the People."

Nika's voice grew firm. "The heavenly father of the whites can never be my spirit father. And though I honor my mother's memory, I do not believe she would want me to be a Christian, if she knew what I know now."

Neither grandmother nor grandson looked at each other or at her, but Nika got the impression that some understanding passed between them. They seemed to know each other so well, that they could communicate without speaking.

They were on the other side of the fire, gazing at it, and Nika's view of them was distorted by the smoke and the heat rising above the flames. Sometimes their faces looked kind — the woman's especially, but in the next instant they looked remote. *And they seem to change in age, as I've noticed before with the woman.* That thought brought to mind one of the other odd things about the woman, which was true of her grandson as well — *neither of them ever look at me directly, eye to eye.*

It seemed to Nika that their faces were becoming more grave, which made her uneasy. *Perhaps it is only my imagination, but I think they've withdrawn from me.* It was not unlike when Tek's spirit and the fawn brought her to the Meadow Woman, and then went away without her.

45

She kept her face still, but internally she sighed. *Well, if it must be so, then I do not mind the grandson so much, because I have only just met him. But I am so very fond of his grandmother, my Auntie, my Meadow Woman . . .*

With these unsettling thoughts, Nika's eyes were drawn to gaze at the fire as well, and this soon had a calming effect on her — not by soothing away the fears, but by helping her choose to accept the decisions of the Meadow Woman and her grandson, as bravely as she could manage.

I will not cry. I will not beg — though she did *wish* she could plead with the Meadow Woman to let her stay here with her. But that would betray her fears . . . *and I do not know yet, whether I actually have anything to fear. All I have are feelings, which could mislead me, and impressions, which could be wrong.*

But . . . if my feelings, impressions are correct . . . there is something I want to say to them, before it is . . . too late.

She bowed her head toward the Meadow Woman and her grandson and told them that all she had learned, while living here in this meadow with her revered Auntie, had strengthened her resolve to stay true to her one and only spirit father, the Good Twin, who had done so much for the People — for her people. She thanked her Auntie for teaching her so much about the ways that should guide her in her life, especially for the words of the prayers — words with which to express her gratitude.

A heavy silence met her words.

Dusk gathered around them. The woman roused first from her contemplation of the fire. She got up slowly and a little unsteadily. Nika scrambled up and went to her, to give her the aid of her arm.

The woman turned away from her grandson to take hold of Nika's arm, and with her back to her grandson she gathered Nika's hands into her own and pressed them in a gesture that Nika hoped was meant to reassure her.

The woman then sighed and handed Nika one of the gum–lined water baskets. Nika understood that she was being asked to fetch

46

some water. The woman often asked her thus, by simply handing her the basket, to bring some fresh water from the nearby spring.

The spring water trickled out of a split in a large low boulder, into a rock–lined pool. Always before the pool had been placid and just deep enough for Nika to fully immerse her basket. But this evening the water in the pool sloshed and rippled.

When Nika dipped the basket into the pool, there was an unexpected tug on it, as if it was caught in a current. She tightened her grip, and was immediately yanked into the pool with it!

Extremely cold water enveloped her. The pool was dark and much deeper than she had ever thought it could be. She let go of the basket and struck out with her arms and legs to get back up to the surface.

She did get her head above the water but was only able to gasp in a lungful of air before something tightened around one of the ankles and pulled her back under.

She reached down to free her ankle, but whatever held it felt like a thick slimy rope, too tight for her to pull loose. She grabbed her short knife from her belt and tried to cut through whatever it was, but it was tough and sinewy, and she was pulled deeper and deeper.

Her need for air was urgent, so she freed her ankle by shapeshifting to owl, and used her wings to fight her way out of her sodden clothes and up through the water.

But as she got clear of her clothes everything went upside down — or at least that was what it felt like. The cold dark water dropped away, dissolving into a heavy rain. She was falling with icy rain through freezing cold air.

A wild harsh wind forced her to tuck herself into a ball to protect her wings from being wrenched and perhaps snapped.

Her feathers were soaked and though the weight made her fall faster, she sensed that she was still very high up . . . and then she understood what had happened.

She was falling from the Sky World.

Down, down she fell until she bounced soggily on a broad dark surface. She rolled and flopped off that like a soggy little ball, and was falling again when, in the light of a sudden red blaze that rippled past her, she saw that she was going to bounce off another broad dark surface that was below her, and that it was made of huge black feathers. It was the wing of one of the two thunder birds, as she now knew was their true name.

* * *

The two masters of storm could have sliced the small she—owl in two with their beaks, or ripped her to shreds with their talons. Falling as she was, she was powerless to prevent it.

But the Good Twin had not given them leave to kill her — at least, not intentionally. In their beak—clashing skirmishes, which flashed shards of lightning and sent thunder bumping off their wings, they swiftly banked and rolled under each other, catching the owl each time on their wings as if it was a hide ball in a rough game of toss.

When they judged they had done enough to ease the owl's way down to the Below, they stopped catching her on their wings, leaving her to be blown about in the sky and to fall from it where she would.

But because her presence in the Sky World had irked them, they left a mark of their pique in the Below.

They dove toward a forest beside a large lake, cupping the wind under their wings. The wind fought back but its only path for escape was through a channel of air so powerful that it snapped and scattered a swath of forest trees in the thunder birds' wake, and whipped the lake into a seething maelstrom.

Chapter 8

Down Nika fell, into the lake. As soon as she realized that she had again plunged into cold, dark water she shapeshifted to girl and fought with all her strength to reach the surface.

She gulped in some air when she did reach it, but high, wild waves crashed over her, forcing her back under.

She would have drowned if she not collided with a tree that had been uprooted and blown into the lake by the thunder birds' savage wind tunnel. The tree — a huge maple, had lopsided branches; the side with the heavier branches stayed below the water, serving as a keel, while the lighter side bobbed lclear of the water.

Nika climbed onto the tree and wrapped her legs around the branches, keeping as much of her body above the rocking, tossing water as she could. The lashing rain and driving wind was cold, but the water of the lake was very much colder.

The storm's wind and rain seemed to go on forever. There were times when Nika did not think that she could hold on to the tree much longer. But as the wind gradually subsided she was able to relax her hold, relying more on balance than muscle strength to keep herself on the bobbing tree.

The rain fell in heavy sheets, blurring all of a dark world around her.

At about the same time that a greyness began to replace the darkness, the tree lurched and shuddered to a stop. It had beached itself on the edge of the lake, but it rocked as if it might work itself loose. Nika moved along the upper branches toward the land and saw, through curtains of rain, that the tree was in an expanse of marsh rushes. The maple's leaves and the rushes had the look of early fall—well past the saturated green of summer. She climbed down into the rushes and swam–sloughed through them.

The rain let up enough for her to see a muzzy grey–green horizontal band far in the distance. It was the start of a raw day with relentless rain. Exhausted and shivering, she stayed as a girl. *I can't fly as an owl in this heavy rain, and wet feathers will give me no warmth,* she thought. *If that greenish band beyond the marsh turns out to be trees, I'll find a hollow there to get out of this cold.*

The cold was already dulling her mind as much as it was stiffening her limbs. She stumbled onto a muddy path that headed in the direction she wanted to go, and hurried along it gratefully. *Moving faster, I can fight the cold better.*

Other paths crisscrossed the one she was following; then her path widened as it skirted a large pond.

Near the center of the pond was a large grassy mound — a beaver lodge. As she took a path veering away from the pond, behind her she heard the distinctive smack of a beaver tail on the pond water.

Through the rain, which was diminishing but still drenching, she could see a few other grassy mounds, and the blurry horizontal band in the distance was looking more like the trees she had been hoping for.

Behind her the beaver continued to rap out its warning, signaling other beavers to hide while a stranger — herself — was passing through. *I'll inconvenience them as briefly as possible,* she thought. *They have nothing to fear from me.* A shiver rattled her teeth; she pushed herself to go faster along the path.

A large beaver stepped onto the path ahead of her. It sat on its hind legs and watched as she came to a stop in front of it. Another beaver joined it and then a third. Soon there were eight of them, all looking directly at her as they chattered and gurgled rapidly to each other. Then they all came toward her and herded her in the direction they wanted her to go. Some of them pushed at her legs with their front paws, to direct her, and hurry her. They were intent and determined.

I'll go along with them, Nika thought, *since they're pushing me in the direction I want to go anyway.* Soon she was hurrying along again, only pausing where two paths crossed to see which one the beavers wanted her to take. Some of them ran out ahead so that she would know which way they wanted her to go.

They didn't crowd her as much, when they saw that she was cooperating with them. But it was in her mind all along — *When the rain slackens some more I'll be able to shapeshift to owl and fly away from them, if I have to.*

The paths wove through the marshy land, skirting wetter areas. They were all beaver paths, Nika realized — marsh grasses beaten down into mud by the beavers' frequent passage.

The rain did slacken slightly, but it was still pelting down when they reached the beavers' destination. It was a structure set incongruously in the marsh, with plain grey walls under a long curving roof with broad eaves. But it didn't seem to have any openings — neither windows nor doors.

The beavers closed in around Nika and herded her to a side of the structure where there was an indentation in the wall, in the shape of a long vertical rectangle with rounded corners. One of the beavers patted the wall there and some small lights flickered across the indentation. Then the wall inside the rectangle dissolved, and the beaver went through the gap. The beavers behind Nika grunted and pushed at the backs and sides of her legs for her to follow the lead beaver in. But she was already following it because as soon as the wall dissolved Nika felt warmth emanating from the rectangle, and she was in desperate need of that warmth.

The wall solidified behind her as soon as she was inside. It was a dim lit area with a ramp leading upward. The silence in the space surprised her — she could no longer hear the rain outside at all.

The beaver that went in ahead of her was halfway up the ramp, chattering for her to follow. When she did not, it came back and pushed at her legs, making more insistent noises. It was not asking — it was *telling* her to go up that ramp.

She went, in part because it got warmer as she went further up, but also because she was not as afraid of the unknown here, in her own world, as she had been when on her own in the Sky World. *At least,* she supposed, *I must be in the Below World now because . . . where else could this be? Though . . . these beavers are very odd, and this structure is unlike anything I've ever seen . . . but this **has** to be the Below World . . . doesn't it?*

It was more than she could bear, to think that she might not be in the Below World. *It just **has** to be. With no thunder birds, no giant snakes, no magic hoops — surely, I can cope with just about **anything** in the Below World.*

It was warmer in here than outside, but a violent shiver racked Nika, that rapidly became continuous. Her mind went blank; she stumbled and fell onto all fours. But the beaver urgently pushed at her until she was crawling up the ramp. Her mind was getting too dull for her to be sure, but she thought the beaver nipped her, in its determination to keep her moving up that ramp. She spoke to it, though her tongue struggled to form the words, saying that there was no need to push, she was going as fast as she could.

The ramp led to another vertical rectangle in a wall. The beaver rapidly patted the indentation when they reached it, and the rectangle dissolved. Nika crawled into a brightly lit room that was *really* warm. The air below on the ramp had only seemed warm to her, compared to the cold outside.

She crouched just inside the room, woozy from the suddenness of plentiful warmth. But she was still shivering. The beaver reappeared beside her with a blanket in its teeth. She wrapped the blanket around herself clumsily. It was very light and soft, and slippery; its fabric seemed to mold itself to her like a second skin.

She swayed with an intense weariness, and was about to pass out. Struggling for some understanding of her surroundings before she collapsed, she could not make much sense of what she saw and heard.

The room had walls and a ceiling that seemed to be made entirely of the finest glass. The air was still, warm and quiet, but she could see everything that was going on outside — the windblown rain pelting the sodden marsh, the masses of dark clouds lowering overhead.

There were a few tables and low seats in the room, all made of some substance that she could see through.

There were two beavers in the room — the one that had come in with her, and another that was nearly twice as large and fat as the biggest beaver she had ever seen.

It was a she–beaver, sitting back in a low, see–through seat that looked like it was floating in the air. This beaver had a gold ring in her nose, and a severe expression on her face.

She patted grumpily at a thin brown rectangle that was set within easy reach of her front paws. The image of a hare suddenly appeared in the air between her and Nika. It looked real, but Nika noticed that it was semi–transparent.

A deep, gruff voice came from the corner of the brown rectangle, speaking a single word in a questioning tone. When Nika looked blank another word was said, and then another, until Nika recognized the word, "What?" and she replied faintly, "Oh. It's a hare."

A dozen more images then appeared rapidly, one after another, with the word, "What?" being repeated for each one. Nika, her head drooping with weariness, gamely tried to give the name for each image that she recognized.

The beaver then divided her attention between glancing over at Nika where she sat on the floor, and patting at her thin rectangle. There was no sound in the room except the faint scratch of her paws on the rectangle until, with a meaningful look at Nika the beaver slapped the rectangle's surface one last time with a flourish, and the disembodied voice said, "So. Here you are at last."

The other beaver came up quietly beside Nika with a cushion in its teeth. Nika's eyes crossed, and when she keeled over she tried to land with her head on the cushion. Because of the beaver's deft twitch of the cushion, she succeeded.

Chapter 9

Nika faded in and out of consciousness, overall preferring the latter to being aware of her surroundings. She was warm, it was quiet. For the time being, that was all she wanted.

In her more conscious moments, she wrestled with the first waves of a profound disappointment. *I was happy in the Sky World with Meadow Woman. I worked hard to earn and keep my place there, and wanted so much to stay. Why did she and her grandson reject me? It's like parting with Tek all over again.*

But no, she realized, *losing Tek was worse. Even in our short time together, he was like kin to me.*

I spent more time with Meadow Woman, but — I always knew — she never allowed it to be more than companionable. I am sad to lose them both, but it is Tek's loss that still empties me.

Later, belabored into more consciousness, she was aware that she cried out for Tek. *How I wish I could sit beside him again. How I wish I could hear the deep growly purr that he made when, in his lynx shape, he tried to soothe me.* With her mind in a swirl of memory, she began to recall that purring rather vividly . . . *almost as if it is real.* And then she realized . . . *it **is** real! I **am** hearing it again!*

Her eyes popped open, and there was Tek in his lynx shape, looking down at her, purring away with his face only inches from hers.

But no, this can't be Tek. And wishing will not make it so. It was a strange coincidence, but by her quick perception she knew this was a different lynx. It had none of Tek's deep scarring, and its head was larger and more fleshed out than his had been. The markings of its face were also different, and had a slightly darker coloration.

55

It was obvious to the e–lynx that the young woman was unhappy about something. She was wrapped in a nest of blankets on the floor of Honcho Beaver's pod, and had been quietly moaning and mumbling. She mumbled something that sounded like 'Auntie' a few times, and then she clearly said 'Tek' in a pained tone, as if this was something lost and gone, and greatly missed. It seemed rather sad to the e–lynx, so he tried to comfort her by purring her into a more restful state.

But the young woman's eyes flew open and she gawked at him. "Tek!" she said again, and this time it was as if she thought it was his name.

He shook his head slowly, and began scratching at his keyb, which was beside him on the floor. Before long an assured man's voice 'spoke' from its corner, "I am Pani, and you are in Honcho Beaver's home."

"That's me," came from the keyb of the fat she–beaver seated in the nearly invisible seat.

Pani continued to 'say' to the young woman, "When you are ready we'll talk. But are you thirsty, or hungry now? We have broth."

The young woman nodded, her eyes wide with amazement. "Broth, please," she croaked.

* * *

Nika watched as Pani turned to Honcho Beaver, who made some passes on her brown rectangle. A dark round hole appeared in the view of the marsh to one side of Nika, and a thick bowl floated out of it and over to her.

She sat up but just stared at the bowl floating in front of her, until Pani 'spoke' to her using his rectangle, "Hold out your hands for it." When she did so, Honcho Beaver scratched some more on her brown rectangle, and the bowl advanced and then descended onto Nika's upturned palms.

Steam rose from the bowl's contents and smelled wonderful to

56

Nika. It was a thick broth full of soft little chunks and lumps that looked like they might be bits of liver and perhaps some tongue meat. She lifted the bowl to her nose and inhaled gratefully, before putting her mouth to the bowl edge and taking a sip.

The broth's taste fully matched its aroma. "Oh, this is *so* good. Thank you!"

Looking up from the bowl, she found that both Pani and Honcho Beaver were looking down at their rectangles, which before long she learned were keybs. Then their gazes returned to watching her solemnly, very much as if *she* was the oddest imaginable creature in this place, instead of *them*.

Pani asked Nika her name, quite casually, while she was still drinking the broth. That at least was a question that was easy to answer.

Nika replied and then asked a question of her own. "What are these walls and the ceiling made of?"

The sun was out and Nika could see clouds scudding across a bright blue sky outside of Honcho Beaver's home, while the marsh rushes swayed in a direction opposite to the reeds in the slower wind closer to the ground. With her keen eyesight Nika could see the marsh's teeming life. Birds flew overhead and down among the reed stalks, most of them in pursuit of insects. A beaver's back could be glimpsed as it moved along one of the muddy trails. Beyond the marsh was a broad fringe of trees in the distance in one direction, and a long flat greyness that was the lake in another.

Nika had thought at first that the walls and ceiling were made of enormous sheets of a very fine glass — for how else would she be able to see the full sky and the marshland that surrounded them, as if she was outside, instead of in a warm, quiet room? But as far as she knew, even a small, imperfect square of glass was a luxury. So how could it be that a *beaver* would have a home with walls and ceiling made entirely of the precious substance?

And, Nika pondered, how could a steaming bowl of broth come

57

in from the outside, through glass?

Pani, who had been watching Nika look around, used his keyb to answer her question. "The walls and ceilings are made of a solid substance called qwunk. It is a black or grey color when the projections — the images — are turned off. Reach over beside you, slowly, just beyond the floor you are sitting on, and you will see what I mean."

Nika gingerly did as Pani suggested, and as her fingers hovered over the edge of the dark, plain floor she felt a slight resistance that she was able to push her fingers through. Beyond it was a soft surface that gave a little bit to her touch. Where her fingers pressed into it, grey dimples appeared at each fingertip — dark voids in what she could see of the marsh reeds outside.

"These are actual images, Nika," Pani continued, "of what is happening outside of the pod. The sounds are turned down, but they can be amplified. Will you show her, Honcho B?"

With a slap and stroke across Honcho B's rectangle the sounds of the marshland rose quickly and filled the room — myriad bird calls and the rush of wind through the marsh grasses. For a short while the volume increased beyond what Nika thought was normal, and then they went back down to a muted level.

"You have never been in a shelter like this. Have you, Nika?" Pani asked.

Nika knew that Pani and Honcho were going to start questioning her in earnest soon, and she had not yet decided how much she should reveal about herself. But this, at least, was another easy question. She could not convincingly pretend to be even remotely familiar with a place like this. She answered with a quiet 'no', and noticed that, even before she answered, Pani was already scratching and tapping away on his keyb, as if her answer only confirmed what he already knew. When the voice came from his keyb again it said, "Then you will not know that there are several other rooms in this structure. And there is one such room that we think you should know how to find on your own. It is called the dirt room. Follow me, and as we go, watch for the small orange squares on the edges of the floor."

Pani pressed something on his keyb, and it rose and followed him as he led Nika to a particular place on a wall, which flashed tiny lights and dissolved, leaving an opening for them to pass through. As they went through it Nika noticed a pair of small orange squares on the edge of the floor that marked where the opening had appeared.

The wall reformed behind them, and Nika realized that, based on the shape of the floor, they were in a narrow curving walkway. Even here, all around them was an unobstructed view of the surrounding marshland and the sky above it. Pani acted as if it was all quite ordinary, but Nika wondered whether this was magic, or an invention far beyond her imagining. Her mind was boggling, and that was *before* she became acquainted with the dirt room.

There were pairs of small orange squares on the floor of the walkway, ranged along its sides. Pani stopped between one pair, and when the wall dissolved, he used his keyb to say, "Welcome to the year 2572, Nika," and then introduced her to the concept and the workings of what he called a typical indoor toileting facility — though he apologized for it, explaining that it was one of the older models. It did not have nearly as many choices of airing fragrances as the newer models.

Nika had to take a great mental leap in order to grasp what Pani was telling her. Just the idea of not going outside to relieve herself was unsettling. All she had ever known, was that only babies, and those who were very sick or dying, were allowed to relieve themselves indoors.

She then had to vault another mental chasm to accept that all she had to do was stand or sit in a certain area in the room, bare between her waist and her knees, and let the sensors and devices whisk away her leavings and clean her up — though the whisking was so efficient that hardly any cleaning was necessary.

59

Before Pani left Nika alone to obtain relief in the dirt room, he assured her that everything in the room was what he called "ultra sanitary".

He then added, in a seemingly casual way, "It is private in the dirt room, Nika. But just about everywhere else inside and around this pod is always recorded, both images and sounds. These recordings are not always reviewed, but they . . . exist. We call it "surveillance", and what that means is, 'no privacy'.

Chapter 10

Nika spent longer in the dirt room than she needed to — not because she was fascinated by the outlandish sensors and devices, or to enjoy the dozens of airing fragrances. It was because she needed some time to herself to think.

Pani had told her that it was the year 2572!

If years were being measured in the same way she was familiar with . . . was it possible that she had fallen from the Sky World into a time that was *eight hundred years* beyond the time she had been born into?

Tek travelled far into the future after his time in the Sky World. Have I done so too? But when Tek did it, he passed from youth to aged man, missing the prime of life . . . looking down at herself Nika was relieved to see that her skin and limbs did not look aged. And though her mind felt old and bemused, she did not feel the actual weight of age on her bones . . .

Tek nearly died from terrible wounds when he was still a young man — he may have actually died — and then he was healed by a spirit bear — or brought back to life. Perhaps something in that was what aged him?

*Both Tek and I have been to the Sky World . . . but there are differences in what happened to us there. The first time he was there, some words were hurled after him for freeing a caged bear . . . had that been a curse? And he brought back some flint from there, while when I left I brought nothing with me, except memories. Possibly **that** was an important part of the difference . . .*

2572 . . . I wonder if Tek felt something like I do now, when he returned to the Below World and found himself in my times, instead of the time he had been born into, long before the whites came and took over. What a struggle it must have been for him to believe what his senses told him, and all that I tried to

61

explain to him . . . what a struggle to adjust to the enormous changes all around him . . .

His being there changed the course of my life . . . was it happenstance? Or was there some reason that he came through time and was there with me — for me?

And now here I am, in a radically changed Below World . . . not knowing whether it is happenstance, or there is a reason for it . . .

She shifted on what Pani had called the 'floating throne'. It had molded itself to her body and was very comfortable.

Eight hundred years . . . I am sure that Pani stated the year 2572 on purpose.

It was one of several 'cues' that he gave me, as if he knows quite well that I am ignorant about things that are common and ordinary here. That seems generous to me, as was his comforting purring.

Honcho Beaver . . . she is not as friendly, but even so, she did not interfere with anything that Pani 'said'.

I think I could like them both.

There is much about them that seems strange to me, but nothing strikes me as false or cruel. I do not think that either of them would deliberately hurt me. They seem intelligent, considerate and trustworthy.

But . . . she sighed. *I should hold back, and find out as much as possible, before revealing myself. There is so much I don't know about them, and this world they live in.*

There are some marvelous things about it, like those invisible walls and ceilings that they call qwunk. But there are disturbing things, like what Pani 'said' about there being no privacy except in this small room . . . and there's the fact that I have not seen any people around here yet. I wonder . . . are there any of the People left?

* * *

"So what family do you belong to, Nika, and where did you come from?" Pani asked her when she returned to the room where they were waiting for her. It was a perfectly natural question, and one that she had been expecting. But she was still not sure how to answer it.

62

"I don't suppose you would be willing to accept that I have no family, and that I just happened to be passing through, when I got, um, a little lost?"

Pani looked politely blank.

Honcho Beaver snorted.

"What I have said is true," Nika maintained, "though I admit it is not very informative."

Honcho Beaver bestirred herself to slap and scratch at her keyb. Her gestures were brusque, and her frown as she concentrated deepened the fat rolls in her face and neck, above the large furred mound that was her seated body. Nika was looking at her and thinking, *she really is a magnificent–looking beaver*, when in a quick glance she seemed to read Nika's thoughts. She growled deep in her throat, though her expression seemed to soften into a pleased smirk.

But when she 'spoke', her tone was curt and grumpy. "Don't treat us stupid! We took samples of you. Know things. Know you do NOT" — with much added volume and depth to the voice for that word — "belong here. Your language — your biology — hundreds of years out of order — all WRONG for now."

She continued, "I speak simple. Your language — some same as ours but old. OLD. Differences, and no words in it for things now. New words I put in — like 'samples'. Ever hear 'samples' before?"

"No," replied Nika uneasily. "But . . . the way you used the word — is it something you have taken from me? I did not —"

Pani hastened to reassure her. "It is nothing bad — just a bit of your sweat from the back of your hand, and a small amount of the air from your exhaled breath. We can use those things to learn a lot about you — about whether you are ill, and some things about you and your family — at least in general, in your case. But to properly explain . . . if you could tell us when and where you were born, so that we will know . . . where to begin?"

"First could you tell me . . . do all animals live like this now," Nika asked, indicating Honcho Beaver's home, "and can they talk to me like you can, with those, um, those flat —"

"Keybs," Pani supplied. "No, Nika. Most animals live outside in the wilderness, as I suppose you are used to them doing, and they cannot use keybs to talk as we do. Honcho Beaver and I are different. We were not born in the usual way. We were birthed in a laboratory long ago, by some humans of the Nation. I am an e–lynx, and Honcho, an e–beaver. We can think like the humans, and we can use keybs to talk with them and with each other. But they stopped making creatures like us, and gradually we have been dying out. There are not many of us left.

"So that is who *we* are. And you . . . ?" Pani then prompted.

But Pani had said something about humans. "Are there any of the People around here?" Nika asked. "Or . . . anyone else?"

There was a profound silence while Pani and Honcho Beaver exchanged a series of odd little glances. Nika had noticed this before: they seemed able to communicate certain things that way, without having to use their keybs.

At length Pani responded, "There are some of what you call the People in the area, Nika. Not many, close in. We will take you to them, at the right time. Perhaps soon. But there are things you should know first, that we will try to explain. And now . . . you are . . .?"

Nika was almost ready to trust them, at least for now. But she wanted to keep secret that she could shapeshift to owl. *If they try to keep me here against my will, I could escape by shapeshifting when they are not expecting it. But . . . they know things . . . what if they already know my secret?*

She closed her eyes, and then looked up into the sky and across the marshlands. "If I want to leave this house, will I be free to go?" she asked quietly.

After some more exchanged glances, Pani replied, "Neither of us would stop you if you insist on leaving here. But we urge you to stay for a while, until you understand better when and where you are."

A gruff 't'cha' erupted from Honcho Beaver. Both of her paws slapped and scratched at her keyb until it piped up testily, "Too nice–nice, Pani!" And then, "You Nika — you Riddle Girl you — VERY DANGEROUS for you out there, until you know better. Now! No more stalling! Family?! Where from?! WHEN from?!"

With a measured look, Nika told them, "I was born into the Peace Tree People about 1730, to the best that I know. My mother was bear clan; my father wolf. They and my little brother died of the smallpox when I was eight. Because I had no other family, I had to work for a white family for six years after that. When I . . . left there I went to . . . another place, that I know of as the Sky World, of the Good Twin. I am not sure how long I was there — perhaps a few years? But then I . . . I fell from there, to . . . here."

Nika wondered, *How can they possibly believe that I was born over 800 years ago? And that I have lived in and then fell from the Sky World? Would **I** believe it, if it was told to me by someone else —but I believed Tek. I'll take some comfort from that.*

For a while Pani and Honcho Beaver were completely engrossed in looking at and scratching on their keybs. Nika glanced over at Pani's, and for the first time she got a fairly good look at it. The keyb had an inner glow, and on its surface she could see floating boxes with strings of words in them, and stacks of numbers and images, that Pani was rapidly re–arranging with his paws.

Pani noticed Nika watching him. With most of his attention still on the floating boxes, he made his keyb 'say', "When you speak we can see your words in our keybs, translated into our language, and annotated." Nika leaned closer to watch, since Pani did not seem to mind. She did not recognize any of the words she saw, but she wanted to. "I can read and write some English words," she said. "But I have never before seen the words for a language of the People."

An exchange of information had begun.

*   *   *

At the outset Nika asked them to 'say' something in her language, and then to 'say' the same thing in their own language, so that she could hear the differences. She hoped, if the two versions were not too dissimilar, that she might pick up their language without too much trouble.

Pani chose something he called the ritual 'Deer Prayer', for thanking a slain deer for giving up its life for the benefit of the People. But Nika could not hide her puzzled amazement when she heard Pani's keyb 'say' the Prayer in Nika's language. Noticing this, Pani suggested that they reverse the process: he asked Nika to say something in her own language, and then the keyb would translate it and 'speak' it in the modern language.

"This is the Deer Prayer that I know," Nika replied. She closed her eyes and softly chanted the short, simple Prayer she had learned from the Meadow Woman, recalling the last slain deer she had prayed over in the Sky World, and thinking of the meaning of its life, and its death. When she opened her eyes at the end, both Pani and Honcho Beaver were staring avidly at their keybs. They seemed engrossed in what they were looking at.

Pani then glanced over at Nika and before long he 'said', "That seems so much more right." Then with a swipe of his paw, Pani's keyb began to 'chant' Nika's Deer Prayer using the words of the modern language . . . in what sounded to Nika something like . . . her own voice!

Nika listened, shocked by and somewhat fearful of a keyb that could capture her voice so adroitly, and speak with it in a different language!

But as she had hoped, there were a number of similarities between the two languages. She asked Pani and Honcho Beaver to 'speak' to her in the modern language, translating to the older one only when she could not understand them. It slowed things down at first, and it was more confusing and tiring for her. But before long the questions and answers went more quickly and smoothly. Pani even commented on Nika's ability to grasp the modern language. "You must have a good ear for it, and a good memory," he 'said'.

But that compliment came much later, toward the end of the first day.

Right after Nika's Deer Prayer had been chanted by the keyb, Pani and Honcho Beaver could not seem to go any further until they had finished 'fussing' over it. With their keybs they began a rapid exchange of words between themselves — almost as if they had forgotten that Nika was there. More than before, Nika wanted to be able to read those words.

When they recalled themselves Pani explained to Nika that the Deer Prayers from the old forest lands had been lost long ago. Only fragments remained. So new ones had been made up to replace them, using parts from the more complete Prayers for other hunted animals. The one that Pani had used was adapted from something that he called a Buffalo Prayer. He showed Nika an image of a buffalo on his keyb — a massive dark animal with stubby legs, an enormous head and short pointy horns, standing in a vast grassland. Nothing at all like a deer! Nika was not surprised that the modern Deer Prayer had become rather odd and garbled as a result.

Pani told Nika that he and Honcho Beaver were very impressed by her Deer Prayer — that it closely matched something he called fragment markers. He asked if Nika would be willing to give them more of the Prayers she knew, later on.

"They were taught to me in the Sky World," Nika responded, "and it would please me to share them with you. But . . . I would like to know: did you believe me when I told you when I was born, and that I learned that Deer Prayer in the Sky World?"

"Ah," 'said' Pani.

"Good question, Riddle Girl!" 'said' Honcho Beaver. "Now we get to the crunch of it! Tell her, Pani."

"Well, we can believe that you were born around 1730, because of the samples we took of your sweat and breath. We pulled some senqs from them, and they tell us that the date is about right, and that your age is about 16 or so, among other things. Of course, we do

67

not yet understand how you have come to be here, 800 years later
..."

"Time can move strangely in the Sky World," Nika prompted.

"Ah, the Sky World," Pani replied. "Yes, well, that is actually more of a problem, because as far as we know it is not a real place." And then he said to Honcho Beaver, "Let's show her."

Honcho Beaver nodded and with a slap of her paw on her keyb the entire wall beside Nika went dark. She could no longer see the marsh and sky beyond it on that wall, though she could still see them dimmed on the other walls.

A picture appeared on the dark wall, of something like a round ball against a pitch black background. The ball was so large that it filled most of the wall. There were splotches of color all over it, mainly blues and swirls and smears of white, but also various shades of greens, browns and black.

As Nika looked at the picture she realized that the whitish smears were moving, mostly from left to right across the big ball shape.

"I've sped it up slightly so you can see the movement of the cloud masses," Pani 'said'. "What you see there is the Earth that we live on, Nika." He next showed some images of the planet Earth and its moon, with the moon moving around the Earth, and the Earth moving around the Sun. He said that those were not actual images; he called them diagrams. Pani gave brief explanations for them, which Nika found fairly easy to grasp as concepts.

Then the big image of the Earth was on the wall again, but this time it looked to Nika as if she was hurtling toward it, closer and closer to a particular part of it. The rapid descent stopped when the entire wall was covered with a motley of greens, with some browns and some black blobs and 'streaks' snaking through the greens. Thin red lines appeared around the edges in a roughly rounded, oblong shape. "Those red lines are the outer boundaries of the Nation, which includes much of what you knew of as the Province of New York, and some other areas besides.

"And now . . . this is where we are." The rapid descent began again and continued until suddenly Nika realized that it was becoming similar to what she could see in her owl flights. Forestlands were getting closer, as if she was swooping towards them, as well as marshlands and a large lake that had changed color from black to a grey blue as it got larger on the wall.

As the images became more like reality to Nika, she began to feel like she was plummeting toward a small dark grey speck that was in the marshland, roughly halfway between the lakeshore and the forest. Soon she could discern beaver lodges in the ponded water that dotted the marsh, with beaver trails lacing through the higher ground.

The plummeting stopped when the grey speck had become large enough to be a round shape filling about a quarter of the wall. "That is the round top of Honcho Beaver's home," Pani 'said', "where we are now." He switched the image to something he called "droner footage", which seemed to slide over the edge of the roof and go down and around the structure at about eye level. Nika recognized the side of the home where she had entered it.

After a pause to allow Nika to absorb what she could of this, Pani continued. "The problem with the Sky World is that there is no place for it in all that I have just showed you. We know of it only as a mythical place — as a place in very old stories, but not as something that is real."

"I did not expect you to believe it. However, I know it is real," Nika replied, speaking quietly and with conviction.

She then reiterated what she had so recently — and so earnestly — told the Meadow Woman and her grandson. "I believe that the Good Twin is my spirit father in the Sky World, as he is father to all of the People. It is he who has given us . . . everything. I will not turn from him now."

She added, "It cannot be explained. It can only be believed."

"Ah," from Pani's keyb.

69

"Talks just like Crazy Red Feather," grumped from Honcho Beaver's.

Chapter 11

The rest of the day went quickly, resolving itself into a wide-ranging series of questions and answers, aided by images projected onto the wall by the keybs.

Nika for her part tried to answer questions fully and honestly — except about things that would reveal her shapeshifting secret. She spoke more slowly and carefully whenever she approached anything having to do with that, making modifications to keep her secret intact. Occasionally at those times, it seemed to her that Pani and Honcho B suspected that she was holding something back. There would be a look in their eyes, or a slight pause in their incessant scratching and slapping at their keybs.

When she told them about Tek being a shapeshifter, Pani replied matter-of-factly, "Oh, yes, we know of shapeshifters. There are always a few of them among the People of the Nation. They usually choose to live apart, off on their own, or in the forests, where their lives are more difficult to study and tabulate. But much is already known about them."

Here Pani stopped to consider what to say next. At length he added, "There are old sketchy tales about shapeshifters, from long before the formation of the Nation, including some rather gruesome ones. Many of the People fear shapeshifters, or are wary of them. They fear that shapeshifters have, or will develop, serious flaws in their character, or that they may be . . . well, evil. And they have a reputation of being unpredictable . . .

"But none of that is true about Tek!" Nika responded.

Pani gave a small shrug and 'said' no more about it.

The questioning continued. Sometimes Pani and Honcho Beaver

got rather excited about what Nika was telling them. Pani would get up and pace; Nika's increasing ability to speak in 'modern' freed him from having to read his keyb's translations as much. Honcho Beaver barely ever budged, but Nika could gauge her excitement by the harder, faster swipes she made at her keyb.

The first time Honcho Beaver did get out of her seat, it was with unmistakable grunts of pain. Her seat lowered and tipped her out; as she made her way slowly to the place on the wall that led to the hallway, her left back leg dragged uselessly, and there was a hitch in her use of her right front leg. When she had gone through and the wall reformed behind her, Pani 'said', "She has gone for relief, and then — it is about time for one of her therapy routines.

"Many years ago she was badly injured — nearly killed by a bear. Most of her injuries could be mended but some — it was impossible. Help came too late. She did not opt for bionic limbs; she doesn't usually move around much, so she has to do her therapies several times each day. It hurts her to do them, but it's necessary."

Honcho Beaver had arranged for meals before she left. Some thicker broth for Nika, with some delicious cooked greens and a small maple sugar cake. Pani had some meat and some hard brown lumps that he called his "kibble", along with a clear bowl of water. Beside Honcho Beaver's keyb was another clear bowl of water and some fat greenish cylinders that Pani said were compacted leaves and bark. They had to be gnawed; that kept Honcho Beaver's front teeth from overgrowing.

While they were eating, Nika asked Pani if he knew why Honcho Beaver had said to her, "Here you are at last," when she first arrived, as if she'd been expecting her. Pani wasn't sure. "Possibly it was from one of her dreams. She puts great store in them."

"How did she get her name?" Nika then asked. "And what does 'Honcho' mean?"

Pani laughed about as much as a lynx can laugh: it was all in the crinkle of his eyes and the gurgle in his throat. "It was the name given to her in the laboratory where she was made, chosen by a brilliant human in one of her more playful moments. Honcho Beaver kept the name because she liked it — it is the kind of name she would have chosen herself. 'Honcho' is not a word from any language of the People, but it means something like 'really big chief'. And that is definitely how she thinks of herself!"

When Honcho Beaver returned her face looked a little drawn but she moved more quickly and deliberately. She backed into her seat and it tilted back and raised her up to the level of her keyb and food. With one paw she grabbed a fat green cylinder and chomped on it; with her other paw she used her keyb to ask, "Did I miss anything?"

"Nothing really," Pani responded.

"Can always check," Honcho Beaver 'said'. This reminded Nika of what Pani had told her earlier — to expect no privacy here except in the dirt room.

Pani coolly told Honcho Beaver, "You are welcome to check the recordings later. But now, let's bring Nika forward in time, about 800 years or so. Shall we?"

Pani skimmed over the first 300 or so years — not that a lot hadn't happened, he 'said', but it wasn't particularly relevant now and could all be delved into later. He began his more detailed history with the year 2066, because that was the year that Joseph Pigean made quantum vector mapping possible, and then practical.

Pigean had been born into a poor and backward family in Ohio, but he was a rare genius as a scientist, and he also had a good head for business. By the time he was 30 he had thousands of registered inventions with millions of worldwide applications, for matter levitation and many other new and clever things. He became wealthier than his entire home country. He was probably the wealthiest man in the world, by a very wide margin.

Quantum vector mapping of plant and animal heredity was one of the many researches that he funded and enhanced with his own discoveries. Senqing became the core building block of this science: it

73

defined and connected the life forms in ways that had never been understood before. And his own senq confirmed what he had always thought might be so — some of his ancestors had been indigenous to the northeastern forestlands of the country.

This part of his ancestry fascinated him, and since he was generous with his wealth he wanted to do something big for his indigenous 'kin'. But when he asked their leaders for a 'wish list' they mentioned piffling things — "Maybe a community building," they said, "or a small health clinic." One of them, speaking for the rest, explained. "We are sufficient. Even you with all your money can not give us what is lacking — the return of the land and our ancient ways."

Genius Pigean shook his head over it. The egg once smashed cannot be made viable again. He gave them a nice little health clinic, and moved on.

But not long afterward, while walking alone in a forest, he came across an odd little clump of a flowering plant — one that he had never seen before. He took a piece of it and delved into its senq, and found that the plant was an impossibility — it had no connection with anything else in the vast teeming oceans of heredity. It wasn't supposed to be there at all. It couldn't exist. And yet there it was, and only there.

Its senq indicated that it had great medicinal potential. His laboratories duplicated its soil and air and persistently tried cloning it, replicating it, transplanting it. But the plant stymied all efforts. It would only thrive in that one place. Nowhere else.

He returned to the place where it grew many times; it became a pilgrimage of sorts for him. And then the peculiar plant did begin to grow somewhere other than its own small bit of earth under the enormous sky. It grew inside his mind, and he began to see the faint outlines of what eventually became the Nation.

"Even you with all your money can not give us what is lacking — the return of the land and our ancient ways."

It had not been said as a challenge, but Joseph Pigean chose to take it up as one.

He formed a cadre of dedicated colleagues, tasked with creating a country populated and ruled by the indigenous. Vast amounts of land in upstate New York were bought, and just about anyone with enough indigenous ancestry was invited to reside on those lands and help found the Nation. All living expenses were provided for. They could come and pursue occupations, or they could come and laze about. It did not matter.

Many did come and stayed; many others came to aid the novel cause before returning eventually to their own homelands.

Genius Pigean and his colleagues passed on but others took up the cause. Over several generations there was an exponential population growth among the indigenous of the fetal Nation. Families with nine or ten offspring were common. As members of the Nation, they did not have to worry about the cost of raising their families. Everything was amply provided for.

Local governments were taken over and changed to adopt the rudiments of the new governing principles. Representation in several state governments grew — mostly in New York but also in the contiguous parts of adjoining states to the west and south.

The fetal Nation became viable and could not be aborted. At length it birthed, wrested with golden forceps from its federal dam. It was a vast territory that included most of upstate New York west of the Hudson River, and parts of northern Pennsylvania and northeastern Ohio. Shrewdly–used money wheedled in the halls of government and funded extensive law proceedings in the courts. Genius Pigean's money talked persuasively and persistently for land and goods. His money ruled in the world. His money *rocked* it.

The non–indigenous who were within its territory at the conception of the Nation — the Others as they were called — they were not forced out. But as they found everything around them changing, many of them took the ample seed money offered by the

Nation and left. Those that didn't leave eventually died off, cared for by the Nation but never full members of it.

Meting out the money and keeping its value up was not always easy, but that turned out to be the easiest part of all, because there was always enough of it. The rest of the Nation's birth and infancy was a constantly shifting, often chaotic, and sometimes violent, mess. Strong personalities emerged and clashed in near constant, brutal power struggles. Blood was shed, some of it innocent. The stress of it demoralized many of the idealists, and unbalanced some of them. But the realists had always known it would be so.

Pani described the Nation's governing structure: it had chiefs (often but not always men) and equally powerful clan leaders (usually women) chosen by the People, with provisions for majority and super–majority rule, and emergency decision–making.

He skimmed quickly over much of the history of the 400–year–old Nation, only outlining the three most significant amendments to the founding principles, briefly mentioning a handful of widespread power plays, and noting the two Nation–wide wars.

"The Nation has been fairly peaceful of late, for the last forty years or so. But there is always chaffing, always plotting going on. There are always insurgents, eager to test the Nation's mettle. Always have been; probably always will be."

In Pani's view, the People of the Nation were about as blessed and cursed as the rest of the human species, in their collective strengths and weaknesses of character. The Nation did have more than its fair share of exceptional leaders, scientists, technologists, warriors and crafts men and women, at least in part because the Nation's money had been used productively to inculcate them. Its leaders knew they were all essential for its survival.

Most of the People of the indigenous Nation led blameless and productive lives. But strife came with being human, sometimes with brutal fighting, vicious backbiting and tragic cruelty. And there would always be those lurking to pick off the weak and the hapless. It was bound to be so.

Chapter 12

Outside, as the shadows lengthened in golden light, Pani began to describe the Nation as it was in the present. As his keyb 'spoke', Honcho Beaver continued to provide assistive images on the darkened wall.

"The Nation is still enormously wealthy. Food, shelter and medical care is available to all of its Members." Images appeared on the wall, of structures something like Honcho Beaver's home, except that most of them were larger and more elaborated, and were clustered together. Pani's keyb 'said' that most of the housing structures were called pods, and that they were all moveable and nearly indestructible.

In some of the images there were people standing or sitting around outside the pods, smiling or looking contented.

"Not all rosy, though," came from Honcho Beaver's keyb. "Sometimes lots of pods moved around — arguments, irritations. Fights."

Pani's keyb continued, "The Nation is closed to Others and is very well defended by its warriors. It has extensive ground defenses, and its entire airspace is shielded. Thus far the Nation has repulsed all attacks from outside its borders." Here the only image was of a scorched and mangled pile of something that Pani said had been an armed invading droner.

"Adult members can leave the Nation and return to it whenever they wish; children can go Outside with their parents. While they are Outside, they are provided with ample living expenses for up to three years, or they can rough it if they wish to. Some never go Outside; many go Outside at least once in their lives for education, or to travel." The first moving image was of some of the People looking exultant, standing and waving atop a fantastically high and forbidding–looking mountain that Pani called K2, adding that they got up there the difficult way — by climbing it.

The second image was of two plump young of the People in brightly colored clothes, smiling and waving, standing next to a huge leering monster that was also waving.

Honcho Beaver commented, "Giant mouse. Very scary."

Pani continued, "Most of the Nation's population live in the Perimeter — a wide band along the outer boundaries of the Nation. That's also where most of the farming and industry is." Here the image on the wall was a map of the Nation, showing splotches of various intensities of a red color all along the outer edges of the Nation, with Pani's keyb explaining that the darker the red, the denser the population. The large central portion of the Nation had no red color at all. "In the year 2238, the Core Accord declared that the center of the Nation would be returned to its natural state."

Several striking images appeared on the wall seriatim, of extensive, unbroken forestlands. Now it was Nika's turn to get up and pace. "Those are rather like the forests of the Sky World," she said.

"Then I suppose the Accord has accomplished its purpose, which was to make the land and waterways there sacrosanct," commented Pani's keyb. "It is called the Core Wilderness, and for good reason — there is virtually nothing 'modern' left in it, and it teems with wildlife. The Core Wilderness — or the Core for short, is difficult for anyone to get through at the ground level, except for the roaming bands of nomars."

In response to Nika's questioning look, Pani's had his keyb explain that nomars were people who lived by choice as primitive hunter–gatherers in the Core. "Very few choose that life, because it is harsh, and often shorter than everyone else's. But quite a number of the nomars are shapeshifters who prefer the wild to living in pods with the rest of the People.

"There's a thinner band that surrounds the Core; that's the Rim Wilderness — or the Rim. Most of it is much more accessible; modern techniques and equipment are used to control some of its growth. Plus there's an extensive fire break between the Core and the Rim.

"Naturalists go into the Core to study it; others visit it to enjoy its beauty, and to feel closer to the ancient ways. But no one, except some primitives, goes in without a security detail for protection, and even then most of them spend most of their time close to the Rim. It can be dangerous to be lost in the Core. Surveillance tracking there is minimal, and of course there are many predators among the wildlife. The People receive survival training in their youth, and many take additional training. But it is still not wise to pit yourself against the Core or even the Rim Wilderness, without careful preparation, ample protective equipment, and in the Core, a security detail.

Nika had many questions about the Core, but Pani was intent on continuing. "Now," his keyb 'said', "something about daily life. The People do not have to work, but most of them have occupations, according to their —"

Suddenly Honcho Beaver's keyb 'said' in her 'voice', "Incoming!" and the entire room went pitch black except for the faint glow of Pani's and Honcho Beaver's keybs. After a crackling noise a disembodied, young–sounding voice was heard coming from Honcho Beaver's keyb, saying in a peeved tone, "It's no use going dark on me! I *know* you're in there!"

"Where else I be?" came Honcho Beaver's response on the same keyb, in push–back, grumbling tones. "You way away in *your* pod, Hacker Boy. Me in *mine*."

"Hacker Boy?! Is'at your new name for me? Well . . . kind of common isn't it, since we *all* hack, Honcho B. You do too! In fact, I should call *you* Hacker Beaver. I got some of my best hacks watching you —"

"Not nice to steal my moves!" Honcho Beaver's 'said' using her keyb. "You got no manners! No —"

Hacker Boy's voice, coming through her keyb, cut in, "But I thought you wanted me to —"

A muffled screech and some garbled yelling came from wherever Hacker Boy's voice originated from. It sounded like Hacker Boy was under attack and getting the worst of it. When the background noises stopped he continued, whispering breathily and hurriedly, "So is Pani there? He's needed here. He's the only one who can — and he's gone silent on me. And —"

"Then why not hack *his* keyb?" asked Honcho Beaver on hers.

"Hacking into yours was faster," Hacker Boy replied, "and he's always with you now anyway, working on those old bones. Which by the way are *so* interesting — you're doing the triple–spiral senqing, right? Or is it the triple–unsulate — what's it called again?"

"No good trying to sweeten me!"

"Yeah," Hacker Boy admitted, "but it was worth a try. That's something else you've taught me, by the way. But then *you* wouldn't answer my queries either, so I *had* to hack in. So, is Pani there? And why don't you turn your lights back on, now that you know it's me?"

"Hacking should never be rewarded."

The boy gave a dismissive t'cha. "Listen, I —"

He was interrupted again by another screech coming from wherever he was located. "You stinking *smelly* rat!" spewed a new voice, a shrill one. "What're you doing with my spare keyb? And — hey! You've taken out the circ chips and the — you've ruined it! You've —"

"No, it's fine, Weqi," the boy said. "It's not broke. I was careful. I was just —"

"Reeking liar! Worst brother *ever!* I'll get you for this and for telling mom about the —"

"I haven't — I didn't — ow!"

Thumping and clattering noises ensued and then there was

silence in the darkness, except for the sound of Honcho Beaver slapping and scratching at her keyb.

Then, "That'll do it," her keyb 'said'. "Hack patched."

The peaceful twilight view of the marsh returned to the walls and ceiling, and, since it was getting dark, some muted interior lighting also came on.

Pani was not there. Nika had noticed his keyb went dark while Honcho Beaver was 'talking' with Hacker Boy, and her sharp hearing caught the sound of Pani's paws going toward the place on the wall that led to the hall.

"Pani'll come back tomorrow. Probably," Honcho Beaver's keyb 'said'.

"Tell me," Nika said simply, "about Hacker Boy."

Honcho Beaver looked reluctant, but she made her keyb 'say', "Name's Wenq, age 14. And yes, he is one of the People. Lives with his mother Wari and a sister Weqi, same age, his twin — in a pod west of here. They're just back from two years Outside. Didn't go well. Tension. You'll meet them. Later. Not yet."

Nika shifted restlessly. "I'd like to go outside now, Honcho Beaver."

"BAD IDEA! Not yet! Only safe in here."

"I won't go far. I'll be safe enough, won't I, if I stay close by?"

"Too DARK!"

Nika said quietly, "There's still some light. I'm going."

"Ah. *Bossing* Riddle Girl," came from Honcho Beaver's keyb, in a grumpy tone.

Now, Nika thought, *I'll find out whether they meant it when they told me I could leave at any time.* She gathered the wonderful blanket up around her and went to the place on the wall where she had come in the day before. There was a pair of orange squares on the edge of the floor there — doorway markers. But Honcho Beaver's keyb 'said', "Not that way. Another way through hall." So she went to the markers for the hallway and went through.

There were three pairs of orange doorway markers in the hallway, besides the pair at the end of the hallway where Nika entered it, and the pair for the dirt room. Nika stood between each pair of markers as she came to them. The wall did not dissolve for the first two pairs, but it did for the last one at the far end of the hall. It opened onto the outside, about ten feet off the ground. An exterior wall of the structure ran along one side of the opening; with a rumbling noise step slabs came out of the wall, along with a gripping rail, leading down to the ground.

But Nika did not use the stairs.

Chapter 13

Nika stepped out onto the small platform at the top of the stairs. An early evening breeze teased through her hair, and she felt the unmistakable itch between her shoulder blades. She hadn't realized how restless she'd become, sitting inside all day. And her mind was jumbled and muzzy with everything that Pani and Honcho Beaver had been telling and showing her. She needed freshening, and what better way than to take a flight — just a short one.

She scanned for other predatory night birds that might be around, and let the blanket fall as she shapeshifted to owl and took flight.

She only wondered after she was airborne whether there might be some of what Pani called surveillance, that would record her shapeshifting to owl . . .

* * *

On her keyb Honcho Beaver watched the recordings of Nika shapeshifting, and of the small owl flying off into the night sky. She darkened a wall and brought up the recorded images onto it, watching them several times, at different zooms. She growled in her chest and t'cha'd. *Bossing Riddle **Owl** Girl,* she mused. The senqing had not been very far off — not far off at all, considering the 800–year gap . . .

She sent a word–message to Pani's keyb before tipping out of her seat and limping off to do her therapy exercises. "Small owl species. Perhaps a tsisté–skew. Probably incoming."

* * *

Nika did not intend to be out long, or go far. She flew a high wide circle around Honcho Beaver's home, which took her over the marsh, part of the lake, and the edge of the woods. She was banking near the tree line to head back, when she spied the distinctive round shape of a pod roof in a small clearing in the woods — except that this roof had the pattern of several smaller circular roof shapes attached to a large central one. She tipped her outer wing down, swinging back around for a closer look.

She circled the pod once, at a distance that she thought was safe. Other than a few baskets left outside under the roof overhang, it was all rather nondescript. She was winging toward a tree branch for a short rest, when one of the smaller roofs on the pod suddenly disappeared, and something exploded out of the pod and hurtled toward her. She caught a glimpse of someone sitting inside a round shape, through a clear dome that was set in the top half of it — a skinny girl with a stormy brow and spiky orange–purple hair.

The flying round shape missed hitting Nika by inches. She spun dizzily in the vacuum behind the shape and, nearly breathless, she tumbled half–fluttering, half–falling onto the floor of the space that the shape had flown out of.

A beeping sounded and the roof rapidly appeared overhead, closing her into the space.

She took a few steps; the moment she moved, a higher–pitched beeping started and the space was flooded with light. A boy stepped through a dissolve in the wall, carrying something that looked to her like a shortened musket. When he pointed it at her she took flight, and was nearly over some crates stacked along a grey wall, when something like a puff of air hit her, and she was held suspended in mid–flight, unable to move her outstretched wings! She could see, but she could not move her eye muscles. Sounds were muffled.

She was rotated, lowered and brought to within a foot of the boy's face. He moved his fingers along the top of the short, musket–like device, to turn her slowly, vertically and then horizontally. Then she was turned to face the boy and was moved in closer to his face until it was just inches away. His light breath riffled her neck feathers.

His eyes darted as he examined her raptly.

If she could have moved in those moments, she would have scratched the boy's eyes out with her talons. She *hated* to be caught and examined like this! Honcho Beaver had been right. It *had* been very dangerous to go outside!

The boy went away, leaving her suspended in mid–air, and soon came back with a large wire cage.

He put the cage on the floor and, using his fingers on the musket–like device, he lowered Nika into the cage. He closed the cage lid and then, kneeling beside it, used the controls on the device to slowly move Nika lower until her talons were positioned just above a rough branch, set at an angle across the length of the cage.

The ability to move came back to Nika in the next instant. She closed her wings and scrabbled with her claws to get a hold on the branch. Every muscle ached, and she was furious with the boy for capturing her and putting her into the cage. She let loose a series of angry squawks and skirls that left no doubt about what she was thinking.

The thick–headed boy only leaned in closer to watch her. Thick–headed . . .

She quieted herself down, shat expressively onto the floor of the cage, and glared at the boy eye to eye through the bars, until the look on his face changed from eager interest to mild confusion and doubt.

Pani sauntered into the room, followed by a spare woman of medium height who carried a basket. Pani stopped beside the cage, while the woman went over to the crates ranged along the wall and started filling her basket, talking as she did so. "We'll have a little peace and quiet until Weqi returns," she said. Her voice's tonals were oddly flat. "What's that you've caught, Wenq? Something interesting?"

"I think it's a baby owl," Wenq replied, picking up the cage and heading for the open doorway.

In the cage, Nika could not stifle a derisive chirrup. *Baby* owl, indeed!

"Too bad you've got to start Braves training tomorrow morning. You'll have to let it and all your other specimens go before you leave."

"I know. I will, Mom."

"That's my good son," the woman replied vaguely. Her attention was more on the crates she was rummaging through, than on anything to do with him.

Wenq took the cage to a small narrow room that had a low battered table in the center, and cages and cases of assorted sizes on shelves attached to one of the two longer walls. Some had occupants — Nika noted mice, a hare and a possum in the lower cages, some small birds in the higher ones, and two snakes in clear–lidded cases in between.

The room's other longer wall had narrow shelves cluttered with objects and several keybs. Nika recognized some of the objects — different types of bird feathers, rodent skulls and cast–off deer antlers. One of the shorter walls was bare and dark; the other one had the open doorway and beside it a small cabinet and some shelving filled with a jumble of boxes, bags and containers.

As Wenq put Nika's cage on the table, Pani followed him into the room.

Wenq grabbed one of the keybs, put it on the table and sat down on a seat that floated out from under the table. Nika could see what he was using the keyb for: he was searching through images of owls and associated words. He kept looking up at her and then back down at the keyb.

She watched him, charging her gaze with as much outraged dignity as she could muster. Every time he looked up from the keyb he saw her baleful stare. He frowned and said to Pani, "The smaller raptors usually focus right in on the caged mice, or the other birds. But this one keeps staring at *me*."

Pani's keyb answered him from under the table, with a purring vocal. "Maybe it thinks you are a big, yummy mouse."

"Huh!"

He kept going through the images and text. "S'not a baby . . . but it's smaller than the common types of owl for around here. I wish I could senq it. Wish I had a senq lab like you and Honcho Beaver." A little later he muttered, "All of these databases must be out of date." He sighed. "Just more of the fallout from being gone two years."

"Try one of the tsistés."

He did. "Mmmm, well, fairly close. But all the subspecies are listed as extinct. Thanks, Pani. That's what I'll enter in my log, for now."

Next he got out a weird little device on a tripod that looked like an eyeball with ears. It was enough like one of the droner images that Pani had shown Nika earlier, for her to guess that the boy was going to use it to make moving images of her.

She did her best to be uncooperative.

She kept turning her back on the device, no matter how many times Wenq moved it on the tripod from one end of the table to the other. Finally he said, "This owl's acting very odd, Pani. It's almost as if . . ."

From under the table Pani's keyb quietly commented, "Maybe it's sick and needs medicine."

Nika understood the warning in Pani's message. She kept herself fairly still on the branch in the cage and tried to look completely natural, which she managed to do except for her fixed stare.

While Wenq was arranging the images of her in the keyb he was using, there was a faint whirring noise from somewhere outside the room. Wenq immediately swiped at a blue keyb on the shelf, and a wall appeared where the open doorway had been. But it wasn't long before there were loud thumping noises right outside the room. Someone was yelling and pounding on the wall where the doorway was.

"Let me **IN**, spew face! **NOW**!" It was the same screechy voice

Nika had heard earlier, along with Wenq's, coming from Honcho Beaver's keyb when it had been 'hacked', as they'd called it. Under the table Pani's keyb voiced one word: "Weqi."

So this is Wenq's twin sister, Nika thought.

Nika herself would have never complied with such an insulting order from a sibling, but Wenq swiped at the blue keyb and sat facing the doorway, with his back to the table. The wall dissolved, and framed in the doorway was a tall rangy girl with bright orange and neon–purple hair. The hair was stiff and shaped into orange spikes going back over the top of her head from the forehead, with big pointy blobs of purple hair over each ear. Beaded tassels hung from the purple blobs and tangled in large gaudy earrings. The girl's nose twitched; even that slight movement made the tiny beads in the tassels clink against the earrings.

It was the same girl who had been inside the flying object that had nearly killed Nika. Weqi didn't look as stormy as she had when Nika had glimpsed her hurtling past; now she just looked harsh. And mean.

"Great Twin," Weqi said, "it *stinks* in here worse than ever! So revolting! Yecchh!" She pulled something from a pocket and spritzed a strong fragrance into the room. A suppressed cough came from Wenq. Under the table Pani sneezed.

Wenq told her, "I put your spare keyb back where I found it. It works fine. I didn't break —"

"I don't care about that, toad head! I'm here to make you show me what you're taking with you tomorrow, 'cause I'm not going to let you take *any* of *my* camp gear. Got that?"

"I haven't finished packing, Weqi. But I'm fairly sure — the only thing that might . . . I'm taking the totem."

Weqi fairly pounced into the room. Standing over Wenq she snarled, "Well, you can't because it's *mine*."

"It belongs to our family, Weqi."

"*I* said it's *mine*. It's mine, fetid runt, because *I* was born first and

89

that makes me the oldest."

"Mom ordered another one — a really nice one — but it hasn't come yet. You can have the new one when it gets here."

"Sure as heck I'll get the new one when it comes — if it really *is* nicer."

"So Mom said I could take the old one with me."

"You rotten scum! You wheedled it out of her!"

"No, I just —"

But Weqi had spun around and was yelling, "Mom?! Mom!"

Wenq muttered to her back, "Like you don't wheedle her every which way all the time."

He thought he'd said it low enough. But she heard him.

She swung back around in the doorway. Her tassels hissed and her face was a charged storm cloud. "That does it," she snarled, stiffening her arms and closing her fists.

She took a stride toward Wenq but had to pull up short because Pani stepped in between them, facing her with a low warning growl.

"Out of my way, Pani! Stop protecting him, like he's your little baby! Your stinking little —"

Pani's growl crescendo'd. His front claws lashed out and his jaws snapped.

Weqi stumbled backward through the doorway, screeching, "How *dare* you, Pani! You've — you've ripped my leggings! And torn my — Am I bleeding?! I'm bleeding!"

But Wenq said, "I don't see any blood."

"There's a scratch —"

"Oh, a *scratch*. So *now* who's a baby?"

"You just wait 'til I catch you without your guard lynx! And I will! And I'm telling Mom! Pani's just too —"

"Tell me what?" came a tired voice from the passageway. Wenq and Weqi's mother appeared in the doorway, taking in Pani in front of Wenq with his hackles raised. There was a spark of comprehension and feeling in the woman's dark eyes, but it seemed to wink in and out through obfuscating layers of something murky. Nika wondered if she was drunk.

Wenq knelt down on the floor beside Pani. He sighed and began, "Weqi started it, Mom."

Weqi cut in and raged on and on, scarcely coherent at times, never letting her mother or brother say a word until she was done ranting about her precious totem and that Pani was too dangerous to be allowed inside. Not that anyone tried to interrupt Weqi — they listened to her tirade with faces wooden and eyes downcast.

Pani had his keyb ready when Weqi's raging petered out. "Wari," he 'said' to Weqi and Wenq's mother, "I will leave if you wish, but if I do then Wenq must come with me, to Honcho Beaver's."

It was Wenq who objected. "I'll be alright, Pani, if you'll just stay 'til I leave for the training tomorrow morning."

"Stinking little baby," taunted Weqi from outside the room, "needs his baby nurse."

Pani's keyb voiced after some scratching on it, "Take warning, Weqi. Brothers have a way of growing up to be bigger and stronger than their sisters."

"S'not gonna happen! He's a runt, and I'm going to be a warrior–woman, the toughest there is! You'll see! You'll all see!"

Wari came into the room and squatted down beside Pani, reaching out to run her fingers through the fur around one of his ears. From the cage on the table top Nika could see Wari's face as she looked fondly at Pani. It seemed like a casual petting, but as Nika watched she thought that something else might be going on. *Yes*, she thought, *Wari is trying to use some of Pani's strength to muster her own wits and resolve.* The spark deep in her eyes steadied, and brightened ever so slightly. But Nika wondered if it would be enough in this battle of wills.

"Thank you, Pani, for helping us," Wari said. Just beyond the doorway Weqi folded her arms and looked daggers at Pani. Wenq got up from the floor and casually picked up the blue keyb.

91

Still looking eye to eye with Pani, as if mustering strength from their bond, Wari spoke. "Pani stays and Wenq must take the totem with him tomorrow." Wenq timed his swipe on the blue keyb so that the wall closed over the doorway just as his mother finished speaking.

There was some furious pounding and yelling on the other side of the door, but it ended abruptly. Not long afterward Wenq, watching the blue keyb, said, "She's gone out in the aeor again."

Wari shifted over to sit on the floor, leaning against the wall of the doorway. Her eyes were closed and she looked drained, exhausted.

"Will it ever end?" she asked. Neither Pani nor Wenq answered, but Pani sat down beside her and purred. Wenq moved around the room, slipping some water and dark brown pellets through slots in Nika's cage.

"I'll take good care of the totem, Mom."

"I know you will, Wenq. Where is it now?"

"In my pocket."

Wari nodded and got up slowly. "You've got an early start tomorrow. So I'll say good–bye now." Wenq went to her and hugged her. She gave him a weak hug back. She seemed to be getting less alert by the minute. "Learn much. Have fun." Her flat–sounding voice began to slur. "Just a week. It'll go fast. And then . . ."

She turned from Wenq, swaying slightly. He dissolved the wall in the doorway for her. She left slowly, bracing herself on the doorframe as she went through. Wenq stepped outside to watch her after she left.

When he came back inside he told Pani, "She made it to her room this time." He sat back down at the table to finish what he had been doing before Weqi's interruption. His face looked closed and brooding to Nika as his fingers slid over the keyb. When he glanced up and leaned in to look at her talons through the cage bars, there was none of the avid curiosity that had been there before. His fingers shook a little and his eyes glistened. He brushed his eyes with his sleeve while he put the keyb back on the shelf.

He moved about, picking up keybs and putting a few of them in a container near the doorway. Pani went back under the table, to be out of his way. From there he used his keyb to suggest quietly that Wenq release the owl that night instead of the next morning. "Owls hunt at night. It would be less disruptive to its natural —"

"But the d'base says that this kind of owl only hunts at dusk and dawn —"

Ridiculous!, thought Nika.

"— so it's already too late — too dark," Wenq continued. "It'll be safer for it if I wait 'til dawn. Besides, if I have time in the morning I'll be able to record it in flight."

Wenq picked up the container of keybs, turned down the lighting, and went out. Pani went with him, and behind them the doorway became a wall again.

Chapter 14

Though Nika felt restless — disoriented and threatened by nearly everything — she forced herself into an uneasy sleep–state for several hours. Inside the room where she was held captive, it was fairly quiet, and outside noises were too muted to disturb her.

She woke up immediately when, well after the middle of the night by her reckoning, the wall dissolved and Pani slipped into the room. He leapt onto the table and knocked the blue keyb off the nearby shelf. Following it down to the floor, he scratched on it busily.

The doorway became a wall again, and a tiny light set above it near the ceiling started blinking and then went dark. Pani leapt back up onto the table and released the clasps along the top of Nika's cage with his paws and teeth. With paws and nose he flipped the top of the cage open. Nika flew up and out of the cage, and shapeshifted to girl in the open space. Pani expressed no surprise at her shapeshifting; he seemed to be expecting it. He was busily patting and swiping at his own keyb.

"Pani, thank you for letting me out of that cage," Nika said. "Can you help me get out of here? Honcho Beaver must be wondering where I am — I didn't intend to be gone long."

Pani used his keyb to respond, "I've already sent her a message that you are here. She's awake, and I'm going to connect with her now."

An image of Honcho Beaver sitting in her special seat, patting and swiping at her keyb, materialized on the far wall of the room — the one that had been bare and dark before. Her gruff 'voice' came out of Pani's keyb, "So you got zapped, Owl Riddle Girl."

"Tell us," Pani's keyb 'voice' added.

First Nika apologized to Honcho Beaver — she wanted her to know that she appreciated her hospitality, and had intended to return to her pod. Then she described how she was nearly hit by something that had shot out of the pod here with Weqi inside it — Pani supplied that it was called an aeor.

"Illegal to fly an aeor with auto–deflection off," Honcho Beaver 'said' with a grimness in her vocal. "Not to mention suicidal. Hurt?"

Nika decided to make light of it. "Some sprains from the near–miss — not too bad. I mainly hurt from being frozen–paralyzed."

Pani and Honcho Beaver both nodded, and Pani made his keyb say, "The technical term for it is Immobilization, but most call it being zapped. We've both felt it. We know how nasty it is."

Pani continued, "Nika, I can't override the security outside of this room. The system is complex; I don't have the right codes, and you're not an included presence. So the moment you go outside this room either as a girl or owl, you will trigger the intruder alarms."

"That'd be bad," came Honcho Beaver's 'voice'. "And if I hack the system to get you out — either way, they'll know it was Pani or me that did it — it'd blow our cover."

Nika did not understand what was meant by blowing cover, but she grasped what they wanted her to do. "You need me to wait in the cage until Wenq releases me in the morning," she said.

Pani and Honcho Beaver both nodded.

Nika was keen to get away from this awful place, and back to Honcho Beaver's, where she felt safe — or at least safer. Wenq had zapped her and put her in a cage, Weqi was mean and violent, and there was something seriously wrong with their zonked–out mother. But she told Pani and Honcho Beaver, "I know you are trying to help me, and you understand everything here much better than I do. I will trust your judgment."

After a brief measuring silence, Pani had his keyb 'say', "We like you, Nika, and there is much we want to show you and explain to you. Most will have to wait 'til you're back at Honcho Beaver's, but

95

there is one crucial thing —"

"Let me tell it, Pani," Honcho Beaver cut in.

"S'like this, Owl Girl. Everybody in the Nation got an ID chip put in them at birth. Required — no exceptions — well, mostly none. You're no exception — nowhere close. So when you came out of the lake, dripping and with no chip, we were supposed to turn you over immediate–like to the Infiltrate Council. You get me?"

"Er, I think so. I have to be kept hidden, or else you'll get in trouble for helping me."

Both Pani and Honcho Beaver nodded solemnly, and Honcho Beaver 'said' through Pani's keyb, her vocal freighted with gravitas, "A whole lot of trouble, very big. You got *no* idea."

But Nika had already had a close call with an aeor, and knew what it was like to be zapped. Added to that all the surveillance, the imbedded ID chips and the rather scary home security — she had a glimmer of how this world might severely punish Honcho Beaver and Pani for not following the more lock–step of its rules.

* * *

Nika knew it had to be early morning because the light in the room had gradually brightened. It wasn't natural light, but seemed timed to mimic the coming of day.

Before ending their late night 'conference', Honcho Beaver and Pani had explained to Nika that Wenq was leaving for his first Braves training early in the morning.

All the Nation's young from ages 10 through 12 spent a week each year in the outer Rim Wilderness on 'Cubbies' meets. The meets were designed to consolidate and further what the Cubbies knew about nature, their culture and basic survival skills. Each year the training got more advanced, but most of it was structured as fun for that age range.

The next phase after Cubbies was Braves training, which was more serious and rigorous, and competitive. For ages 13 through 17, boys and girls went annually to the inner Rim, to separate sites, for week–long camping trips. There was some nature study, but the emphasis was almost entirely on physical endurance and on honing survival skills.

Because their mother had chosen to take the family Outside for two years, Wenq and Weqi had missed two annual trainings. She took them away with her to try to outrun her sorrow, Pani explained, because of her husband's death in an accident, and the death at nearly the same time of their youngest child, a toddler, from a blood cancer. But after two years away she came back in worse shape than ever, and was taking strong medicines that made her 'not completely there' much of the time.

The two annual trainings that Weqi and Wenq missed were the last of the Cubbies meets, and the first of the Braves training. They had both made up the last Cubbies meet, with boys and girls two years younger than they were. Weqi had already gone to her first Braves training the previous week, with girls a year younger. And this morning Wenq was going on his first Braves training.

* * *

When the wall inside the doorframe dissolved and Wenq came rushing in, Nika pretended to be just waking up. She gave one of her wings a beautifully long, full open stretch. It attracted Wenq's attention, as she'd hoped, but the moment he saw the blue keyb on the floor he picked it up and looked at it instead, frowning.

That's bad, she thought. *The blue keyb on the floor is the weak link in our cover up of Pani's late–night visit.* Pani had to use the keyb right before he left, to restart the surveillance camera that he'd turned off when he'd come in. But he couldn't use the keyb while it was on the shelf where Wenq had left it — the shelf was too narrow, and there was too much clutter around it. So they rearranged the clutter and tried to make it look like the keyb had fallen off the shelf by itself. They hoped that Wenq would be in too much of a hurry to puzzle over it being out of place, or check its recording.

Wenq was looking between the floor and the shelf, with more of a frown, and his fingers started moving over the keyb. In moments he was going to find the gap in the surveillance recording, and see that Pani had come in and turned it off. That was what Nika had been trying to distract him from checking and finding.

It's not working, she decided. *Time for Plan B.*

Nika was supposed to throw herself against the cage wires and emit squawks, whistles and shrieks, to draw his attention away from that blue keyb, and to alert Pani to come and help her distract him.

But watching Wenq's flying fingers and his face bent over the keyb, Nika sensed that Plan B wasn't going to work either. *It won't be enough. This boy can easily do everything at the same time — observe a berserk caged owl, deal with whatever Pani does when he arrives, and bring up the recording.*

She scrapped Plan B and tried to intrigue Wenq by doing something an owl would never do. She began whistling and chortling her way through the tonals of a common chant.

Immediately she ran into a problem. She had never tried to 'sing' as an owl before, and her owl 'voice' could not hold the right pitches for the chant. Her tonals warbled unpredictably. She had even less range than the flutes she had made and learned to play in the Sky World. Improvising, she switched to one of her simpler flute melodies.

With the warbling–off it didn't sound very much like her flute melodies to Nika, but it did seem to be distracting Wenq. His fingers paused over the blue keyb, and he stared at her. She redoubled her vocal efforts, and was rewarded when Wenq put the blue keyb aside and set up the eared eyeball that he had used the night before. He adjusted its tripod, pointing the eyeball at her.

To keep him interested, she began to vary the melody. And to draw him away from the blue keyb, she turned her back on the eared eyeball and 'sang' more softly. She also started making some 'dance moves' — head bobs and twists, leg squats and stretches, hops along the branch, all in time with her weird little 'melodies'.

Wenq *did* hurry to bring the eared eyeball around to the other end of the table, just as she hoped he would.

His fingers fumbled as he adjusted the tripod. He thrust his face close to the cage bars in an odd fidgety way, and he seemed to twitch and sway while listening to her and watching her.

It was odd, as was the effect on the caged animals on the shelves. The birds edged closer and watched in silence with their heads cocked to one side. The mice and other mammals restlessly paced along the side of the containers closest to Nika's cage. But the snakes coiled and uncoiled, batting themselves against the lids of their containers.

The last time Nika had seen something like that, was in the Sky World, when certain of her flute melodies agitated and drew those who heard it, instead of soothing them.

She continued her 'singing' and little dance moves — *the longer he stands there watching, the less time he'll have to examine the recordings on that blue keyb.* But she tried to scale it back, using the reaction of the caged animals to gauge whether the effect was diminishing.

Suddenly Pani's head popped up on one side of Wenq. He too was twitchy and fidgety, but he shook his head as if trying to clear it. He managed to nod at Nika — their prearranged signal. Nika stopped singing and moving, except for a big fluff up of her feathers, before settling them back into place.

Wenq blinked and shook his head. He rubbed his ears and eyes. "Great Twin, what just happened?" he said muzzily. Pani nudged him. He looked down at Pani, tensed and said, "I'm late?"

When Pani nodded emphatically Wenq took the eared eyeball off the tripod and jammed it into his pocket. Then he started taking the other cages and the cases out of the room, bringing them back empty.

The first time he was out of the room Pani knocked the blue keyb off the table and scooted it underneath, out of sight.

When Nika was the only caged creature left in the room, Wenq paused in his hurry and stood by the table looking at her. "There's something odd about this owl, Pani. I wish I could —"

"No time left now," Pani's keyb 'said'. "Your ride will be here in less than three minutes. And they'll mark you down if you're not ready on time."

Nika could see that Wenq did not want to release her — that he was trying to think of some way —

"Pani, I don't suppose that you could —"

"No."

"Maybe Honcho Beaver could —"

"No. Better hurry. Two minutes now and counting down."

"Horse puke and piss. It's not *fair!* Pani, this owl type is *not* live in the d'base. And if it's migratory I'll never get it back. It could be some kind of breakthrough discovery —"

"An ordinary little owl."

"No." Wenq's jaw set; his face became distinctly mulish. He rummaged in the cabinet and grabbed something brown and flat. It popped open into a small rectangular box with little round holes along the sides. He quickly set its open end against the door in Nika's cage, and Nika felt herself go numb all over. In a matter of seconds she was sucked off the branch and into the box. The numbness left her almost immediately, but not before the box was closed up. She was carried in the box out of the room, down a hallway and into the aeor's space. The aeor wasn't there and the roof was open. Through the holes in the box Nika could see a pile of cloth bags beside the doorway. Wenq set the box down beside the bags.

When Pani came up and asked him what he was going to do with the owl, he said he was going to take it with him to the training.

"You should let it go, Wenq, even if it is a new type."

When Wenq made no response, Pani added, "This isn't like you."

"I know, Pani. I can't explain it. But I just can't let it go."

The shadow of a round shape darkened the sky overhead. After hovering for a few moments the shape descended into the aeor's

100

space and settled onto the floor. A clear dome on its upper half rose.

Nika supposed it was another type of aeor. It was similar to the one she had seen Weqi flying in, but this one looked larger and far less streamlined. Wenq raised two lids in the rim around the dome and put his bags into scooped–out areas. The aeor then 'spoke' to him, instructing him on adjusting the weight of the 'cargo' between the two 'holds'. He kept moving the bags between them until the aeor 'said', "Close enough" and closed the lids. Then it 'said', "Passenger cleared to board".

Wenq said goodbye to Pani. Pani used his keyb to wish him good luck, and to 'say', "Release the wild owl as soon as possible, Wenq."

Wenq didn't answer. He climbed into the aeor with a keyb and the box holding Nika. The aeor's dome closed over him as he got into the middle of three seats. As soon as he snapped on a harness the aeor rose into the air and headed in a southeasterly direction. It was moving quickly, but nothing like as fast as the smaller one that Nika had seen Weqi flying in.

Wenq didn't seem to be interested in where the aeor was going. He was using the keyb. Through the holes on one side of the box Nika could see words and a few images on his keyb's surface. Through the holes on the other sides the box she could see that they were flying rapidly well above the trees, gradually arcing around to a northwesterly direction.

She cast back in her mind over the adamant way Wenq had said he could not let her go, and Pani's response. Pani had said that it wasn't like him . . .

I managed to pry his attention away from that blue keyb with my 'song and dance', but . . . it worked too well. She recalled his fidgeting close to the cage and the way that Pani was twitchy and drawn to her as well. *I did not want my melodies to have that effect on them . . . I wonder if my 'song' is the reason Wenq did not release me.*

If that's what it is, I can only hope that it will wear off quickly.

Chapter 15

Des was the In Charge for his region's Braves training. He'd been doing it for more than twenty years, but it never got old. He liked working with the newbie Braves best of all — like this group, getting ready to leave for their first training in the Inner Rim.

Sometimes there were bumps and hiccups. But so far today everything was going exceptionally well.

Now it was time to get everyone into the big transport aeors. He tapped the speaker icon on his wrist band, and his amplified voice rang out, stilling the murmur of the milling crowd.

"Attention! Attention! Take off is set for 0700, in about five minutes. All Staff other than Squad Leaders — take your assigned seat and harness in. Squad Leaders, maintain your designated locations with your Standards.

"And now — listen up, all you Newbie Braves!

"Line up in front of the guy or gal that's holding up a banner with a picture of the *same* animal that's on your armband. Got that? Bears to bear, wolves to wolf, skunks to skunk."

He tapped off the speaker and stood watching the newbies. Most of them did not have to look at their armbands before finding their Squad Leader, and some of them seemed to get that the bit about skunks was just a joke. Ah, such a tired old joke . . . he remembered it from when he'd been a newbie Brave, and it was probably a tired old joke *then*.

Ten Squad Leaders, ten newbies in each squad. 100 newbie boys altogether in this cluster.

Sometimes he could tell at this early stage, which of them were going to get through the challenging week ahead just fine, and which ones were going to lag, or maybe even flunk out and have to take their first Braves training over again.

Right now his guess was that none of these boys would have to go remedial. Most had good backgrounds, and he could see that they were all eager and excited, and helping each other. There were bound to be tensions below the surface — always were. But everyone was keeping that in check, for now.

It always boded well for the week, when things started out this well. Just a few minutes more and they'd be on their way.

Except that something was wrong. There were only nine newbies in one line of boys. They were short one newbie bear.

How can that be? Des wondered. *Surely I'd have been notified by now if any of the boys had not checked in.*

The Bear Squad Leader had just given him a "Problem Here" hand signal, when Kaien the Record Woman reached his side and told him, "The Kah boy hasn't arrived."

"Kah, Kah . . . you don't mean Wenq Kah, the catch–up kid from the tsye marshlands?"

Kaien nodded, and Des almost groaned out loud. Of all the boys to be missing! Because if that boy was anything like his awful sister — they'd had nothing but trouble with her in *her* catch–up. She had just barely squeaked through it — in fact he thought her Squad Leader probably 'tweaked' her record in order to turn an actual 'fail' into a 'barely passed'.

Putting aside the unpleasant recollections associated with the boy's sister, Des checked his keyb. "Why do you say he hasn't arrived? This shows he got here 30 minutes ago and checked in. What's his game? I'm sure you checked the dirt rooms. Where do you think he's gone? Through the fence?"

Kaien shook her head and said grimly, "That's what somebody wants us to think— that he got here and then left the grounds to hide out somewhere with friends. But I've been following an extra procedure, ever since the Haun kid went missing last month. It's antiquated, but foolproof. It can't be hacked."

She pulled a crumpled sheet of paper out of her pocket. It had a handwritten list of names on it. She held the paper up, pointing to an unchecked box beside the name Wenq Kah. "I was very careful, Des. I personally checked each boy in, using this list. The Kah boy is not checked off, and I'd even bet that the aeor we sent for him is *not* back in the hangar with the others, even though its records say that's where it is. Remember? We sent one of the three-seaters, but he was the sole pick up from his area. That boy never got here, Des. I'm sure of it."

"And here's another odd thing," she continued, whipping a keyb out of her pocket. "I got a special clearance to track his ID chip, just before I came out here to report. It was showing him in range, about a half mile south of here, and then the marker did a really weird jump, showing him about a mile to the east instead. Here, let me show you. I'll play it back." She tapped the tracking record. Initially it hung up with an error message; when that cleared, they watched the recording and Kaien exclaimed, "Why, it's changed! It wasn't that way before! It's smooth now but I *know* it jumped before."

"Then it's been deep hacked," Des said.

Kaien agreed. "The whole thing's been hacked to pieces. And that'd take quite a bit of skill. And access."

"Better alert Interagency. And keep a lid on it for now. Let's get one of the stand–bys slotted in. We'll pick him up on our way to camp."

* * *

Wenq had dozed off in the aeor. When he woke up he swiped at his keyb to check the time, but nothing happened. The screen remained dark. The aeor's panel was dark too.

He sat up sleepily and looked around outside. The aeor was moving steadily over dense forestlands. It looked to be about mid–morning, judging from the position of the sun and the length of the tree shadows. *But it can't be that late,* he thought. *And there's something*

104

about the sun and those shadows that doesn't look right. He puzzled over it, and then realized, *The sun isn't where it's supposed to be. It should be ahead of me, since I'm travelling southeasterly toward the launch place for my Braves training. But it's behind me.*

He rummaged in his pocket for a tiny compass — one of the items he was required to bring for survival training. The compass needle confirmed what the sun and tree shadows had already told him. He was travelling almost due west.

Maybe they changed the launch place for the training at the last minute? But no, they would never do that without announcing it. That has to be the least likely explanation.

Or . . . could one of the aeor's processing chips be malfunctioning? I linked my keyb to the aeor, so if that's it, it would explain why my keyb isn't working.

But then Wenq remembered: all aeors have a series of fail–safes and alerts in case of malfunctions — programs that automatically run on back–up and, if necessary, get the aeor safely out of the sky and landed as close as possible to an occupied location. *So if that's it, then there should have been an alert, and some of the panel would be working — otherwise the aeor would have landed by now.*

There were some other possibilities, but in terms of likelihood . . . Wenq next considered, *Could someone be playing a trick on me — hacking the aeor to make me miss my Braves training? It'd be a really hard hack to do . . . and I can't think of anyone good enough at it, who'd want to do it to me. . . so if it's that, then this probably isn't personal . . .*

Hacking was a national pastime, but most of it wasn't destructive. It was more about counting coup to show off one's tech-savvy. Only a few ever went beyond the legit hack sites. The Nation stymied unsanctioned hacking with cutting edge cybersecurity, shielding and redundancies. The few hackers that got past all that were either the 'good hats', which included some of the Nation's best engineers, or 'bad hats' — shadowy rogues who occasionally wreaked havoc. Wenq himself had some notions of joining the good hats someday, if he could ever get good enough at it . . .

When an exceptional bad hat got through and ran amok, the good hats could usually shut him (or her) down and restore everything fairly quickly. But in the meantime . . .

Wenq still wasn't sure whether this was a hack, but he glanced around the inside of the aeor suspiciously. *If this aeor* **has** *been hacked then the hacker will be able to spy on me from the cameras. Well, if that's so then at least I can spoil some of that kind of 'fun'.*

He got a few pieces of gum out of his pocket and chewed them until they were pulpy soft. Then he put wads of gum over each camera's 'eye' — small bumps on the dome's interior that he could see in raking light, and then feel with his fingertips.

When he sat back down he pulled a small bag of processing chips out of his pocket. Since he'd begun to hack he always carried them. *I'll try to get my keyb working again. I feel practically naked without a keyb.*

He flipped the keyb over, pried off the back, and started replacing its chips with ones from the bag — an assortment of spares, and some chips he had modified for hacking.

A light scuffling at his elbow made him look over; the noise was made by the owl he'd brought with him. Through the holes in the box, the owl's eyes were watching what he was doing with the chips.

It certainly is an odd little owl. But Pani was right. I should have released it. I still don't know why I felt I had to keep it with me. But at least I don't feel that way anymore.

"I'm sorry, little owl," he told it in a whisper, while working with the chips. "I should have let you go." He was used to talking to Pani and Honcho Beaver, so it didn't seem at all odd to be talking to the owl. But he whispered, just in case there was a hacker listening in.

He tried every chip combination he could think of, but his keyb remained dark and inert.

"Nothing," he told the owl, under his breath. "It's almost as if its tilm has been deliberately fried."

Frying a tilm was a serious hacking offense, and because of tracking redundancies it was something that — as far as he knew —

no bad hat *ever* got away with. *The problem is, sometimes it takes a while to track some of them down. So that isn't going to help me now.*

He turned his attention to the aeor's panel. Everything was still dark and unresponsive — communication controls, flight options, overrides. *But unlike my keyb, this aeor is functioning — it's flying — which means that I ought to be able to hack it. And if I can get control of it, I might even get myself back home in it. Or — probably more realistic — if I can get the aeor to find a safe landing place, then I can get at my spare keybs in the holds, send out a distress signal with one of them, and just wait for rescue.*

But the problem with hacking this aeor in mid–flight is that if I do something really wrong — like messing up the fail–safes, then I could end up in a crash landing.

He looked outside. The sun had gone behind some clouds, and the forest he was overflying looked dark and forbidding. The tree branches of the canopy were tightly interlaced; the few breaks in the canopy were cluttered with fallen trees and thickety brush. For as far as he could see, there was no good place to crash land an aeor . . .

He removed some access panels and used his small pocket light to examine the chips and read the circuitry markings inside their shallow cavities. His hopes rose when he found a small keyb wedged inside one of the cavities. It was only about two inches square, but he thought, *I might be able to run some diagnostics on it.* A strap over the keyb was brittle with age. He eased it out and tried to activate it.

It flickered on and then numbers, letters and symbols of code sequences scrolled rapidly across its surface. It went off and when it started itself back up the coding flashed instead of scrolled. Some of the flashing coding stayed the same but other parts rapidly changed into different code sequences. Then the keyb went off and back on again, this time with scrolling again. Wenq knew basically what this meant. *The programs in this little keyb are trying to regain control of the aeor's systems. But a hack is actively breaking in, real time. With each off – on cycle, the hacker is getting closer to taking it over completely.*

Well, at least I know now. This aeor's been taken over by a bad hat.

Wenq envisioned the hacker — probably a him — in a private place somewhere, surrounded by several hack towers and stacks of interconnected keybs, all at his fingertips and all meticulously programmed to break in and break apart code, and re–write it.

Why would anyone hack an aeor like this one? he wondered. *And where is this aeor taking me, and for what purpose?*

His thoughts turned uneasily to the girl, Áka Haun, who went missing last month on her way to a Braves training.

It happened while he was away at his make–up Cubbies meet; he heard about it when he got back. She was a few years older than he was and lived in a more populous part of their region. He knew her slightly from the mingling and games in previous years, at the annual community meets. When she disappeared last month there'd been searching and questioning — some by the authorities, a lot by her family, who insisted that she had not run away to the Outside, like the authorities were saying she had. By the time he was home it had all quieted down and almost everyone except her immediate family seemed to think she had gone on an Outside fling after all.

Now he wondered, *What if something like this is what happened to her?*

He decided he had two choices. *I can let the aeor take me wherever it is going, or I can at least try to take control.*

He pried the back cover off the little keyb, popped the main chip out and put in his best hack chip.

For a short while he made some progress. He got the keyb's frantic program to move a bit slower, with fewer restarts. He even got started on a few tags for program takeovers. But he soon realized that the hacker was just messing with him, like a cat playing with a cornered mouse. *The hacker let me slow things down and make those starts, just to see what I could do. Now that he knows how limited that is, he'll force the little keyb's programs into overdrive.*

Within moments, that was exactly what happened. The keyb's program crashed, with no hope of resuscitation.

Well, you've made your point, whoever you are. But I'm not quite done yet.

As the aeor continued on its westerly course, Wenq returned to studying the chips and the circuitry markings behind the aeor's access panels. His plan was to try to trigger a fail–safe landing, by removing just the right chip, or series of chips, from the aeor's circuitry.

In a fail–safe landing an aeor's programming is supposed to automatically plot an optimal landing site, and bring the aeor down to it safely.

The sky had darkened, and there were splatters of rain on the aeor's clear dome. Now Wenq really needed his pocket light to see what he was doing.

He was methodically working his way through the circuitry when the aeor shuddered and in the pit of his stomach he felt a sudden drop. It corrected almost right away but he immediately replaced the circuit he'd taken out and scooted to his seat. He snapped on the harness and hunched over in his seat with his arms wrapped around the owl's box. *If the aeor's going to crash, I need to be ready.*

The aeor's systems tried to keep it airborne but they failed. Clunks and stuttering noises rapidly cycled on and off. Wenq didn't know whether he had caused it, or the hacker had. Or some combination of both.

After a brief recovery from the first drop, nothing counteracted the aeor's plunge from the sky. It hit uppermost tree branches and then wallowed crazily, sliding, bouncing, and spinning through snapping, groaning branches, all the long way down to the ground, where it thumped once heavily on its rim, and then tipped and settled itself sideways against a tree trunk.

Chapter 16

Investigator Rahra Kwar directed his aeor to approach the tsye marshlands from over the lake.

Water, water everywhere. Rahra was not overly fond of large lakes and marshlands. He knew, of course, that the Nation was fortunate to have such an abundance of fresh water. Out in the Western lands of the Others, where some of the Res Peoples still had their territories, water was scarce. For centuries the Nation's scientists had provided expertise and technology to help their brother and sister Peoples conserve and enhance those precious water supplies, but there never seemed to be enough. Tensions were often high over water among the Peoples themselves, and with the Others.

Rahra fully appreciated the extensive and myriad life supported by the lake and marshlands he was flying over. But as a wolf shapeshifter, he preferred water in moderation. Not too wet underfoot, nor too deep. And definitely not all–immersing. He ground his teeth at the thought of water pressing in on him from all sides.

Unlike many wolf shapeshifters who preferred dark forestlands and their isolated meadows as their natural home, Rahra had always worked hard to remain firmly in the People's normal world.

He had applied for, and been granted, the right to have his senq records modified, so that only those with the highest clearances had access to the records of his shapeshifter overlays. This gave him a better chance of assimilating, since many of the People had an innate fear or distrust of shapeshifters, simply because they were not as "normal" as themselves. Other than his immediate family, only a chosen few knew for certain that he was a shapeshifter.

Now in his mid–twenties, he felt reasonably settled into his niche in life. He was a devoted and supportive son, brother and uncle. He was a reliable and diligent worker in Investigations. He had his forest jaunts as a wolf to compensate for the likelihood that he would never find a woman who would want to mate with him for life. His was a world and life-choice that could not be easily shared.

For the most part he kept his Investigations work as a man separate from his forest forays as a wolf, though some overlap was inevitable, and synergetic, because he always had the heightened senses of a wolf. Even now; in his musings about the waters of forest and meadow, he sniffed as if he could smell all the earth secrets beside a babbling brook, and his toes twitched for the springy give of the forest's mosses alongside those brooks and streams. Over the faint hum of the aeor he 'heard' in his recollection the forest's constant flow of messages — the potent and the slight all mixed together in an exciting puzzle, to be worked out for the prize of continuing life, with death as the penalty for failure.

Death. With a mental wrench and a sigh, he recalled himself to his purpose in coming here. Youths and children, inexplicably missing and perhaps dead. And the latest one — a fourteen year old boy who'd gone missing earlier this morning.

The boy's home was in a pod near here. It had been a while since he'd been to this area, but he remembered it fairly well. He slowed his aeor somewhat and used the zoom screens to get closer views of the marsh. He noted the muddy beaver paths, several beaver lodges in the deeper water behind their dams, and of course the solitary marsh pod where Honcho Beaver lived. Yes, it was much as he remembered it.

There was also supposed to be an old constituted lynx somewhere around here. Both the e–beaver and the e–lynx had been lab–made by a noted scientist, Tsi Kah, at least 100 years ago. But they had stopped making those constitutes; in fact these two might be the only ones left. Both had ward status with some of Tsi Kah's descendants — specifically with the Kah family unit that included the missing boy.

He had met Honcho Beaver only once, ten or so years ago, but he actually knew her fairly well through some of the hacking networks that they both used. From those contacts he had a high regard for Honcho Beaver's hacking skills, and he suspected that the wily old constituted beaver was an even better hacker than she let on. He'd already been thinking about consulting with her about a Missing Girl case he had. Now he was eager to talk to her about it, along with the new Missing Boy case. After this morning's events, he suspected that both cases were the work of the same rogue hacker.

But first he planned to visit the Kah family unit, in the woodland next to the marsh. He mentally reviewed what he'd already found out about the family. Not much detail about them in the files — usually that was good. It meant the family followed the rules and kept a low profile.

The family unit was isolated, with only three members, recently returned from two years Outside — the mother in recovery and fourteen year old fraternal twins — girl a hellion, boy apparently a quiet type. The pod they lived in had originally been a research station; the location had been used by some part or other of the Kah family for at least seven generations.

Investigator Rahra did not do many in–person visits. Rarely was there a need for it. Most of his work could be accomplished by a video patch, rather than in–person. And that suited him, because as a wolf shapeshifter the plethora of scents he was exposed to on in–person visits could be extremely distracting. Though occasionally edifying . . .

But there was no question of doing a video patch in this case. All communication with the family's pod had been jammed since early this morning — even when it hadn't seemed to be.

Someone had been rather clever. When Investigations was notified that the Kah boy was a no–show for his Braves training, their queries to his home got a video of his sister saying he'd been planning some stupid hack — something to do with his Braves training. She looked and sounded bored, and irritated by their queries. She didn't know what her brother had been planning, but she was sure it was just some stupid thing or other. She assured them that it wasn't anything that anybody should be wasting their time on.

But the Records woman for the Braves training had insisted that there was some kind of big honkin' problem, and that they should be checking *everything* out quickly and *in–person* . . . the woman herself had shown up at old Kanr's workstation *in–person*, waving some crumpled piece of paper around like a war flag. Word was that she practically had Kanr in a head hold until he capitulated and contacted the Kah pod to arrange aeor clearance for an in–person visit . . .

Rahra smiled to himself. *I'd have liked to be patched in on Kanr's wall view and seen that exchange between the Records woman and my boss's boss . . . maybe I can hack the recording of it sometime . . . if Kanr doesn't manage to hack it out first . . .*

It was that second contact with the pod that blew the hack wide open. Clearly, the hacker hadn't expected an aeor clearance request for an in–person visit; he (or she) made several glaring mistakes while trying to counter it in real time. In the second video projection of the boy's sister, hasty hack splices were obvious: some of the sound was disjointed and nonsensical, while the images went all hack–patchy. An engineer dove in fast, before the hacker was able to cover his tracks, and salvaged enough markers to establish that the first contact had been hacked as well.

Yep, if it hadn't been for the Records woman, it would probably be days instead of hours before we realized that the pod's communications were hacked and jammed.

It was still going to be difficult to unravel and trace back the hacks they had uncovered so far — the hack of the Braves training aeor, the records at the Braves training launch, and the hack at the Kah pod.

But the engineers had more to work with this time, since it was all fairly recent — still only a few hours old. They had put in tight data lockdowns and created more backup redundancies, exponentially increasing the data checkpoints and making it much harder for the hacker to completely evade detection. They had a much better chance of catching the hacker this time.

Meanwhile here I am, nearly at the Kah pod, with an open–ended assignment to investigate quickly and report my findings in case they'll be of any help to the engineers.

Rahra thought he knew why he'd been chosen to do the in–person. *My boss knows I'm still working the Haun girl's file, even though it was shelved in the press of other work.*

The girl — Áka Haun — had disappeared in the middle of the previous month. She had been gone for three days before anyone realized she was missing. Her family thought she was at her Braves training, but the training records showed her as postponed due to illness. It was only because one of the girl's cousins was also at the training, and sent out a 'glug' asking how Áka was feeling on the third day, that they finally caught on to the hack.

By then the hacker had covered his/her tracks. Three days was plenty of time to make the hack look straightforward and mundane to the Investigations bosses — suspiciously straightforward and mundane, in Rahra's opinion.

It was made to look as if the girl had done the hack herself, to give herself enough time to get Outside of the Nation. Border records, at a likely spot for an unauthorized exit to the Outside, showed a hack on the second day she was gone, that they were able to connect back to the hack of her Braves training records. Supposedly the girl just wanted to go Outside without permission and live with some of her Outside relatives.

She hadn't actually contacted those relatives, and had not shown up at their home. But once it *looked* like she had gone Outside . . . there was just too much other pressing work for Investigations to pursue it. Outside, there were so many places she could go, and lots of things could have happened to her, that the Nation could do nothing about. So Outside Consul had been notified, and the case was shelved for the time being.

Rahra believed the girl's mother when she said that she knew her daughter and was certain she would not have done this. *And though the girl did have advanced hacking skills,* Rahra thought, *the hack was too sophisticated for her to have done it all by herself.*

* * *

Rahra circled above the Kah family's pod in his aeor, signaling an on–the–spot request for landing. When there was no response, he set his aeor to go outside the pod's security perimeter for a ground landing at the first available spot.

The aeor's program put it down about a half–mile away from the pod, just outside the woods, in some brush that petered out into the marsh.

He briefly reported in and was getting out of the aeor when Kanr himself came on his panel screen. Apparently, the Records woman and her paper banner had really fired him up.

"I've been doing some checking with the other Sectors," Kanr told Rahra. "There might be more to this than we thought. There've been disappearances in the other Sectors that had seemed random at first, but now we're not so sure. Information is being shared. Though nothing is certain, precautions should be taken."

Over and out.

Rahra was gathering up the gear he wanted to take with him when the aeor alerted him that there was a small 'In Range And Approaching', by land. Looking in the indicated direction, he saw a beaver coming along a muddy path toward the aeor. It stopped about twenty feet away and watched him. Another beaver joined the first one, and then a third.

Then the aeor indicated a larger 'In Range And Approaching', and a lynx came into view, with a keyb dangling from its neck.

115

The lynx was hurrying. It went right past the beavers and up to the aeor. Looking directly at Rahra, it made an upward jerking motion with its head, as if it wanted him to raise the dome lid.

Rahra guessed that this was the e–lynx — what else could it be? Normal lynxes didn't act like this. He intercomed to it, "You're the constituted lynx? You want to talk with me?" and the lynx gave a brief nod after each of his questions.

Its eyes looked quite intelligent. Rahra weighed the odds that the lynx was trustworthy and . . . civilized. Well, the three beavers seemed to think so . . .

Rahra raised the aeor's lid just a little.

The lynx cocked its head, as if to say, "Really?" So Rahra raised it some more and the lynx jumped up, scrambled its way through the opening and squeezed into the small space beside his seat.

Rahra's wolf instincts caused him to tense uncomfortably, but the lynx showed no menacing inclinations. It got itself situated and started pawing at its keyb.

"Thank you," the keyb 'said'. "I'm Pani. ID, please?"

Rahra blinked, but did as the e–lynx requested. He held his forearm over its keyb, so that his ID chip would reveal his name and Investigator status.

The e–lynx studied the ID box for what seemed like a long time, while also scratching at its keyb. As Rahra watched the keyb, which was right next to him, a text box appeared on it from a sender named "HB", with the words "Legit" in it. Then after the lynx had scratched at its keyb some more, the keyb's vocal 'said', "Officer Rahra, we need help. Outside communications have been down since early this morning, and a fourteen year old girl named Weqi Kah is missing."

Chapter 17

Wenq's shoulders were sore from being jerked against the harness during the crash landing, and his neck was stiff, but other than that he thought he was alright. He gave a little prayer of thanks to the Good Twin, and to the engineers responsible for the safety features in aeors. Aeors rarely crashed, but even so their seats were fitted with pneumatics to absorb much of the force of a crash landing.

He found he was dizzy, though, when he released the seat harness and tried to move around inside the tilted aeor. He fell over sideways, and had to crawl until he reached the emergency release for the dome.

He half fell, half stumbled out of the aeor, with one arm curled around the box holding the owl. It was almost as dark as night, with the overcast sky and dense growth of tree branches overhead. He could hear rain drip, but not much of it reached the ground under these particular trees — massive pines.

He only planned to be outside long enough to let the owl go, if it was able to fly, and to get some of his gear from the holds. *Then I will close myself up in the aeor,* he thought, *signal for help with one of my other keybs, and wait for rescue.*

Trees seemed to wobble and gyrate around him. Sitting on the ground to steady himself, he opened the owl's box. The owl immediately flew out and up to a tree branch. It looked down at him with its large, baleful eyes, that spun and twirled in circles. Then it split into two owls. *That can't be,* he thought.

"You are free now," he told the doubled owl. Using a formal farewell he added, "And I am thankful that you go well." He closed

117

his eyes, hoping to steady his vision.

Instead he passed into unconsciousness.

* * *

Nika was not feeling nearly as 'well' as the boy Wenq seemed to think. During the crash she had anchored her talons in the springy mesh at the bottom of the box, and kept her head tucked down. Even so she had been jerked and buffeted.

She supposed though, that she had withstood it better than the boy had. *At least I am conscious. He is slumped over, oblivious to the rain, and exposed to any danger that this densely timbered forest might serve up.*

With her exceptional vision she could see that the forest was very old, and untamed. Her sharp hearing caught a cacophony of rustling, and other sounds of life and of movement in the rain, both far and near. She sensed though, that it was quieter than normal.

This crash has disturbed the forest's normal noises and rhythms, she thought. *All of its creatures within hearing have paused to assess what the disturbance might mean. Even now some of its larger predators may be approaching, circumspectly, to find out if it is a challenge to be dealt with, or an unexpected meal.*

* * *

Wenq felt someone prodding and tugging at him, and there was a voice that sounded urgent, saying, "— in danger, Wenq. Hurry. Danger. Hurry." The voice sounded harried and sincere. He tried to cooperate, to move himself in the direction that he was being pulled and pushed. He was lifted, leveraged and rolled about.

He was inside the aeor again before he remembered that he had been outside of it when the prodding and tugging began. Someone had gotten him back inside. But his keybs . . . "My bags," he mumbled.

"I'll get them. Better keep your head down," someone said. It was a firm voice — *a woman's voice,* he thought, *oddly accented.*

He faded out of awareness for a while, and then woke to a thrumming of rain against the outside of the aeor's dome. When he opened his eyes, he found that he was lying wedged between the closed dome's inside curve and its narrow surround rim. With the aeor canted at an angle against a tree, he was hammocked awkwardly in the bottom–most part of the dome's curve.

Looking down at him from the middle of the aeor's domed space was a girl or woman, wearing some of his clothes, including a pair of his socks. Because of the aeor's cant, she was perched on the back of the middle seat.

Wenq rubbed his eyes. At least they were focusing better. He saw only one of her, instead of two.

She would be rather nice–looking, he thought, *if her skin wasn't so scarred.* All of it that he could see — her face, neck and hands — was covered with shallow, roundish splotches, the size of a fingertip. It made him think of some old images he'd seen once, of someone with small pox scars. *But it can't be that — small pox was eradicated centuries ago.*

She looked like she was still a girl to him because of her size: she was thin, slight and small–boned.

But he wondered if she might be a very small woman, because the expression on her face was not like anything he would associate with someone who was still a girl. Her large dark eyes under her frowning brow looked age–old and preternaturally wary, as if she was used to being ever alert for dangers that he could not begin to fathom. A notion flitted through his mind, that she must think that the world had very few places in it that were truly safe.

There was a blur of movement outside the aeor, and a thump and scuffling noises at his back, muffled somewhat by the rain.

"That was one of the wolves," the girl/woman told him.

Wenq was groggy. He had to think about what she'd just said for nearly a minute. "Wolves," he said at last. "Well, that's probably not good."

With a wan smile the girl/woman nodded agreement. And for a moment her whole face was transformed — beautified by the little

119

smile. But it faded quickly. "I tried covering us both up, hoping that if they couldn't see us in here, then they might lose interest and leave. It didn't help, and more of them have arrived, perhaps a separate pack."

Wenq got up slowly and climbed up to sit on the back of one of the outer seats. The girl/woman shifted to the other outer seat; she explained that she did it so that the aeor would not roll sideways.

"Sometimes the wolves jump up against the aeor, and it shifts slightly," she told him. "I'm Nika, by the way."

Looking out through the rain–beaded dome, Wenq could now see the restless, shadowy shapes of wolves moving about in the darkness.

"My name's Wenq. I count four or so wolves out there, so far."

"There were six or seven at first, with more arriving recently."

"Mmmm. Well, I guess you'd know, Nika. So, okay then. Could I please have an update now?"

Nika brow wrinkled, and she looked at him as if she thought his brain was addled.

"Well, we — you — crashed landed," she said carefully.

"Yes, and then I climbed out of the aeor to . . . to do some things, and then someone helped me get back inside it," Wenq said, matching Nika's slow and considered way of speaking. "And then you were left to stay with me and . . .," he prompted.

"But there's no one else. I'm the one who got you back inside."

"You?!"

It didn't seem possible. She was so small and frail–looking — to Wenq she looked as delicate as a little fawn. In comparison, he felt as big and lummoxy as a yearling moose.

"Without any help?" he asked, still in disbelief.

"I'm stronger than I look," she answered gravely.

Wenq struggled to organize his thoughts. Perhaps because of Nika's quiet, serious demeanor, he had been assuming that she'd been left to wait with him while someone else went for help. Though that didn't explain why she was wearing some of his clothes . . .

His thoughts turned uneasily to the fact that the aeor had crashed in the first place, because his trip to Braves training had been hacked . . .

"Who *are* you, Nika?" he asked.

Nika did not answer right away. When she did, she said, "Wenq, you must first promise me that you will never reveal my secrets, without my permission."

Wenq blinked at her. He knew he was somewhat young for his age, and that thus far he had led a fairly sheltered, privileged life. But despite his youth and inexperience he also knew it was extremely unwise to ever make a 'blind promise'.

And yet . . . there were two things about this girl/woman Nika that he thought he could be certain of, despite barely knowing her. *If I don't make the promise, she is not going to tell me anything.*

He also *felt* certain he could trust her, though he did not understand *why* he felt that way.

Am I fooling myself? he wondered. *I want to trust her and give her my promise . . . but what if she is tricking me, and is actually in on the hack that caused me to end up here? I don't like to think that she is part of it. But what if someone forced her?* This made him wonder again about why her eyes seemed so old, and so wary . . .

"Isn't there anything you can tell me that isn't a secret?" he asked. "Your age, for instance?"

"I can safely say that I am not much older than you are, in lived years. But I think that's all I should reveal, until I have your promise."

While he was trying to decide what to do — how to respond, a fight broke out among the wolves. Escalating deep–throated growls and feinted attacks erupted into a frenzy of snapping jaws and lunging bodies. Fangs found purchase in necks, backs, flanks and legs; the smell and taste of blood crazed the wolves into a mindless swirl of savagery. The aeor was buffeted whenever a wolf was flung or flipped across the aeor's dome, leaving bloody smears.

The fight ended almost as quickly as it started. The wolves broke free from each other, snarling. Some slunk away into the darkness, while others stood beside the aeor, licking their wounds or panting with their tongues lolling. A few turned their heads to gaze steadily at Wenq and Nika.

"I'm thinking that was a fight between two different packs," commented Nika, "and that the second pack to arrive was the one that won. Now they probably think they've *earned* the right to eat us."

Wenq had never seen wolves fight with such fury, and so close up. He agreed with Nika — their gaze now had a possessive, *hungering* glint.

He told her, "Thank you for getting me back into the aeor before *any* of those wolves arrived."

"You are most welcome," she replied formally. "So," she continued, pressing what she perceived was an advantage, "what about that promise?"

"I can promise you that I won't reveal any secret of yours as long as it is not illegal or, or just plain wrong," Wenq offered.

Nika shook her head. "That's not enough, Wenq. The wellbeing of two others besides myself is involved."

Seeing that he looked totally baffled, she added, "Two that you care about as well."

Two . . . care . . . "My mother and sister?" he asked quickly.

At the shake of Nika's head, he next asked, "Pani and Honcho Beaver?"

He read the answer in her eyes before she looked away, saying, "I probably shouldn't have —"

"Are Pani and Honcho Beaver friends of yours?" Wenq asked.

"Well, yes, I think so."

"Nika, do your secrets have anything to do with the hack that kidnapped me on my way to Braves training?"

Now it was Nika's turn to look baffled. "Oh," she said, "is that

122

what happened?" Her face then lit with partial understanding. "Is that why the aeor crashed?" she asked.

Wenq gave himself a few moments to think. Then, taking a deep breath, he gave Nika his unconditional promise.

She then told him, "One of my secrets is that I do not have an ID chip. Another is that I am an owl shapeshifter. I am the owl you captured yesterday, Wenq, and that you let go after the crash."

Wenq's jaw moved up and down but no words came out of his mouth. This was so far from anything he could have imagined . . . *his* Pani and Honcho B, harboring a girl who had no ID chip . . . and she was a shape who? A shape what? A shapeshifter . . . he knew a few existed, but they were freaks. They kept themselves apart . . . and he had never heard of any of them being a *bird* before . . .

His mind was boggling over her being that weird little owl . . . which meant that *he* had brought her here . . . and *that* was why she was wearing his clothes . . .

While Wenq was staring at her speechless, Nika's mind had been busy. "Wenq, we'd better hurry up and plan *something* . . . do something. Because if we're *here* because you were kidnapped . . . then those wolves are probably going to be the *least* of our problems."

'*Our* problems.' It registered with Wenq that Nika said '*our*' problems. So he wasn't going to have to face the wolves, and whatever else was out there, alone. He was grateful for that, he supposed, although he wasn't sure how much help a skinny girl, who could turn herself into a tiny owl, was going to be.

"Well, the first thing to do is to signal for help." He rummaged through the bags for one of his keybs.

None of the keybs were usable. "The aeor's transmitter must have been shut down by a hack, or damaged in the crash," he told Nika, "and we don't seem to be close enough to anything else that will transmit a signal."

Wenq was wrong in thinking that his keyb's signal went

unrecognized. It was picked by the hacker Stealth, and only by him.

Chapter 18

This latest round of Stealth's hacks for the New Order had not gone quite as well as he planned. But with a few on–the–fly adjustments, they were all executing smoothly again. The aeor with the Kah girl in it had already landed at the cave, and he was going to pluck her twin brother from the crash site and deliver him to the cave himself.

How fortunate for him that his cover occupation was that of a Wilderness Seek and Capture warrior. He never had to go begging for help like the other Chosen, when problems cropped up in *their* assignments. He had everything he needed to take care of everything by himself.

Now as always, he had all the skills and equipment ready to hand, and had hacked the records perfectly so that none of the Nation's engineers or its good hats would ever know about this mission of his for the New Order. Only he had the tracking record for the crashed aeor. No one else could have done these brilliant hacks, but it was easy for him, because he was the best hacker not just in the Nation, but in the entire world.

Stealth had always known that he was marked for greatness. He had the towering intellect. He was a bold conceptualizer but could also untangle minute intricacies. Not to mention his quicksilver reflexes for dealing with those inevitable, er, glitches.

In short he had it all. And despite his years of extensively shadowing and tinkering with the Nation's records and systems, very few of its engineers and good hats were even aware of his existence, and then only barely so. He was a Shadow Teasingly Ephemeral, Always Lurking, Tantalizingly Hidden — STE–AL–TH. His private joke — ha, ha. No one had ever come anywhere close to finding him, much less catching him!

And yet that was the conundrum that stymied him. He was the greatest hacker ever, but no one else knew it. He — stealth personified — stood on a pinnacle. But no one could see him there.

Until two years ago. Then everything changed.

Leader found Stealth, and informed him that he was marked for greatness, as was Leader himself.

It happened at a routine Seek and Capture seminar. Stealth was on the fringe of some warriors who were standing around jawing during a break in the demonstrations of equipment updates. He was bored nearly to death, but kept to his usual 'blend in', 'lie low' act. The others were boasting about how many coups they'd scored on the latest hacks, put up on the sanctioned sites the preceding day. Boast, boast, blah, blah . . . when there wasn't even one *first class* hacker in the bunch! *Ah,* he thought, *if they only knew that the greatest hacker in the world was right here in their midst . . .*

Somebody asked him what his coup score was. He just murmured that the hack looked so difficult, he'd decided to skip it.

A voice behind him said, so softly that he alone could hear it, "But you and I know better than that, don't we, Stealth?"

Stealth stiffened — *No one but me knows my hack name!*

"But of course I know it," the voice continued, "and I know what you can do. I have sought you because of who you really are. You see, I am Leader, and I need you. I have come for you."

Stealth turned and saw a tall, good–looking man smiling down at him, as if from somewhere much above his actual height. The man exuded a superb pride and confidence, while his eyes danced with the rich fun of sharing Stealth's great secret with him.

Leader wanted Stealth to be among his first recruits — one of the Chosen — for his New Order.

The New Order was going to overthrow the Nation, succeeding where all other attempts had failed. In the New Order, all of the

126

Chosen were marked for greatness. All of them would have enormous personal wealth, and the recognition they deserved — not to mention the tremendous power they would wield.

Stealth eagerly joined the New Order. He had vision — this, he could see, was what he had been made for. The New Order needed the best hacker in the world, and clearly that was him. He never questioned his belonging to the New Order's super–elite — that was, after all, why Leader had hand–picked him. And besides that, he had Leader's personal promise and guarantee that he was the New Order's top hacker.

The first big assembly of the New Order occurred about a year after Leader recruited him. It was held in a large cave located deep in the Core Wilderness — in a wild, impenetrable area. The cave was almost impossible to find unless you knew its exact coordinates.

Stealth was kept very busy doing the hacks to make sure that the assembly stayed all hush–hush, clandestine.

At the assembly, overall Stealth was rather impressed with his first look at the other Chosen — they were warriors, scientists, administrators and others with special expertise, from all over the Nation. It was uncanny, their range and depth. Everyone at the assembly sensed their combined greatness. It invigorated, intoxicated. The crowd in the large cave room fairly frothed with excitement.

But Stealth was disconcerted to find, from listening to the eager talk of the others, that many of them believed that they had exceptional hacking skills, in addition to their main expertise. Clearly, they thought their services to the New Order would include some high–caliber hacking.

For Stealth, this was like finding a fly in his soup. Their hacking skills were bound to be inferior, and he foresaw much trouble as a result. Overconfident, they would crowd him with their stupid, know–it–all ideas. They would criticize him for the smallest glitches in his on–the–fly hacks, and claim that they could have easily done better. They would always be trying to undermine him, get him ousted. He had not been expecting this. For the first time since he met Leader, he began to have doubts.

Then a few minutes alone with Leader completely restored his faith.

He didn't recollect exactly how he came to be in Leader's dim antechamber, with just himself and Leader present. He supposed Leader's Second fetched him there. Leader's Second was a formidable woman who reminded Stealth very much of an ugly old hawk. She had a prominent beak–like nose, a cold gaze, and long curving nails on her sinewy hands. During the assembly at the cave, she seemed to always be somewhere on Leader's periphery, carrying something for him, or delivering his messages.

The antechamber's only illumination was reflected off surfaces, from a torch set in the passageway outside. The lighting was fitful, but somehow it was enough for Stealth to be able to see just what he needed to see.

There was a strong odor in the room — something like a pervasive incense — that Stealth could have done without, but then he decided it wasn't too bad. In fact, he came to think it was bracing, in a manly kind of way.

Up until then Stealth had only seen the public persona of Leader. In that inner sanctum, he felt highly honored to be consorting with Leader in private, at his leisure. Leader lounged on the skin of what must have been an enormous snake. The whitish mottled pelt was arranged in great crisscrossed folds. As Leader leaned back against its expanse, the huge diamond–shaped scales seemed to wink at Stealth in the befuddling light.

With a gesture Leader invited Stealth to seat himself on a mound of luxurious pelts of bear, wolf, and panther.

Leader's amused eyes shone out of the darkness, mildly admonishing Stealth for his doubts. "I chose you; *of course* I am going to reward your absolute, unswerving loyalty. My confidence in you is unshakable." Then, in a 'just–between–the–two–of–us' tone, Leader

128

gave Stealth his personal promise: "You, and you alone, will be the New Order's top hacker. None other."

Leader gave Stealth something to wear around his neck on a leather braid. It was a small wooden hoop, thin and no bigger than the palm of his hand. "You must always wear it," Leader told Stealth. "It makes my promise to you unbreakable."

Stealth slipped the braid over his head and let the hoop drop under his shirt.

Back in the assembly room, Stealth no longer worried about hot–shot hacker wannabes.

The meeting reached a strange, beguiling state. Everyone — including Stealth — talked loudly, past and over each other, vying to be heard, clamoring about what they thought was essential to be done. At the same time, they were aware that momentous decisions had just been made, though they weren't exactly sure what they were. But everyone was bursting with confidence and enthusiasm, including Stealth, though in his case it was not because of anything that was being decided at the assembly. It was because he had Leader's promise.

It wasn't until after he had returned home from the assembly, that he learned what his part was going to be, in the next phase of the New Order. About a month after the assembly, Leader's Second visited him, and all was made clear.

Stealth wished that Leader himself had come. But Leader's promise was still fresh in his heart. Stealth accepted that, with so much to be done, Leader could not be everywhere and do everything himself.

Leader's Second scraped her sharp, curving nails across her keyb to bring up a text box with Action Point 217 in it, which stipulated that an ample supply of workers — minions, she called them — was needed for the cave, to perform important work for the New Order, and to be 'trained up' to join its lower echelons, if they proved themselves worthy. Stealth didn't remember anything about an

Action Point 217 being discussed at the assembly in the cave, but no matter — Leader's Second was there to go over it all with him.

Each and every moon cycle, some of the Chosen — including Stealth — must deliver to the cave two young, healthy minions , no older than their teens. Minions should be at least five or six years old, up to age fourteen or so — easier to train up that way. A few up to age sixteen would be alright, especially if they were changers, as Leader's Second called shapeshifters.

In plucking these minions from the Nation's population, utmost secrecy was essential — records must be flawlessly modified, subterfuges executed with cunning. The Nation must not catch on that the New Order was orchestrating these disappearances until later on, when the New Order was ready to reveal itself and take over.

Naturally, Leader was expecting Stealth to be exceptionally good at collecting minions, because of his extraordinary hacking skills.

Leader's Second also relayed a personal request from Leader. Leader wanted Stealth to aid two of the other Chosen in their assignments to purloin minions for the cause. Stealth was to guide their hacking efforts, rate them, and report his findings back to Leader's Second.

Stealth was not pleased to find that, besides doing his own assignment, he was supposed to help two other Chosen with theirs. He always worked alone. But since it was a personal request from Leader, he acquiesced as gracefully as he could manage.

One of the two that he was asked to work with, turned out to be alright. Stealth did not really mind helping Shaw, because from the start Shaw had the right attitude. He was always very humble about his hacking. He readily admitted that Stealth's skills were vastly superior to his own, and he always deferred to Stealth. Shaw was a big lump of man, apparently brilliant at strategic chemical munitions, but clearly struggling with his minion assignment. Stealth actually went far out of his way to help Shaw. When he discovered that Shaw's problem – besides his lousy hacking — was that he was too softhearted, Stealth coached him, bucked up his resolve, and practically delivered his first minion for him. Then, as Stealth had rightly surmised, Shaw got over his squeamishness and took take care of delivering his allotment of minions each moon cycle on his own.

It was Lako, the other one of the Chosen that Stealth had to work with, who became a real thorn in his moccasin. Working with her perfectly illustrated why working alone was always preferable. Lako was Shaw's near–opposite: she thought very highly of her hacking skills. She always insisted she needed no help from Stealth, and then took all of his suggestions and claimed that she'd thought of them herself. She wormed information out of him, about his own minion assignments, that he did not really want to share. And then oh, how she gloated when the least little thing went wrong with one of his hacks!

Lako'd gotten even worse in the last few months because, as a logistics specialist, she went completely covert for the New Order. According to the Nation's records she was Outside, three months along in a two–year educational trip. But in fact she was at the cave, developing and maintaining a comprehensive system of her own design, for monitoring the minions.

Stealth had shown her how to do the hack that permitted her to go covert. Since it worked perfectly, she gave him no credit for it — claimed she had done it all herself. And she was insufferably smug about being on–the–job and in–the–hub at 'Central', as she called it.

Stealth would have liked to block all of the encrypted voice messages she sent him. Unfortunately, he had to be in communication with her from time to time, about the minions he was delivering each moon.

She never missed an opportunity to needle him. Earlier today, in one of her messages she complained about the Kah girl he'd sent to the cave. "Weqi Kah just arrived — or should I say, made an entrance. Such a drama queen! She'll be useless — except for laughs and slopwork. But mmmm, here's an advise, Stealth, just between us ol' pals — minions that are only good for laughs and slops — that gets old real fast here at good ol' Central. Yeah, you've done a double and almost caught up on your quota but, *really?* Weqi Kah was the best you could do? I wish I could make you take her back! Ha, ha, ha!"

Later, when she informed him that the Kah boy had not arrived on schedule — "The aeor bringing Wenq Kah to the cave has disappeared from my screen, Stealth. Apparently, one of your hacks has wiped the trace. Tryin' to hide something from me? Got a little rip in your britches goin' on there?"

Despite Lako's nasty jibes, Stealth knew he had everything back under control. He had his aeor homed in on the Kah boy's crashed aeor, and was nearly there. He'd get the boy and deliver him personally to the cave, which wasn't too much farther west by aeor.

The Kah girl, he felt sure, wasn't as useless as Lako said she was. He'd break down that petty lie of Lako's when he delivered the boy. He also wanted to spend a few moments with Leader while he was there. He had Leader's promise, but it wouldn't hurt to remind him of it, in–person.

Then he would move on to Phase 3 of the Kah double hack, to wrap it all up. He'd make it look like the mother and her two kids had gone back Outside. Phase 3 had been delayed because of this little hiccup in Phase 2 — getting the Kah boy to the cave. But he'd smooth it all out. Talk about counting coup! It was a brilliant two–for–one. He'd bet that no one else was managing their minions assignment nearly so well.

Chapter 19

When Stealth's aeor alerted him that it was in a hover over the crash site, the trees completely blocked his view of it. At most he could see a few freshly broken branches in the canopy, where the aeor carrying the Kah boy had fallen through.

He programmed his aeor to land as close to the crash site as possible.

Most aeors had to seek a fairly open area in order to land, which might be an irksome distance from the true destination. But Stealth's Seek and Capture aeor was specially designed and equipped for landing close–in, even in rough terrain. And, being Stealth, he had done some brilliant hacks to its complex programming, to make it even more pin–point capable.

Even so the landing felt like a dicey, bumpy, shimmying plummet through the massive old trees. Several times his aeor got hung up in interlaced branches, making him feel like some kind of goofy bird stuck high up in a nest, instead of what he really was: an ace Seek and Capture guy working his way down in an enhanced, state–of–the–art aeor.

Whenever the aeor shimmied free of a 'nest' of branches, it lurched, tilted and dropped precipitously, causing Stealth to wonder if he'd made a few *tiny* mistakes in his hacks on the aeor's landing programs.

But the last twenty feet or so of a landing was what really mattered, and the aeor performed that part flawlessly. It settled gently onto the shadowy forest floor, and through the gloom Stealth could see the crashed aeor not far away. Only a few large tree trunks partially blocked his view of it.

The crashed aeor was intact, but canted against a tree trunk. Stealth sent a recon droner over to it. The droner readily detected three wolves milling around the aeor, but the aeor's dome interfered with detection of the boy's body heat inside it.

Using the droner's spotlight and visual relay, Stealth could see on his screen a blanketed figure inside the dome, lying across the backs of the three seats. That would be the boy, apparently asleep. Stealth wondered if he'd been injured in the crash. *Serves him right if he's bumped up,* Stealth thought. *He should have known better than to mess with someone else's hacks on an aeor in midflight.*

While Stealth was getting out of his aeor, one of the wolves started to come in his direction. Then it hesitated, and was veering away when Stealth pointed his Rif in its general direction. The Rif locked onto the wolf and Stealth killed it while waiting for his Skim's platform to finish unfolding. He stepped onto the Skim when it was ready and set it to pursue the other two wolves.

As Stealth rode the Skim past the crash site it flushed a pair of pine martens from a tree hollow. Stealth whipped the Skim around and picked them both off with his Rif. He was ready for target practice whenever an opportunity presented itself.

Locking his Rif in on each of the two wolves in turn, he killed them as they tried to slink away. The Skim was swift and agile, fully shielded and loaded with both kill and capture gear. Stealth was indisputably the top predator in this forest.

But things had changed at the crash site in the short time he was away from it: the aeor's dome was open, and the boy was no longer inside it.

Stealth surmised that the boy had tricked him, lulling him into going after the wolves so he could escape. *But he can't have gotten very far away,* Stealth thought. *I'll catch up with him in no time.*

He used the equipment on the Skim to scan for the boy, but its furthest range in this density of woods was only about 100 feet. Unsurprisingly, he did not get a detect.

No matter. I'll just track him using his ID chip. Much easier really. He rode the Skim back to his aeor to retrieve the keyb that had his hack on it for the boy's ID chip. He immediately got a blip on the chip and set off on the Skim to pursue the boy.

* * *

Stealth did not know it, but he was going off on a 'wild moose chase'. He *was* following Wenq's ID chip. But the chip was no longer inside Wenq.

* * *

Removing Wenq's ID chip from his arm was the first thing that Wenq and Nika decided on after agreeing that they should leave the aeor as soon as possible. In response to Nika's questioning, Wenq confirmed that his ID chip could be tracked fairly easily, within about a mile range, which meant that an aeor programmed to cruise a search grid at tree–top level in this area would locate his chip fairly quickly.

The chip could be felt as a slight bump under the skin of Wenq's forearm. Cutting a chip out was supposed to be done only by a qualified medic, and of course it was a major crime to remove one without buckets of special approvals. But Wenq agreed with Nika that it needed to be done right away. He still didn't know why he'd been waylaid, but on top of everything that had already happened to him, he did not want the hacker or his buddies to be able to find him so easily in the forest.

Nika strapped Wenq's forearm to a seat armrest. Wenq turned away and as some of the wolves watched through the aeor's dome, Nika excised the chip, making a slit cut with Wenq's sharpest knife. It hurt him, but the thought of being cut into was worse than the actual pain. The wound bled a lot but most of the blood soaked into a pad underneath his arm. They used an antiseptic clotting unguent on the wound, from the aeor's first aid pouch, along with some Liqui–Derm that was applied over it.

They next went through the gear and divided what they planned

135

to take into two piles. Most of it would go into their pockets or two of the shoulder bags, but in addition they each attached a short knife to their belts, and Wenq would carry the low caliber Immobilizer he had brought, on a shoulder sling. It did not have much power or range, but it might slow down a smaller predator, or help keep a larger one at bay.

Nika then shapeshifted to owl, and Wenq opened the dome just enough for her to slip out and take flight. She was going to reconnoiter, and would also dispose of his ID chip.

Nika was watchful in case a wolf lunged at her, but the wolves showed little interest in her. To them she was a strange Two–Legger that stank pungently of owl, and sometimes even looked like one. In any matter of doubt, they let their noses rule them. As long as she smelled like an owl, she was not one of their preferred prey. It was the other Two–Legger that they were keen on. They salivated over the scent of his blood that wafted through the temporary crack in the structure that contained him.

Wenq did their packing while Nika was gone, while marveling over the first shapeshifting he had ever witnessed. It was a transformation that he never could have imagined until he actually saw it. But once seen, it seemed so natural, almost inevitable. Many things about Nika — her slight size and frame, her large round eyes and her pervasive wariness — seemed seamlessly connected to her ability to shapeshift, so beautifully, into a small owl.

He hadn't seen much of her human body before she shapeshifted. She just seemed to shrink down into the clothes she was wearing, and then came scrambling out of them as an owl.

She returned fairly quickly. She had taken the ID chip north to a small riverway that meandered through the forest, heavily overhung with trees and brush. On its bank she shapeshifted to girl and selected a sound branch from the litter, about as thick around as her wrist. She broke off a piece about a foot long and bound the chip into a crevice with some woven lengths of willow. Then as an owl again she labored to get the branch to the middle of the river, where she dropped it into the flow. The branch was likely to float a considerable distance before snagging somewhere along the bank.

Nika took the chip north because, as she had explained to Wenq, she thought their best land route was in another direction — not the exact opposite direction, because that might be too obvious. The route she recommended went southeasterly toward a boggy area, and then easterly into hillier ground that was studded with rocky overhangs.

"But first," Wenq had asked, "how am I going to get past the seven or so wolves that surround the aeor?"

"With the pad that got soaked with your blood, when your ID chip was removed," Nika answered. "I'll carry it away, upwind, and the scent of your blood will draw them away from here."

They sealed the pad inside a pouch that they sprayed on the outside with some No–Scent. Nika left the aeor again as owl, with the pouch in her beak. She flew westerly about a quarter mile, since the wind was from that direction. Shapeshifting to girl on a large tree branch about fifteen feet off the ground, she removed the bloody pad from the pouch, and let the wind carry the scent toward the aeor.

Inside the aeor Wenq kept himself covered with a blanket. From underneath it he watched as the wolves lifted their heads nearly as one and faced west. Then, barely glancing at the aeor, they streamed away in that direction.

Wenq quickly arranged some of the bags under the blanket to make it look like someone about his size was lying asleep across the aeor's seat backs. If the wolves came back, he wanted it to look like he was still inside.

He sprayed some No–Scent on himself and their gear, and quietly left the aeor. He closed the dome behind him, hiding its manual crank where he and Nika had agreed, under the aeor. He then left the vicinity as fast as possible, heading southeast. He kept the Immobilizer at the ready, but he hoped the No–Scent would work long enough, so that the wolf pack would not pick up his scent. He did not want to test this Immob's capabilities against them. It was only intended for small wildlife studies. In this forest, it felt like a toy in his hands.

Out in the open the No–Scent would only work for a half hour or so, and there wasn't enough of it left for another full application.

It was one of the things he'd brought with him for the Braves training, for use in the Evasion Challenge. The boys sprayed it on themselves and were given a head start in some light woods, before some scent–tracking droners went in after them. The boy from each Squad who lasted longest before being found counted coup, and got to wear a genuine wolf tail at that evening's meet around the big campfire.

Wenq had dreamed of evading the droners long enough to earn the wolf tail. But now that paled, compared to evading the real wolves that had watched him so avidly through the aeor's dome, as if he was a big chunk of fresh meat which, sooner or later, was destined to end up in their stomachs.

Chapter 20

Wenq had been in the Core before, but only as part of large, well–protected groups that came in bus aeors to visit designated scenic sites, just for a few hours and in optimal conditions.

This is a lot different, he thought, as he hurried from the crash site.

He had been taught about his heritage — about how long ago, his ancestors had filtered into forests like this one, surviving as hunter–gatherers with crude weapons and the roughest imaginable shelters. But he had not understood what it felt like to constantly live with the danger of savage death. *It's no wonder,* he thought, *that in those primitive times they stayed in groups as much as possible — more safety and better odds together, than alone. There would have been times, though, when they couldn't help being alone and exposed, like I am now.*

He tried to use his senses to improve his chances. He eyed his surroundings, and assessed the sounds that reached him. He gauged the direction of the air moving across his skin, to intuit the likely direction that a keen–nosed predator might come from, when the No–Scent wore off. That included any wolf, bear or panther that was downwind of him . . . and those were just the first predators that came to mind.

At first he moved fairly quickly through the forest. He was fresh and the going wasn't too rough. His journey got more difficult after a mile or so on a gradual down slope. More light filtered through the trees, thickening the underbrush. He had to skirt some of the denser scrub, making it hard to keep his southeasterly bearing.

He worried that Nika would have trouble finding him if he strayed too far off his course. He wondered why she had not caught up with him yet. He could only hope nothing had gone wrong for her.

There was still no sign of her when he reached some quagmires, where he was supposed to change course and go more easterly.

The clumpy grasses and bushes were taller than he was, because the area had few standing trees. The ground was spongy and uneven, and littered with trees that had fallen over, exposing gnarled, compacted root masses. Wenq had learned about this in the Cubbie meets. It usually meant there was something impenetrable, like shale or rock, not far below the mucky soil, so the roots massed near the surface, and then the tree would blow over in a strong–enough wind storm.

It was taking him much longer to get through the tangle of brush and fallen trees. Worse than that, the tall grasses and bushes blocked his sight lines, and the noise he was making masked other sounds.

That was why the moose was very close before he realized it was there.

Grunts and huffs approached rapidly, along with some clicking noises. A large bull moose hove into view, his antlered head already low, whipping from side to side, with his dewlap swinging below his neck. A loathing smoldered in the moose's eyes as it charged.

Wenq had a split second to decide what to do.

Firing the Immob'll just infuriate it. So, ball or tree?

He probably should have rolled himself into a ball — a moose charge is so fast, even over rough ground, and this moose was already much too close.

But he tried to reach a downed tree, to put it between himself and the moose. He waved his arms to look bigger and unafraid, and spoke in a low–pitched singsong that he hoped sounded firm but nonthreatening to the moose, all the while backing away.

His maneuvers did slow the moose slightly. But then he tripped and fell.

He did a desperate overhead roll to get clear of the first kick when the moose reached him. The lethal hoof sliced past his leg,

140

knocking him sideways. He did another roll toward the tree. He was almost there but not close enough.

The moose's next kick would have been fatal if Nika hadn't gotten there in time.

*   *   *

Nika dove in as owl and sank her talons into the moose, right behind its antlers, emitting a screech to startle it further, and to alert Wenq that she was there.

The moose bellowed and bucked and ran to free itself from the sudden pain in its head. It ran a long distance before bogging down in some mire. At that point Nika broke free of it and winged back to Wenq.

Wenq was gathering up the gear that had been scattered when the moose charged. Nika shapeshifted to girl and helped him, taking up her share of the load. Other than slipping a blanket over a shoulder and tying it under her opposite arm, she did not pause to dress herself.

"We must hurry," she told Wenq. "There're other dangers, besides that moose."

They made better time getting out of the boggy area, than Wenq had managed on his own. Together they went directly over the downed trees, instead of skirting them. The first to reach the tree set up a foot lift for the other to scramble onto the trunk; then that one helped the other up and over with an arm pull.

They reached some woods where the land began to slope upward. Less concentration was needed to get through the ground cover there, so Nika told Wenq about what had happened at the crash site, before she came to join him.

Their ploy to draw the wolves away from the crashed aeor had worked. "All seven of them came to where I was waiting for them with the bloody pad. Just before they arrived, I tore the pad into two and snagged half of it on the branch. Then I shapeshifted to owl and carried the other half further west, with some roving to spread the

141

blood scent. That was to confuse the wolves and keep them casting for a trail well away from the aeor, for as long as possible.

"But on my flight back to the aeor, I found that three of the wolves were already on their way back to the aeor. I reached the aeor not long before they did, and settled onto a branch to see whether they would pick up your trail leading away from it.

"They didn't. The No–Scent worked perfectly. They sniffed and looked around the perimeter of the aeor, and then took up positions around it. They thought that you were still inside!

"I was about to leave to join you, when I heard some strange noises high overhead. I flew up and saw an aeor making its way down through the trees."

Nika then described how she tried to keep herself inconspicuous, and at a safe distance, while watching the aeor's descent, and the man inside the aeor.

The aeor was much smaller than the 3–seater, and had a symbol etched into its curved rim, which Nika committed to memory.

It looked very trim and sleek, and seemed to have barely enough space inside its domed area for the man at the controls. The space all around him bristled with tiers of panels, levers and other gadgetry that Nika could not guess the purpose of, except for one item that worried her: it looked like a larger version of Wenq's Immobilizer.

The passenger was a full–grown man, wearing clothing that was bulked out with bulging pockets. A marking on each shoulder of his shirt was similar to the symbol etched on the aeor's outer rim, but not exactly the same.

The man was too preoccupied with working the aeor down through the trees, to notice a small owl flitting about in the vicinity, at a discreet distance. As he worked to control the aeor's descent, he reacted nervously to its occasional tipsiness, and steep downward lurches.

Nika tried to assess his nature. *What kind of person is this?* she wondered.

142

He was obviously working his way down to the crash site. *Could he be a rescuer, even though we weren't able to send out a distress signal? Or is he connected to the hack that kidnapped Wenq?*

Nika inclined to think the latter. *His movements seem both cocky and furtive. And every time his aeor takes a sudden dive, his face looks harried, as if he knows he's responsible for the sudden drops, but doesn't want to admit it, even to himself. Especially to himself.*

He reminded her strongly of Sedric, her old master's son, and Sedric had certainly not been a decent, trustworthy person. All in all, it was Nika's guess that this man wasn't one either.

When the man landed, he launched a tiny device from his aeor that flew like a hummingbird over to the crashed aeor and gyrated around it. Nika supposed it was what Honcho Beaver had called a droner. She kept herself very still, as she watched it from a nearby tree. If the device registered her presence at all, she hoped it would note nothing more than a small, harmless—looking owl.

The device returned to the man's aeor, and when the man stepped out of his aeor he proceeded to load himself up with so much gear that he looked bloated with it. His head was encased in a hard—shelled covering; a sleeveless jacket had even more bulging pockets than his shirt had. His hands and arms were covered with bulky gauntlets that had levers and buttons, and small inset keybs. His feet and legs had similar coverings clear up to his thighs.

The man was carrying something that looked like the larger version of Wenq's Immobilizer. He promptly killed one of the wolves with it.

The wolf had been moving circumspectly in his direction, casting for scent. It was obvious to Nika that the wolf was more hesitant than menacing.

Beside the man, a thin box—like device unfolded itself into a platform, with a rod sticking up from it. When the man stepped onto the platform and grasped the rod, the platform rose with him on it and he was able to travel on it, about two feet from the ground, for the most part. He stood upright and used one of the keybs on his gauntlets to control the platform. It was all nearly silent, except Nika could faintly hear that the man spoke a few words inside his head covering, and there was a low–pitched whining as the platform moved. The sound rose in pitch and became more piercing the faster or higher in the air it went.

The man eagerly pursued and killed two pine martens — gratuitous killings that shocked and appalled Nika. She allowed that he might have felt threatened by the wolf, but what harm could the pine martens be?

When the man darted off on his zippy platform in pursuit of the other two wolves, Nika acted quickly. Conscious that the man's aeor might be recording the crash site through the intervening trees, she shapeshifted back to girl behind the aeor and cranked it open. She quickly got the blanket and bags out and stuffed them into one of the holds. She left the aeor with its dome open, and hid the crank again, always trying to keep what she was doing hidden from the other aeor's direct 'view'. She had to risk that that there might be some fleeting recorded images of her.

She had barely shapeshifted back into owl when she heard the whine of the platform that the man rode on; a few seconds later he arrived.

She watched as he surveyed the open aeor, and then retrieved a keyb from his own aeor. She feared that he was going to use it to view surveillance imagery, but instead he rode off to the north on his platform. She guessed correctly that he had gone off in pursuit of Wenq's ID chip. He still might view surveillance imagery later on — if in fact it existed, but for now he didn't seem to be aware of her existence.

Before she left, she took a quick look at the dead wolf and the martens, and also went in the direction that the man had gone when pursuing the other two wolves. She found one of them, dead, and thought it likely that the man had killed the other one too.

144

The bodies were oddly stiff, lying in positions that belied a natural death. Their torsos and limbs were rigid, as if locked or frozen in motion before they toppled to the ground. In a strange way, they looked as if they'd been discarded like refuse.

It reminded Nika of when she had been zapped by Wenq's Immobilizer. The dead animals looked like they too had been caught in motion, but instead of being held in stasis, they had died.

It seemed to Nika an ignoble kind of death. To her, it was not a good part of what the Nation had become.

She took a last look around, but there didn't seem to be anything to be gained by remaining. She dared not approach the man's aeor, in case he had some kind of surveillance running on it.

She headed west, just in case she was being recorded, but soon whipped around to the southeast, to catch up with Wenq.

Chapter 21

When Nika described the symbol on the man's aeor to Wenq, he told her it was a badge for one of the Seek squadrons, but he didn't know which one. "There are about a dozen different Seek squadrons, and I don't know the badges for most of them," he admitted.

When she described the symbol on the man's shirt, Wenq got excited and said they should return to the crash site, because he recognized that one — most people did. It was for the Seek and Rescue Squadron.

They slowed somewhat while Wenq argued for going back to be rescued, and Nika explained why she thought that was a terrible idea.

Soon Wenq agreed with her, and they resumed their rapid pace eastward. Nika's observations of the man's mannerisms while he maneuvered his aeor — those might have left Wenq in some doubt, despite his new, high confidence in her. But it was the killing that brought him round, particularly the killing of the pine martens.

"It's against the Nation's principles to harm pine martens, Nika," he told her. "They're not a threat to the People. We're not supposed to interfere with them."

Nika asked, "And shouldn't the badge on the aeor match the badge on the shirt?"

"Oh! Yes, it should. Always. So that's another thing that's not right about this guy. The badges should match, because although there's overlap, each type of Seek squadron has its own specialization. The protocols, equipment and training have similarities, but also differences. Someone say, in a Seek and Detain squadron that operates along the borders, wouldn't be using an aeor for a Seek and Rescue squadron, or vice versa."

He continued, "It's my guess that the badge on an aeor would be harder to fake or change, than the badge on a uniform. So I'm thinking the badge on the aeor is the correct one. Could you describe it to me again?"

When she did, Wenq shook his head. "Maybe I'll be able to figure it out if you draw it for me later, when we stop for the night."

Though shadows were lengthening, it looked to Wenq like they had several more hours to go before night's darkness came. He just hoped he could keep up with Nika that long.

They had to put as much distance between themselves and the crashed aeor before nightfall. The greater the distance, the wider the search circle, and the harder it would be for the Seek guy to find them.

They planned to shelter overnight somewhere where the heat of their bodies could be hidden from either a heat–sensing droner, or an aeor scanning for body heat. Then, in the morning, Nika would reconnoiter as an owl further east, looking for one of the old signal towers, or she might find a research station, though Wenq knew there were precious few of those in the Core.

The signal towers had been built hundreds of years ago to boost signals transmitted across the Core's expanse. Even though they were no longer needed for that, except as an antiquated, auxiliary back up, the Nation continued to maintain most of them. Each had a structure anchored to the base, large enough for several people to shelter, along with equipment to signal for rescue.

Most of the towers were hundreds of miles apart, placed along two fairly straight lines, one running east–west, and the other north–south, not unlike a great compass cross. Nika thought that with some time and persistence she might spot one of them from the air. Wenq meanwhile would have to wait, keeping himself hidden.

Wenq hated to think that he would be hiding while Nika was out taking all the risks, even though it was probably for the best. With their scant gear for survival and protection, he was many times more vulnerable in the Core than she was. Her sight and hearing were superior to his, and in a bind she could rapidly take flight, while he was slow, clumsy, and earthbound.

He was also finding that she had a lot more stamina than he did. They had travelled many miles through difficult terrain, yet she still moved lightly and quickly.

He was in better shape than he might have been. He'd been jogging along the beaver paths in the marsh, to prepare for Braves training. But his legs were increasingly leaden and uncooperative, and breath came more often in ragged gasps.

A walking staff helped; each of them had found a likely branch on the ground and broken it down to size. Wenq intended to carry his for protection, but he used it instead for balance, and to eke out a little more speed.

He pushed himself harder than he ever had, determined to do his best and not let Nika down. If they failed, he did not want his weakness to be the reason.

I don't really understand why Nika is helping me, he thought. *She's Pani and Honcho Beaver's friend, not mine.* **And** *I zapped her and put her in a cage, which is an awful thing to do to someone — although I didn't know at the time that she* **was** *a someone.*

I wouldn't have blamed her if she'd flown off and left me at the crash site when I released her from the box. But I'm grateful that she stayed. If I have to be stuck in the Core and nearly defenseless, I can't think of anyone I'd rather be with, than this Nika — well, except maybe some Core–hardened hero–warrior type, all decked out with the latest gadgets and equipment. But there's no chance of anyone like that showing up anytime soon. I have the next best thing. Nika is smart and quick, and she's as brave as someone many times her size. Great Twin, she even attacked a moose!

I can trust her with my life, he realized. And then came the worry. *I hope her life'll be as safe with me, as mine is with her.*

But when we get out of the Core — if we get out of it alive, that is — she'll avoid me because I zapped her. It's hard to ever forgive someone for doing that.

And besides, she seems miles and miles more mature than me. To her I'm just a kid.

At first he had thought that the scarring all over her body was unattractive, but he hardly noticed it now. He had seen her without clothes on twice now, first when she shapeshifted from owl to girl after her first recon, and then in the bog before she got the blanket tied on. And the blanket still left one side of her and most of her legs exposed to his view. He was not too interested in girls as *girls* just yet, but he did think now that she was rather pretty. *It's just too bad that I zapped her.*

He had been admiring her ankles — how trim they were and the way they flexed and rotated to meet the uneven ground. She seemed to float rather than walk. Then her calves and the back of her knees started to look interesting to watch in motion. But that took his eyes further from the ground and he promptly tripped on a root. He barely kept himself from pitching forward, and staggered and wheezed as he strained to catch up with her again.

Nika slowed a little for him when he stumbled. He didn't like it, but he was relieved all the same. It was so hard to force his muscles to keep up the work. He put aside thoughts of twinkling ankles and flashing knees.

By then Nika was doing most of the scanning for danger. She heard and saw things so much sooner than he did. When she signaled to pause they would both listen, and he would look intently in the same direction she did. Sometimes he never heard or saw whatever it was. But when he did, it was always much later.

Mostly he saw nothing more than distant shadows passing between tree trunks, and heard only faint rustlings, or noticed only that the bird twitter either went silent or got more agitated for a while before returning to normal.

A few times he saw some deer in the distance, that were heading in about the same direction as they were going. Nika said that was good sign, because deer knew the safest ways through the forest.

149

To Wenq, the forest seemed fairly quiet and free of other animals; when he said so, Nika's response was that it seemed that way only because of the fall abundance, with deer in particular being plentiful. "A surfeit of deer keeps most of the larger predators satiated, and less likely to pursue two Unknowns — us — moving swiftly through the forest together — at least during the day. As for the smaller prey animals — they hide themselves or leave quietly long before we pass through."

Once when Nika signaled a pause, she had Wenq climb a tree, giving him a foot lift so that he could reach the lowest branch. That was when he realized that, in addition for scanning for danger, she was choosing routes that were close to something that offered him some safety — like a climbable tree, or a dense thicket that he could force himself into, in a pinch.

From what they could glimpse through occasional breaks in the tree canopy, the wind was hauling in heavier clouds from the west. What had begun as a fairly mild, early fall day with occasional smatters of rain, got much colder as the afternoon progressed. About the same time that they started through a hemlock stand, a chill, drizzly rain trickled down on them, through the feathery branches. There wasn't as much brush under the hemlocks, so the going was much easier.

Many of the hemlocks also looked fairly easy to climb. Nika seemed to relax her vigilance a little, commenting that the rain would help keep their scent down. She took Wenq's suggestion to stop long enough for her to put on some of his spare clothes, to protect herself from the rain and the increasing cold. Wenq welcomed the short break to rest his weary legs.

When they continued their trek Nika asked, "Tell me about the weapon that killed the martens and wolves."

"They're called Rifs. They send out a more powerful pulse than Immobilizers. An Immob can never kill, but a Rif can be set to either immobilize or to kill.

150

"Rifs have much more sophisticated Finder capability, and some fail–safes for Lock In accuracy — though those can be overridden. They also have much greater range.

"Once a Rif locks in on a target, it can 'follow' it as long as it stays within range, and at least partially in view in open air, in the general direction that the Rif is pointing."

"What if the target goes completely behind something like a tree, or a large rock?" Nika asked.

"A Rif can't hit a target that's completely blocked by inerts with enough density — like wood, stone, earth, or fairly deep water. And most buildings block their pulse as long as there are no openings in the direction the Rif is pointing. Likewise, a hard, clear substance blocks it, such as the dome of a closed aeor. See, it's intended mainly for open-air use, where the user would usually have other equipment for mobility and speed. If the Seeker knows or suspects a target is behind a rock, say, he would just go fast around the rock."

When Nika asked whether the weapon had any weaknesses, Wenq told her, "Not any serious ones. All it needs is a partial line–of–sight through air, in the target's direction. Rain like this wouldn't matter. A downpour or heavy snowfall might interfere with its longer–range effectiveness, but up close it would still kill."

Wenq added, "I've been meaning to tell you, Nika, that I'm sorry I zapped you with the Immobilizer. I didn't know —"

"But why would you ever zap anything? Don't you know how it feels?"

"Well, I've been told it's very unpleasant —"
Nika scoffed.

"— but it's the safest way I have for obtaining small wild animals, to study them."

Nika started to give Wenq an 'earful' about the experience, but she stopped in mid–sentence and slowed her steps, looking puzzled and tense.

They had come to a place where the high overshadowing

151

hemlocks gave way to the lower, denser growth of an upland bog. Running through the transition area was a broad path of extensive, unnatural damage. To Wenq it looked as if something large — as much as fourteen or fifteen feet wide and as tall — had forced it way through, breaking and mashing everything in its way. Some of the crushed vegetation had been sizable bushes and fairly large trees. The destruction did not proceed in a straight line; it undulated a little to one side and then the other.

The damage looked to be only a day or two old.

Nika stepped gingerly onto the fallen tree limbs and crushed brush, looking both ways along the mashed trail. Wenq squatted nearby to rest his legs. They both sniffed; despite the light rain, there was a stink on the trail like meat going off.

Nika asked Wenq, "You've studied snakes?"

"Snakes?!" Wenq popped up from his squat and stepped quickly away from the debris, thinking that Nika had spotted a snake slithering through it. "Er, well, yes, I've studied them. I know the main types and their habitats."

"What's the largest one that you know of, that might be found in the Core's forests?"

"The largest . . ." Wenq took another step back from the debris. "Well, that would probably be a rat snake. I've never, er, had one of them to study. But let's see, um, some of them get to be, oh, as much as ten feet long when full grown. They're not venomous, but their bite can be fouling. They don't usually bother humans; they kill by squeezing their prey to death, usually rodents, lizards and such."

Nika listened to everything Wenq said, but began shaking her head slowly as soon as he stated the rat snake's length.

"What is it, Nika?" Wenq asked. "What's the matter?"

"Wenq, do you know of anything that could have caused this kind of damage?"

Wenq shook his head. "Not really, at least not here in the Core. The Nation has some big machines for logging on the tree farms of the Perimeter. But those machines wouldn't be able to go over uneven ground like this, and besides they'd cut a narrower, straighter path, that'd be covered with wood chips, instead of torn up mash like this. No, Nika, I can't think of anything that could have done this."

"Try thinking very, very big snake."

Wenq looked doubtfully both ways along the path. He tried to gauge the size, the weight and the brute force of a snake big enough to make a path like this through the forest. At length he said, "It would have to be a mythically huge one."

"Yes."

Wenq looked directly back at Nika. It was a measuring moment, of sizing each other up. Wenq could see that Nika was dead serious. This was not some kind of joke at his expense.

He already trusted her implicitly. So if she thought that a really big snake had done this, he was inclined to believe it, even though it seemed totally crazy to him at the same time.

Nika must have read the leap of faith in his eyes.

"Let's keep going," she said. "I'll explain as we go along."

They crossed the crushed vegetation, continued easterly through the bog, then entered another stand of huge old hemlocks.

Wenq was thinking, *I can't help it if I'm a clumsy oaf–kid to her, but I have to find a way to make my face less readable. I don't mind so much that she could see what I was thinking about the snake. But I have other thoughts — private ones about her, that I don't want her to see so easily.*

Chapter 22

Nika was thinking, with some relief, *At least we're not travelling in the same direction as whatever made that trail. The crushed brush all fell westerly. Whatever it was, it travelled mainly west, and somewhat north.*

And it did not go through the hemlocks, so in the hemlocks we should be safer from it. Probably it was because the hemlocks are so large, and the trunks so close together. Instead it took an easier path through lighter growth.

After reminding Wenq of his promise to keep her secrets, Nika told him some more of them.

She kept her history brief, matter of fact, until she got to the part about the giant snake in the Sky World.

She told Wenq that she had seen the same kind of damage before, when a giant snake had pursued her in a forest of the Sky World, before she was taken to the Meadow Woman, and lived under her protection.

She described the Sky World snake fully, so that Wenq would understand why she feared that the same snake — or a similar one — was now in the Core, and would be a formidable enemy if it ever came after them. She told him of the explicit thoughts — the heady and enticing, though utterly false thoughts —the snake had tried to entrap her with. "That's probably the snake's most powerful weapon, Wenq, even more than its strength and swiftness, and the substance it spits which paralyzes its prey."

Wenq did not interrupt her with questions — though he had many. And because he was listening intently, he was better able to understand that the shakiness in her voice, as she spoke about the snake, was because she was re–living it, in telling it to him. He asked himself, *What chance would I have, up against something that scares this owl*

154

girl so much?

They travelled in silence for a while, leaving the hemlock stand for a more open area of birch, maple and ash, where they had to be more alert. Shadows were lengthening and the light was fading. It was time to find a place to stay overnight.

Wenq kept up with Nika more easily now. His legs were still leaden and shaky, and his breath was labored, but he had tapped a reserve of strength while they were going through the hemlock stand. He hardly noticed it at first, while intent on what Nika was telling him. He was still looking forward to stopping for the night, but his need for it was less urgent.

They had been travelling gradually downward, not far from a winding, broadening stream. Nika commented that they seemed to be following an old road bed, and after observing the lay of the land, Wenq agreed with her. It was heavily overgrown, but there were still traces of a broad shallow dip that ran straight or curved slightly.

"They stopped using most roads in the 2100s," Wenq mentioned. "Certainly the longer distance ones. No need for them. Most everything moves by air. Some roads in the Perimeter were torn out. In the Rim and the Core, they were left to be overgrown by the forest."

Abruptly the forest they were walking through ended along a ridge. Below was a wedge of marshland, and beyond that was what looked in the gloaming like a wide riverway.

They followed the ridge for a while, casting about for a good place to stay overnight. They had almost decided to head back into the forest, to dig out a shelter under some boulders they had passed, when they came upon an unnatural, slightly raised area. It was discernible only because the forest that had overgrown it did not lay quite as naturally on it, as it did on the surrounding land.

Nika thought it might be the foundation of a rectangular building. The foundation itself had filled in and did not offer shelter, but nearby there was a dip below a smaller mound in upsloping

155

ground. With Wenq's help she cleared some of the debris from the center of the dip, revealing a low, narrow opening that was partially blocked by a long heavy branch.

"I think we're in luck," she told Wenq. "This looks like an old root cellar, and it doesn't seem to be already occupied."

Wenq had a small light that he shone inside before they squeezed themselves past the branch. It was indeed a small root cellar, with a low barrel vault buried under four or five feet of earth. In days long past it overwintered fruits and vegetables. Now it smelled heavily of rodent. Tree roots rippled the clayey floor and grew through the vault's stonework, but it was dry and both Nika and Wenq felt it was a better place to stay overnight than a scoop–out under a boulder. The earth overhead would mask their body heat from detection by an overhead droner or aeor, and they could barricade the opening against predators.

Wenq set to work clearing a space on one side of the root cellar, while Nika shapeshifted to owl and overflew the area. She returned quickly; she did not see a signal tower but was able to guide them to a streamlet for water. They filled their water bags and carried them back to their shelter in the dark. Nika, with her excellent night vision, led. They closed themselves in, leaving an opening for Nika to go in and out easily as an owl.

Besides the water bags, their gear included some dehydrated food from the aeor's emergency kit, a shallow dish and some basic utensils. Wenq supped on some of the food, but Nika took a gob of it and put it as lure near one corner, where she'd heard mouse rustlings. She hoped to dine on a mouse or two later on.

There was no question of starting a fire; even a small amount of heat or smoke rising from the root cellar might be detected on a droner or aeor scan.

They discussed whether Wenq should try to use one of his keybs to signal for help. They might now be within range of something that would accept or at least boost a keyb's signal.

The problem was that anything in range might include the equipment of the guy they dubbed 'the marten killer'. No, they decided, the risk was too great, especially since they planned to be here for several hours. If a keyb signal enabled the marten killer to pinpoint their location, he could get here swiftly by aeor.

"I've been wondering about something," Nika said. "You're certain it was the marten killer who took over control of the aeor we were in. Well, couldn't he also take control of the equipment at the signal towers? So that if we find one of them, he'll know it when we send out a signal for rescue?"

Wenq didn't think so. If someone tried to hack that equipment, he thought it would send some kind of priority breach signal. That would alert whoever maintained the equipment to go check on it.

"At least, I hope so," he told Nika.

"At least, it's a comforting thought," he added.

He sighed.

"But it's probably not worth the risk," he admitted.

There was only one blanket but that wasn't a problem because Nika didn't need one. She shapeshifted to owl for the night.

Wenq was asleep almost as soon as he got himself wrapped up in the blanket.

* * *

Nika listened to Wenq's full, deep breathing while she waited to catch her dinner. She could have easily gotten two mice, but stopped at one. She did not want to be overfed, for that dulled the senses. She thought, *I need to be ready, in case something unexpected comes up.*

It was a good thing she passed on that second mouse.

157

Chapter 23

Nika roosted in the fork of one of the branches they used to block the root cellar's entrance. When she wedged that branch in, she pointed the fork toward the inside of the cellar, so she would be protected from the outside by both the main part of the branch, and by other branches between it and the outside.

After a few hours of sleep she awoke to sounds alerting her to a stealthy presence close to the root cellar. Through the glop and splatter of desultory rain her ears caught the sound of the near–silent press of weight on sodden ground, not far downslope from the entrance. After a silence the sound came again, a little closer. Then again. It was the steps of something large and heavy, that nonetheless moved in near–perfect silence through the murky darkness.

She could also hear lighter steps coming from the mound over the root cellar. There was at least one other near–silent presence in the darkness there.

It wasn't the near–silence of predators passing through the area. It was the near–silence of an imminent attack.

Even with this foreknowledge the attack was sudden and shockingly powerful. Something large and dark crashed down on the branches in the root cellar's entrance. Nika glimpsed a long–clawed bear paw as she was nearly yanked out of the entranceway with the branch she'd been roosting on. Just in time she released her hold on it and flitted over to where Wenq was.

The large heavy branch that blocked most of the entranceway was yanked out of the way as if it was a mere twig. A few more swipes of the bear paw cleared the entrance completely. Nika saw the tip of a large bear's nose, and heard its deep–chested breath as it took a whiff before backing out of her sight line.

It wasn't quite as dark outside as it had been earlier. Some ragged moon glow came through where rain clouds had broken up.

Judging from the size of the bear's paw and snout, it was much too big to come through the entrance. But Nika knew it was not out there alone.

*　*　*

Wenq bolted awake and pulled out his belt knife, scrambling for the Immob. Nika, close by him, stayed as owl for the time being.

A hard, angry voice from outside said, "Both of you come out with your hands and pockets empty."

Neither Wenq nor Nika moved a muscle.

"*Now!*" grated the voice, and there was no mistaking its harshness and fury.

"I'm coming," Wenq called out, as calmly as he could manage. "Give me just a moment." He started emptying his pockets.

Nika shapeshifted to girl and snatched up the blanket. "You're sure we should go out at all?" she whispered.

"There are so many ways to flush us out," Wenq whispered back. "Better just do it, not make him angrier."

"It's odd, Wenq. There's a large bear out there, and maybe more than one." Nika placed herself between Wenq and the entranceway. Wenq thought she might have some notion of going out first and attacking whoever or whatever was out there. "I should go out first, Nika," he whispered to her.

His voice had a calmness he did not feel, but he was sure he needed to be the one to go first, to face whatever was out there. After a few moments Nika moved aside, to let him.

He was expecting to see the marten killer, loaded from head to toe with the latest in Seek equipment.

Instead, the first thing he saw in the darkness was an old but large and powerfully–built man, without anything covering him whatsoever. The man stood facing the entrance, about thirty feet

159

away from it. *A safe enough distance from uncertainties,* Wenq thought, *if he has good reflexes. And he looks like he probably does.*

As Wenq got just beyond the entrance a slight sound above him warned him that something or someone was on the mound over the root cellar, probably poised to pounce on him.

For a moment he considered scurrying back inside, but it was already too late. Whatever was overhead could easily drop on him. He walked toward the big man, because he supposed that was what was wanted. But he moved slowly because the man's face matched the fury he had heard in the voice, when it had ordered him to come out unarmed. It was a smoldering anger, barely contained. Wenq did not want to get too close to a man that angry, for fear he would lash out and knock him down.

"Stop there," the man growled at him, when Wenq had covered about half the distance. "Now the old bird woman. Out!"

When Nika joined Wenq, the man looked at her intently. Uncertainty flitted across his face; his angry glare lessened slightly, though his eyes narrowed with suspicion.

He nodded to someone behind them. Wenq and Nika risked turning slightly; the man did not object so they watched as two young men dropped down off the mound and ducked to go inside the root cellar. One of the young men looked full grown, fairly tall with a lean build; the other was stockier and looked several years younger, like he might not be too many years older than Wenq. The taller one was as naked as the older man; the stockier one was fully clothed in traditional woodsman garb. He looked like he had stepped out of an old story about ancestors, except that he pulled a small, ultra–modern light from a pocket and shined it around inside the cellar.

It didn't take the two young men long to go through Wenq and Nika's gear. They did so in silence, though there was an occasional snicker. When they came out the taller one shook his head at the big man. He was carrying the Immob, which he tossed down at the big man's feet. Then he tossed something small at the big man, which

160

the man caught easily in one of his large hands, even though the throw was wide.

The big man examined the small object and made an odd grunt in his throat, which sounded dismissive, derisive. Suddenly he threw the object at Wenq. It hit Wenq squarely in the center of his chest. Wenq fumbled for it but wasn't able to catch it. He had to pick it up from the ground. It was his family's fawn totem, that he had taken out of his pocket and left with his other belongings.

The stockier young man was carrying a couple of Wenq's keybs, and was already running his fingers over one of them. Wenq could see a slight glow on the keyb's surface; apparently the guy knew how to use a keyb, or at least how to get a startup screen.

The guy grabbed Wenq's right arm and passed it over the keyb. But because Wenq's ID chip had been removed from his arm, the keyb did not register his keycode. The stocky guy grunted "Keycode," at Wenq.

Wenq wished he had seen what the stocky guy was doing with the keyb sooner. He might have been able to stop him from starting it up in time. He turned to the big man and tried to explain. "There's a Seek man after us — a hacker. We don't know why he's chasing us but we think he's dangerous. Just by starting up that keyb, the Seek man probably knows where we are now. He could get here any —"

Wenq was not able to finish because the stocky guy cuffed him to the ground, growling "Keycode!" at him again.

Several things happened nearly at once. Nika shapeshifted to owl and whipped her talons up toward the stocky guy's eyes, causing him raise an arm defensively and stumble backward. The taller young man shapeshifted to wolf, sprang and snapped his jaws at Nika as she keeled away and pumped her wings to reach a tree branch. And the big man scooped up the Immob and nearly zapped Nika with it. He only missed because she saw him in time and got the tree's trunk between herself and the Immob's pulse.

She then flew further away, careful to keep tree trunks between

161

herself and the Immob.

*   *   *

Having failed to immobilize Nika, the big man whispered instead.

At first while he was whispering, he looked straight at Nika, so she knew he was doing it on purpose. When he whispered she was too far away to hear what he was saying.

Before long he squatted down next to Wenq and spoke to him — still whispering. He didn't seem as angry as before, or at least he didn't seem to be angry at Wenq.

Wenq got up and started walking in the direction the big man pointed him in, which was the direction that Nika had flown. The big man followed a short distance behind Wenq, without the Immob, giving him directions until Wenq was standing below Nika's tree. The two young men trailed behind the big man. Nika noticed that Wenq was carrying their blanket.

When Wenq could see Nika he told her, "These are three nomars, Nika. The big, older one is Tehwe. He's their leader, and he wants you to come down and for us to go with him. He says we should hurry, because he agrees with you — the guy we've been calling the marten killer might come. He says there's been a misunderstanding, and he needs to know from you about the giant snake."

Nika shapeshifted to girl on the branch.

"Has Tehwe told you that he is a bear shapeshifter?" she asked.

"He hasn't mentioned that yet," Wenq responded carefully. "But we haven't had much time. The thing is, I trust him, Nika, and I think you will too."

While Nika was considering, there was a subtle change in the surroundings. It was indefinable but Nika felt it. Everything — the dark mistiness, the rain drip, the air sweeping unevenly through leaves and across myriad surfaces — was the same as before. And yet it wasn't.

Nika could tell that the big man felt it too. He had stilled and

162

raised his head slightly. The taller young man noticed the change in the big man, and began to glance around suspiciously. Wenq and the shorter young man seemed unaware of any difference.

"Something's coming," Nika told Wenq. When she glanced at the big man, he nodded.

Chapter 24

Stealth landed his aeor on a narrow wedge of land between a tree–covered ridge and a marshy swath. The signal from one of the boy's keybs had come from nearby on that ridge.

He was surprised that the boy had been able to separate from his ID chip, and had made it this far from the crash site. But there were logical explanations for both. The ID chip — that had to be a record mix–up. The kid had probably been granted a bracelet chip — unusual but not unheard of. And he must have found an exceptionally easy way through the forest between the crash site and here. That was all. That had to be all.

Stealth was sure it was nothing more than luck, because he'd done a thorough check before he went after the boy and his twin sister. They were from an ordinary family that made the mistake of isolating itself. Easy pickings. The mother was in a downward spiral, all because she lost her husband and one of her kids. An obvious weakling. The boy's sister was a loud, gawky, ridiculous idiot, who would have been shunned if they lived in a pod community like nearly everyone else. And the boy? A plodding nonentity.

They were no loss to the Nation. Before long, a few of his keystrokes would make them completely disappear.

The boy'd had some fluky good luck — more, Stealth was certain, than his fair share of it.

Ordinary people sometimes did have a phenomenal run of luck. But this kid's luck ran out when he stupidly turned on one of his keybs. He must have travelled like a dumb–luck lug well into the night, and then turned his keyb on when he finally bedded down, barely fifteen minutes ago. Stealth's programs immediately hacked the keyb so that no one else would be able to trace it; he was sure he was the only one who had a fix on its location.

He'd been dozing in his aeor, letting droners do the plodding night search work for him, when the alarm he'd set on the boy's keyb addresses bleaped and roused him. He turned it off and immediately set his aeor to go to the keyb's coordinates

Enroute Stealth brought up data about the site where the boy was. Some old, quaint maps and diagrams popped up for the coordinates, but the text was in English, with translations that were a difficult for him to understand. This kind of data was usually deciphered only by fusty old Fire Keepers.

Stealth sussed out that many centuries ago, there was a cluster of Anglo buildings on the site — some kind of estate built for river trade. Most of this information was not useful, but there was an image of a hand–drawn map showing where the buildings had once been. Stealth thought it likely that the boy had hunkered down in one of the old foundations.

When he arrived, quick scans by his droners indicated no large animals in the area. Good. He scaled his Rif down to immobilize in the boy's size range, rather than kill. After all this trouble, he did not want to accidentally kill the kid, though he did plan to rough him up some — maybe a lot — for causing him this extra work. In any event, success was assured now. First thing in the morning, he was going to up his minion score by one, by delivering the boy alive to headquarters in the cave.

He got out of his aeor, finished suiting up and started off on his Skim.

* * *

Nika, stationed on a tree branch near the root cellar's entrance, watched as the marten killer approached the ridge on his Skim. Wenq and the three nomars were hiding in the root cellar.

Nomars. Pani had told her yesterday — *Was it only yesterday?* — that they were primitive hunter–gatherers who preferred to live wild

165

in the Core. Wenq had hurriedly told her that this nomar threesome was a war party from a nomar band. There had not been time to find out what their war was about. Tehwe, the bear shapeshifter, was the leader of both of the war party and the nomar band. The young man who was a wolf shapeshifter was Tal, and the stockier young man was Sirk.

Wenq and the nomars had hurriedly concocted plan that depended on misdirection. They wedged the activated keyb into the inside corner of the building foundation that was close to the root cellar. They expected — or at least hoped — that the marten killer would go to where the keyb was, after a cursory check around. The moment the man got off his Skim there, Nika was to give a distinct chirrup signal, and the nomars would rush out of the root cellar and attack him.

But the man on the Skim barely paused at where the keyb was hidden. Instead, he was spending a lot of time circling the root cellar. Too much time.

They had piled up some branches at its entrance, to make it look naturally blocked, although the branches could be easily shoved outward from the opening. Perhaps it did not look natural enough, or perhaps the man somehow suspected that the keyb's location was being used as a decoy.

The man paused about twenty feet from the root cellar's entrance, and pulled something small out of one of the many pockets in his jacket. Nika thought, *It's probably some kind of droner.*

It was. When the man pressed it and tossed it up, it settled in the air about a foot away from his left wrist, hovering nearly silent while the man pressed and swiped at a small keyb set in a wristband. Nika knew enough to understand what he was doing: *He's going to send the droner into the root cellar, through gaps in the branches that block the entrance.*

Once inside, the droner will send the man images or body heat signals. The nomars will lose the advantage of surprise. They'll be vulnerable to the Rif and whatever other equipment the man has with him. And they won't be able to rush

166

him — he's still on his Skim and can quickly, effortlessly back away.

Nika sensed more than heard movement inside the root cellar. *The nomars realize something has gone wrong with their plan. They're probably deciding whether to rush out and take their chances. They can't know that the man has his Rif pointed directly ahead of him, at the root cellar's entrance.*

With scant seconds to decide and few options, Nika did not know why she made the choice that she did. In fluid instants she decided against shapeshifting to girl on the branch and calling out to distract the marten killer's attention away from the root cellar's entrance. And she rejected swooping down on him as an owl. Perhaps it was because she'd seen the Rif's speed and accuracy when it killed the agile pine martens.

Instead she chose the 'song' that had mesmerized Wenq the previous day. There was a chance that it might work on this man, or at least confuse him, or slow his reactions.

She launched into it with all the verve and volume she could muster. It was something like the melody that had riveted even the Meadow Woman when she had played it on her flute in the Sky World. Now she performed it as well as she could within the limitations of her owl 'voice'.

She could not see the man's face through his head covering, but his head snapped around in her direction. So did his Rif. She flitted behind the trunk of the tree but feared the man would quickly skirt it. She flew higher and further away, and heard the Skim's whirr as it rose to follow her. Now and again, when she could, she gave another burst of her 'song'.

The man made hectic slaps at a keyb on his armband. The Skim homed in on Nika and accelerated. It whined like a mosquito in the ear as it went higher and faster.

Below her and behind the Skim, Nika caught a glimpse of a huge bear and large wolf racing after the Skim. She wheeled up and around, in a desperate dive back toward them.

The Skim pirouetted flawlessly, following her around and down.

167

The man's Rif caught and immobilized her, just as she raced over the bear's head.

* * *

The Skim followed the owl, as Stealth had directed it to do. He had no time to re–direct it at the bear that appeared out of nowhere, though he managed to reset the Rif to 'kill'.

The bear, so unexpectedly close, reared up to an amazing height and swatted Stealth off the Skim. Stealth rolled and was raising his Rif when a wolf sprang on him, clenched its jaws on his throat, and threw him to the ground.

The wolf's fangs could not bite through his neck armor, but it was strong. It kept him down with his Rif stuck half under him. In an instant the bear was on top of him and ripped through all of his defenses, while the wolf kept hold of his neck.

Stealth was going into shock, but even so he was aware that this was no ordinary bear, and no ordinary wolf. Bears and wolves never hunted together. These two seemed to know how all of his protective gear worked, and where his pocket devices were for close–in fighting. They never gave him a chance to reach any of them.

Near the end he felt large hands releasing his helmet's strap and yanking the helmet off. The hands then broke apart his jacket stays and exposed his chest.

The wolf had released its hold. A big hand at his neck held him down, though he probably could not have gotten up by then anyway. He had been pummeled and had long bloody gouges running down his arms and legs, and across his hips through shredded clothing.

Someone came up and tossed a large knife. Stealth saw it wink through the air right before the other large hand over him caught it and swung it away, out of sight.

A face came down toward his face, as if through a long, sinuous tunnel. For some reason the tunnel reminded Stealth of Leader. But not the face. The face was passionate, merciless rage. The face was death.

A hoarse voice sounded in his ears, though he was past understanding the words. "You serve the snake, the snake that killed my Anq. On her dead body I smelled the snake's stench, as I smell it now on you."

The knife came up and plunged into Stealth's heart.

*   *   *

Thus died the greatest hacker in the world, one of the Chosen, a kidnapper of minions for Leader, and a killer of wolves and hapless pine martens.

Chapter 25

It was Wenq who released Nika from immobilization.

He was supposed to have stayed in the root cellar. Everybody else had agreed among themselves that he was too weak and slow to be of any help, and might actually impede things by getting in their way.

But he followed the three nomars, when they rushed out of the cellar to pursue the man on the Skim.

While waiting in the root cellar for Nika's signal, they had realized that things were not going according to plan. Tal the wolf shapeshifter risked a head bob at the entranceway, and had seen the man on the Skim, facing the root cellar's entrance. They were just about to burst out when Nika's odd 'song' began, loud and strident.

After the first few notes Wenq felt his head going muzzy, and he knew why. "Cover your ears!" he hissed to the others, while cupping his hands over his ears and shaking his head to clear it. "Quick! Plug 'em! Her music is — it'll take your mind! Hurry!"

Wenq's urgency must have convinced them; they were quick to react. They gouged up clayey soil and smeared it into their ears.

Tal shapeshifted to wolf and burst out of the cellar first. Tehwe shapeshifted to bear as soon as he got past the confinement of the small entranceway. Sirk scrambled out right after Tehwe.

Tehwe and Tal were out far ahead, but Sirk wasn't as fast. Wenq just barely kept Sirk in sight or hearing as he plunged through the brush after them.

Wenq got there in time to hear what Tehwe said to the man, and to see the downstroke of his knife.

Tehwe and Tal knew Wenq was there. The breeze was behind

him; Wenq supposed they smelled his presence. Tehwe gestured for Wenq to come closer, asking if he knew who the dead man was.

But where is Nika? Wenq wondered. He caught his breath when, as he approached the dead man on the ground, he saw Nika nearby, suspended in flight. *She wasn't killed! But she looks very stiff — probably the Rif was set to immob something bigger. She must be suffering.*

He'd intended to take a quick look at the body and then grab the Rif, which was nearby on the ground. It went almost that smoothly, but not quite.

The dead man's face had been left unmarked, but the knife stood upright in his chest and most of the rest of him was a mass of gouged flesh, and bloody misshapen limbs. Wenq was barely able to say, "No idea who —," before he turned aside to retch. His reaction to the gore embarrassed him, but he couldn't help it.

He wiped his mouth on his sleeve and told the others that he needed the Rif to free Nika. Sirk snatched it up, telling Wenq to show him how, that he'd do it. But Wenq insisted that he should be the one to do it, that he could do it faster and better, for Nika's sake. Sirk wanted to argue about it, but right about then Wenq noticed that Sirk had a braided leather cord wrapped around his hand, with a small round hoop dangling from it. Sirk's hand, the cord and the hoop — were smeared with the dead man's blood.

"Did you take that off the man's body?" Wenq asked Sirk. Sirk didn't answer, but his expression told Wenq that he had.

Wenq turned to Tehwe. "Nobody should touch that little hoop," Wenq told him. "Nobody should be anywhere near it. It could have something to do with the snake."

Sirk dropped the hoop and its braided cord as if it was burning, and stepped away from it.

"What?" Tehwe asked harshly. "What's it to do with the snake?"

"You'll have to ask Nika. Let me free her. That's all I'll use the Rif for. I won't use it against any of you, but Sirk can cover me if you don't trust me."

171

Tehwe looked at Sirk and jerked his head toward Wenq. Unwillingly Sirk gave the Rif to Wenq, but he crowded Wenq, to snatch it back if he thought Wenq made a false move.

Wenq didn't care how close the guy was. "I'll show you how," he told him. The Rif's current setting was kill with no fail–safes; Wenq realized that the dead guy had gotten very close to killing either the wolf or the bear shapeshifter. Wenq carefully re–set it to Immob and pinned it on Nika, explaining what he was doing as he went through it. He eased the Immob level back and lowered Nika to the ground as smoothly and quickly as possible. He positioned her a bare inch above a little mound of moss, so that if she fell over when she was fully released, she would fall harmlessly against its springiness.

". . . and so, see, you move your finger along here, very slow until . . . now. And then you snap this. Release is complete."

Nika fell faceward with her wings still outstretched. She made odd gurgling noises, and was trying but failing to get her wings folded in. Wenq set the Rif aside and picked her up, easing her wings closed. He opened his jacket and tucked her inside it. All three nomars stood close by, watching him. From their expressions he could not tell what they were thinking.

"She needs to be warm and to rest for a while," he told them.

* * *

A grey smudginess at the horizon meant the new day was about to dawn. Tehwe insisted that they leave right away. He told Wenq to bring Nika; he would take them to his camp. A day's journey if they kept up a good pace.

He said he had a child there, that had been bewitched by the snake, or by the hawk woman that accompanied the snake. He wanted Nika's help in removing the bewitchment.

Wenq was not sure whether Nika would be able to do anything about the child. But it was obvious to him that it was best to go along with what Tehwe wanted. Tehwe was a big, powerful man who was determined and in a hurry. Tehwe would make it difficult for Wenq

172

to do anything other than what he wanted.

Even so, Wenq quietly resisted Tehwe's expectations long enough to decide for himself whether going with the nomars to their camp was his best choice for himself and for Nika.

He did not want to stay here. If the dead man had confederates, this place would be swarming with them before long.

It would be useless to try to use the man's Skim, or his aeor. He would need more than the ID chip in the man's arm to activate them. He would need codes that only the man knew. Wenq still didn't know which Seek squadron the man belonged to, but based on the type of gear he had, it was one that went out on tougher, more dangerous assignments.

Wenq still could not fathom why the marten killer, alone or with others, would want to waylay him and take him off somewhere to the west. *I just want to be rescued,* he thought. *I just want to go home. But if I send out a distress signal on one of my keybs, will real help come, or will more guys like the marten killer come? There's no way to know for sure.*

Wenq decided. *For now, I think that Nika and I will be safer if we go with these nomars to their camp.*

Wenq dug a shallow hole and buried the hoop and its cord in it, putting a heavy stone over it for good measure. Sirk stuffed his pockets with the dead man's devices. Tehwe dragged the body back to the root cellar, and Tal carried the mangled Skim back.

With the dead man and his Skim deposited inside the cellar, they put some heavy branches over the entrance, this time without trying to make it look natural. Wenq retrieved the keyb that had been wedged into the nearby building foundation, and crammed it into the branches at the cellar's entrance.

They worked quickly and in near–total silence. They soon left the area with their own gear and the Rif, heading west–southwest.

* * *

Tehwe told Wenq that they had a long way to go and would be traveling fast.

173

Wenq sighed to himself. Not only would he be practically retracing his long arduous journey of the preceding day, he would be going in the general direction that the dead man had been sending him when the aeor crashed.

At least I won't have to worry about predators while I'm travelling with these three nomars, and they'll know the easiest routes through the forest. I just hope I can keep up with them.

The day started out grey and cold. Likely there would be rain before long. He was stiff and sore but fresh enough for the time being. With his staff in one hand, he kept his other arm against his jacket, to cradle Nika from the buffeting as he hurried after the nomars.

Chapter 26

Lako did not wake up until it was nearly seven in the morning —
two hours after her usual time! It wasn't at all like her to sleep in. But
she had worked later than usual last night, and it was easy to lose
track of time in the cave. It wasn't so much the lack of natural light,
but a feeling of being cushioned from everything — including time
— that she attributed to living under tons of rock.

She could indulge herself by sleeping in now and again. She was a
top administrator — one of the best at making things run smoothly.
Leader understood how extraordinary she was, so it no longer
mattered to her that no one else did.

At her old logistics work, someone always dumbed down her
brilliant planning, claiming it was impractical. She knew they called
her 'The War Chief' behind her back. It was not a compliment, but it
rather pleased her. She knew what needed to be done and was willing
to bust ass about it, and yes — be vicious. She was strong, utterly
ruthless, and proud of it.

As she got out of bed the first thing she did was check to see if
Stealth had replied to the messages she sent him last evening. He
hadn't! She smiled to herself. This was a great start to the day. It was
looking more and more like Stealth had finally messed up big time.

He thinks he is such a great hacker, she thought huffily, *but I can hack
circles around him — in my sleep! He is so overdue a big fall.*

She wondered if it was too soon to report to Leader about
Stealth's failure to deliver his latest minion on time. *I'm really looking
forward to ratting him out. But it's probably just a little too soon. I'll give it
another hour or so, and meantime get some grub and check up on the minions.*

When she arrived here to reside, three moon cycles ago, she set to work finding out what everybody else was doing. She wanted to know everything, and as fast as possible. But she never did get a clear idea of what was going on.

From a distance she would see the other Chosen, busily engaged in conversation or reviewing sheafs of documents, presumably working at breakneck pace to finalize the great plans for taking over the Nation. But when she approached them, in a blink they were much further away, or were suddenly far behind her instead of in front. And there was a strange hollowness in their faraway voices.

Misgivings besieged her, until she had a meeting with Leader, which calmed all her fears, banished her doubts. Thereafter she paid little attention to anything other than her 'minion herding' duties, as she jokingly called them. She no longer chased after the glimpses of indistinct bustle, or the echoes of muted voices. And it did not bother her that the few here that she was able to talk to, knew as little as she did of the great plans.

This morning it was very quiet in the tunnelway just outside her little suite of rooms, as it always was lately. *Much too quiet,* she mused.

Lako shivered as doubt spiked in her mind, like an atypical resource in a coordination chart. She hastily soothed it away by fingering the hoop that Leader had given her, that she always wore around her neck, on its braided cord.

As she slowed her breathing, she indulged in imagining what it was going to be like someday soon, when her ridiculous family, and all her old acquaintances, woke up one morning and found that their precious Nation no longer existed. Gone — poof! And in its place, the New Order, with her standing proudly in its pantheon, close in beside Leader — perhaps very, very close.

Leader is smitten with me. It is too soon for him to openly declare his love, but there is no mistaking his smoldering gaze, his tantalizing smile.

These charming thoughts were cut short when she turned the first corner beyond her rooms. The minion Miti was standing there, looking scared and miserable. And definitely not where she was

176

supposed to be!

Miti was one of the few minions that Lako had some hope of training up. The girl might even become a member of the New Order someday, though in a lower echelon. She had been grooming Miti, giving her privileges — one of which was that her ankle band had more range than the other minions. But Miti was supposed to be serving in the canteen now — not loitering around here. Clearly, the girl needed to be brought down a peg!

"What are *you* doing here?" Lako demanded.

"I, I, I don't know, know anything, except —" Miti replied shakily.

"What's wrong with you? What's going on?" Lako shrilled.

Her sharp questions frightened Miti. The girl became incoherent.

Lako briefly considered smacking her, to jolt her out of whatever her problem was. But that might make her worse. So she took a deep breath and opted for the warm, fuzzy approach.

She shook the girl and grabbed her head, holding it rigid between her hands, forcing the girl to look directly at her.

* * *

Miti tried speak but she could barely move her mouth in the tight grasp of Mean Woman's hands.

Mean Woman. That was what the minions called this woman who ruled over them in the cave.

Áka had woken Miti up early this morning and told her where to wait for Mean Woman, and what to say to her. The older girl had smiled at her, smoothed her hair and hugged her gently, and told her that it was safer for her if she knew nothing else. She took Miti to the turn–off to Mean Woman's rooms and patted her shoulder before leaving her there to wait for Mean Woman to come out.

There Miti had waited alone. No one else came or went.

At nine years of age, Miti was one of the youngest minions. She had been snatched from a playground near her home and brought to the cave, where she was put to work, mainly in the canteen. She did

177

not know how long she had been here, but she thought it was about two moons, based on stick notches that the other minions used to keep track of time.

It was a strange, fearful existence. She was afraid of the grownups that came to the canteen for meals. They were all abrupt and their faces had odd, distracted expressions. Miti sometimes wondered if they were on drugs.

And the cave 'shudders', as she called them, terrified her. That was when there were heavy rumbling noises and a shaking under her feet, while a fine dust filled the air. The shudders always made her think that if the walls of the cave collapsed, she would never see her family again.

Most of the time after the shudders, there would be one fewer person in the cave. Usually it was one of the other minions, but sometimes it was one of the grownups. The minions talked among themselves about it, but none of them knew where any of the missing ones had gone.

They all agreed, though, that Mean Woman never seemed to realize that the missing minions were completely gone. She would continue to talk as if they were still around. She might ask where a missing one was, and then whip out a keyb to check her records. Then she would start fingering the hoop she wore on a cord around her neck. Her face would go slack, and she would either shrug or say something like, 'That minion must have been assigned to the mines after all.' That was apparently where she thought they all went, which was really strange because as far as the minions knew, the only mines in the cave had been inactive for centuries.

Miti lived in a state of constant fear and dread. She had terrible dreams sometimes, especially after the cave shudders. And she couldn't help crying when something reminded her of her family. The other minions tried to help her and comfort her, especially Áka after she arrived, about a moon cycle ago.

Miti trusted Áka more than anyone. So when Áka asked her to

178

wait here with a message for Mean Woman, she decided to do it, no matter what.

Clearly something was wrong, but she had no way of finding out what it was. She was frightened, and nervous, and then about halfway through her wait for Mean Woman, there were some cave shudders.

By the time Mean Woman got there, Miti was frantic. But despite Mean Woman's rough ways, Miti managed to deliver Áka's message. "There's been a collapse in the mines," she said, "and everyone has gone there to help out."

"Why wasn't I notified immediately?!" Mean Woman snarled as she shoved Miti away from her. "Worthless girl! You should have come for me right away, or sent someone for me!"

None of the minions' ankle bands permitted them to go any closer to Mean Woman's rooms, but Miti knew better than to say this to Mean Woman now. She was still tottering backward when Mean Woman seized her upper arm and yanked her toward her. "You're coming with me," she said. "I might need you."

But Áka had told Miti not to go with Mean Woman!

She held back as best she could. She dragged her feet, she limped. But she was pulled along, until she made a desperate attempt to break free. She threw herself against the back of Mean Woman's knees. Mean Woman went down, and with a twist Miti got loose from the woman's hold on her upper arm.

She started back the other way, but there was a wolf was coming toward her — a wolf with bright orange fur on the top of its head, and neon purple fur around its ears!

With a cry Miti backed against the wall and put her arms up defensively. The wolf rushed past her and went after Mean Woman, who had seen the wolf coming and was pelting away, yelling her head off for help.

*　*　*

Being able to shapeshift into a wolf was all very new to Weqi, but one of the first things she discovered about it was that she had much

179

more patience in her wolf shape, than as a girl.

As a girl she had practically no patience at all. Zip times zilch. But as a wolf, a hunting instinct seemed to lodge in her bones. And a hunting wolf always knew when and how to be patient.

She had waited patiently, just around a corner from where Miti was stationed to await Mean Woman. Even when Mean Woman arrived and was rough with poor Miti, Weqi stayed put, though she could hardly repress a snarl. When the woman went rushing off, dragging the sobbing Miti with her, Weqi followed silently, at a distance. But she was not going to let the woman take Miti with her very far. She was just waiting for the right opportunity.

Miti gave it to her when she twisted free of the woman. *Then* Weqi's patience was repaid. *Then* she surged toward the woman, intent on exacting some overdue revenge, both for herself and the other minions.

Chapter 27

During the patient waiting, Weqi had plenty of time to think about the incredible changes of the last twenty–four hours — the very worst and the very best of her life. Was it just the previous morning that she'd been at home as usual? It seemed so long since then, and such a different life, just this short while later.

She remembered how extremely unsettling the night before had been. The air of her room at home seemed drenched with strong, revolting odors, and filled with annoyingly amplified sounds, worse than ever before. She'd had a terrible dream of having fangs instead of teeth, and of sinking those fangs into the neck of a big fat rabbit — which to her horror became her brother in the dream. She had killed him! The dream then shifted to her desperate, panting flight through dark dream woods, pursued by shadowy hunters, all of them with Rifs set to kill her.

She'd woken up with thudding heart and immediately checked the pod's security summary for the hallway. The only notations were of Pani padding around — good. Her brother was perfectly safe. It had only been a dream. Nothing real.

She supposed that her dreams were punishing her. She had been inexcusably nasty to her mom lately, and mean to her brother. She hated herself for it, but they both made her so mad. If only her mom would stand up to her, instead of going vague and helpless and hollowed out. And if only Wenq would punch her back for once, she'd — well, at least she'd have some respect for him, for trying.

But she would not lie to herself. It was her fault, not theirs. She was the one who was a total mess.

After the awful dream she was nervy and in her worst possible mood about everything. She rushed out in the aeor at daybreak to get away from her family, to get away from everything. Taking the aeor out on manual with its fail–safes off, zooming around in it madly, was the only thing she could think of, that might help her settle down.

She buzzed the few beavers that were already out and about in the marsh. She skimmed so low over the lake's surface that the aeor nearly flipped in wave chop. She zoomed over to the woods and shaved treetops so close, she could feel the jolts as the topmost branches whacked and scraped the aeor's smooth bottom.

When she got her fill of nearly crashing the aeor and killing herself, she took the aeor off manual, set it on cruise, and got busy with her keyb, posting angrily on NetNation about how extremely inconsiderate smelly people were.

That engrossed her for a while. Then her keyb went dead without warning. She was immediately furious with Wenq. He must have meddled with it; she was sure he was to blame for its malfunction.

But when she sat up to set the aeor to return home, she found that it too was malfunctioning. It was taking her west, and nothing she could do would change its course. All of its panels were dark. None of the controls were responsive.

She wanted to blame Wenq for that too, but she was fairly certain he hadn't been messing about with the aeor. Uneasily she thought back to the beating it had taken at the treetops. There had been one clunk in particular . . .

She was banging on the aeor's control panel and kicking it underneath when she suddenly got the feeling that she was being watched.

She glanced up suspiciously at one of the aeor's pin cameras, and then quickly looked away. If somebody *was* playing some kind of crazy joke on her, by taking over her aeor and flying her somewhere stupid, she needed to show them she could be calm and aloof, like the true Warrior Woman she was. Or at least, like she was going to be when she got older.

She did not have to think very long or hard, to come up with a few kids who might want to play this kind of joke on her. She hadn't exactly made any friends since her family had returned from the Outside a few months ago. In fact, at the make–up Braves training some of the others there had made it clear that she had seriously annoyed them. But she didn't think that any of them had anywhere near the hacking skills needed for something like this.

One of them might have an older relative though, with the right hacker knowledge and access . . .

She seethed inside, angry with whoever was doing this. At the same time, she worked very hard to act like she didn't have a care in the world, like a real Warrior Woman would do.

It became increasingly difficult to act that way though, because it turned out to be a long trip. Most of the morning the aeor trundled along monotonously, ever westward over the Core's huge expanses of forest. When it finally slowed and descended to land, still deep inside the Core, Weqi was almost vibrating with impotent anger.

She knew she should control herself better, especially in this weird situation that she did not yet understand. But she doubted she would be able to stop herself from venting on the first person she came across. It was as if she stood outside herself and saw another girl, visibly shaking with barely contained fury.

It wasn't just this sick joke. Anger had been building in her for a long time.

Over her 14 years Weqi had absorbed enough of the constraints of her people's culture and her gender to feel uneasy whenever she struck out too boldly on her own unproven course. Like the rest of her generation of the Nation, she had been born into privilege and nurtured with a sense of responsibility to be a credit to it — or at least, to avoid disgracing it. Beyond that there was little to guide her future. It was a simple, seemingly generous precept that the Nation entrusted to its youth, and many of them had no trouble using it to find a fitting path for their lives. But lately Weqi had come to mistrust it, because no matter which vocation she tried to embrace she found that it hemmed her in against her inclinations and spirit, until she boiled over in frustration and rebelled and added another notch to her stick of failed attempts. Everything from science to song. And now on top of all of that, was this insult.

She was tinder—ready to flare, only needing a spark.

The aeor settled down in a small clearing beside a massive outcropping of rock. The place looked deserted, but before long a large, beefy man came out of the bushes, dressed in soiled, wrinkled forest camouflage and carrying a big Rif that he pointed at her. Weqi sized him up. Looked to be about ten years older than she was. Could be brutish, she decided, but more fundamentally was just a weak and soft jerk.

Brutish and weak — it was an unpredictable combination, but she was not afraid. She was sure she could handle him. Even though he carried a Rif, it was inconceivable that he would actually use it on her.

Part of the aeor's control panel sprang back to life, and the man motioned for her to raise the dome. She opened it, but only a crack.

"Get out of there!" he ordered her. "Do exactly as you're told."

"Like heck I will! I'm going to report you! I'm going to —"

She was zapped before she got any further, and the beefy guy just walked off and left her that way!

Weqi had never *ever* been immob'd before. It felt as terrible as she'd heard it would be. It was like she was made of wood instead of flesh and bone, except it ached so, worse and worse the longer she was immobilized.

And she was left immobilized for a long while.

Finally a dumpy woman, past her prime, came out of the bushes carrying a Rif. She looked habitually sour, with an unpleasant glint in her eye as she sauntered up, as if she was looking forward to having some 'fun' at Weqi's expense.

She slowly circled the aeor, cradling the Rif awkwardly.

"Well, well, well," she drawled, "So here's the Missy Big Mouth. I hear you're uncooperative. *And* you've threatened to report us. Oooooh, that makes me *so* scared —"

"— *not!*" The woman's voice hardened to flint. "Around here you'll keep your mouth shut and do what you're told. Or you'll be very, very sorry. Oh, and that orange and purple hair — definitely not your colors, dear. We're going to shave it all off that silly head of yours! So how'll you like that? Hmmm?"

Weqi could hear her, though it was muffled, as if she had plugs in her ears, and of course she could not speak. Which was the way the woman wanted it.

The woman went on to tell her that her name was Lako, and that she — Weqi — had been brought here to be a servant for some kind of Order, and that if she was smart she would stay in the woman's good graces. Then everything would go better for her.

"I'm going to release the hold on you," the woman continued, "and you're going to open the aeor the rest of the way. Then you're going to come along with me like a smart little minion."

The woman fiddled with the Rif's controls for Immob. Weqi was released from its hold with a sudden jerk that felt like a harsh blow. She nearly cried out, and for a few moments she could do nothing but sag in the aeor's seat, unable to move on her own.

"Still not cooperating?" the woman said, raising the Rif.

Weqi managed to show that she was trying to do what the woman wanted, enough to avoid being zapped again. She got the dome up and stumbled out of the aeor. But the woman was impatient. She kept saying, "Hurry up." "Not fast enough." "Move it." All the while jabbing Weqi with the end of the Rif.

Weqi was barely able to move at first. She could not stop the woman from searching her pockets. Then she was prodded down a short path and into a cave.

There was an off–smell around the woman while they were still out in the open, something like meat going bad. As soon as they were inside the cave, the smell got stronger.

The beefy man was sitting on a rock just inside the cave, next to a jumble of camp food cases, and the area around him was littered with empty food packaging. There was a concentration of the bad smell around him too. Neither he nor the woman seemed to notice it. He glumly took his Rif back from the woman and, looking bored, settled down to stare out of the cave, with the Rif laid across his thighs.

The woman pushed and prodded Weqi further into the cave and down a dimly lit tunnel. They passed a few tunnels that were somewhat smaller than the one they were in.

Weqi could barely walk at first, but the moment her limbs became less wooden she felt an instinctive need to escape before they got to wherever the woman was taking her. The bad smell was revolting, and the woman's constant jabs at her back loosened her grip on her pent–up fury.

She knew it was foolhardy, but with a stream of passionate insults she turned on the woman and wrestled her down.

She had just barely gotten her down when the woman zapped her with a pocket Immob. It was not very powerful, but was more than enough to stop someone like herself, who had not yet recovered from a much bigger zap.

"I *knew* you were going to be difficult," the woman said while getting up and straightening her clothes. "I'm taking you straight to slops! And that hair — it's all coming off tomorrow, girlie!"

The woman's chest was heaving; apparently some of Weqi's insults had gotten to her. *Good,* Weqi thought, with a fleeting moment of satisfaction. *No matter the cost, I'm glad I tried.*

When Weqi was able to move again she was prodded and poked even more harshly. They retraced their steps part of the way and turned down a narrower tunnel that had a long curve around to the right. At length the tunnel opened out into a large room that smelled of filthy drains, where the air reverberated with the slosh and splatter of water.

There was a dirty boy there, who was slowly sluicing water down a long, sloping waterway that was filled with all kinds of foul lumps. He used a long thin paddle to move the soggy lumps along the channel until they dropped off the end and plopped into a deep pool. He did not look up from what he was doing.

The woman snapped a band around Weqi's left ankle, after first entering a code and pressing some buttons on it. She told Weqi to do the same work as the boy, and that she'd be punished if she didn't do at least half of it. The woman then turned and left without another word.

Weqi went out right after her, but the moment she got beyond room the ankle band sent jolts of pain up her leg, causing her to fall. The jolts only stopped when she managed to drag herself back into the room. Looking up she saw the woman standing in the tunnel not far away, watching her agony with a smile on her face.

Weqi screamed some insults at her.

The woman's smile froze and she took out a device that made the ankle band send more jolts into Weqi's leg.

"Pretend it hurts worse than it does," the boy told her in a low murmur. "Otherwise she'll ramp it up more."

A proud Warrior Woman never flinched at pain. But something cruel in the woman's smile, and the demented gleam in her eyes, made Weqi decide that under certain circumstances, a 'strategic retreat' was nothing to be ashamed of.

She did as the boy suggested. She dropped fully to the ground and writhed and rolled and wailed and — though it embarrassed her to do it — she whimpered.

It worked. The woman stopped the leg jolts, and left with a petty nod of her head. Weqi wailed some more for good measure.

"There're cameras with audio record," the boy then told her, again under his breath and with his head down. He had never stopped sluicing and plying with his paddle. "Come over closer. Take

187

the other paddle and pretend that you're working, so we can talk. If we talk low, the watery noises will cover what we're saying."

Chapter 28

The boy quizzed her, and then told her about himself and the other 'minions' there, as all the adults here called them.

His name was Desag, and he was about a year older than Weqi. He'd lost track of exactly how long he'd been here, but he was sure it was at least a full moon cycle. He was from the western side of the Nation; he'd been seized and brought here when he'd been on his own, camping in the Rim Wilderness. He used to go camping with his dad, but his dad had gone Outside for a while. Probably by now his family thought he'd been eaten by wild animals. He was sure they thought he was dead.

He'd resisted doing the work that the adults here wanted him to do, by being slow and clumsy at it. So Mean Woman punished him by assigning him to slops.

For a while there had been two minions regularly working at slops. Lately it had just been him, until Weqi arrived. Food was usually brought twice a day — early in the morning and then at about seven or so in the evening. Usually Áka, an older girl minion, brought it. If there was any news, it was exchanged then in undertones.

After the next meal they'd have to work for another hour or so. Then a twitch from their ankle bands would signal that they could rest. The bunks were in one far corner of the room, the dirt hole in the other.

The ankle bands made it impossible to escape. "The moment you get beyond your allowed area, your leg will start hurting, and it gets much worse the further you try to go. And us slops minions are always confined to the slops room, because, well, because we stink of the slops."

Desag had lost count of how many minions there'd been, but there were only five of them now — six counting Weqi. Besides him and Weqi, there was the older girl named Áka, another older boy who was a bit slow in his thinking, and a younger boy and girl.

"There were at least double that many minions when I first got here. And a few more were brought in after me. But one after another, minions have been disappearing.

"There aren't many adults left in the cave either. Maybe only three or four. It's hard to tell for sure, but it seems to me that there are less slops lately, than ever before."

"So if they're gone, then where did they go?" Weqi asked.

"I think that maybe they've been eaten, perhaps by a giant snake," Desag replied. "And yeah, I know you'll have a hard time believing that, but that *is* what I think."

Desag described how there would sometimes be a rumbling in the tunnels, and how afterward there would often be one fewer person in the cave.

"One night I woke up to rumblings that got closer and closer to the slops room. I was watching the room's entrance, with nothing to protect myself but my paddle and a small knife that I'd found and kept hidden. Suddenly something flicked around the corner and into the room, and then back out.

"The rumblings receded after that, though they went on for a while. The next day, one of other minions was no longer here.

"The thing that flicked into the room — I think it was the tongue of a giant, hungry snake. It happened very fast, and there wasn't enough light to be certain. But I can't think of anything else that could look and move like that."

"A whip maybe?" Weqi asked.

Desag shook his head. "I think the snake didn't like the stink of the slops room. So even though slops is the worst work of all, it might have saved my life that night."

* * *

Weqi was not ready to believe in giant snakes. But everything else Desag told her was grim and believable enough.

Time dragged on miserably for her in the slops room. The mal odors were nearly overpowering. She swayed and stumbled, and had dry heaves. She would have definitely puked if there had been anything in her stomach.

Mean Woman had told her to do half the work, but for the most part she just went through the motions. That made her wonder about how closely she and Desag were being observed. The cameras were probably recording, but there didn't seem to be active monitoring.

At last they were able to take a break when an older girl arrived with two food buckets and a thin blanket. "That's Áka," Desag said under his breath.

Áka put the blanket on one of the bare wood bunks, and set the buckets down.

Weqi had no appetite but she went with Desag to the food buckets to meet Áka, and for any news. Áka reported that the only news was Weqi's arrival.

When Áka noticed that Weqi wasn't eating, she took something out of her pocket and surreptitiously passed it to Weqi. "Nose wads," she said quietly. "Go round to the dirt hole, where you're out of camera range, to put them in."

When Weqi got back she was able to eat a little, and she asked Áka questions about the ankle bands. Desag had told her that Áka knew the most about them. 'Were they ever taken off?' 'What did she know about the controls for them?' 'How many control sets were there, and where were they kept?'

"The ankle bands are never taken off," Áka muttered with her head down. "Mean Woman always carries a special keyb with her, that controls them. I think it's the only one, because she doesn't like to share her 'power' with anyone else."

"Where does she sleep at night?"

"I know where, but it's out of range, especially at night. At night

191

we're all confined to where we're assigned to sleep. Believe me, Weqi, I've tried. I had to turn back."

Áka left, and after several more hours of drudgery their ankle bands buzzed.

"Mornings are usually better," Desag mentioned, as he went to the bunk area. "Less smelly, at least at first." He had noticed how difficult the smells were for Weqi, even with the nose wads. All through the long day and evening he tried to take care of the most odiferous slop, so that Weqi wouldn't have to.

Weqi saw what he was doing, and was grateful. She was touched by both Desag's and Áka's attempts to help her in this strange, awful place.

Desag switched bunks with Weqi so she'd be closest to the room's entrance, where the air was slightly less stinky. That was the only reason she didn't barf up her dinner when she took the nose wads out.

She didn't think she would be able to sleep in such a disgusting place, but before she knew it she was dreaming.

In her dream she again had sharp, glistening fangs instead of teeth, but instead of feeling that there was something wrong with that, she happily sank her dream fangs into one of Mean Woman's legs.

Her dream then took an odd twist, or so it seemed at first. The boy Desag threw his blanket over her and whispered urgently, "Over here! Over here quick! And don't — don't bite me!"

Weqi was disoriented and Desag's blanket covered her head and kept her arms pinned to her sides. As he dragged her, struggling, from her bunk he whispered, "You never told me you're a wolf!"

"I'm sure as heck not a wolf!" was what Weqi wanted to say, but a deep growl came up her throat instead, breaking off in a confused grunt. Desag shushed her frantically and told her to stop struggling and twisting so much, unless she wanted Mean Woman to find out what she was. By then he had gotten her into a shallow niche in the

192

wall near the bunks. "The cameras don't cover here," Desag whispered. "So I'm going to loosen the blanket now. Just don't, don't fight me, Weqi."

Weqi didn't fight him, because a great calm had come over her. She was fully out of the dream she'd been having, and she knew that she really *was* a wolf, as Desag had said. And she was so *happy* about it. Suddenly, all the knots twisted up inside her loosened. She was a wolf shapeshifter. So much about herself now made perfect sense.

She knew that shapeshifters were thought to be odd, and were shunned, but she didn't care about that. She thought it was wonderful.

This was why everything was so smelly, she thought, *and sounds were so amplified. And now, I can smell everything even better. And I can hear an incredible range of sounds, even through layers of other sounds. I can see in the dark too. This is fantastic!*

Weqi looked down at long furry paws that poked through her sleeves instead of two hands, and through her pant legs instead of two feet. Her clothes weren't too comfortable at the moment, especially on her legs. But she felt powerful chest and leg muscles bunching and rippling under her fur, for racing and lunging and bringing down prey. Prey like Mean Woman.

She looked again at her back legs, and saw that the ankle band was not on the left one. It had been tight around her ankle, but it slipped right off her wolf leg!

She shapeshifted back to girl while Desag watched, amazed.

As soon as Weqi could speak she assured Desag that she hadn't known that she could shapeshift before — that she would have told him if she had known. "And," she said, "I'm going to get the controls for the ankle bands away from Mean Woman, or die trying."

* * *

Desag had never met a shapeshifter before; he had only heard stories about them, mainly from his father. Many of the stories told of how dangerous they could be. In a few of his dad's stories, though, shapeshifters were solitary heroes.

So this is new to her too, Desag thought, *and it's probably at least as strange to her as it is to me. Yet the first thing she says, is to reassure me. And the first thing she wants to do, is to help us all out, by disabling the ankle bands.* His fear of her lessened, even though he knew her idea was hopeless.

He shook his head. "They'll catch you. They'll see you in the cameras."

"Only if they're actively watching them, or if they have them rigged with movement alarms. You said yourself that there aren't many adults around, and the two I've seen — they don't have much on the ball. I'm willing to take the chance, Desag. If their security is lax, and I can get the controls for the ankle bands, then with any luck at all, we can all be out of here by morning."

"Out of here?!" Desag was stunned by the idea. As grim as his existence had been in the cave, he had become inured to it.

He felt a flood of surprise, then elation.

And then, fear. Dismay.

"Even if we can escape," he said, "we'll still be in the Core."

"Better than staying here," was Weqi's quick response.

Desag shook his head slowly. "You don't know the Core, do you?"

Weqi had to admit she didn't.

Desag weighed the alternatives. *Stay here and get picked off one by one, maybe by that giant snake I believe in. Or take our chances in the Core.* He shuddered, and took a few moments, before deciding.

"Alright," he said. "I'm in. But this is what I think we ought to do."

Chapter 29

Weqi shapeshifted back to wolf and left the slop room, slinking in the shadows along the walls, where cameras would be less likely to get a clear image of her. Before shapeshifting to wolf again she'd undressed and readied a blanket to take with her, tied in a loose loop so that as wolf she could nose it over her neck, or shrug it off. She left her clothes behind; they'd be too restrictive.

Once she got away from the slop room her nose cleared and it led her right to Mean Woman's rooms. With no ankle band to stop her, she went right in.

She wanted to take a great big bite out of the horrible woman, but Mean Woman had a camp shell around her bed, which made her unreachable. The most Weqi could do was shapeshift to girl and take the control unit for the ankle bands from the room, along with the woman's other pocket devices.

Desag had suggested that she also look for Mean Woman's store of medical supplies. She found an ample kit on a shelf and dumped its contents along with everything else into the blanket she'd brought. She twisted the blanket and looped it for carrying it around her neck after she shapeshifted back to wolf.

As wolf her nose then led her to the small room where Áka slept.

Weqi began to shapeshift to girl to wake Áka, but Áka was already getting up.

* * *

Áka had not been sleeping well lately, and heard a slight noise just outside her room. As she watched the open doorway a shadowy wolf came in, which changed as it got closer into the new girl with her distinctive orange and purple hair.

"I thought I was dreaming!" she whispered to Weqi.

Áka wasn't as afraid of shapeshifters as most others were.

A cousin of hers was one — a wolverine shapeshifter whose name was Wuju. When she was a child her mother had taken her to meet him once — because he was family, her mother said. He lived by himself in the Rim Wilderness, in a primitive hovel. When they visited he was so abrupt and snarly that he frightened her mother into leaving almost at once.

Áka, though, had rather liked her cousin. She saw that Wuju was testing or fooling with her mother with his rough ways, and was disappointed when her mother failed to understand that he was asking her to accept him the way he was. She remembered turning back as they were leaving and smiling shyly at him. He had winked at her, which she had understood to mean, 'Come back when you are older, little cousin, if you wish. *We* might get along.'

The years slipped by and she had been too busy to go back. But lately she'd been thinking, *If I ever get back home, I'll make a priority of going to visit Wuju.*

Now Áka wasn't afraid of Weqi, and she noticed right away that Weqi's ankle band was gone. It gave her a flutter of hope.

As soon as Áka had the gist of the situation, she agreed with Weqi and Desag that they should act while they had the advantage of surprise, and that escaping into the Core Wilderness was probably better than staying on in the cave. And she agreed with Desag's suggestion that, in addition to deactivating the ankle bands, they should sedate Mean Woman before they left.

Sedation patches were standard issue in medical kits. Áka found several of them in the medical supplies that Weqi had brought. "Just one," she told Weqi, "will put Mean Woman out for at least five hours. We'll use two — we'll need at least that much time to get well away. Otherwise it will be easy for Mean Woman to track us using our ID chips."

While they were talking Áka hacked into Mean Woman's control unit for the ankle bands, and deactivated it.

She went and got the other older boy, Geh, from where he was sleeping in his nearby room. Together they worked on fully disabling the control unit for the ankle bands, as well as Mean Woman's other devices. Though Geh wasn't very sharp, he was able to help Áka with some of the more mundane hacking tasks. They spoke in whispers and tried to hide what they doing from the cameras, but Áka wasn't overly worried about being recorded. She reassured Weqi that the cameras and audio were not monitored in real time. "We'll be okay, at least until Mean Woman reviews the recordings," she whispered.

* * *

While Áka did some fancy hacking to keep the control unit from re–setting or re–charging, Weqi went to get Desag. But he was already on his way there, carrying both slop paddles and his knife. "I kept trying to leave the slop room," he said. "When I was able to, I knew you'd been able to shut down the ankle bands."

They cut off the hated ankle bands while laying their plans.

Little Miti was to be left in the tunnelway at the turnoff to Mean Woman's rooms, with a message to direct her toward what the adults all called the mines. After 5 a.m. most of the minions were allowed to go in that direction, so Mean Woman would not be suspicious if she was told they'd gone that way.

There was a disused niche room along that route that had been fitted with an old–style door. It had probably been a storeroom when the cave was actually mined, centuries ago. Its old–fashioned lock no longer worked but the door itself was still sound. Desag and Áka were to wait in the niche room until they heard Mean Woman coming toward it; Weqi would be following her. When Mean Woman was nearly to the room the three of them would surround and subdue her. Their plan was to leave her sedated and hidden in the room, with the door pulled shut.

Weqi proposed that they kill Mean Woman instead of sedating her, but Desag shook his head, and Áka looked at Weqi with a faint smile, saying, "That's very tempting, Wild Woman. But there's no justice in it."

"What's justice got to do with it?!" Weqi groused. But she gave way, and privately enjoyed the new name Áka had given her. *Wild Woman. Still Wild Girl actually, but someday . . .*

I **do** *have a wild side,* she thought, *and I love myself this way. But I want to be a smart kind of wild — not stupid and heedless wild.* Weqi already had a notion of what she wanted to grow into — wolf wild, but with a smart woman's ways.

Her attention returned to the planning. The other two minions — the older slow boy Geh and the younger boy, were to wait in a crawlway not far from the canteen, along the route to the one exit that they knew of, that was guarded by the beefy guy. They were to wait there with the gear and supplies they had hastily gathered up.

Weqi snuck Mean Woman's disabled devices back into her room, and everyone except Áka settled into their hiding places. Áka woke Miti and set her in place with the message for Mean Woman. She then joined Desag to wait in the small room along the way to the so–called mines, armed with the long paddles and the knife.

* * *

Their trap laid, they did not expect to have to wait very long, because it was nearly the usual time that Mean Woman got up. But the wait stretched out and became nerve–wracking. They fidgeted, they fretted. They worried about all the ways that things could go wrong — that might have *already* gone wrong.

After an hour or so of waiting a heavy rumbling rolled through the cave, coming from the direction of the so–called mines. It was frightening, but at the same time they felt safer where they were, than where the ankle bands would have forced them to be.

Desag and Áka fully closed the small room's door and kept it closed until the rumbling went past them.

As it went down a tunnelway near where Miti was waiting, she trembled and cried and pressed herself against a wall, but kept to her post.

Weqi, hiding nearby, got her first inkling of why Desag thought there was a giant snake in the cave. And besides hearing and feeling the rumbling, she got a strong whiff of the off smell that permeated the cave.

The rumbling passed within a few feet of the two minions waiting in the crawlway near the exit. It was like a terrifying earthquake, with rocks grinding and shifting like they were about to fall on them. Geh cried out, but his cries were lost in the noise.

About an hour after the rumbling died away, the waiting finally ended.

Lako — Mean Woman to the minions — came out of her rooms, shook Miti until her teeth rattled, and dashed off toward the 'mines' with Miti in tow. Weqi followed them silently, at a distance.

When Miti broke free and Lako became aware of the wolf, she ran hollering for help. When the wolf had nearly caught up with her she whipped out her pocket Immob. Weqi, knowing the device was disabled, rushed up and bit it out of her hand. Lako, horrified by her bloodied hand and fingers, let out a screech and fled.

Weqi chased Lako, and Desag and Áka burst from the room up ahead and ran toward them.

But suddenly there was someone else — a tall gaunt woman — rushing up behind Desag and Áka, carrying a large hoop.

* * *

In an instant Weqi decided that the gaunt woman was a much worse threat than Mean Woman. There was something indefinable about her that Weqi as wolf understood. It was kill or be killed. She sprang past Mean Woman, Desag and Áka, going for the gaunt woman's throat.

The woman glared at Weqi with contempt, tossed her hoop into the air and croaked out some words that caused the hoop to disappear — except that Weqi could see a round-shaped distortion in the air, floating between herself and the woman.

199

At the last instant before reaching the roiling air, Weqi twisted away from the round shape's center, and got past it by slipping alongside it at the wall, though it pulled at her powerfully along her flank.

*   *   *

Behind Weqi, Áka called out to Desag, "Help Weqi! I'll keep at Mean Woman."

Desag could not see the round shape that the woman had conjured in the tunnelway, but he did see Weqi twist violently, nearly in a back flip, and then go low along the wall. So he crouched and hugged the wall in the same place, as he hurried after her. He too felt a strong pull on himself away from the wall, but forewarning and momentum got him past it.

The woman pointed at Weqi with one claw–like hand while waving a knife at her with the other, speaking in a rapid, rasping guttural. Weqi and Desag reached her before she was able to finish her utterance. Desag smacked her knife hand down with his paddle, while Weqi sank her teeth into her pointing hand. The knife spun crazily through the air, weirdly seeking Weqi. Only when Weqi got the woman between herself and the gyrating knife, did the woman utter some hasty words that caused it to clatter to the ground.

The woman seemed to capitulate but Weqi and Desag were wary. Weqi menaced her while Desag tied her up. When the woman's lips started moving Desag said, "Oh no you don't!" He snatched the cloth off her head and gagged her mouth with it. Ever since he'd come to believe in a giant snake, it did not take much to convince him that there could be other kinds of magic going on in the cave.

Desag and Weqi heard a faint cheeping noise behind them. What they saw, when they turned toward it, was bizarre. Mean Woman was suspended in the air, making the cheeping noise and sluggishly flailing her arms and legs. Áka was standing beyond her, with Miti, round–eyed and shaking, at her side.

"What's, what's holding her in the air like that?" Desag asked.

200

"I don't know," Áka responded. "I had her up against a wall, but she dashed your way to get the other woman's knife when it fell. She was ahead of me and just got, um, stuck there like that."

Weqi, shapeshifting to girl, told them, "There's a round shape there that's holding her. I can't see it now that I'm not a wolf, but you should stay well away from it, Áka, and keep Miti away."

Áka nodded, and moved further back from it with Miti.

Desag put two sedation patches on the gaunt woman, and Weqi helped him finish binding her. They worked quickly, all the while listening and watching in case other adults came. But everything seemed quiet. Eerily quiet.

"Let's put her into the round shape with Mean Woman," Weqi suggested. "The shape — it captures things. It might hold her better than these cords, when the sedation wears off."

The woman was already groggy from being sedated but she mightily resisted being taken toward her round shape. She jerked and twisted as they dragged her to it.

"We're getting close," Weqi warned, when they had almost reached it. "Don't let her swing you around in front of her."

The woman tried to do just that, with a sudden writhe of her shoulders and flex of her bound arms. She might have succeeded if the sedation was not taking hold. Weqi and Desag linked their arms behind her and pushed her forward until her tossing head got close enough to be caught in the round shape's center. It gripped her and drew her up, making it easier for Weqi and Desag to shove her the rest of the way into its hold.

"Use your paddle for the last bit," Weqi suggested. "Don't let your hands get too close."

Soon both women were held in the round shape. They floated, bunched at its center, slightly apart from each other. Mean Woman was still struggling to get loose, but the other woman was fully sedated and still.

"Somehow we've got to sedate Mean Woman too," Desag said.

201

"Otherwise she might get loose from this shape before we've had a chance to —"

"Shhh," Weqi warned. "Mean Woman can probably hear what we're saying."

They sedated Mean Woman by sticking the patches on the end of the paddle, and transferring them from the paddle to her neck.

Weqi then guided Desag along the wall so they could join Áka and Miti. As they edged past the shape, they again felt a pull on their hair and skin, toward where the gaunt woman and Mean Woman were held, but it was not as strong as before.

Chapter 30

The four of them hurried along the silent tunnelways to where the other two minions waited in the crawlway. After gathering up their gear and supplies, they all approached the exit as silently and cautiously as possible.

When they were nearly there Weqi went ahead as wolf. *It should be fairly easy,* she thought, *to catch the guard unawares if he's sitting like he was yesterday, staring out at the greenery. Or he might be asleep, or —*

But the guard was not at his post. The cave opening was quiet and empty.

Weqi was wary of trapping devices or an ambush. But her nose, eyes and ears reassured her. The place reeked of the bad smell, but neither that nor the scent of the guard was super fresh. What was still rather fresh was the smell of bruised leafage and oozing sap from mashed vegetation outside the cave.

Weqi signaled the others to approach. They came and looked around. The guard's Rif was on the ground just outside the cave opening. Beyond it was a large area where bushes and small trees were flattened, as if something heavy had rolled right over them. Further away was a wide trail of destroyed vegetation leading west.

Desag gave his paddle to Áka and picked up the Rif. As he powered it up, he looked over the crushed vegetation. "Told you," he said. "Mega snake."

Weqi as wolf and Áka exchanged glances. They were still not convinced of Desag's big, hungry snake notion. But they were starting to give it more credence.

All of them except Weqi had been in the cave so long that just being outside felt strange and awful. The sky above was clouded over, but even so the brightness stung their eyes. And the cold air felt too thin to breathe, and hostile somehow.

The darkness of the forest beyond the open area looked brooding and threatening. All manner of danger lurked in there, which could easily overpower and kill them. In the cave, at least there had been walls of solid rock to put one's back against.

They felt an odd impulse to rush back inside the cave, even though getting out of it was what they had pined for, dreamt of, for so long.

Weqi was not as afraid of the forest as the others were, but even she hesitated. From where she was standing her gaze could not penetrate its darkness, but a riot of scents and sounds rolled out of it, most of which she could only broadly identify. She knew that some were benign, while others signaled danger. But there were more that she was not sure of — so many more all mixed up together and overlapping.

She fought down a rush of panic. *Every wolf shapeshifter must feel this way at first,* she told herself, shakily but sternly. *Just . . . get used to it. Get used to it. Get —*

She made a low keening sound without realizing it. Áka and Desag, on either side of her, moved in closer, until their legs brushed lightly against her flanks.

"You can do this, Wild Woman," Áka said.

"Yeah," Desag added. "And we'd better get going,"

Reassured, *Desag is right,* Weqi thought. *We need to get away from here.*

She nodded. *Ready or not.* She loped off in a southerly direction.

She would have preferred to head west, into the wind, but whatever it was that left the trail of crushed vegetation had gone west.

The others gathered up the gear and supplies, and followed her south, into the dark wilds of the Core.

* * *

204

When the sedation wore off Lako found herself tied up and lying in the tunnelway. *How did I come to be tied up here?* she wondered. *Oh. I suppose the minions did it.*

Her first reaction was severe disappointment. *Apparently none of the other Chosen were smart or fast enough to stop the minions from escaping. I'll have to do all the work of getting them back myself. But first someone will have to untie me.*

She shouted for help, and before long Leader's Second came.

Another disappointment! *I wish it was anyone other than Leader's Second. She always stares so, as if I'm from a lower order of beings. But she's just jealous. By now she must know how much Leader loves his 'darling little minion minder', as he playfully calls me in private. Leader's Second must suspect how high up Leader is going to place me soon, so very soon.*

Lako tamped down her disappointment and called out brightly, "Untie me, quick! The minions have escaped, and I've got to trace them before they get out of range!"

Lying there with Leader's Second coming toward her, Lako knew something was amiss. Then she remembered that Leader's Second had been bound and gagged when they were both stuck in that strange floating trap. But now Leader's Second was walking around freely, while she herself was all tied up . . .

Well! Lako thought angrily, *so she's jealous **and** spiteful!*

Even so, Lako felt she had to make a show of getting along with Leader's Second — at least until Leader raised her up. "I'd really appreciate it if you'd hurry," she urged, straining to keep an acidic edge out of her voice. "Soooo much valuable time is being lost. As soon as you untie me, I'll get to work on getting all those minions back for our dear Leader. I'll stop at nothing. I'll —"

Leader's Second knelt down beside Lako, but instead of untying her, she yanked her scarf from her neck and gagged her with it.

"Enough from you," Leader's Second murmured. "The minions, too long gone for easy back. And Master is so very hungry. He must have something *now. Anything* now." She t'sked absently while looking over Lako's bound body, pinching and prodding her arms, thighs and buttocks.

Lako squirmed trying to escape those strong fingers. *That really hurts, and is so insulting! How **dare** she! And just who is this 'Master' fellow? And what does his being hungry have to do with anything?! Really!* Angrily she twisted around to glare at Leader's Second.

Leader's Second gazed coolly back at her.

"Master has been insulted – such an extreme insult, that his appetite, it spikes. Normally, he's very picky. Nothing but the best — or at least, the best of what's available. The young, or the changers — but especially the young changers. The flavor — so much better. But now, at war. Ravenous. Anything. Everything." Her hoarse voice trailed off, while her eyes again strayed appraisingly over Lako's body.

Suddenly Lako understood that Leader's Second was not just being mean and spiteful, and that she had no intention of untying her. She struggled violently to free herself, but with a long string of guttural words and a wave of her hands over Lako, Leader's Second stilled her.

*   *   *

Leader's Second stood up and grabbed Lako by her hair. Dragging her further into the cave along the tunnelway, she murmured, "Yes, you'll have to do, for now." And then with a sigh she added, "And then we'll have to go out again, and hunt for more. Always more."

Chapter 31

Earlier that day, in mid–afternoon, two aeors arrived at the obscure Anglo historic site deep in the Core Wilderness.

Honcho Beaver was at the controls in one of the aeors. Her floating chair latched into its main seat; the controls were within her shorter reach, and responded to paw touch rather than fingers. Pani was with her, in the small space for either cargo or a small human–sized passenger.

Rahra was flying his Investigations aeor, which Honcho Beaver had hacked so that no one else would know about this trip they were making to the old Anglo site — at least not yet.

According to protocols, Rahra should have notified his bosses to contact Seek and Rescue when, very early this morning, they broke into the rogue hacker's hacks. But Honcho Beaver had 'said', "Let's keep this quiet until we know better what's going on."

Rahra had agreed with her at the time. They did not know how widespread this rogue hacking was. And if someone in Seek and Rescue was involved, in addition to the rogue hacker in Seek and Capture, then the search for the missing children and youths could be undermined or blocked.

By now though, flying incognito to the old site, they were fairly sure that they were up against only one rogue hacker with a few confederates, and it did not look like any of them were in Seek and Rescue. *Probably I should have let my boss know by now . . . but,* Rahra reasoned, *it's still not a sure thing, and it won't be until we get our hands on the rogue hacker's keybs.*

Ever since Rahra arrived at the marsh the previous morning, he and Pani had worked with Honcho Beaver in her pod, trying to pin and work back from the rogue hacks that were responsible for Wenq and Weqi Kah being missing. Rahra quietly went off duty after filing a 'stable' report — no viable leads to follow at present. Pani found a discreet relative to come and stay with Wenq and Weqi's mother, leaving him free to be at Honcho Beaver's beck and call. Sleep and rest came in snatches for the three of them, as Rahra and Pani helped Honcho Beaver set up and monitor every tech net they could think of, to snag tracings left by the rogue hacker in the Nation's vast networks, no matter how ephemeral.

They went deep and they went wide — drudging, sloughing work done across dozens of hacking keybs that Honcho Beaver linked together. The keybs were spread out around the three of them, some of them in piles and stacks. It looked chaotic, but it was actually tightly organized. Rahra marveled at how adroitly Honcho Beaver kept everything coordinated and operating at breakneck computing speeds.

In the wee hours of this morning their spirits were flagging.

It was around then that Honcho Beaver broke the silence to comment via her keyb, "Somewhat difficult, getting into these hacks."

Pani chuffed in derision at how much of an understatement that was.

"They're septuple, octuple wrapped," Honcho Beaver groused. "Even the hacker'd have trouble keeping 'em all straight. *And* there are nested layers of programs running that erase or snarl over the hack 'footprints', nearly in real time."

Rahra commented, "So to break in we've got to, like, *know* there is a tiny bone needle hidden somewhere in the cast of one giant pine tree, out of the cast of thousands, even millions of pine trees. And *then* we have to be already set up to pinpoint and grab that one tiny sliver fast as lightning — faster actually — before it slips away for good."

"You got it, Rahra," was Honcho Beaver's terse reply.

"It's impossible."

"Only nearly so."

They had been at it for so long, and thus far it had all come to nothing. But Honcho Beaver still led them, pushing herself, Pani and Rahra to create and monitor for every conceivable trace. Pani and Rahra sometimes made suggestions; the three of them worked well together, anticipating what was needed and bolstering each other's efforts.

Their break finally came when, not long before dawn, one of Wenq's keybs suddenly activated.

Honcho Beaver had backdoor hack access to all of Wenq and Weqi's keybs — something she had set up years earlier. "For their protection," Honcho Beaver explained to Rahra. "Because you never know what's out there."

"Sure don't!" Rahra agreed. "Like for instance, this rogue."

Throughout the night Rahra had thought that Honcho Beaver was working in overdrive. But when Wenq's keyb activated, the old e–beaver practically leapt out of her seat, in an all–out frenzy to shove through millions of snag and copy nets — her own and the ones she'd assigned to Rahra and Pani. For a crucial minute they worked nearly flawlessly, until the boy's keyb went dead again.

Honcho Beaver sat fully back in her floating chair for the first time in hours.

"Got something," she 'said' with a grim sigh. "Now the *real* work begins."

She immediately set to work reconfiguring the hacking keybs. She kept Pani on monitoring — no small task, and brought Rahra in on the grinding work of unwinding the hacks they'd bled out through Wenq's keyb.

It took many hours, until nearly noon. Honcho Beaver was adroit, but she was also cautious, and relentlessly thorough. In a spare moment Rahra mused that this fat old e–beaver might well be the best hacker that ever was. The rogue hacker was an exceptionally good one, but Honcho Beaver was many times better. Like a wily old spider, she was intimately familiar with every far–reaching strand, ready to pounce at the slightest vibration in her hacking 'web'. Rahra knew enough about hacking to appreciate the incredible amount of knowledge, skill and organization it took. And the intellect required for it was astounding.

By noon they had pieced together that one of the Seek and Capture warriors had gone rogue and was involved in the disappearances of a number of youths and children, including Áka Haun, the girl who had gone missing last month from their region, and Wenq and Weqi Kah, who disappeared early yesterday morning. The hacker called himself Stealth in his hacks, but Honcho Beaver got his real name and his S&C badge number: Aten Erh, in the 74th Seek and Capture Squadron.

According to the squadron records, which Honcho Beaver slash–hacked right into, the guy was out on a sick leave for a sprained ankle, and his S&C aeor was grounded for maintenance upgrades.

"His name and his being in that squadron looks real enough, but I wouldn't bet on him having a sprained ankle," Honcho Beaver commented dryly. "And we now have our own hacked coordinates for his aeor being at that old Anglo site. I'd stake a lot on our coordinates being the right ones."

Most of the rest that they were able to access were messages having something to do with delivering 'minions' to work for something called the New Order.

"I dunno, but does that sound to you like, maybe, some kind of cult or something?" Rahra hazarded.

"Let's hope that's all this is," Pani 'said' grimly. "Some kind of crazy cult. Then we'll stand a much better chance of getting those children back alive."

None of them wanted to dwell on what could happen to children when at the mercy of pitiless adults. Better to have hope.

Honcho Beaver 'said', "So we've gotten about as far as we can without actually having the hacker's equipment. Oh, and I should mention, this Stealth guy is probably . . . incapacitated."

Pani simply nodded in agreement, but Honcho Beaver's statement surprised Rahra.

He was used to being several steps behind the wily old e–beaver in everything they'd been doing. Besides her superior hacking skills, Rahra also saw that both Honcho Beaver and Pani took it very personally that the rogue hacker had snatched the Kah brother and sister, whom they clearly considered to be part of their own family.

But from the work they'd been doing, Rahra could not understand how Honcho Beaver could know something like that about the hacker. "Ah, clarify?" he asked.

"Elementary, my dear Rahra. You haven't been doing much of the monitoring, but look at it now. Look at what's been running — just automatics really. Stealth hasn't been active on his hacks recently. If he had been, he'd have made it much harder for us to get this far into them. So this Stealth guy isn't using his equipment, which for a hacker like him is highly aberrant.

"My hunch — he's got a big ass hacking base somewhere. But it'd be too much to lug around. So he'd control it from some keybs he keeps with him. Probably in his aeor. We need to get to those keybs. And the coordinates we have right now — both for Stealth's aeor and Wenq's keyb — are for that old Anglo site."

* * *

The two aeors gave the signal for approach. Honcho Beaver and Pani in one aeor, Rahra in the other, turned their attention to the visuals and the monitors.

The aeors came in over the river under a sodden, bruised sky. Even before they canted slightly away from the river and over a long wedge of marsh in a smattering rain, they could see through their aeor domes that an S&C aeor was indeed at the coordinates they had pinned to. Their monitors informed them that the area was clear of all larger warm–blooded animals, other than a scattering of deer.

211

They landed close in beside the S&C aeor. Visuals of the insignia badge and code on its rim confirmed it was the S&C aeor assigned to Warrior Erh. It was closed up, with its sophisticated dome set to opaque.

Being in Investigations, Rahra had a manual Crank–All in his aeor for use in emergencies. He got out of his aeor with it and was kneeling down to put it in the S&C aeor's crank port for the dome, when Honcho Beaver asked him stop.

"Stealth might have programmed the aeor to do a data wipe upon manual entry, unless he initiates an override," Honcho Beaver 'said'. "But now that we're here there are a few things I can try to hack open his aeor."

The coordinates for Wenq's keyb were a short distance away, up on the ridge running alongside the wedge of marsh. Pani and Rahra went to look for it, while Honcho stayed behind to work determinedly at her hacks for opening up the S&C aeor. "Let me know right away if you find anything up there that will help me get into this aeor," she 'said' as they were leaving.

Rahra took some scent droners and other equipment with him, but neither he nor Pani needed any aids to smell the blood and the many other recent scents on the ridge, well before they reached the root cellar where they found Wenq's keyb wedged into branches covering its entryway. Rahra removed the branches and after a brief look inside, he watched as Pani messaged to Honcho, "Stealth found bloodied and dead here. His body in an old root cellar. Some scent of Wenq and Nika here but it goes off west, with the scent of three strangers, two of them Mix–Scents. Possibly nomars?"

Mix–Scents. That was the term that Honcho Beaver and Pani sometimes used for shapeshifters.

Honcho Beaver's grim response was, "Bring Stealth's body. Using his ID chip will make this hack a lot easier. And bring all the equipment that you and Rahra can find. Everything, and quick."

"Who's this Nika?" Rahra asked Pani. "And why did you tell her

212

two shapeshifters, when we have both scented three?"

"I'll explain once we get everything to Honcho B," was Pani's reply.

Chapter 32

Using Stealth's ID chip, along with some of Honcho Beaver's hacking chips inserted into the mangled Skim that Rahra brought from the root cellar, Honcho Beaver hacked the S&C aeor enough to open its dome without causing a catastrophic wipe of Stealth's hacks. Honcho Beaver immediately went inside the S&C aeor on her floating chair and got to work with Rahra helping her. Rahra badly wanted to shapeshift to wolf and follow the scents going west, but it was Pani who went off to do that with some scent droners that Rahra set for him.

Before leaving, Pani gave Rahra the essentials about Nika, as he had promised.

"So you're telling me," Rahra said, "that she's a young woman who is an owl shapeshifter, but she was born 800 plus years ago, and she has informed you that she recently came from a mythical place that does not actually exist. *And* you did not immediately report her to Infiltrate even though you *knew* she has no ID chip. *And* Honcho Beaver expunged the young woman's scent from her pod before I arrived there yesterday, so I wouldn't scent her there."

"That's right," was Pani's measured reply. "It was a matter of staying focused on finding Wenq and his sister. And until you and I scented her on that ridge just now, Honcho Beaver and I did not know whether she was still with Wenq. Plus we did not want to put you in a position where you might feel it was necessary to report her to Infiltrate yourself."

Rahra was dismayed that Pani and Honcho had not trusted him enough to tell him about this mysterious Nika person until they absolutely had to. But he admitted to himself that in a similar

214

circumstance he might have done the same.

Pani then left and returned after about an hour, reporting that he had found where Stealth had been killed, and giving coordinates for the direction that Wenq, Nika and the other three went when they left the area. "But there's nothing to indicate why Wenq and Nika went away with those three that we think are nomars," he commented.

The unspoken question they all had was whether the unknown three were friend or foe.

By then Honcho Beaver, with Rahra's help, had full control over Stealth's hacks, and had unrestricted access to his files.

"It's an insurgency of some kind, but a very strange one," Honcho Beaver 'said' through her keyb. "It's been kidnapping children and youths from all over the Nation, apparently to work in a cave far to the west of here, and a little northerly, that's probably their headquarters."

Rahra had been studying the available topography files on one of their keybs. "But Wenq and the others that left here this morning on foot — they're heading more southwesterly. It's not a route that would take them directly to the cave."

Pani looked over the topo files and agreed with Rahra. "It doesn't make any sense for them to have gone southwesterly if their destination was that cave. That would only put more obstacles in their way, including those large marshlands and a wide river."

They were eager to follow the leads they'd developed. "We should split up," was Honcho Beaver's suggestion. "Rahra could go to the cave with Seek and Rescue, while Pani and I follow the five that went southwest from here on foot."

"So you agree that it's time to brief my boss, and bring Seek and Rescue in on this?" Rahra asked.

Honcho Beaver and Pani knew that Rahra was going to take some flak for not bringing Investigations and Seek and Rescue into this sooner.

"We'll back you, Rahra," Pani 'said' for both of them. "We really didn't have enough to go on until now."

"Have both Investigations and Seek and Rescue put their best IT on it," Honcho Beaver added. "I'll send them all the files as soon as you let us know where to send them. Full Cooperation mode now."

* * *

By early evening three Seek and Rescue squadrons were swarming in and around the cave, as well as back and forth over the strange, huge tentacles of mashed vegetation that stretched far from the cave in several directions.

Rahra and two of his Investigations bosses watched all the activity near the main entrance to the cave — S&R aeors zipping around, S&R warriors on the ground and careening about on their Skims, and an uncountable number of droners flitting hither and yon. Rahra thought, *They look like flies of different sizes buzzing over putrid meat.* He couldn't help thinking of it that way, because the whole place stank like meat going off. He kept expecting the S&R warriors to drag some big old carcass out of the cave, to account for the terrible smell. But so far nothing like that had happened. The source for the stench was not yet apparent.

He and his bosses were kept in isolation; S&R wasn't telling them *anything*. Rahra's bosses in Investigations had grudgingly accepted his explanation for the delay in being notified, but S&R resented that his delay was because he thought they *might* have a rogue hacker in their midst.

But they were dedicated professionals, and caring people. Despite their pique, and some grumblings about dire repercussions later on, they immediately got to work on finding the missing kids.

Rahra noted that S&R was not nearly as hard on Honcho Beaver and Pani, as they had been on him. Just in case they were not already aware of Honcho Beaver's 'hackumen', he had made it very clear in his reporting that without her and Pani's help, they'd be nowhere. He needn't have gone to the trouble. S&R's IT were already aware of her

216

hacking skill, and in awe of it.

S&R had grudgingly shared with Investigations that three of those travelling with the Wenq boy were among the most primitive of the known nomars. (Rahra had left Nika out of his reporting, for the time being.) Because nomars could be unpredictable and savage, S&R agreed that Pani and Honcho Beaver should be the first to make contact when they were tracked down. They were the ones most likely to get in close without alarming the nomars. For the Kah boy's safety, Honcho Beaver and Pani were in the lead, following the trail left by him and the nomars. Some S&R aeors kept pace not far behind them, ready to assist if needed.

Meanwhile at the cave, S&R made it clear to Rahra and his bosses that S&R wanted them to leave. 'We will notify you if and when S&R has anything to report,' they'd been assured.

But they stayed on, sheltered from the cold drizzle by an open–sided pop–up hut. They cared too much about the children and youths who had gone missing to leave. They had worked on some of the cases themselves and felt haunted by all of those missing and their families. By staying here and quietly using their senses and their own portable devices, they felt they might notice something useful. Or — less likely — S&R might eventually condescend to include them.

An S&R cadet glumly waited with them, clearly not pleased at being relegated to making sure they stayed put and out of S&R's way. She did not interfere, though, when they sent a few of their own scent and ID–tracing droners around the area.

Their ID–tracing droners did not get any pings, but their scent droners confirmed what Rahra had ascertained with his nose. A small group of kids had left here early this morning, heading almost due south into a part of the Core that was marked on the charts as being one of its most dangerous and impenetrable areas. Several heavily shielded S&R units had recently gone in that direction, presumably to track them. The S&R cadet sighed and fidgeted, obviously wishing she was going with them instead of being stuck here with her lowly, dreary assignment.

Data from the scent droners were matched with IDs for six of the kids. It worried Rahra that there were no scents around for any of the other missing kids. If they had ever been here, it had been long enough ago that their scents had dissipated. S&R might have already found some senq traces for them inside the cave, but if they had they weren't telling Investigations about it.

Other than the Kah boy, there were nearly two dozen missing kids altogether, that they knew of. But only six of them had gone off into the Core early this morning. And with every passing minute, it seemed less and less likely that any of the other kids were going to be found alive inside the cave. Already there was much less S&R activity going in and out of the cave, and much more of it in scouring widening perimeters outside of it.

Rahra had been pondering about what could have caused a bunch of kids — according to records the oldest was sixteen — to go off into the Core instead of staying in the relative safety of the cave. Surely some of them knew how dangerous the Core was. Even he, with his wolf shapeshifter senses and reflexes, usually forayed in the Rim Wilderness, avoiding the central Core altogether.

He and his bosses had noticed that the scent data found here for the Kah girl — Weqi — had recently developed a shapeshifter overlay. She had become a wolf shapeshifter like himself. But as a shapeshifter she was practically a baby — much too young and inexperienced to survive in the Core by herself, let alone with a bunch of helpless kids who, if she stayed with them, were probably slowing her down and distracting her. It was insane for any of them to have gone off into the Core, unless they had to because of something worse here . . . Rahra eyed the massive areas of crushed vegetation, this time really working over the scents drifting from it.

Honcho Beaver and Pani had not reported in for a while. At last contact they were still following the scents of the group that included

218

the Kah boy, generally heading southwest, which would take them south of where the cave was.

And the six kids from here had headed south from the cave . . .

Rahra was not an especially imaginative man, but he had a mature wolf's hunting instincts, including a keen sense for the immediacy of dangers lurking in the forests. Now it was giving him a feeling of dread, that he had learned to pay attention to over the years. It was telling him — faintly but definitely — that something was in motion, something that was dangerous and that was probably going to go after those six kids.

He turned to his immediate boss, who was the only one here who knew he was a shapeshifter.

"I'm thinking about going in after them." he told her.

She did not respond right away, but when she answered her voice was decisive. "It's crazy. Don't even think about it."

But Rahra then told her, not caring that the other Investigations boss Kanr and the S&R cadet could hear him, "S&R is the best of its kind. But they could miss something. Riding on their Skims with their equipment and all they're, like, one step removed from the, er, the real thing. The real scents. The real sounds and, and all. And there might not be much time. Great Twin, those are kids out there in the *Core*, and there might not be much time."

"I wouldn't stop you," his boss said slowly, "but —"

"Then I'm going. And I think I need to leave, like, *now*. In fact I think I really ought to have already left."

* * *

The S&R cadet's assignment suddenly became more exciting. She reported promptly and succinctly to her higher–up, "The low guy in Investigations just went off in his aeor. Into the Core, heading south."

Her supervisor took it in stride. "Suicidal," came her response. "But . . . let's track him."

Chapter 33

Weqi had lost her panicky fear of the Core not long after
plunging into it that morning with Desag and Áka at her side, and the
three other kids close behind. Sooner than she thought possible, she
was confidently sorting through the dense forest's scents and sounds,
and combining them with her sharper vision into manageable
patterns and probabilities.

Throughout the long day as they travelled through the forest,
they coped rather well with its abundant dangers. Time and time
again Weqi led the others clear of large predators before they got
close enough to be in serious danger. And with an aggressive
feistiness that came naturally to her, she stood down wolf packs in
two skirmishes that were unavoidable. Both packs had ultimately
backed away from her strange mix of wolf and human scent, and
from the tight defensive formation made by the odd–smelling Two–
Leggers travelling with her, who bristled with pointy, foreign–
smelling objects.

Weqi was inexperienced, but not naive. She suspected that the
corpse–scent hanging about them was at least as much a deterrent
for the wolves as her brazen snarls. They seemed to be chary of the
odor — an odor so alien to the living.

She knew that survival depended on her, because the contrast
between herself and her companions could not have been greater.
She had wolf-keen senses of smell, hearing and vision, deadly fangs,
and elastic strength and swiftness. The others were clumsy and
hopelessly noisy, even under hemlocks, where there was little brush
to entangle them. There, where they whispered to Weqi that they
were gliding over the spongy ground as if on cat–paws, they actually

sounded to her like buffaloes stampeding across a plain. They were so inept and unaware of everything going on around them that it actually embarrassed her, though at the same time she felt fiercely protective of them all. Even Desag, who was more capable than the others, completely missed some of the Core's most basic warnings. If not for her, he would have been unaware of several stalking dangers until they were much too close to be avoided.

Weqi wondered where the strong protectiveness she felt for them sprang from. *I have no duty to lead them, or to put myself between them and danger. It's not a motherly feeling — far from it! It's more like good against evil, but I don't understand why it feels that way.*

And yet she knew that she would die trying to save any one of them.

This was an entirely new experience for her. Like a lone leaf fallen from a great tree, she had thought of herself as a pointless piece of nature's cast, and had striven only to assure her own comfort, and to satisfy fleeting whims. Apart from a strong but vague notion of becoming a great Warrior Woman someday in the misty future, she'd had no greater goal for her life. She was a spoiled, uncaring and unthinking girl.

But as a wolf shapeshifter everything rearranged itself and coalesced into a new Understanding. *I don't have it all worked out, but I am **not**, sure as heck **not**, going to be like some damned dead leaf!*

Life suddenly exploded with meaning, and was precious. She resolved, *Whether it's long or short, I must always be doing Something Useful with my life, right up to when some force greater than me prevents me from doing that any longer.*

Finding herself in the desperate situation of being in the Core with five nearly helpless humans, that 'Something Useful' for the time being was simple and stark. *Somehow I must lead them out of the Core to safety, or die trying.*

* * *

So far in this journey they had done alright.

221

For the most part they travelled through varied but dense forest lands, with only an occasional bog, meadow or stream to vary their dark and chill course under densely interwoven tree branches. Even with some early fall yellowing of leaves, most of the forest floor was shaded by the untamed growth. They were grateful whenever they came to a place where they could see grey mottled clouds through the old growth canopy, as if through a small moth hole in a dark smothering mantle. Sometimes it was when passing through a marshy pocket, other times in a swath of blowdown. Weqi's nose kept them mainly on deer trails, which were difficult enough to travel on in some places where bushes and tree branches hemmed them in.

All of that was normal for the Core. What was not normal was another wide curving trail of mashed vegetation that they came across, similar to what they had seen outside the cave early that morning. This damage was at least several days old, but seeing it made them all uneasy. Several of them, including Weqi, felt a superstitious dread as they stepped across it, as if they were treading on human bones instead of shattered branches. Weqi gurgled a half–remembered prayer chant to the Good Twin, asking for his understanding and protection. It was unintelligible in her wolf throat, but Desag and Áka seemed to understand that she was trying to nix a jinx. They followed her lead, both of them softly crooning their own prayer chants.

Whatever flattened the vegetation had been travelling westerly, so Weqi led them much more southeasterly when they were past the mashed trail.

In mid–afternoon their way was blocked by a stream too swollen with recent rains to be forded. For a while they went more directly south, until they found a broad dilapidated span that most of the stream still passed under. It was sound enough to bear their weight; once across, they resumed their southeasterly course.

They had kept their wits about them and been rather lucky. Desag and the slow–witted boy carried the two young ones, Mitzi and the younger boy, most of way, so as not to be slowed by them. Despite the roughness of the terrain and raw weather, they had travelled far, at least by human standards.

But Weqi was not lulled by their modest successes. The Core was practically shrilling at her, as the light of day began to wane, that they must find a place to hole up for the night. Travelling in the Core at night would be the surest way to meet with death.

She found a passable shelter about an hour before full dark. It was a deep horizontal shelf in a sheer wall of slabby slate, set about ten feet above one side of a shallow but fast–moving creek. To climb up to the shelf they notched a knobby, heavy branch and leaned it against the slate wall. Weqi had to shapeshift to girl to be able to climb it. After they had all climbed up onto the shelf, they hauled the branch up after them with rope.

The shelf was only about three feet high, cramped and dank. But the blankets they had brought with them from the cave were waterproof, and the niche was likely to protect them from predators.

They lit a small fire and kept it going only long enough to boil some water for reconstituting dehydrated rations. They ate in near silence and then they tried to sleep, all except Desag, who took the first watch of the night.

Weqi had shapeshifted back to wolf and was curled up fairly comfortably at one end of the niche. Foot–sore and bone–weary from the exertions and strain of the last day and a half, she had surely earned some rest.

Chapter 34

Weqi was nearly asleep when the heavy beat of feathered wings brought her head up. Only the strong wings of a large raptor bird would make enough noise to wake her.

A large hawk landed on the branch they had notched, which was lying along the outer edge of the niche.

Desag also heard the bird and saw it, but it was gone before either he or Weqi could react. He did not even have time to point the Rif at it, and Weqi's hackles were still rising when the hawk flew nearly straight up and wheeled away to the north.

"Odd," Desag whispered to Weqi. "Much too odd," he quickly added. "Because that *was* a hawk, right? And hawks don't hunt at night. And it couldn't have been nesting here . . . what could it mean, Weqi?"

Weqi shapeshifted to girl and whispered back glumly, "Not just any hawk. It had the scent of that woman — the one we left tied up in that hoop with Mean Woman, back at the cave this morning. So she's a shapeshifter, and she's found us. She's probably gone for reinforcements."

Desag said a filthy word. Not to be outdone, Weqi said a filthier one. At least she had learned a few useful things in her wayward, spoiled girl life. It brought a rare smile to Desag's face, though a wan one. "You won't be second in anything, will you?" he asked.

His smile faded. "But we've come so far. And we had nearly a full day's start. How could she have found us?"

"Not likely by our ID chips or the chip in that Rif — I'd have heard it if a droner or anything like that was following us. Possibly it was our fire, the heat rising after dark . . . maybe that's something a hawk could see from a great distance."

"Possibly was it, um, well, magic?"

Weqi thought back to the strange guttural words the woman had uttered that morning, before Desag gagged her. She still didn't believe in magic — to her shapeshifting wasn't magic, it was something totally natural. "She might just be an exceptionally good scout. I mean, with the eyesight of a hawk and the advantage of flight, and maybe a few lucky guesses from the ground trail we left . . ."

Desag then voiced what neither of them wanted to think about. "So we can't stay here, can we?"

Weqi sighed. "Yeah, we'd better move. I'll listen for her wings, in case she returns, while you wake the others."

Without much discussion they all moved to another niche in the jagged slate wall, further down the creek and around a bend. They waded in the creek in the darkness, so as to leave no tracks. The new spot was lower down in the wall, so it would not be as defensible against a ground attack. But it had the advantage of being almost completely hidden from view from the sky.

In the new place Weqi got a few hours of rest before waking up in the middle of the night to something new — a profound feeling of unease and danger. She came a little closer to believing in some kind of magic, because this dread felt out of balance somehow. It was something that did not belong, even in the wild forests of the Core. And yet it was here, and it was hunting, and not just for any and all belly food. *No,* she sensed, *it hunts for lives, and some lives are more valuable than others. It wants young lives, with complexities. My life as a young shapeshifter would be worth more to it, than the lives of the others.*

She did not know how she knew this. It wasn't anything that she could explain to Desag, who was still on watch, but she herself understood it.

It was a foreign danger, near and coming closer, and many times worse than anything she'd encountered in the Core thus far. And it

225

was much too strong for them, when and if it found them.

Weqi knew what had to be done — it was very simple. *The others must keep themselves hidden, while I go out and draw the danger away from here. I'm not really fast enough, or strong enough. But I have to do it anyway.*

Desag did not want her to go out on her own. He argued that they should all stay together, no matter what.

When that failed to persuade her, Desag insisted that he would go with her, bringing the Rif for their protection.

Weqi shook her head. "I have to be fast, Desag. Very fast. And unencumbered. Tell Áka when she wakes."

Desag didn't agree, but he nodded reluctantly. There would be no stopping Weqi.

She shapeshifted to wolf and jumped down into the creek. She swam and waded some distance before leaving the water. It was not a sure thing that the coming danger was something that could scent her, but the odds were good that it was. She went west and slightly north of where she thought the danger was approaching from, into the wind so that her scent would lure the danger toward herself.

Unencumbered by the others she charged through the nighttime Core at top speed for several hours. She was nearly thirteen miles away from them when she began to hear a distant groaning and crackling noise. For a while the volume remained low but then the noises sounded louder with every passing moment. Whatever was out there was coming in her direction!

She continued west, approaching a bare rise where her scent would flow easterly. Everything went unusually quiet, before the woods around her erupted with closer thrashing, crashing noises, all approaching from the east.

A dozen or so deer streamed past her, surging over the rise in heedless leaps, their eyes glazed with a desperate fear.

A large pack of wolves rushed past a little to her right, like a surging river, nearly silent and running like they were being chased themselves. Just as suddenly two bears loomed out of the darkness, crashing and lumbering almost directly toward Weqi. They swept past her, paying her no heed, hurrying, hurrying. Clearly fleeing from something.

In an odd backwash of scent trailing them, Weqi caught traces of the smell of meat going off, which brought the smell of the cave vividly to mind.

Instinct told Weqi to crest the rise quickly and keep running west, on and on, low to the ground. But as she listened to the rumbling noise in the distance, she thought it was turning more southward, in the direction of the creek, where she did not want it to go. Though her hackles rose and her legs trembled she rushed to the crest of the rise and stayed there, letting the wind carry her scent toward the hidden danger.

Below her, the way she had come, the land sloped down and then back up again to a distant, slightly higher rise. On it some of the larger trees swayed and bent, while smaller ones snapped and toppled. She could see that the groaning, crackling noises she'd been hearing were branches and tree trunks breaking and tearing.

With her night vision she caught glimpses of something large, pale and mottled oozing along under some of the larger trees. It was angling south as it forced its way along the rise's crest, but as she watched the half–hidden shape stilled, and the pale head of an enormous snake rose above the trees. The forks of its tongue flicked through the air like a pair of giant whips.

The snake's head went back down into the trees, and the snake re–set its course, heading west, directly toward Weqi.

Weqi turned and ran for her life.

Chapter 35

Weqi's brother Wenq had spent most of that day laboring to keep up with the three nomars, all the while trying to keep Nika as comfortable as possible inside his jacket.

Much of the time he lagged so far behind the nomars that he had to guess at where they were ahead of him, by the faint sounds they made, and the distant blur of their movement. The only reason he never completely lost track of them was because *they* kept track of *him*, deliberately slowing just enough so that they would not outpace him. Whenever he began to go off course, Tal the wolf shapeshifter would let out a desultory whoop to guide him back.

Despite his aches and the foul, raw weather Wenq did his best to keep up, plying his staff to keep upright, and eke out a little more speed.

Wenq knew the nomars only tolerated him because he was carrying Nika. She was too strained from the harsh immob to fly or to go with them on foot, and she would only let Wenq carry her — no one else.

Every once in a long while the nomars stopped and waited impatiently for Wenq to catch up. After the first time he knew what it meant: when he reached them Tehwe swept him up as if he was as light as an empty basket, plunked him onto his back and carried him through a place that he would have found impassable on his own. Once past the rough area, Tehwe shrugged Wenq off his back without breaking his stride.

The first time Wenq got slung onto Tehwe's back he'd been too surprised to fully buffer Nika, and she got pressed between his ribs and Tehwe's back. She squawked pitiably and Wenq immediately shifted his elbow to give her more space, whispering an apology. Tehwe's only acknowledgement of having hurt her was, when he next slung Wenq onto his back he did it slightly slower, giving Wenq a little time to get Nika better positioned.

These few interludes of being carried by Tehwe were not at all restful for Wenq. Often the difficult areas were full of thick rope–like vines that hung from trees and bushes, in a dense weave of vine, tendril and leaf. Tehwe seemed to know just the right places to force his way through them. Wenq had to keep himself very close against Tehwe's back, and to shift and duck, to keep from getting snagged in them.

It was while porting Wenq and Nika that Tehwe spoke in curt, grunt–like phrases, sometimes with words Wenq could not understand. Wenq soon realized that Tehwe was telling Nika what he knew about the snake. He seemed to take it for granted that once he told Nika these things, she would know just what to do, to un–witch his child when they reached his camp.

Tehwe said that he had first encountered the snake about four stick–notches previous, when travelling west with his band on their long meandering journey to a lake shore where they usually wintered. As darkness came on that night, Tehwe noticed an unusually large, tawny hawk flapping from tree to tree in the gloaming, behaving as if it was following them. It was an odd thing for a hawk to do, particularly with the approach of night, but the hawk went away as they were settling in, so Tehwe thought no more of it.

During that night a great rumbling and crashing started up, coming towards their camp from almost due north. Tehwe, sensing a strangeness and a great hostile strength in the disturbance, split his band into small groups and sent them off in different directions.

Tehwe did not say as much but Wenq guessed that Tehwe and a few others stayed behind so that they would be closest to the coming danger, to draw it away from the others. But the danger swiftly rumbled past them in the darkness and attacked his woman Anq,

229

who was fleeing with their youngest child.

Tehwe caught glimpses of the creature as he pursued it. He described it to Nika as a giant snake, pale with some darker splotches. It was as long as several of the tallest trees laid end to end, and as wide around as a bundle of five or six of the biggest tree trunks of the forest. The snake gave off a sickening stench of rot and death. Most of the time it moved slowly, having to force its way through the denser parts of the forest. Only occasionally when its way was clear, it travelled very rapidly.

Anq had fled east along the path they had come by. Tehwe knew his Anq so well; he knew she was trying to reach some old burrows in a river bank where she would be able to hide with their child. But the snake caught up with her before she got that far.

When Tehwe arrived she was bedeviling the snake with her bludgeon, standing beside a hollow tree that Tehwe knew, from its scent, was where Anq had hidden their child. In the next instant the snake's head rose up with Anq in its jaws. She wielded her bludgeon against the snake's mouth until the snake dashed her against the trunk of a large tree.

Her body went limp. The snake flung her aside and then coiled itself loosely around the hollow tree.

Tehwe's voice, as he described his wife's recent death, shook with an implacable fury. For a while he became incoherent, until Nika chirruped to him from Wenq's jacket, a strange little noise that sounded to Wenq like a strangled cry. It silenced Tehwe for a while; when he continued his telling, his voice still held the fury, but it was more contained.

The snake's head was tucked inside its massive coils, and the coils kept Tehwe from reaching his child in the hollow tree. He and those with him attacked the snake's side, first with arrows and then with their bludgeons. The others in the band that were close enough came rushing in and joined the battle.

But the snake's thick scales deflected their arrows and bludgeon

230

blows. Even after Tehwe and some others in his band shapeshifted to rip at the scales with claw and fang, their efforts seemed no more than a mild irritation to the snake. Other than a few sudden spasms that forced them to back away, the snake paid them no more heed than if they were pesky gnats.

After a while the snake uncoiled itself and slithered away, while overhead the tawny hawk circled once and flew off in same direction as the snake. It was as Tehwe ran to Anq that the hawk's scent drifted down and he scented an aged woman combined with the scent of the hawk.

Nothing could be done for Anq. Her back was broken.

She said something though, which Tehwe could not understand until he guessed that she was trying to say their child's name, Onera. Only a few labored breaths after that, she died.

Still in his bear form Tehwe called out to Onera in his bear 'voice'. She did not answer his call or come to him. He went to the tree hollow to retrieve her, but she was not there.

He picked up her scent and followed it. In a short time she had gone a surprisingly long way. He found her hurrying, following the snake's trail, stumbling but moving fast as if driven, as if in a trance.

Onera had nearly reached a strange hoop shape that Tehwe could see floating upright across the snake's trail. He snatched her back from it and carried her away. At nearly the same instant the hawk swooped down, skirling angrily, going for his eyes with its talons. Tal had caught up with him, however, and together they snapped and lunged at the hawk until it gave up and flew off.

From inside Wenq's jacket Nika made a sound that was something between a hoot and a whistle. Wenq could not fathom what it meant, but Tehwe nodded, as if to say it had been a close call with the hawk woman and her hoop.

Tehwe had thought the worst might be over for the time being, but he soon realized that his Onera had been bewitched. She kept trying to escape from them and go off, presumably to wherever the snake was. Most of the time she attempted to go north, but sometimes at night when they could hear a distant rumbling in some other direction, she would try to go in that direction instead. She would not eat, or sleep. She struggled and cried incessantly, and would not heed any of them. Before long they had to tie her to a rack to keep her from wandering off.

Night before last they heard the rumbling again; the snake was travelling east. The next day Tehwe secured most of his band in a safe place and went with Tal and Sirk to go after the snake.

They struck the snake's trail and were still following it at dark when it arced back around to the west, and they came to where Wenq and Nika's trail crossed it, going further east.

Tehwe could scent that Nika was a bird shapeshifter with strange old scents. He immediately assumed she was another of the giant snake's servants, like the hawk woman.

The snake's trail would be easy to follow even after it aged, but Nika's trail was light, barely leaving a trace when it was fresh. So they hurried after Nika and Wenq, catching up with them at the root cellar where they had bedded down.

Tehwe was surprised to find that Nika was so young, and was frustrated that she and Wenq seemed to have nothing to do with the snake. But soon afterward the heavily–armed man came in his aeor searching for Nika and Wenq — a man who stank of the hated snake. He saw that there was some connection after all.

And then Nika had beguiled the man with the strange song she made . . .

Tehwe told Nika that he thought her song could counter the snake's foul witching of his child. He'd heard enough of her tune, before he sealed his ears to it, to know that it was not ordinary sound. It echoed weirdly through the forest, with a foreignness to it, not unlike the terrible emanations of the snake. Even after sealing his ears, he felt it like an uncomfortable vibration, pulling at him. He thought its effect on him was not strong, because he was old, and knew much. But the pull would be strong and irresistible to the young, especially the very young, like his Onera.

When Tehwe was finishing explaining this they were nearly out of a rough, mucky area that Tehwe had been carrying Wenq through. Wenq asked Tehwe a question that he thought Nika would have. "But what happens if Nika's song makes the child cling to Nika? Wouldn't that —"

With a grunt Tehwe simply dropped Wenq and kept going.

Nika squawked miserably, and Wenq apologized to her for the rough landing. He picked himself up and sloughed the rest of the way out of the muck as well as he could.

Tal had been directly behind him, since the nomars often went single file through the rougher areas, letting the one in the lead clear or set the way through.

As Tal passed to one side of Wenq he muttered an answer to Wenq's question. "Better a small owl, than a giant snake."

Chapter 36

Wenq, Nika and the three nomars had travelled most of the day and long after dark, when the rumbling began. It was quite far off, but in the general direction they were going. Unmistakably, it was the snake. It was on the move somewhere out there in the darkness.

Nika scrambled out of Wenq's jacket. He handed her some clothes as she shapeshifted to girl. The weather had worsened; the wind had picked up and they were pelted with cold rain. He gave Nika his staff to use, making do without one until he was able to find another.

Nika shivered and moved stiffly at first. But she kept pace with him as they followed the nomars.

Wenq had been looking forward to talking with Nika. There was much he wanted to talk with her about — not the least of which were the rumbling noises, and whether she thought she could un–witch Tehwe's child.

But the Nika walking beside him was withdrawn and preoccupied — far different from the Nika he thought he knew. She barely acknowledged his existence, and didn't seem to care about him at all.

He cast about for an explanation. *She's been under a lot of strain, and that last immob was a bad one. But somehow that doesn't quite explain . . .* Reluctantly, he thought of the common warnings about shapeshifters — that they were unpredictable and full of vagaries, that they had flawed spirits. And that some of them, sooner or later, became evil.

Could something like that happen to Nika? he wondered. *If it did, how would it begin? Like this? Have I been completely wrong about her? I've been hoping that she might become one of my truest friends, but what if I'll have to fear her instead?*

If Nika was aware of his misgivings and doubts, she gave no indication. When she began to move a little more easily she asked Wenq for a small knife. Then she began to peer intently at the bushes they were passing. It wasn't long afterward that she called out to the nomars, "Wait! I won't be long."

They heeded her; Wenq could hear that they had paused up ahead, while she went to a particular bush in the darkness and cut several lengths of branch from it.

When they continued on the journey Nika hurried Wenq until they caught up with Tal, long enough to borrow a thin blade from him. She asked Tal as she did so, "How long until we reach your camp?"

"Two or three hours, depending," replied Tal.

"And the rumbling noises, are they in the same area as where your camp is?"

Tal shook his head. "That's further off, and more to the south."

Nika nodded, and she went back to walking a slower pace with Wenq, while she trimmed down the branch lengths and reamed out the soft pith.

When Wenq asked her what she was doing, she made no reply.

Nika's whittling slowed her pace too much to suit Tehwe. He came stomping back and roughly asked what she was doing.

It was not so easy to ignore the question when it was Tehwe's.

"Making a flute," was her answer. "A flute's better, for the song. One of these," she said, indicating four branch lengths, "ought to do well enough."

"So many?" he asked.

Nika shrugged. "Trial and error."

Tehwe grunted, heaved her up onto his back, and swept away with her. Before Wenq lost sight of them he could see that Nika had quickly settled herself with her toes hooked in Tehwe's rough belt, her knees under his arms, and her wood shavings dribbling with the rain over his hair and neck.

235

Wenq was struck by how natural and unflappable Nika looked, with her elbows braced on Tehwe's shoulders as she cut at the branch lengths. It was as if it was the most ordinary thing in the world for her to be whittling away while perched on the back of a great, bear–like nomar.

They are all at home here in the Core, Wenq thought. *They move through it so easily, while I have to plunge, stumble and trip my way through.* But even as he thought that, he knew better. *I **have** learned a few things about the Core. I **could** make my way through without quite so much clumsiness as before. The others are much better at it, but at least I'm getting some grip on the Core.*

Or rather, he thought ruefully, *the Core is getting its grip on **me**. Little by little it is pulling me into its ways, and its rules.*

But I'll never feel at ease in the Core. Those long–gone ancestors of mine, who survived and sometimes flourished in forests like this — I don't feel any connection with them at all. It's as if we're from different planets.

While Wenq was mulling over this he had to push himself to keep up with the others. Tehwe set a faster pace than before. Now that Wenq wasn't carrying Nika, none of the nomars seemed to care whether he was with them or not.

*   *   *

Nika was sorry to have drawn away from Wenq, but she felt she had to distance herself from him, and the sooner she did so, the better.

She thought, *I can probably release the hold that the snake has over Tehwe's child, or at least lessen it.* It was what might well follow that deeply unsettled her.

Tehwe said that my 'song' carried great distances through the forest, in an unnatural way. No matter how softly I sing it, or play it on a flute, the snake will hear it, and come for me. And this time there will be no Tek or the wind fawn to repulse it, and no Meadow Woman to shelter me. There will be nothing at all, except possibly . . . just possibly . . .

Nika thought further and called over to Sirk, asking him if he knew whether there was anything in the Nation's arsenal that could trap and imprison the snake.

"Trap it? 'mprison it? Huh! More like, blow it all to bits — smithereens!" He made some weird pishing and gurgling noises, which Nika supposed were meant to be the destructive sounds of the Nation's powerful weaponry. He prattled on about things that Nika had no understanding of — sigtoray calibrations, evapitig yields, magnum scrorchers and pin tine devasts.

Nika cut in, "But what if the snake is mythical?"

"Mythie — who?"

"What if the snake is from the Sky World?"

Sirk replied disgustedly that there was no such thing as the Sky World — that was all just stories for children. "The Nation is ultra–modern in its weaponry," he assured Nika, "It can destroy *any living thing* no matter where it came from."

"What do *you* think, Tehwe?" Nika asked. "You have seen and felt the snake's power up close."

Before answering her, Tehwe wanted to know why she thought the snake was from the Sky World.

"Because I have seen it there myself — or one very like it," she answered simply.

Throughout the day Tehwe had been the driving force, moving the others forward on their journey with all possible speed. Now he abruptly slowed to a stop and stood silently, gazing into the distance.

Nika continued to whittle, making minute adjustments to the size and spacing of the breath and note holes. She blew softly into two of the hollowed–out branch lengths, testing the tones.

The far–off rumbling seemed to crescendo ominously into the silence around them. It seemed to have a deep rolling cadence to it, of 'Soon.' 'Soon.'

"The snake is on the move," Nika commented. "It is on the warpath."

Chapter 37

Tehwe stood still so long that Wenq was able to catch up with Nika and the nomars. When he reached them Tehwe was lifting Nika down from his back and turning her around to face him. His movements, usually so brusque, were slow and precise. His big hands lowered Nika and placed her on the ground as carefully as if she was made of a glass filament. He crouched in front of her so that they would be eye to eye. His was a great and hulking shadow to her small, waif–like one. Wenq could barely see their details but, with their excellent night vision, it seemed to Wenq that they were watching each other tensely, warily. It struck Wenq that each of them wanted something very badly from this exchange, as if they were engaged in some kind of contest for astronomically high stakes. Tehwe's great shoulders hunched further forward, and Nika was still, having left off her whittling.

Wenq went to stand beside Tal, who was also watching them. Sirk was nearby, but he seemed sullen and bored.

Wenq whispered to Tal, "What's —"

"Hsst!" Tal cut him off. "S'about the snake."

Tehwe spoke to Nika in a charged voice. "You say you saw the snake in the Sky World. But *you* are not of the Sky World."

"Correct," replied Nika in a crisp, taut voice. "I was only there for a while — a visitor. I never *belonged* there, as the snake does."

"A Sky World snake cannot be killed," Tehwe stated slowly. "And it will never die."

Nika nodded. "It belongs in the Sky World, where its powers can be . . . checked. But for some reason, it is here, where it is by far the most powerful creature of all."

"Then it can only be avoided. Fled from. Hidden from," Tehwe said slowly, deliberately.

"Especially now that it will kill any and all of the People that it can find."

"Explain," Tehwe growled.

"Tehwe, the snake marked your child Onera for himself when she was in that tree hollow. A strong will can sometimes resist being marked, but Onera — she was much too young. Once she was marked, she belonged to the snake. She was bound to go to him."

Nika continued, "But you snatched her back from following the snake's path. You . . . well, that insulted the snake, because you — a mere creature of the Below — stole something that belonged to him. You stole something from a powerful creature of the Sky World."

Tehwe angrily thumped his chest and roared, "My child! My —" but Nika withstood the blast and cut across it. "He goes by his rules — not ours. And by his rules — because of a brazen human thief, he will rampage against *all* of the People. He will attack and kill any and all of us he can find. Inside the Core, outside of it, all the same. He will kill multitudes, Tehwe, before he is satisfied. If he is ever satisfied."

An uptick in the snake's distant rumbling seemed to underscore Nika's words of warning.

She added, "No one can blame you for this rampage, Tehwe. No one can blame you for trying to save your Onera."

"But *you* know of a way to stop him," Tehwe said forcefully, as if challenging Nika to admit it. He had been watching Nika carefully. Something in her expression must have suggested this to him.

"I do know of something, but it might not work," was Nika's careful response. "And it's dangerous — very dangerous."

She was fully present, but at the same time it was as if part of her was far away, dwelling on possibilities that the rest of them could only guess at. She continued, "It's a kind of trap that belongs to the Sky World, so there's no way of knowing whether it will work here.

239

And if it doesn't work, I won't know that until it will be too late to save myself from the snake. If the trap fails, Tehwe, the snake will devour me, and anyone else who is nearby."

Tehwe leaned away from Nika. The only sounds were the falling rain and the snake's distant rumbling.

In those moments Wenq thought Nika actually disappeared into the darkness. He saw both Tehwe and Tal narrow their eyes and look more keenly at the spot where she was — or had been. Perhaps it was a trick of the shadows, but it seemed that she definitely wavered in and out of sight. It only lasted a few rapid eye blinks, but it seemed to Wenq that she became even more remote from them, both in time and place. It seemed to him that if any of them tried to touch her, they would not be able to. Even Tehwe with all his brute strength, and intelligence, would not be able to reach her where she had gone.

Tehwe seemed to realize this, because for the first time, he spoke to Nika as an equal or perhaps, as someone who was above him. "Fight the Sky World snake with Sky World trap," he said. It was his considered judgment, not a demand.

Nika nodded, and there was a relaxation of the tension between them. This contest of theirs seemed to be going in a direction that satisfied them both.

Nika was still abstracted, but when she spoke, her words were careful and precise.

"You hear him out there, Tehwe. He is hunting. I may not be able to stop him, but I think I should try. And I should do it as soon as possible, because innocent lives are at stake.

"There are only two things you can help me with. They are important. But then you must leave me to face him alone."

Tehwe disagreed. "S'my fight too," he growled angrily.

"It won't be anything like that — a fight with tooth, claw, weapons. And this time, Tehwe, the snake will not brush past you as he did last time. He will simply devour you too, if you are there and if what I do fails.

240

"Tehwe, help me get ready to face the snake, but then you and the others must get well away. You should flee from the snake, keep yourself and your family hidden. Dying with me would be pointless, and a waste."

"Tell me what you plan, what you need," Tehwe said brusquely.

Wenq noticed that Tehwe, in his answer, had neither agreed nor disagreed with Nika. Wenq was fairly certain that Nika noticed this too, and chose not to make an issue of it.

"I think I can make the snake come to me," she told Tehwe. "*That* part should not be difficult. But then comes the part that I'm not at all sure of. *If* I can get the snake to put his head through a hoop I set up, then he *may* be trapped. And then he *may* be unable to harm us, or others."

She continued, "I will need some vines to make the hoop— four of them about twice your height in length, and as thick around as my wrist. And I need you to direct me to an open place, of fairly smooth and even ground, where I can set up my trap."

The craziness of what Nika was saying almost took Wenq's breath away. The idea that she was going to face a gigantic snake alone, and that some kind of hoop would trap its head and — how could she possibly think it?

Wenq glanced over at Tal for some assurance that he too thought it was crazy . But he could make nothing of Tal's expression, other than some murky misgivings.

Wenq was sure that Tehwe, at least, would think it was crazy.

But Wenq soon found that, whether Tehwe believed in Nika's plan or not, he acted as if he was going along with it. Tehwe ordered Sirk to take Wenq with him to their camp. Tehwe then told Nika that he and Tal would go with her to gather the vines, and would then tell her how to get to a place he called the Face.

Sirk started off right away as Tehwe ordered, but Wenq refused to go with him. Tehwe roared at Wenq, cuffed him flat and then picked him up and threw him in Sirk's direction. Wenq crawled back.

He was determined not be separated from Nika. Even though she was so strangely remote, and might have some dangerous shapeshifter flaw, he had decided, *I'm going to be as loyal to her as I intended to be, before I had doubts about her.*

And I don't trust the way Tehwe has fallen in with Nika's plan. I don't believe for a moment that he's going to do just as she asks.

When Tehwe and Tal set off to take Nika to the place where they would cut some vines, Wenq followed them.

Nika deliberately kept back with Wenq, to talk with him. "I owe it to Honcho Beaver and Pani to ask you, for their sakes, to go with Sirk," she said. "It's still not too late."

Wenq shook his head. "You don't know Honcho and Pani like I do. They would expect me to stay with you."

"You seem very sure of that."

"Did they have a chance to tell you how Honcho Beaver came to be crippled?"

"No."

"She was saving Pani from a rabid bear – one of the large ones. Imagine that, Nika — a beaver going up against a large rabid bear — or any large bear! Certain death. But by some fluke both Honcho and Pani survived it."

"It was a marvel, Wenq. But this is much different. This is going up against a Sky World creature. If you come with me and I fail, then you *will* die too."

"I'm coming," was Wenq's stubborn response. "And I think Tehwe is going to stay with you too. Not sure about Tal."

"Crazy Tehwe. Crazy Wenq," Nika said in an oddly resigned sing–song.

"Crazy owl!" Wenq shot back.

Nika surged ahead to join Tehwe and Tal, leaving Wenq follow as best he could.

Now Wenq really labored to keep up with the pace set by Tehwe. He had the shakes, and was nearly spent from all that had happened to him over the last two days. And his mind moved more wearily than his body.

He directed all his energy, all his strength, to keeping up with Nika. He would not permit himself to be separated from her now.

He had thought of it as a loyalty to her, but there was more to it than that. *I've been in the deep wilderness for less than two full days, but it feels like a lifetime. My old life seems far away, unreal. It's as if the wilderness has taken hold of me, and dictated new rules. Nika and I, we're part of something, and I must be loyal no matter what happens.*

Wenq was realistic enough to know that he might not be of much help to her, or — worse — that he might unintentionally cause serious problems for her. *But we've been joined by what we've been through, and by the wilderness's code. I can't leave her to face this crisis alone.*

Chapter 38

Tehwe and Tal took Nika to a place that was festooned with thick, ropey vines. In a cold fretful rain they cut the four vine lengths that she wanted. Tehwe caught up the cut lengths of vine and told Nika that the way to the Face was too rough for her to get there alone. He told her that he and Tal would help her take the vines there.

Nika made no objection.

As they were leaving, Tehwe tossed one of the vines to Wenq and ordered him to carry it. Tehwe left carrying two of the vines; Tal and Wenq each carried one.

Wenq realized that tacitly, the plan had changed. Nika, having clearly warned them all of the danger, was not *insisting* that they keep themselves safe by leaving her. And Tehwe, when he told Wenq to haul one of the vines, seemed to have accepted Wenq as a member of Nika's ragged little band. The pace Tehwe set when they left the vine area was not as fast as before, and there was again the occasional whoop from Tal to keep Wenq from losing track of where the others were out ahead of him in the darkness. He still lagged behind despite his best efforts to keep up, but he did not have to worry as much about getting separated from them.

When Wenq reached the Face after the others, he could easily see how it got its name. Even in darkness that was beginning to curl with mist under a glowering sky, he could see that it was a massive slab of nearly solid rock that looked somewhat like the flattened, lopsided face of a prone giant. The sloping, broadly oval expanse had a long crease for a bitter mouth, a broad lump for a mashed nose, and two misshapen eye hollows forever staring toward the western sky.

Near the center of the Face, Nika was directing Tehwe and Tal in helping her make a hoop from the vines. Wenq's vine was added when he arrived. The tough, supple bark was peeled off and used to bind the lengths of vine together, overlapping each vine half–way around to make a hoop that was two vines thick. Nika let Tehwe, Tal and Wenq peel bark and hold the lengths of vine tightly together, but she did all the binding work herself, muttering some kind of incantation as she did so. She knelt alone inside the hoop, while her three helpers knelt outside it.

When the hoop was finished Wenq looked down at it critically. *It looks sturdy enough considering what it's made of. But it's only about 8 feet in diameter. How could a gigantic snake even get its head inside it, let alone be restrained by it in any way?*

* * *

Nika stood alone inside the hoop, worriedly casting her eyes over it and slowly twirling one of the flutes in her hands. She stood facing rumbling noises, which were now more from the west than the north.

She asked her three companions, "Are you going to do as I advised, and get yourselves as far away from here as you can?"

They all looked back at her steadily, shaking their heads 'no'.

"Well then, you must go some distance away at least, because there are some words I must say that you are not allowed to hear."

They started to move off — big burly Tehwe, tall lean Tal, and beside them Wenq, looking small and young.

"Wait!" Nika called out.

They turned back to her to find her eyes flitting over the three of them. Her mouth silently opened and closed, and she looked as if she had just had a sudden, surprising thought.

"Wenq," she asked, "do you still have your family totem with you?"

Wenq's hands were sticky and grubby with vine sap. He wiped one hand on his pant leg and took the totem from his pocket, holding it out so that Nika could see it. The carved wooden fawn seemed to be quietly resting on its side, nestled in his palm.

Nika then addressed each one of them in turn, with a slight bow.

"Tehwe, go to the north side of the Face. Tal, to the west side. And Wenq, to the south."

Tehwe stood for a few moments frowning at Nika. Then he said, "Ah, the four winds. But . . . you have no panther for the east wind."

Nika stepped out of the hoop on the east side of it and turned to face west with the hoop on the ground in front of her. "My owl beak and talons will have to do for that," she said.

Tehwe shook his head. He could not agree with her about that. But he jerked his head at Tal and they both left to take up their positions. Wenq went to the Face's south edge, leaving Nika standing alone in the dark near the center of the massive slab of stone.

Nika's thoughts were grave as she ran her fingers along the length of the flute she had chosen to play. The snake moving through the forest rumbled like thunder. The hoop at her feet looked . . . pathetic. Too small. Too weak.

She pocketed the flute and knelt. Lifting the hoop she held it vertically, and softly sang the Meadow Woman's chant for a hoop snare.

The hoop stayed vertical when she released it, but just barely. It was not firmly in place, as it was supposed to be. The bottom sagged against the worn stone of the Face, and the rest of it wavered in the breeze, as if it was about to flop over.

She saw her mistake. *I've been too tentative, too uncertain whether the charm will work here in the Below World. This charm needs complete, unreserved confidence — almost — even — bluster.* She remembered that now, from all that the Meadow Woman's little tongue clicks had taught her, when she had first learned the charm.

In the Sky World the confidence seemed natural and came easily. Here it is going to have to be dragged up and punched out somehow into a convincing fullness.

246

She also remembered, *Besides needing confidence, it is more the rhythm of the words than the words themselves that the chant draws strength from. But the rhythms are not the same here as in the Sky World. I felt that immediately, as I sang through the chant here. But I don't know what the correct rhythms are . . .*

Then she thought, *Perhaps the rhythms have something to do with what the hoop is made of. In the Sky World, the hoops were much smaller, and a supple length of willow always sufficed.*

She put both hands on the hoop and closed her eyes, hoping for a better understanding. For a while she felt nothing but emptiness, and inadequacy.

Chapter 39

"Better try further uphill," Honcho Beaver suggested.

Pani nodded, slipped out of the aeor, and was immediately swallowed up by the shadowy, dense brush of the Core.

Honcho Beaver watched Pani's complete disappearance into the night with an irrepressible stab of fear that she might never see him alive again. He was her oldest and best friend. She had never been anywhere as close to anyone else. Life without him would be . . . unimaginable.

They were the only ones left of Tsi Kah's creations, made over 150 years ago with human intelligence in animal bodies, to bear witness for the People. Over the years, each of them had honed their strengths to complement the other's, and had grown inseparable.

Highly valued by the Nation's Fire Keepers, they spent most of their lives dealing with a myriad of uncomfortable truths that the Nation should not shirk. It was cerebral work, done for the most part from the quiet and safety of Honcho Beaver's pod in the tsye marshlands. *Nothing like what we've been doing throughout this long day of searching for Wenq and Nika*, Honcho thought. *But here we are, risking our lives for them.*

Forests were anathema to Honcho Beaver. She sighed. *If only the search was in flooded marshlands filled with rushes, reeds and swale grass.*

But at least Pani has been more than equal to everything we've encountered in the Core — so far. Even now that it's night. In fact, he's in every way perfect for night hunting in forests just like this one.

That thought comforted her, as she concentrated on the blip on the aeor's monitor, that tracked his progress — or lack of it. There was no knowing how much longer it would take to locate Wenq or

Nika. *Conserve strength, conserve energy,* she reminded herself. *The rest of the journey is yet unknown.*

Due to the cold, off–and–on rain, tracking had been extremely difficult — not just for Honcho Beaver and Pani, but also for Rahra and the Seek Squadrons that were following the trail of Weqi and those with her. The scent droners frequently lost the trails and had to cycle back through their programs with slow, thorough cross checks, before picking one of them up again.

Each time the scent droners lost the trails, Honcho Beaver and Pani analyzed the terrain using topo maps and locale–detailing droners, and Pani went out and scouted their likeliest hunches. More often than not, Pani picked up one of the trails before the cycling–back scent droners did, gaining them a little time. Slowly throughout the day and into the night they had been closing the gap. The trails were noticeably fresher.

Two Seek and Rescue aeors followed them at a distance, sometimes sending out their own droners but mainly being close by in case their help was needed.

Wenq's scent was the main one they followed. His was usually the last trail through, and he left more scent than the others. Honcho Beaver envisioned how much he was floundering around. If it wasn't for the cold and the rain, Wenq would have been quite easy for the scent droners to track.

As the day stretched into night both Honcho Beaver and Pani were impressed by Wenq's stamina — he had travelled a much greater distance than they thought possible. They knew he had been preparing for his Braves training by jogging along the beaver trails near his home, but that would not have prepared him for this grueling trek through the Core.

"Something's driving him," Pani commented.

"Something strong," was Honcho Beaver's reply, with a grunt for emphasis.

Neither one of them 'said' it, but both of them thought that whatever it was, it had something to do with Nika.

The only pause in their search came near dusk when the trail they were following crossed the first of two broad swathes of mashed down trees and brush.

"Seek sent us some visuals and data for something like this," Honcho Beaver commented.

While the scent droners moved out ahead, they stayed to assess what could have left such a massive trail of destruction. Honcho Beaver landed the aeor on it, and they sent out analysis droners in both directions along the broad, forced passageway through the trees. While waiting for the droners' return they sat with the aeor's dome up, looking, listening and scenting. The scale of the destruction awed them, as did the foulness of the off odor that lingered, even though it was several days old.

Without 'saying' anything to each other, Honcho Beaver accessed a snake database on her keyb, while Pani accessed old myths on his, using the keyword "snake". After they sent each other a few files, Pani 'said', "Honcho, do you think maybe . . . something to do with Nika . . . and Sky World . . ."

Honcho Beaver shuddered. "Sure hope not!"

Not long afterward, S&R sent them tracking for a huge snake that had been located far to the west. Some S&R aeors and drones were following it at a safe distance. They were only monitoring it for the time being, but all of the heavy duty, armed Seek squadrons had been activated.

*　*　*

Honcho Beaver and Pani started picking up Nika's scent well after dark, giving them five scents instead of four to follow. It was not long afterward that the main trail seemed to veer away from the direction it had been heading. It was no longer going through the most likely terrain for reaching an area that they had begun to think might be the travelers' ultimate destination.

Something had apparently changed their plans. That made

Honcho Beaver and Pani's work harder, until they got a better sense of what the new destination might be.

Pani's blip on the aeor's monitor had been stationery for a while. Then, "Found something," came Pani's 'voice' over a keyb. "Four trails — Wenq, Nika and the two nomars that are shapeshifters. They stopped here and cut some wild grape vines. Cuts still fairly fresh."

Honcho Beaver programmed the aeor to go to Pani's coordinates, and signaled the scent droners to follow. On the way she studied data for the terrain west of Pani's coordinates. But she could not make any sense of it. *Why would they be going that way? And why had they cut some vines?*

"How big around are the vines?" she asked Pani over the keyb. "And can you tell how many?"

"Fairly thick, about the same as my tail," was the response. "Hard to tell how many they cut, or what the lengths were."

"Puzzling."

Honcho Beaver was still mystified when her aeor came up beside Pani, and Pani leapt inside.

They directed the scent droners westward while they studied the terrain maps.

Rahra's voice came over the open channel. "Five of the kids found! All except Weqi," he reported. "Going after her now. West."

They both began to notice that a rumbling, though still distant, had increased and was almost constant. They'd been patched in to the signal for the giant snake. It had recently turned and was going steadily west, away from Rahra's coordinates.

"Where's it going?" What's it after?" groused Honcho Beaver. And then, *Weqi?* she wondered.

She and Pani had been studying the topos for exposed rock formations close by. There were several of them spread out over a broad area, bare gashes of exposed bedrock in the forest.

"The trail we're following might be heading for one of those big slabs of exposed rock," Pani commented. "There's just not much else

251

—"

"Which one's the biggest?"

"This one," Pani 'said', sending the file to her keyb. "But why would they be going to such a place?"

"No idea." Honcho Beaver could make no sense of them going there, or of the cut vines they were taking with them. *But at least the giant snake isn't heading in that direction.*

Not long afterward, the blip tracking the snake moved much faster, still heading west. *If it can move that fast,* Honcho Beaver worried, *then it can also change direction quickly, and reach those bare rock formations before we could.*

It was all giving Honcho Beaver a pressured feeling, which rapidly built into a strong dread that their window of time for finding Wenq and Nika alive might be closing fast.

"Want to take a leap — go to those gashes?" she asked Pani.

"That's quite a hunch. But . . . it's not that far and . . . are those vines bothering you too? What could they want them for?"

"Dunno. Maybe a sling to drag something? Too thick for rope . . . a net to catch something?"

An involuntary shiver seized Pani and his fur stood on end. He 'said', "Catch death." They both felt the dread.

Rahra's voice came over the channel open to Honcho Beaver's aeor and the S&R Squadron's hub. "Got her! We got Weqi!" Moments later he added, "Closely pursued by the snake! Requesting Seek diversions — but not too close. Snake's blazing fast!"

Silence, as both Honcho Beaver and Pani watched the snake scope. Then Pani 'said', "We've got to find Wenq and Nika — got to get them out of here. Let's try the biggest of those rock gashes."

"Yes. Fast as we can."

Chapter 40

Nika was not sure how long she crouched next to the hoop, searching for the vine's full cadence to use in the chant. Part of it she found right away — the strong, heavy clinging parts. The quieter parts were harder; she supposed it was because she was so weary. Her existence had not been restful since falling from the Sky World, barely three days ago. Her spirit was strong and buoyant, but no spirit is inexhaustible.

She began to make some headway when she asked herself, *How would the Meadow Woman in the Sky World go about thinking this through?*

Nika thought about the quieter vine parts, which at first seemed too fragile and whispery to matter. Then she understood: they had an insinuating stickiness that was the vine's real strength. A vine first sends out small, delicate tendrils that sway in the wind until they touch a branch or leaf to curl around. Then the lacy tendrils embrace the host, still liable to be snapped away, but usually strengthening into an iron grip that binds the vine securely to its host even in gale force winds, a hold strong enough to bear the weight of the vine while it grows higher, closer to the sun.

Ah, the strength and the lacy in–betweens, Nika thought. ***Now** I understand the vine's essence — at least enough of it to begin again.*

She readied herself to reinforce the chant, calling upon some last reserves of strength.

To tap these reserves, and muster the confidence she needed, she imagined herself to be the Meadow Woman, well used to charms and chants, and supremely confident and efficient with them all. She took hold of the hoop and willed its vines to give over to her the pulse of weak, subtle tendrils that reliably hardened into unbreakable strength.

She felt this come to her, and she sang it back into the hoop, with what she imagined was something like the Meadow Woman's verve.

The hoop rose clear of the ground, with flickers running along its circle. It exuded strength that had not been there before, and Nika was satisfied that it was as strong as she could make it. Whether strong enough for her purpose, she could not know.

She stepped back, taking her flute from her pocket to begin, but paused when she became aware of a disturbance somewhere behind her, coming from the east.

Within moments a small aeor hove into sight over the trees beyond the edge of the Face, slowing as it got closer.

Nika looked carefully at the aeor's dome and thought she saw —

She set down her flute, shapeshifted to owl and flew to the aeor. Closer in she confirmed — it *was* Pani and Honcho Beaver inside the aeor!

She circled the aeor as it settled onto the Face about halfway between its edge and where she had been standing. Its dome rose. She landed on the aeor's front rim and shapeshifted to girl.

"I need your help, Pani, if you are willing. And will you, Honcho Beaver, wait on the south side of the Face with Wenq, and be at the ready to take him and Pani away from here?"

* * *

Tehwe, Tal and Wenq had left their positions and approached the aeor. Tehwe arrived first in his bear form, then Tal as wolf. Wenq was as usual last.

The moment Wenq saw that it was Honcho Beaver and Pani in the aeor, he had a sudden childish urge to jump into the aeor and beg to be whisked away from this nightmare, back to his old life.

The urge faded as quickly as it arose. *My old life is gone. If Nika is right — and she usually is — the snake is a killer that can't be stopped by anything in the Nation's arsenal. No one is safe from it. I've seen the path it's left . . . its destructive power is unearthly, and if it's unleashed on the settlements outside of the Core . . .*

Nika's scheme to stop the snake is wild and impossible, he thought. *But the snake **itself** is wild and impossible.* His thinking, muddled by exhaustion, was that if two wrongs could ever make a right, this would be the time for it!

And Nika has asked me to place myself on the south side of the Face. Something to do with representing the fawn wind spirit. That much I can do — and will do, whatever the cost.

He had barely reached the others when they dispersed again. Pani slipped out of the aeor and chuffed in his direction before disappearing into the darkness on the east side of the Face. Tehwe, Tal and Nika were returning to their former positions, leaving Honcho Beaver and Wenq alone where the aeor had landed.

"Get in, Wenq," 'said' Honcho Beaver. "I'll take you back to your position."

"It's great to see you too, Honcho Beaver," Wenq said as he climbed into the aeor. He wanted his voice to sound jaunty, but he couldn't keep some wobble out of it.

"We'll have much to talk about later," Honcho Beaver 'said' as she piloted the aeor to the massive slab's southern edge.

"If there is a later for us. What do you think, Honcho Beaver, of the chances that this will work?"

"Oh, very bad odds. Terrible. Especially for Nika. Some of the rest of us might manage to get away, but only with extraordinary luck."

The aeor landed. Honcho Beaver put the dome up and they sat looking toward the center of the slab. Wenq could just barely make out a smudge there, that was Nika beside the hoop — a small darker dot against a slightly lighter band of darkness.

"Feel it?" Honcho Beaver asked. "Something — an expectation?"

Wenq shook his head and sagged into the jump seat beside Honcho Beaver. The only thing he sensed was that the area had gone unusually quiet, apart from the constant distant rumbling, which had more of a frenzied sound to it now.

* * *

This is it, thought Nika. *It's time to begin. Success or failure. Life or death.*

I prefer success, of course, and life.

Or do I? she asked herself. *I always have . . .*

Standing in the darkness on that bare cold rock, she felt low, pummeled, weakened. And now she was suddenly uncertain of the most basic question of all — whether to strive, or wither.

She had done her utmost to display confidence for the others, but she could not believe in herself now. She had slipped out of harmony, and would surely fail if she could not regain it.

She searched, adrift from time and place. Now more than ever she missed her family. Her mother, quiet and loving, with a will stronger than oak. Her father, bowing his head to the whites, doing their demeaning tasks for his family's sake in a hopeless world. Even her little brother, in his brief and innocent life — she had loved him so, and knew he loved her back. His chuckling laugh, his serious conversational babble as if he was laying down judgments in a language all his own. His eyes so sharp, so wise sometimes in one so small and young. She *knew*, she just *knew*, that his death was a great loss not just to her but to his People — their People.

Her family, her bedrock, was gone. As were Tek, Phoebe and Ruth, whom she had come to know and love, and then also abruptly lost.

Then there was the Meadow Woman — though somehow Nika had always known that her time with her was a world apart, a time apart, and that it too was bound to end, as it in fact did end abruptly. She'd been allowed to stay there for a while. That was all.

For what purpose? she asked herself. *Or was it mere fluke or circumstance? A whim of the Meadow Woman's? Surely there was more to it than that.*

She recalled how the fawn and Tek's spirit rescued her from the snake and took her to the Meadow Woman. She felt again her anguish as they left her there, and remembered turning to find the Meadow Woman startlingly close to her, inspecting her with such avid curiosity. Appraising her. Recognizing her fear and uncertainty, the Meadow Woman had turned away confidently, and casually dropped an object that it was impossible for her to possess — her mother's fine maplewood comb, with the three broken teeth and the teething marks left on it by her little brother.

Recollections flooded Nika, of all the Meadow Woman's ways, of all she had taught her, both directly and in that odd 'not teaching' way of hers. And with those recollections Nika felt herself slip back into harmony, out of all the hectic confusions she had found in the Below World after re–entering it. She could not believe that it had all been for nothing. And now she had this opportunity to restore a much greater balance than her own inner harmony. It might be beyond her ability. But whether she succeeded or failed she felt certain that this was exactly what she was here to do.

Exhaustion receded somewhat. A small surge of strength brought her up from the dark well she had been spiraling down into.

She lifted the flute and began to play.

Her first notes was the signal for the others to plug up their ears. Pani's ears had been plugged before he left the aeor, with little tabs in the plugs so he could hook them out. They were all to keep the plugs in until the vibrations caused by Nika's otherworldly fluting stopped.

New notes sounded, and with them came an immediate change in plans.

The four representatives of the winds could not hear the notes with their ears plugged, but the heavy vibrations caused by the notes made the earth sway under their feet, and spoke to their minds with authority.

They removed their ear plugs.

They could not do otherwise. The eerie vibrations caused them do it, and caused them to advance toward the center of the slab.

Chapter 41

Weqi felt fully in her element, probably for the first time in her life, leading the snake away from where the other kids were hidden. The snake had been coming after her for some time but she was not even winded, and she was well out ahead of it. Exhilaration fueled her naturally buoyant confidence. She had strength and stamina in her limbs, and sharpness in her wits. Relying on nothing but her own body and mind she kept well ahead of the slow lumbering beast. Despite all the stresses and strains of the last day and a half, she felt she could effortlessly keep this up for hours and hours, leading the snake ever further away from where her friends were hidden. The snake was big and hideous, but it was not so tough and scary after all.

From time to time she noticed a big hawk tracking her in the darkness, and guessed that it was the same hawk that had found their first hiding place, and that it was now hunting her with the snake. She had some respect for the hawk's hunting prowess. It seemed to be shrewder than the snake, and a lot more agile. But she had not seen or heard the hawk for a while, and had begun to think that it had lost track of her.

Then her bubble of elation burst. *This is just too easy!* she thought. She became convinced that the hawk and snake had set her up, and were biding their time until everything aligned to their advantage.

That time came soon afterward when Weqi dashed from cover to cross a boggy swale. The hawk swooped with a piercing screech. Behind her was a flurry of crashing trees amidst heightened rumbling. Within seconds the snake reared up over the trees behind her. It was nearly directly over her and coming down on her with its maw open wide.

She saved herself only by pulling up short, flipping sideways and backward into a thicket of tag alders along an upward sweep from the swale. The snake's tongue flicked over the tip of her tail as his body slid right over her. Crushed alder branches ground down on top of her, driving her into the earth. The full weight of the snake's body would have killed her if she had not rolled into a depression, where some spring in the flattened alders cushioned her from the snake's heft.

The snake whipped back around in a tight loop. The hawk circled close in to mark her exact location for snake — though at this range he would not miss a second time. Dizzily, Weqi scrambled out of the shattered alders, stunned from almost being crushed, but also reeling from strange images searing her brain — something about the snake actually being an incredibly desirable man who wanted to be her wild and sexy lover. All she had to do was smile up at him —

'Ewwwww! Gross!' she chuffed indignantly.

Her mind cleared, but her legs wobbled and the hawk screeched and flapped around her head to confuse her. She was too stunned to even try to flee. The snake flicked its tongue above her, taking a few moments to anticipate her as a tasty morsel, before swallowing her whole.

The hawk chittered angrily, as if warning the snake that the only sure kill was a dead one.

Seemingly out of nowhere an aeor slipped in under the snake's chin at top speed, catching Weqi up in a drag net and zooming out and away alongside the snake's sticky tongue. The tongue lashed out at the aeor but its saliva was not gummy enough stop it, though it did knock the aeor spinning and wobbling off to one side of its intended course. The aeor brushed the hawk's wing in its erratic flight away from the snake, injuring it enough to send it pinwheeling away.

* * *

Rahra sent his aeor scudding along the top of brush toward a dense stand of old growth hemlocks.

259

"Got her! We got Weqi!" he reported over the channel.

* * *

Rahra had spent the evening and much of the night searching for the six kids who had gone off into the Core from the cave. He worked alongside some Seeks but, like Honcho Beaver and Pani, in the inclement weather he consistently proved faster than the technology at finding their trail each time it washed out. He 'hunched out' likely trails, and constantly got out of his aeor and shapeshifted to wolf to scent for trail wisps. As the search wore on the Seek aeors gave him the lead, and provided back up.

He found five of the kids holed up along a creek bank, first finding their earlier shelter and then intuiting and scenting out their second location. The boy Desag, while telling Rahra that Weqi had gone out to lure the snake and its companion hawk away from their hiding place, jumped into Rahra's aeor to go with him. The Seek aeors were already coming in to rescue the other four kids — the older girl Áka, the younger one Miti, and the two other boys.

Rahra told Desag to get out of his aeor. "It's too dangerous," he said bluntly. "Stay with the others. Let Seek get you out of here, to safety."

"You'll need me," Desag insisted. "Believe me, handling a wolf shapeshifter like Weqi — that could be even tougher than the snake."

"Well, actually, I think I can handle her, because, see, I'm a wolf shapeshifter too," Rahra replied evenly.

'Eh, just my luck,' Desag muttered. "But you'll still need me," he insisted. "I can help you with the hawk. You watch the snake. Me — the hawk."

Standing nearby and listening to them, Áka backed Desag. "He's right," she told Rahra. "You should have one of us with you. I'd come, except Desag's already volunteered."

"And we'd better hurry," Desag urged. "Even seconds could make a difference."

260

Rahra knew the two kids were right about not wasting time, but he really did not want this boy to come with him. He made one last effort to get him out of his aeor. He suddenly shapeshifted to wolf and snarled and snapped aggressively, to frighten the kid into scrambling out of the aeor.

He succeeded in thoroughly scaring the kid — he could smell the fear in him. But the kid sat tight in the seat, though he leaned as far away from Rahra as he could.

"No fair!" yelled Áka angrily.

"Yeah," said Desag, trying to keep a brave face though his voice squeaked. "And, and let me tell you something. You think you're tough? Weqi's worse n' you! Lots worse!"

Rahra shapeshifted back to man and said, "Fair's got nothing to do with this!" Then he grumped, "Had to try." He impatiently flipped the switch to lower the dome. "Well, if you're coming, harness in."

When they were underway Rahra asked Desag, "You were bluffing me, right? About this Weqi girl being worse than —"

"Tons worse!" Desag cut in. He was furious with Rahra for trying to scare him out of the aeor.

Rahra wanted to probe this some more, but finding the girl was the priority now.

He decided it would be faster to follow the snake than track after Weqi. One of the aeor's monitors gave the snake's location, not far away.

Suddenly the snake's blip on the monitor quadrupled in speed and both Rahra and Desag sensed it was closing in on prey — perhaps on Weqi.

Rahra risked going above the trees for speed and visuals. They arrived just as the snake was whipping around to make its second pass at Weqi, who also showed on their scopes now that they were close enough to pick up her ID chip.

Rahra's felt his blood freeze at his sighting of the giant snake.

261

Seek's calculations had prepared him for its size, but the speed and sinuosity of the monster chilled him to his core. He hadn't quite believed how fast it had moved as a blip on his aeor's panel, until he saw it whipping around. It was faster and more agile than any aeor could ever be.

Their only advantage would be surprise. The snake had not yet detected their approach.

"Let's go in!" Desag urged. "Safeties off!"

"Yeah. Under the chin," said Rahra.

"The *chin*?! Oh . . . *yeah*! I *like* that."

"Then get busy and set up the drag net, Tag Along," Rahra snapped.

"*On* it. *Told* ya you'd need me. And by the way, you're too old for Weqi, y'know."

"Too — what?!"

"*Old*," Desag repeated firmly. "And don't call me Tag Along. Call me Sidekick Who *Rocks*."

"Oh, gimme a break!" Rahra muttered.

Although Rahra was never going to admit it, he was really glad now to have the kid's help.

In no time they had chucked the snake's chin and gone spinning away from its lashing tongue, with the dazed wolf–girl netted. Then the chase was on. The snake crashed after them, gaining because Rahra re–engaged the collision safeties and set the aeor's flight to skim under the trees. The aeor's dodging of brush and boulders slowed them, but Rahra knew they were safer below the treetops than out in the open above them. He had seen the snake lunging over the trees lightning fast, unimpeded by vegetation.

Rahra risked a short flight over a rivulet, hoping to gain some distance. It nearly ended in catastrophe. With a sudden charge the snake caught up with them and bulleted through marsh alongside the rivulet. As it coiled sideways to lunge at them Rahra swerved into the trees along the other side of the water. With safeties reduced but not fully off, Rahra and Desag deftly but desperately piloted the aeor under the trees.

Several Seek aeors showed up on their scopes. The Seeks had orders to maintain a safe distance but they were coming in closer to lure the snake away from Rahra's aeor. Rahra got on the channel and warned them to keep well away.

Honcho Beaver's 'voice' came through on the panel to report. "Got Wenq here," was her curt message. Rahra turned that over in his mind — the odd flatness that Honcho Beaver programmed into her message.

"S'at Weqi's brother Wenq?" Desag asked. "He went missing too?"

"Yep," Rahra confirmed.

Honcho Beaver's 'voice' came through again. "Get Weqi and yourself out of there and don't come this way, Rahra!"

"Trying!"

But even as he said it Rahra felt a vibration that moment by moment built inside his head until it sounded to him like the breathy notes of a flute.

All thoughts of escaping drained away. A glance over at Desag confirmed that the boy was also affected by the vibrations. And behind them the wolf–girl began a plaintive howling, which he interpreted to mean that she was also under the same compulsion that he was. He set the aeor to go toward the vibration. The Seek aeors that were nearby set their course to follow.

He had momentarily lost track of the snake, but a glance at the monitor showed that it had changed course and was no longer chasing them. It too was heading toward the vibration's source — to the flute, though it was not rushing now. Rahra wondered if the snake was trying to resist the compulsion.

Weqi's howling became more urgent. Rahra sent the aeor above the trees and set it for top speed to their destination.

Chapter 42

From the first notes there had been nothing tentative about Nika's playing. She launched in, firm and confident. Some of the confidence was borrowed from her recollections of the Meadow Woman's self–assured ways — no matter. She drew strength from all the Meadow Woman had taught her.

She was prepared for the powerful vibrations emanating from this flute melody. She had guessed it would be so in the Below World. Nearly immediately she heard the sudden pause in the snake's distant thrashing, and then a roiling frenzy. The snake was coming to her.

She was not prepared, however, for the effect of the flute's melody on the four who were with her, representing the winds. They had agreed to stop their ears, to be immune from the flute's notes. But they were *not* immune.

Tehwe in his bear shape roared — wild roars of tempestuous challenge, for a fight to the death.

Tal in his wolf shape howled — not as forcefully as Tehwe was roaring but as if the howls were being forced out of him. There was a surprised sound to them, though he kept trying to bolster them enough to match the intensity of Tehwe's roars.

The lynx Pani shrieked and yowled with such unrestrained fury that the fine hairs on Nika's neck rose. The sounds were outsize, much more panther–like than anything that she could have expected from a lynx. She learned, at that moment, that in every lynx, there lodged the heart of a panther.

The boy Wenq could be heard shouting something insistently, though whatever it was, it was largely drowned out by the flute and the cacophony of the other three.

The four vocalists did not stay in their places of relative safety. They all approached Nika — not rushing but coming firmly, steadily, as if partaking in some kind of stately ritual. As they came, their vocals changed from a discordance to something brusque and brash that melded their primal and defiant calls, each to the other. Power seeded and seemed to flit and fluctuate among them.

Observing all this, Nika also heard the snake's approach. By the sound of its thrashing through trees and brush it was nearly there.

She did not understand what power the four vocalists were raising. Nor did she know how that power might affect either the hoop or the snake. But she was certain that she had to keep playing the flute. She dared not stop now.

Tal's vocals were the weakest — weaker even than Wenq's hoarse shouts that were barely audible over the flute and the others' din. Clearly he was struggling to fully grasp what he was supposed to be howling about, though he desperately tried to keep up his part in the ensemble.

An aeor zoomed in and immediately the howling of another wolf could be heard — a higher more melodious voice, a surer one. It was Weqi, netted to the outside of Rahra's aeor. The aeor landed on the west edge of the Face, which Honcho Beaver had suggested to Rahra when she saw on her panel that his aeor was approaching.

Rahra and Desag jumped out of the aeor and the moment they freed Weqi from the net she raced to Tal and took the lead there. Her howls were charged and eerie, drawn from her soul, rising with blood–curdling crescendo, and meshing perfectly with the roars, shrieks and shouts of the others.

She's . . . she's awesome! Rahra thought.

"Stay with the aeor," he told Desag. He shapeshifted to wolf and raced to join Weqi and Tal. Together the three wolves approached the center of the Face from the west. Led by Weqi, Tal and Rahra's howls bulked hers out until their howls together matched the

265

strength of the roars from Tehwe, and buffeted the shrieks and yowls from Pani. Wenq's shouts did not add much overall but they were as essential in their way as the more obvious power of the others. His power was more like the sturdy breaths of the young, with their innate will to survive.

The power of the four steadied and grew, briefly frail but strengthening into something invincible. They felt it. Nika felt it. It was breathtakingly powerful, but at the same time they all knew its vulnerability: it was unbreakable for only so long as they were able to keep up their bold and raw 'song'.

* * *

Desag was left at Rahra's aeor, yelling after him tauntingly, "Old! Way too old!"

Honcho Beaver contacted him on the open channel and advised him to stay at the controls in the aeor, at the ready to aid the seven at the center of the slab. Both Honcho Beaver and Desag could see, on their aeor panels, that the snake was nearly there and that Seek aeors were coming in — from the look of it, all of the Seek Squadrons were converging on the Face.

* * *

Honcho Beaver sent out a priority advise for the Seek aeors to stay at least a mile away from both the snake and the Face. In her curt post she said that something was underway to contain the snake, and they should not interfere with it. But if that effort failed, their services would definitely be needed. She also suggested that they send in observation droners to monitor what was happening at the Face.

Seek Command probed for more information; Honcho Beaver responded, "You've seen the snake from a distance and you've gauged its strength from the broken path it leaves wherever it goes. You have to know that it is not of this world. Give this effort to contain it, its chance."

She knew her request would be hard for Seek Command to

accept: they were not used to taking second place in *anything*. It went against everything that they stood for — to charge in to aid and protect. Would they defer to her, for the time being? She, who had broken into the terrorist Erh's hacks, and given them the start they needed to find cave and track the missing kids? She, who was the only reason they were here at all?

After some moments of silence, Seek Command complied.

They formed up close in but on standby. And their observation droners proceeded to the Face with all possible speed.

*   *   *

With the addition of Weqi's howls, supported by those of Tal and Rahra, the song of the four winds became whole. The winds' four representatives — Tehwe for the north bear wind, Weqi, Tal and Rahra for the west wolf wind, Pani for the east panther wind, and Wenq with his totem for the south fawn wind — reached where Nika played her flute with the hoop floating vertically in front of her.

They halted about ten feet from her and turned to face outward, never abating their roars, howls, shrieks and shouts. Within moments their song changed subtly to coordinate not only with each other but also with Nika's flute music.

Power built exponentially and Nika felt a strong protection settle over herself and the hoop. For a few moments it felt wonderful! It was the first time she had felt completely safe since she had fallen from the Sky World. But it was completely at odds with her plan to draw the snake close enough to ensnare its head in the hoop. For how could the snake reach the hoop, with this protection in its way?

Her confidence faltered, and it was then that the floating hoop dropped to the ground in front of her.

She was appalled to think that she had caused the hoop to go inert, but she dared not stop playing her flute long enough to try to revive it. The snake had arrived.

It broke through the forest along the northwest edge of the great slab of rock, bunching itself with its head up, weaving to and fro against the sky, its tongue flicking avidly. The hawk flew in clumsily, its wings beating unevenly as it shrieked an angry skirl. The hawk brushed close to the group and then flew to the snake. Nika understood that it was reporting to the snake what it had seen with its superior sight, in a series of squawks, skirls, caws and grating acks; there could be no other explanation. Some of its yabber had a fiercely mocking quality to it, but whether the derision was aimed at the snake, or at the group and its flaccid hoop, it was impossible for Nika to know.

Chapter 43

The snake began to move. Wenq, along with the other representatives of the wind, kept watch on it. It did not approach the center of the Face directly; instead it circled, going north first and then around to the east. Before it reached the south and then the west sides of the Face where the two aeors were, the aeors nimbly skirred further away.

The snake ignored the aeors. As it went fully around the Face it focused entirely on the noisy center. Its head tilted sideways as it listened intently; all the while its tongue flicked constantly.

When it reached the place where it had first burst through from the forest, it extended its head toward the group at the center. Weaving its head slightly from side to side, it suddenly spat some gooey liquid off its tongue toward Tehwe. Nika had warned them about its spit, which could paralyze any living creature that it touched!

Nika sounded an alarm with her flute, and the four representatives of the winds, who had all been watching the snake closely, modulated their song and raised a whirlwind. Most of the spit got caught up and swirled harmlessly away, but one small drop landed on the back of Wenq's left hand.

Wenq hurriedly wiped it off but a feeling a stiffness and numbness spread rapidly past his wrist and up his arm. He understood that as soon as the numbness spread to his chest, he would not be able to shout out his part of the wind song, and part of his mind also realized that when the numbness reached his heart he would be paralyzed, and helpless. He did not know what to do, except to rub every trace of the drop off the back of his hand. He dropped to his knees to rub the back of his left hand against the rough stone under him. He still desperately shouted out his part of the song, as the numbness passed his elbow.

Something butted him squarely from behind, sending him sprawling toward where Nika was standing beside the hoop. He nearly dropped his totem, which he'd been holding in his right hand. Glancing behind himself, he saw the faint outline of a leggy fawn, with an indistinct wisp of rope around its neck. It seemed to be gazing at him, trying to tell him something.

Busily rubbing his hand against the slab he felt another strong push from the fawn, and then another.

Nika subtly changed her flute notes, and jerked her head and flute at him in a 'come hither' gesture. Between that and the continued pushes from the fawn, Wenq thought he understood what he should do.

He crawled closer to Nika on his knees and his right arm; his left arm felt like wood nearly to his shoulder. He tried to keep up his shouts. He reached Nika but now the fawn pushed him sideways toward the hoop at her feet. It caught him off balance and mid–shout he fell into the hoop's circle and it swallowed him up. He was no longer there!

* * *

Wenq found himself crouched in a cool dark tunnel, with a smudgy yellowish glow ahead of him. All around he heard echoey soundings of what he had been hearing before he fell into the hoop — a flute, roars, howls, shrieks. A faint bleating blended into the rest, that he had not heard before.

He wanted to go back to his companions, but when he looked behind him there was — nothingness. He was not sure how he knew it, but he felt a great emptiness there. Clearly the best way for him to go was toward the yellowish glow. The tunnel was too low for him to stand upright, but he stumbled to his feet and went in that direction, bent over.

270

The echoey sounds of flute and roars and such faded. There were new sounds as he went along — natural sounds like the wind brushing through leaves, fish darting in gurgling water, land animals padding softly, silently, accompanied by bird and insect twitter. Though the sounds were strangely muted they were all quite ordinary, except for some humming, as if someone was absently singing under their breath. It was all so faint and whispery that Wenq sometimes doubted whether he heard it at all, or had instead been hearing nothing more than the sound of his own breathing.

For a long time the glow did not seem to get larger but finally it did, and then it came to look more orange with red glints. It was an open fire up ahead, that he was trudging toward.

Suddenly he was there beside the fire's glow and felt its warmth. He was inside some kind of lodging made of stout wooden poles with bark walls lashed to the framework. It was a compact rectangular shape with the fire at its center and a smoke hole above the fire in the curved roof. He was at the edge of the fire's reach, where the air behind him felt sharply cold, as if it was the dead of winter outside.

An old woman sat on the other side of the fire, with her head bent over some kind of handwork she was doing. When he stepped a little closer to the fire, she glanced up at him and then back down at her work. Although her glance was brief it was sharp and inquisitive, and Wenq felt that the woman summed him up in an instant . . . and found him wanting. As if in confirmation of that, the woman t'sked, which seemed to Wenq to mean, 'What *is* the youth of today coming to?'

Wenq knelt quietly on the other side of the fire from the woman, and respectfully greeted her, calling her grandmother.

The woman seemed to ignore him, so left to himself, Wenq looked around.

The more he looked, the more he felt like he was sitting in one of the elaborate walk–through holograms, found in museums, that

271

depicted the interior of the longhouses that his ancestors had lived in, long before the Nation was formed, and even before the coming of the whites. Except that this felt real, while the museum 'grams always looked rather bare and sterile. This place looked really lived in, and it smelled lived in, with the odor of burning wood mixing with earth, wood, pelts, and many nameless but not unpleasant odors.

From what he could see of the structure he was in, it was like a truncated longhouse. Wenq's back was to the main door. Along both longer walls on either side of him were platforms built out from the wall at sitting height, with other platforms above them fairly close to the ceiling, stuffed to overflowing with stored items. The platform at sitting height on his right was hung with pelts and held mats and pelts for bedding; the one on his left was mostly empty, with just a few rolls of pelts and some baskets stacked in it.

There were all kinds of things leaning against the walls or wedged into corners — drying racks, skinning hoops of various sizes, and long straight sticks with shaped stones lashed to one end. Various tools were lying about but many more things were hanging from the walls and from the wooden poles — lumpy bags and baskets of all sizes, bunches of herbs, clothing made of pelts, and woven hats.

Wenq's eyes kept going back to one item in particular among the hanging things. In the flickering firelight he saw, hanging from a pole for the sitting platform on his left, what looked to him like a supple hide bag, perforated with circular patterns, with the ends of two flutes sticking out of its loosely gathered top.

As soon as Wenq realized that he was looking at a pair of flutes in a bag, he thought of Nika and her fluting. Then as if thought could beget reality, Wenq felt certain that he could hear Nika's breathy flute music as he stared at the flutes at rest in their bag.

The old woman glanced at the bag, and then at Wenq. She put aside her handwork and stood up.

Suddenly she was kneeling beside Wenq, prodding his left arm. He had no feeling in that arm and hand; it was numb to his shoulder, and useless to him. He was worried about it, but also relieved that the numbness had not gone any farther than his shoulder.

The old woman felt along his arm and t'sked and clucked over it gravely. Her face was so serious that Wenq asked her, "Will it get better, grandmother? Will the numbness go away?"

She did not answer, but the expression on her face clearly suggested that she did not think it would heal by itself.

Wenq could definitely hear flute music now. It made him restless. Some breathiness in its lilting, haunting melody made him feel that he had to get back to the others — that he had already been gone too long from them. For a while he had felt that he was in a suspended state where time did not exist — in the tunnel and here by the fire. But now he felt he had to go back — surely they were needing his shouts.

He started to get up, saying, "I must go, grandmother, to help my friends." But with a surprisingly firm hand on his shoulder the old woman kept him down, and spoke one word: "Wait."

Or at least that's what Wenq thought she meant. Her word was somewhat like the word he knew for 'wait'; it was her gesture that made her meaning plain.

She motioned for him to take his jacket and shirt off; while he did so she dragged out from under one of the sitting platforms a large, tightly woven basket that was full to its brim with a jumble of smaller baskets, and hide and woven pouches of various sizes. Odd smelling fungi and lengths of gnarled roots also tumbled out as the woman rummaged. Strong, sharp odors of all kinds welled out from the basket's contents in the fire's warmth.

While the old woman went through the contents of her basket Wenq struggled with his jacket and shirt. With one arm and its hand wooden and useless, it was difficult to get them off.

To be able to grab at his clothing better with his good hand Wenq carefully set his totem down in his lap. The moment he did so the woman's rummaging stopped and her dark eyes were riveted on

273

it. Her eyes seemed to burn with intense avarice. It was obvious that she wanted his totem very much, which was strange because the few people he had shown it to over the years had seemed hard–pressed to show anything more than a bored, polite interest in it. About the size of a walnut, its simple carving was so worn that it looked more like a small tree burl, than a carved fawn. Only Wenq, knowing that it was his family's fawn totem, was able to trace the baby animal's neck bending around, with its head at rest over its tucked–in legs.

But now this woman clearly wanted it. Wenq was a bit worried that she might reach out and snatch it — her gaze was that covetous. But it was sacred to his family, and he needed it to represent the south fawn wind for Nika. Perhaps, if she understood how important it was to him . . .

He picked up the totem and held it in the palm of his good hand for her to look at in the firelight, telling her it was his family's totem, and that he needed it to do his part to help his friends. He was not sure how much she understood of what he said, but she shook her head vehemently, as if she emphatically disagreed with part or all of what he'd said. But she did not attempt to take his totem away from him.

It was during this exchange that Wenq noticed that the woman would never look directly at him, eye to eye. It struck him as odd, because in all other respects she seemed to be very direct and sure of herself.

She had gone back to rummaging in her basket, and from near the bottom of it she drew out a bulging, tightly woven pouch. From that she scooped out a handful of a greasy, smelly substance that she slathered onto Wenq's bare left arm and hand. As she rubbed and kneaded the concoction into his skin, his muscles and sinews began to burn and clench, and his bones ached horribly. He clenched his jaw to keep from crying out. It was agony, until he realized that it was actually a *good* thing that he could feel the pain. His arm and hand — they were no longer numb!

274

While the woman worked silently on his hand and arm, it seemed to Wenq that tendrils of flute music hovered all around them, but he could not find their source. He looked several times at the bag of flutes hanging on the post, but those flutes were always still and silent.

The woman seemed to know exactly how much of the ointment to use, and how much rubbing and kneading his arm and hand required. When she was done, she stopped abruptly, stood up and stepped aside. "Go," she said simply, and gestured at the door. This time Wenq understood her word because it was virtually the same in his own language.

Wenq did want very much to rush away. But he knew he should not leave without thanking the old woman.

He did so, thanking her sincerely for allowing him to warm himself by her fire, and especially for curing his arm and hand with her ointment.

The woman listened with her head down and her face blank, but her gaze was fixed on his right hand, which held the totem. Nothing could be clearer. She wanted him to freely give her the totem, as a thanks and parting gift. But she was not going to insist on it.

Wenq did not understand where he was or how he got there, but he was fairly certain that once he left he would probably never see this old woman again. So whatever he chose to do now, would be his final contact with her.

He opened his right hand and with the fingers of both hands he rubbed over the contours of the small carved fawn. It was not lost on him that he could feel the totem with the fingers of his left hand only because the old woman had healed it.

He was humbly grateful to the woman for healing his arm and hand, but he had nothing else to give her in return that she wanted, except for the little totem.

But how could he part with it? It was the most sacred possession of his family, passed down through countless generations, its carving worn by the reverent fingers of his ancestors before him, and oiled by their hands. It had been entrusted to him. And besides that, he needed it to represent the south fawn wind in Nika's big attempt to trap the huge snake.

He could see in his peripheral vision that the old woman was shaking her head vehemently. It was as if she had read his last thought and was disagreeing with it, just as she had before when he tried to explain that part of his need for it to her. He looked up at her. She did not meet his gaze but she said, "Belongs," and solemnly crossed her arms across her chest. Wenq understood this word of hers as well, but was not sure what she meant by it. How could it be that his family's totem belonged here with her?

The flute music trilled more urgently; time must be running out. He had to decide now about the totem, once and for all.

He felt bound to keep the totem, for his family's sake. But then he thought of Nika, who had come into his world with no possessions at all, and didn't seem worse off for it. With a wrench he decided that his family did not really need the totem, that his family could make its way without it.

After that he understood that he no longer needed to possess the totem to be able to represent the south fawn wind. Having it with him had helped him before — it had given him confidence. But now he could agree with the old woman's adamant head shake. At least here and now, he thought he could shout the fawn's part without having the totem in his hand.

Stolid, cautious Wenq took a great leap of faith, hoping it was the right choice. He stepped up to the woman and with a bow he put the totem into her hands, telling her he wished her to have it on behalf of himself and his family.

She accepted the totem, quickly slipping it into a bag on her belt. Then her hands closed over his, and a chuckle rose from deep in her chest as she tipped her head toward Wenq.

Wenq was aware that if he looked at the woman's face now he

would be eye to eye with her, but suddenly he sensed that he should avoid that. Something warned him that a direct look could be lethal.

Chapter 44

The woman shrugged a cloak she'd been wearing off her shoulders and nimbly stepped to where an assortment of racks and hoops leaned against a wall. She selected a large thin hoop and came back to where Wenq was standing, all the while muttering words in a sing–song. Her every movement was swift and the set of her face was eager and determined. She set the hoop on the ground beside the fire pit and motioned Wenq to hurry up and step inside it. As soon as he did so she stepped inside it too and pulled him to her. Even so it was a tight fit for both of them within the hoop's circle.

She snapped her fingers and the hoop rose rapidly. By the time it cleared their heads they were no longer in the woman's home beside her fire. They were on the Face beside Nika, within Nika's vine hoop. The snake loomed overhead, despite the din of flute, roars, howls, shrieks and bleats. Wenq only had time to notice that a small fawn stood bleating in his former place on Nika's south side, before a violent storm gathered overhead from nowhere. Wind and torrents of rain beat down on Wenq. Or was it the old woman's strong arm that pushed him down, and did he hear her say, "Stay" in between the violent gusts of shearing winds?

He hunkered down and watched as the old woman grabbed her hoop, which was hovering above her head, and stepped out of the circle of Nika's vine hoop.

Both the woman and her hoop grew to an enormous size as she took that step. Vivid lightning split the sky from end to end and earth–shaking thunder drummed the Face. The snake reared back from the enormous woman, hastily uncoiling itself.

The woman said a word that was lost in the winds but it caused

Tehwe, the three wolf shapeshifters and Pani to instantly cease their vocals and scramble to join Wenq inside the circle of the vine hoop. There was barely enough room for all of them. Wenq stood up, the better to accommodate the wolves and Pani. Tehwe brought Wenq close against his great body and Wenq thought, somewhat wildly, *It is always the bear that is most protective of the fawn.*

It seemed to Wenq that the world outside the vine hoop went mad. The only relatively sane thing in it was Nika, beside them, still plying away on her flute — a different tune now, one still filled with a trenchant 'Come, come,' but sounding wild trills and sobbing hollows. Wenq wondered how she could stand upright in the storm, but then noticed that the lashing rain and buffeting winds barely touched her.

Lightning flashed, illuminating the snake and weird giant apparitions against the dark seething sky. The snake darted its head back and forth, avoiding the old woman's feints at it with her hoop. She and the snake were ringed by a great shadowy bear that paced through cold winds driving in from the north, while a giant wolf wove with dark hunting eyes among the winds of the west, and a huge panther chuffed blasts of wind at them from the east. The fawn in the south, grown very large, had its soft breath whipped away by the others' stronger winds. Overhead the lightning lit up enormous, raven black wings of two birds so large that in their violent swift wheeling they seemed at times to fill the entire sky.

The old woman spoke another word into the storm. Lightning became almost continuous and, before the sound of the woman's word eddied away, another giant strode up — a gaunt man so tall that the tallest trees in the forest only reached his ankles. In the strobing lightning Wenq saw the old woman toss her hoop to the man, while the snake tried more desperately to break away. The bear, wolf and panther winds hemmed the snake in, and the woman herself stood between it and the fawn wind to the south.

The giant man caught the old woman's hoop mid–air and held it out, speaking guttural words. The snake was drawn to the hoop, though it tried mightily to resist its pull.

The giant man shook the hoop and spoke more guttural words. With a sudden dash the snake tried to force its way alongside the hoop instead of through it, but with a rapid lunge and twist of wrist the man caught the snake's head inside the hoop.

The snake thrashed itself against the Face and the forest beyond, pulverizing a huge area of forest, but its anger was in vain. It was defeated.

The winds died down, the rain slackened. With incredible strength the man hoisted the hoop high over his head, one–handed, and with his other hand he took hold of the snake further down its long writhing body. One of the huge dark birds descended and grabbed the snake in its talons, near the center of its length. The man let go and the bird pumped its enormous wings, taking the snake aloft with it. It disappeared into a sky still pulsing with lightning, accompanied by another bird as large and dark as it was. The snake's hawk could just barely be seen, flying up after the snake into the rain–filled sky. There was no sign any longer of a great shadowy bear, wolf, panther or fawn among the treetops.

As the snake was taken up into the sky Nika stopped playing her flute. The old woman and the man turned to her. She knelt and bowed to them. Those with her, seeing what she was doing, stepped out of the vine hoop and did the same.

With a snap of the old woman's fingers the vine hoop rose from the ground and flew to her hand. It grew in size as it flew until its diameter was slightly larger than she was tall.

She spoke to them — it sounded to Wenq like a parting, something like a 'Go in peace'. They all looked up and in the night's fading darkness they saw the man step through the hoop and disappear. The old woman also stepped through it and disappeared. And the vine hoop dissolved, into a soft, light wind.

Chapter 45

Two aeors approached and landed — Honcho Beaver was flying her own aeor and Desag piloted Rahra's. A silence prevailed. Everyone had been straining every fiber of their being, and now that it was over they felt empty and disoriented. It was a while before Honcho Beaver even thought to notify Seek Command that the giant snake had been 'dispatched' — as she put it, with her reassurance that she did not think it was likely to come back anytime soon.

Tehwe and the wolf shapeshifters all reverted to their human forms. Tehwe, into a big powerful man, brooding over his wife's death and angry because he had not yet fully avenged it. Tal, into a tall lean young man, feeling out of place among so many strangers, but covertly watching Weqi, and wishing for the first time that he was not already married. Weqi, back into a gawky girl with splotches of orange and purple hair, but showing promise of a unique beauty when her chest and shoulders filled out, and caught up with her lengthening arms and legs. Rahra, into the quiet, resigned young man he was, not daring to hope that this beguiling young wolf girl would ever see him as anything other than an older friend, or possibly an honorary uncle.

Nika, herself, felt a great need to get away from everyone — from everything. The urge to shapeshift to owl and fly up and away was nearly irresistible. But, being Nika, she wearily approached each of her companions in turn. She was not sure what she should say to any of them, but the words she needed came to her once she was with them.

She put her small hands into Tehwe's. With him she did not use words. In silence she commiserated with his loss, and allowed him to read the depth of her own losses in her eyes.

To Tal she expressed her thanks and advised him to be happy in his family and the rich life that he had. She added, "Have Sirk contact me through Honcho Beaver if Tehwe's child Onera does not recover, now that the snake is gone."

She told Rahra that he was a fine man and a true friend, and that she looked forward to getting to know him better, later on.

When she touched Desag's arm she intuited an image of Desag in the woods camping with a man he resembled. She told Desag that his father had never given up looking for him, and that he was going to be very happy to see him again.

To Weqi she said, "You howl beautifully," and Weqi laughed.

To Wenq she said softly, "Crazy Wenq," to which he responded gamely, though tears rolled down his face, "Crazy owl!"

Pani chuffed when she told him that she was very glad to see him again.

When she reached Honcho Beaver, as globular as ever and ensconced on her custom–made aeor seat, Honcho Beaver told her gruffly to just get in the aeor, that they were going home and would talk later. Wenq and Pani squeezed in and Nika stumbled in after them, shapeshifting to owl with her last reserves. Now completely exhausted, she let Wenq pick her up and tuck her into his jacket, where she instantly fell asleep.

Some Seek aeors landed nearby to offer assistance. They approached the odd group respectfully but bursting with curiosity. The blip for the big scary snake had abruptly vanished from all of their scopes, and Seeks in some of their closer–in aeors reported strange visuals during the tremendous lightning storm. But all of the observation droners had jammed, leaving them without answers to their many questions about what the *heck* had just happened.

Honcho Beaver promised to fully brief them once she got her charges home and herself rested up. But she warned them that they were probably not going to believe it. Even with the destruction in the forest done by the big snake, and the images of it that they had captured from a distance, it was going to be hard for the science–hardened ones of the People to take anything on faith.

Tehwe and Tal declined rides in Seek aeors, but they accepted some constitute rations to take with them before they left, silently melting into the forest.

Desag was asking some Seeks if they had contacted his family yet, and was about to accept a ride in a Seek aeor when a civilian aeor came zooming in. It landed with a hasty thump and Desag's father sprang out of it, crushed Desag to his chest and told him, "My son, my son. I never, *never* believed you were dead!" They went away together, not long after Desag introduced his father to his new friend Weqi.

Weqi hitched a ride with Rahra since they were both going back to the same cantonment.

When all of the civilians had left, the Seeks had their droners scour the Face and its periphery for clues and hints. But the droners detected nothing unusual, other than an elevated level of ozone.

Chapter 46
(Six months later)

It was very early spring. The wolverine shapeshifter Wuju knew his sap ought to be rising, but it was not.

He knew why. It was because he was fed up with being alone.

For many years he had reveled in his near–total solitude, but lately he had admitted to himself that he needed something more than being a wolverine. He needed to spend more of his time as a human, and live with other humans again. He needed to have friends.

But he had been a solitary wolverine for so long by now, that he was not sure how to be human, or how to find a real friend.

As a child and then as a youth he had always been uncomfortable around nearly everyone, including his family — *especially* his family. No one in his family seemed to go to the trouble to really get to know and understand him. No one ever came anywhere close to sharing his unique sense of humor — though he would be the first to admit that some of his pranks had been a *little* too aggressive, a *tad* disagreeable. They never seemed to turn out quite as he intended them.

As soon as he was old enough, he camped out in the woods near his family's pod, rather than live in the pod with everyone else. When his family exhorted him to come back inside and act more 'like a normal person', their exasperation hurt his feelings. He snarled and snapped back at them until they left him alone. Later when he became a wolverine shapeshifter it surprised no one, least of all himself. Nor did it surprise anyone when he impulsively announced one morning that he was 'going nomar', and immediately set off for the forests of the Core.

Nomars usually travelled in small bands, but Wuju was

determined to go his own wild and solitary way. It was with a sense of relief and release that he bid his family good–bye. He never wanted to see any of them again, and he confidently assumed that the feeling was mutual.

Later, after the passage of time, it sometimes saddened him that none of his family tried to talk him out of leaving.

He still felt it had been the right decision. His years alone in the Core had been good years, which he'd spent mostly in his wolverine form, travelling great distances every day. It was only lately that he'd been having a hollow feeling. It puzzled him at first, and then it worried him, because it grew until he felt more empty than full.

He understood that it had something to do with his human side, which he'd been deliberately ignoring for years.

He began spending more time in his human form, and thinking about the emptiness in his life, and wondering if there was anything he could do about it. He still travelled great distances every day, but he ranged further out of the Core and more into the Core's Rim and the inhabited Perimeter, where he was more likely to come across other people.

Sometimes at night he'd creep up on an isolated settlement and watch and listen to the people as they went about their everyday lives. He tried to understand what they were thinking about, whether they were happy or sad, mean or kind. He wondered if he could ever come to like any of them enough to spend time with them, and get along with them. He worried that instead they would all turn out to be like his family. Or worse.

Winter finally passed — an unusually hard and harsh one. But with the coming of spring he did not feel his usual vigor surging back. That hollow, incomplete feeling was getting in the way.

He wanted to do something about it, but he had been alone and wild so long that did not know how to go about relating to people again. He was not even sure where his family was. He had gone to where they had been, but their pods were no longer there. Aspens and birch brush had already reclaimed the place where the pods had once been anchored.

He sometimes thought about his little cousin Áka, from the time when her mother — the most tiresomely prim of his aunts — went to great lengths to contact him, about a year after he left his family. Áka's mother had brought Áka with her to a prearranged place, just so the girl could later say that she'd met him, since he was family. At the time he thought the whole thing was silly, and the way his aunt stared at him made him nervous — and rambunctious. He shapeshifted to wolverine and playfully ran around her and then clambered up the front of her shirt, baring his teeth at her. It should have been obvious to *anyone* who wasn't wound up too tight that it was all in fun . . . he hadn't meant to scare her quite as much as he did.

He had taken to Áka though, in that brief meeting, from the way she smiled at him and then silently laughed along with him when her mother squealed and tottered back from him. Over the years since then, it had always comforted him that at least Áka had gotten his joke, even though her mother hadn't.

* * *

On a chilly day early in the Bud Moon[1] Wuju was aware that an aeor had been following him for about an hour. He was in the Rim in his wolverine shape, hunting rabbit. The aeor stayed above the trees but it was definitely following him, and that irked him. He hadn't seen an aeor this close to him in ages, and he definitely disliked being tracked by one.

He heard a faint sound getting closer to him. It was some kind of droner, probably sent down to observe him, by someone in the aeor. He stopped, his fur bristling, and the droner hovered about ten feet in front of him. He snarled and bared his teeth at it.

A disembodied voice came out of the droner. "Hiya, Wuju! It's

[1] April, usually

286

Áka. Remember me?"

*   *   *

The aeor landed in a clearing near some massive willows lining the edge of a stream. Áka and a boy about her age got out of it. The boy waited at the aeor while Áka approached Wuju, very casual, relaxed and smiling.

Áka? Could this really be Áka? Yes, it was her scent — it had to be her. But she was no longer a child. She was a young woman now.

She seemed friendly, like before, but Wuju worried. *What if now that she's older, she's become all prim and fussy like her mother?*

Wuju was still in his wolverine form, and very skittish, nervous. This was so unexpected, and he was not used to being around people.

Áka knelt down to be at his level when she reached him, and her calm, smiling face and her first words did much to ease his mind. "I've been meaning to come for so long," she said quietly. "Ever since I first met you, I've wanted to really get to know you, and be friends, cuz."

She was carrying some loose clothes for him and a blanket, in case he wanted to use them. "Clothing — covering — optional," she assured him. "Whatever you're comfortable with, Wuju, is fine with me."

He shapeshifted to his human form and fingered the clothes curiously, but he chose the blanket. It felt odd to be wearing anything, but at the same time it felt comfortable to have the blanket buffering him like fur in the chill air. Áka nodded and tucked the clothes away. "Let's sit in the sun," she suggested. "There's so much I'd like to hear about, and tell you about."

Wuju glanced back at the boy waiting by the aeor.

"Desag will join us later," Áka said, "if it's alright with you."

"Is he your . . . your . . ." Wuju was not used to talking. He formed the words awkwardly, and he couldn't think of the word for a boyfriend.

"We're just friends," Áka told him. "Good friends — friends for life. We got to know each when — when we were in a trap together, Wuju, that we had to escape from. I'd — we'd — like to tell you about it. But first I'd like to hear about how you are doing, and maybe catch you up a little on family."

* * *

Áka was relieved to find her cousin Wuju's spirit much as she remembered it, though he seemed subdued now and his eyes were much more anxious than she remembered them being before. She understood right away that he was lonely, but also very shy and unsure of himself. Slowly, carefully, she did her best to reassure him. She wanted him to know that she was fully committed to being his fiercely loyal friend.

She had not undertaken this lightly; it was no idle whim. She had consulted long and thoroughly with her mother and her two closest friends — with Desag and Weqi, about how to ease the way for him, after his years apart in the wilderness.

They had given her a number of helpful suggestions. Her mother had long since gotten over Wuju's scramble up the front of her shirt. And she had lost a lot of her prissiness in the intervening years. She was actually very observant, and she understood and cared about Wuju much more than he realized.

Desag's suggestions were more about the timing for the meet– up, and some of the finer points of how a guy's mind might work differently than a girl's.

Irrepressible Weqi filled Áka in on how Wuju's shapeshifter mentality would affect the way he saw things. And Weqi was the one who got Honcho Beaver to hack in on the location of Wuju's ID chip. "For which I owe her so big time," Weqi groused, not very convincingly.

After that it was only a matter of a few weeks before Wuju's ID chip showed up on a Rim monitor. Then Áka and Desag were able to track the wide–ranging wolverine well enough to go in an aeor to meet with him.

A laugh gurgled up Áka's throat and her eyes sparkled. "Remember when you climbed up mama's shirt? That was so *funny!*"

Wuju laughed too, though his laughter had an odd sobbing catch to it that surprised and embarrassed him.

Áka didn't seem to notice it. "But there's more," she continued. "Because you know what mama says now? She *says* that if you ever do that to her again then she'll be ready for you. She's going to bare her teeth right back at you!"

Áka was already laughing, and the image of Áka's mother baring her teeth at anything was hysterically funny to Wuju. They both laughed until tears leaked from their eyes, and they had to catch their breath. To Wuju's relief, his laughter no longer sobbed.

And suddenly the spring sap surged in Wuju, filling up the hollowness. Because surely, if this girl cousin could laugh with him like this, then there *had* to be — there just *had* to be — others out there as well. Possibly Áka's mother, or even this friend of Áka's, this Desag fellow. The sun was shining and he was so glad to be alive. And to have a true friend . . .

Chapter 47

During the year following the capture of the giant snake by the Earth Mother and her grandson the Good Twin, the great slab of rock called the Face was left, for the most part, free of human presence. It existed as it always had, weathering imperceptibly under cycles of sun, rain and snow. Other than the occasional nomar band crossing over it on its way somewhere else, there were a few visits by the Nation's investigators, scientists and archival Fire Keepers. They came in their aeors from time to time and walked over it, trying to absorb something from it because 'this is where it was said to have happened' — 'this is where the most incredible of the events connected with the giant snake took place.'

They stood on the Face's weathered rock, mulling over the story told by 'those there', as the witnesses had come to be known. None of the Nation's advanced recording devices had captured any close up images to prove or disprove what the witnesses said. And most of the physical evidence could have other plausible explanations — except for those massive trails of destruction winding through the dense forest. What, other than the giant snake of the 'those there' accounts, could have crushed and flattened everything in its path, including stands of such tall, stout trees?

With little to go on other than the accounts and those strange winding trails, they came to the Face, where they wavered between belief and disbelief. Most of them left with essentially the same convictions that they had come with — either skeptical, or believing, in part or in whole. There was nothing there to change their minds — nothing other than an expanse of rock which, as large as it was, was only a small scar on the forest's dense, lush, teeming growth.

During the first few weeks after 'Snake Night', as the night of the capture of the giant snake was dubbed, physical evidence and 'those there' accounts were meticulously and exhaustively gathered and analyzed. In the planning and coordination of this work, Honcho Beaver's preferences were deferred to, because she was the one who had been instrumental in breaking open the renegade kidnappings. The Nation also respected that this was, after all, one of the purposes for which Honcho Beaver and the other e–animals had been constituted — to provide generation–spanning wisdom and perspectives for the People.

There was an unusually high degree of coordination, with investigators, scientists and Fire Keepers working together nearly seamlessly.

Within a few months a comprehensive report was released, and the Nation learned that a charismatic man had led a small group of followers calling themselves The Chosen, who believed they were going to eventually take over the Nation. They kidnapped children and youths to work for them in a large cave hidden deep in the Core. They succeeded for a while because an exceptionally good hacker among them erased all system traces of their crimes. Ultimately though, an even more talented hacker broke into the hacks and, in coordination with Seek, zeroed in on the renegades, rescuing the kidnapped children and youths who were still alive.

Up to this point in the report there was nothing to strain the Nation's understanding. Insurgencies were not unheard of. But the report proceeded matter–of–factly to describe a giant snake (approximate dimensions — impossibly — about 90 feet long and twelve wide), and an owl shapeshifter from another time that had fallen from the Sky World and played flute tunes that drew the snake irresistibly to her. Large shadowy giants also came, captured the snake and had a thunder bird take it back to the Sky World.

In this part of the report qualifying statements appeared, to the effect that, 'Physical evidence neither supports nor disproves witness accounts.' And with respect to the flute tunes, it was simply stated that 'recording devices were onsite but failed to record them', and 'the shapeshifter steadfastly refuses to play the tunes for them, maintaining that they are sacred.'

The report proceeded to exhaustively document the events leading up to 'Snake Night', and then the events of that night, in the same matter–of–fact manner. Regarding what occurred on the slab called the Face, 'all sensory equipment failed to record anything', which by itself was unprecedented and defied all logical explanation.

The Nation had a tradition of issuing its reports with a maximum of source material and objective analysis, and a minimum of conclusions. The mantra was: 'Release the information without bias, and let those interested form their own conclusions.'

It certainly was an unusual report — very likely a 'once in a millennium' one for most who took interest. It received its full share of doubters and scoffers, proponents and enthusiasts, and those who were uncertain, bemused or confused by it.

Quite a sensation at first, the hubbub eventually died down, and 'those there' breathed a collective sigh of relief. All of them had told what happened to the best of their ability — even Tehwe, Tal and others of the nomar band allowed themselves to be interrogated — once — by some intrepid investigators and Fire Keepers who tracked them down in their travels through the Core.

The 'those there' stepped back from the wave of public attention that crashed down on them when the report was released — all except Weqi who at first rather enjoyed the prying curiosity, and some of the fawning by a few sycophants. But even she became satiated within a few weeks, and longed with the others for their lives to return to normal.

Chapter 48

After the report was issued, most of the Nation moved on from it rather quickly. But there was a dedicated group whose interest was more enduring. Among them were a number of the Nation's leaders, shamans and Fire Keepers; it was they who requested that a commemorating ceremonial be held at the Face, approximately one year after the seminal 'Snake Night'.

Thus it was that a fleet of large aeor transports silently converged on the isolated Face late one afternoon in the Fat Moon.[2] Just as silently, Tehwe and his entire nomar band filtered out of the forest on foot.

The sky had been a crystal–clear blue dome all day, and the night promised to be fine and unusually mild.

All told, there were nearly four hundred of the Nation who came. All of the 'those there' came, along with their family members and close friends. The rest included a range of chiefs, clan leaders, shamans, scientists, teachers, Fire Keepers, a contingent of Seeks and sundry others.

The families of some of the lost children also came, as part of honoring their memory.

Not all of those who came were believers — in fact quite of few of them had at least some doubts, particularly of the events of the 'Snake Night'. However, they came not to question or argue, but to take part in the ceremony.

Under the direction of the event's formidable organizers, a security perimeter was established, and the transports were unloaded.

---

[2] October, usually

Everyone busied themselves with preparations for the ceremony, including a plethora of pop–up shelters and cooking stands. Gradually a murmur of voices filled the Face, punctuated more and more often by an excited shout of recognition from a friend, or by a rippling exchange of laughter.

Tehwe's band kept apart at first. Their lives were so very different from the non–nomars, and Tehwe disliked the press of strangers' curiosity. He also did not want his band to be tempted — any more than it already was — by the lure of modern Nation life — the endless array of convenient gadgets brought here, and the references to the pod homes with their safety and comforts, and the conveniently free and plentiful food, clothing and other supplies.

Sirk the 'Gadget Guy' was the first to slip away to mingle with the non–nomars. Then little Onera broke from the band and made a dash for Nika and the Kah family.

Onera had spent several months with them. Not long after 'Snake Night' Honcho Beaver relayed a message she received from Tal, via 'Gadget Guy': Onera no longer had to be racked but, as Tal put it, "Her mind is twilight. She pines. She will not eat."

Nika went right away in an aeor and played her flute for Onera — quiet, subtle tunes, like those she had played to help the Meadow Woman rest at night. When Onera showed some feeble response to it, Nika convinced Tehwe to let her take Onera away with her for a while, to Honcho Beaver's pod. She would continue to play her flute for the child, to try bring her mind back gradually, in small, quiet increments.

If it had been anyone other than Nika, Tehwe would have flatly refused, even though he could plainly see that his child was wasting away. As it was, he insisted that Onera's exposure to modern things be kept strictly to a minimum, and that she be returned to him at the earliest possible moment — certainly no later than midwinter.

A long difficult month followed for Nika and Onera. Nika's flute music gradually soothed and drew Onera to her, enough that she was willing to eat again, though she did so without interest.

Once Nika lessened the snake's hold over Onera, she tried to gradually reduce her own hold over the child, which to some extent only replaced that of the snake's. She subtly changed the melodies she played, from those that she knew drew the child, to ones that were similar but had a weaker 'pull'.

In this she received some unexpected help from Wari, Wenq and Weqi's mother.

Nika had been visiting Wari at her pod frequently, once they were properly introduced. Wari was striving to become less dependent on medications, and Nika's presence was like a soothing balm. She was drawn to the young woman by her many kindnesses.

One day when she'd been told that Nika could not come to her that day, she ventured out on her own to visit Nika at Honcho Beaver's pod. Nervously she set out on the old path in the woods and went along the beaver trails through the marsh, arriving while Nika was playing her flute for Onera.

Usually Nika made sure that only Onera, Honcho Beaver and Pani were around when she played her flute for Onera. Honcho and Pani both told her they found it soothing, but Nika was not sure how others might be affected by it.

Wari was drawn powerfully to the music, and since she was musical herself, she was able to explain to Nika what parts of it had the strongest pull. Together they dissected its flows, and from then on Wari became essential in Onera's healing. Before long Onera became more receptive and engaging. Soon she was comfortable prattling with both Wari and Nika.

It was a wrench for the three of them when Onera was returned to her father, Tehwe, not long before midwinter. Nika and Wari took her to him in an aeor; by then Wari was much less dependent on her medications and was getting out more and more often.

Onera searched plaintively for her mother, even though Nika and Wari had prepared her for her absence. But she was very happy to be with her father and the rest of her family again. She wanted Nika and Wari to stay, and to live with her in the band, but they assured her that they would visit from time to time, and that they would stay with her this time until she fell asleep. Overall she adapted to the changes like the brave little girl that she was.

In the aeor on their way home, Wari and Nika cried over the sadness of parting from Onera. They had both become very attached to her in their few months together.

Wari came further out of her shell after that. She had not been told about Wenq and Weqi's abduction until after they returned home, for fear of making her frantic and deepening her depression. In consultation with her healer, her children told her what happened to them, and Nika told her about her unusual life thus far, little by little.

When Wari knew all, she was appalled to have been so lost in her meds, that she was not aware of her children's ordeal until it was over. But she was amazed by her children's pluck and resourcefulness, though they made little of it.

Wari began to want to live without the buffering meds, so that she could be fully present in the lives of her two living children, and a good mother to them. She still sorrowed over the sudden deaths of her husband and youngest child, but she knew she had been wrong to neglect the living in her grieving over the dead.

She saw how much Weqi had been railing against her absence from hers and Wenq's lives, and how much Wenq had been trying to protect and shelter her while she was so weak. Wenq, she saw, should carry that burden no longer, and he needed to be drawn out of his ways of quiet worried vigilance. Weqi, on the other hand, needed to hear her mother's guiding, steadying voice, as well as to have her firm hand in reigning in her rowdiness.

It was Nika who showed Wari how to manage Weqi's outbursts. Wari had never imagined it possible, but this was just one more surprise rendered by the small young woman who they all — she and

296

her children, Honcho Beaver and Pani — soon came to think of as part of their family. Nika was like a shrewd older sister to Weqi. With a few well–placed words, and even better–placed silences, Nika showed them how to stamp Weqi's blazes out, with the least offense to them all.

Wari and Wenq in particular learned from Nika's methods — so much so that Weqi complained that losing her temper was not nearly as satisfying as it used to be. But in truth, Weqi was glad to leave all that behind. She liked herself better, when she kept herself in check. Now that she was a wolf shapeshifter, and had Desag and Áka as good friends, she was finding much better ways to release her high spirits. And she absolutely loved having her mom 'back' —taking an interest and having a real personality again. She felt wrapped in her mother's rejuvenated love like it was a mantle made specially for her.

Honcho Beaver and Pani looked on and helped when they could, ever thoughtful and observant.

They would always be apart from the Nation, but were fully committed to its welfare. In form they weren't even human, but they devoted their considerable human intellect to furthering its knowledge and — hopefully — its collective wisdom.

Having Nika with them began a wondrous, fruitful time, full of fascinating insights into the Sky World that they now believed in as fully as they believed in the mottled orb that revolved in outer space around an endlessly burning ball of fire.

It had been a year of exceptional sharing with the Fire Keepers and others interested in all that Nika brought into their lives.

Honcho Beaver and Pani were grateful to Nika for patiently allowing them to satisfy their nearly insatiable curiosity about her life. They were grateful to her as well for bringing an unexpected but refreshing level of harmony into their lives. They responded in kind to her affection and love. And they heartily approved of her good effect on the Kahs.

And yet they saw that there was always a part of Nika that she would not allow any of them to reach — at least not yet. They were very observant and long–thinking ones, and they guessed that Nika's reticence had to do with her past losses, from the time she had been born into — the loss of her parents and little brother, and then being parted from that extraordinary shapeshifter Tek, and the women Phebe and Ruth. But not the Earth Mother — the Meadow Woman as Nika still called her sometimes. In fact, Nika had told them more than once that when, on 'Snake Night', the Earth Mother stepped out of the hoop in front of her and then suddenly grew to tower over the Face, so large that Nika was no taller than her little toe — it was then that Nika understood that the Earth Mother always had been, and always would be, her companion and guide in life.

Chapter 49

The one–year commemoration ceremony on the impassive Face
began with talks by two elders, a chief and a clan leader, patterned
after the thanksgiving that opened so many of the People's traditional
celebrations. They dwelt on the common purpose of those gathered
in gratitude to their great spirits. Wild tobacco was placed in four
small cornhusk baskets and burned at the center of the Face as a gift
to the spirits, and to send their prayerful words upward toward the
Sky World.

As the light faded a large fire was built at the spot where the
tobacco had been offered, and the chanting and dancing began, led
by the six who had represented the four spirit winds on 'Snake Night'
— Tehwe for the north bear wind, Weqi, Tal and Rahra for the west
wolf wind, Pani for the east panther wind and Wenq for the south
fawn wind.

The plan called for the 'four winds' to dance in their quadrants,
joined by other dancers who would fan out beyond them. Soon after
the dance began, by an unspoken, common urge the 'four winds'
dancers began to weave past each other in two great circles around
the fire — with Tehwe going from north toward east, Wenq from
south toward west, and the others going in the opposite direction
from their starting points. As they danced they exhorted the crowd to
join them, shouting above the chanting that 'All must join because
the wind must rise.' *Where did that come from?* They did not know.

The circle of swirling, weaving dancers expanded wider and wider
until nearly everyone was dancing.

The dancing went on for a long time, as was fitting. It was very
good, strong dancing, yet it lacked something until near the end when

Nika slipped out of the dancing and, standing near the fire, began to play her flute.

Her melody sent low breathy tendrils through the accompanying drumbeats and the hiss of rattles. Everyone felt the change. The music lit the dancing, and even the best dancers there had never danced as they then danced, never with so much joy and devotion.

And the winds *did* rise. Everyone had to shift back from the fire as it whipped and roared in the wind buffeting the whirling dancers.

And a thunder grew and rolled in the sky, though the night was clear and the sky utterly cloudless.

Gradually the thundering quieted, the music slackened off and the dancers slowed their steps. Everyone understood. Their dancing had been accepted. Now it was time to bring it to an end.

As soon as it was over, those who were recording the ceremonies rushed to check whether their equipment had malfunctioned, as had the recording equipment on 'Snake Night'. They needn't have worried. The ceremony's sights and sounds had all been faithfully captured for the Nation's posterity.

Singing ensued, and feasting.

More talks were given at intervals through the night, recognizing the beneficial spirits and thanking them for all they did for the People.

And then at dawn, out came the netted long sticks, and a hide ball. A stickball game was about to begin.

The two goals were marked on the Face while the two leaders chose their teams. Rahra was one team leader, Seek Commander Katsit the other. Everyone who wanted to play got on a team, because there was no limit to the number of players and both captains took the 'lesser players' — those whose skill level was unknown or, because of their small size or other disadvantages, were not expected to be especially good at stickball. Wenq and the wolverine shapeshifter Wuju were among the 'lesser players' and both ended up on Rahra's team.

300

The team wagers were displayed. Side bets were laid, most of them friendly.

The game began with some broad joking and larking around.

It quickly settled into a quiet intensity, though both leaders and most of the players did their best to keep it from getting *too* intense. At a ceremonial like this one, the purpose of the game was to offer up a spirited game to the Great Twin. It was supposed to be in earnest, but not *too* earnest. It was so very easy, though, to get carried away.

The game went on for two hours. With five minutes remaining, the score was tied. It was still that way when time ran out, so the game would continue until one team got a goal and won by breaking the tie.

The ball went wide into the forest on the edge of the Face. Half the players from each team went in to scramble after it, while the other half ranged themselves to aid or intercept whoever came out of the bushes with the netted ball.

There were shouts and scuffling under the trees, and then — improbably — it was Wenq who emerged with the ball in the net at the end of his long stick. Players from both teams quickly followed him out of the woods. Wenq ran doggedly for the other team's goal. He was so small, and it was so certain that he was going to be heavily checked by the other team's players, that the cheerers for *both* teams cheered him on.

The blockers in front of Wenq reached him at about the same time that the players behind him caught up with him. He disappeared into a scrum of body and stick checks — flailing arms and legs, and long sticks all scuffling for the ball. When the confusing mass broke up Tal had the ball in his net and was racing for the opposite goal. Wenq got up and limped closer to the goal he'd been trying to reach. He was banged up and nearly spent, but wanted to be ready to help make a goal for his team, if somebody managed to send the ball back that way.

When Tal was about halfway to the Rahra team's goal Rahra himself body–checked him — the ball popped away from them both. Weqi was close enough and snared it in her net on the fly; she sprinted back toward the other goal. There were several successive checks, sending the ball back and forth near the middle between the goals, until Wuju came out of a scuffle with it, and ran like the very wind with it. Áka and Desag followed shouting encouragement, unable to catch up with him but urging him on. He was fast, he was agile, and there was a fanatical gleam in his eyes. The other team's captain and two of its best players loomed up before him but he dodged them, weaving past them in such a way that it reminded many watchers of the weaving steps of the night's dancing.

The other team's goal guardian was the only player in Wuju's way. He gave the ball the fastest whip shot that he could. It nearly got in but the guardian flicked it back. Both teams converged on the goal, sensing that this was where they needed to be. The ball went every which way among the closely laboring sticks, then it chipped to the fringe where Áka caught it in her net. She rushed it as close to the goal as she could and spun–whipped it. The guardian had plenty of time to net it but her spin on the ball rolled it over his net's stick and home to goal, winning the game for Rahra's team.

Suddenly it was over.

The feelings of some on losing team were as bruised as their bodies. But there was remarkably little rancor. The leaders and the strongest players from both teams set a 'well met, well fought' tone, and most of the players were able to fall in line with it.

The players left the field together as the morning brightened, many of them limping.

Wagers were settled, followed by a feast, which further soothed the disappointed, and settled down the victorious.

After the feast and some brief talks, the gathering would disperse.

* * *

Nika was feeling that itch between her shoulders. She scanned

302

the sky. No hawks or eagles in sight. She told Honcho Beaver that she would take a flight, and be back before it was time to leave.

"Bad idea," came from Honcho Beaver's keyb. "Stay put. Safer to fly back at home."

Nika replied, "Yes. But I'm going."

"Not too far, Bossing Riddle Girl," came from Honcho Beaver's keyb, as she gave Nika a long stare.

Nika remembered. That was the name Honcho Beaver had used for her when, soon after she arrived back in the Below World, she had insisted on leaving Honcho Beaver's pod, and was nearly killed by Weqi's hurtling aeor, and was immob'd by Wenq.

But she had learned much since then, about this Nation of her People, as it had come to be.

"Yes, not too far this time," she replied with a small smile.

Up in the air Nika as owl circled the Face, higher and higher, until she felt she was flying at about where she was as a person — suspended somewhere high between her past and the Below World as it was now. Fully belonging to neither.

She did not see things as everyone else saw them. She was apart from them, because of the distant time she had come from, and all that she had lived through.

Perhaps, she thought, *the distance between myself and this Below World will eventually close to nothing, or nearly nothing. But I do not think it will ever fully close. And for now, being in the sky like this is where I am most comfortable, and most at peace with myself.*

It has been a good year for me. I have lifelong friends now, that love me as family. Yes, perhaps with time I will not feel as much apart from them.

* * *

Wenq saw a small owl flying high above the Face and guessed that it was Nika. He watched it until it got too high to see, as did Honcho Beaver, Pani and a few others.

He exchanged glances with Honcho Beaver and Pani. They all loved her, and wanted to help her. But they knew that was not

303

enough for her, at least not yet. For as long as she felt she had to, Nika was going to have to go by herself to where none of them could follow.

End of Book 3
And perhaps a beginning.

Acknowledgements and Afterword

I offer my heartfelt thanks to friend and fellow author Sandra Keisling, who more than all others, helped me tame the rough edges enough for this story to shine through.

As well to my family, especially spouse John, who helped immeasurably with edits to clarify and hone the story further.

*　*　*

In this book both Tek and Nika spend some time in the Sky World, the mythical home for the creative and destructive forces of the People. Tek has been summoned there, but Nika is unwelcome until Tek's spirit intercedes for her.

In my imagining, things are not always logical in the Sky World. Events will rarely dovetail neatly. Elemental forces, like the Thunder Birds, are subject to some broad rules laid down by the Good Twin, but for the most part they do as they please. There is goodness and order, but danger and chaos lurk. Largely the Sky World is unknown, left open, to wonder at, be unsure of.

It is not a 'heaven'. In the myths it existed long before the Below World was formed. Some of the people in the Good Twin's knat would be related to him, but that is not gone into in this story. (Knat, by the way, is a made-up word, for a settlement of the People.) The Good Twin's grandmother lives off by herself, as do some others like the snake and his hawk woman. In this story, the snake is a version of the Bad Twin. In the myths the Bad Twin is often viewed as a monster of some kind or other.

Time is fluid in the Sky World. The fact that Nika could spend a few years there, and then find herself 800 years beyond her own time when she returns to the Below World, is part of that fluidity.

Something similar happened in Book 2 of the series (**Nika Rising**), when Tek went with the spirit bear to the Sky World. This was after an unknown passage of time that occurred while he was being healed by the spirit bear. When he later fell from Sky World he

305

found himself a thousand or so years beyond his own time. And yet Ruth met a bear that fell from the Sky World at about the same time that Tek did, and she met that bear roughly 20 years before Tek arrived back in the Below World. The point is, that anyone or anything falling from the Sky World can fall anywhere, both in time and place.

The Good Twin is a benevolent force, but usually he is much too distant to directly aid the People of the Below World. He may provide certain raw materials, but then has no further involvement. Near the end of this book he comes to the Below World when summoned by his grandmother, but only at her behest.

His grandmother is the Earth Mother, initially known to us in the story as the Meadow Woman. She also tends to work indirectly, but in a different way. In the Sky World she usually lives alone in a meadow, but by nature she is more of a sharer, a nurturer. She teaches Nika several powerful things relating to hoops, that she knows she is not supposed to teach her. Why did she do it? She is ancient, inscrutable, with her own notions of fitness. There is no certain answer; she herself might not know why, but she doesn't answer to anyone. She also did not stop Nika's flute playing, even though some of Nika's melodies had a power over her. But that is a key aspect of sharing and nurturing: one never knows what it will lead to, what it will yield. While she and Nika were together, neither of them could know the effects that some of Nika's melodies would have in the Below World, or that a Sky World snake was going to wreak havoc down there. In the same way that the Good Twin cast sacred ashes to the wind, which resulted in a plant that inspired Joseph Pigean in the distant future, his grandmother gave some of her knowledge to Nika, which served Nika in the Below World in unexpected, but needful, ways.

If You Liked It, Say So!

If you enjoyed reading this book, please take a few minutes to leave a brief review on a few online sites where reviews are accepted.

www.ingramcontent.com/pod-product-compliance
Lightning Source LLC
Chambersburg PA
CBHW022021240626
47154CB00007B/2206

*9 7 9 8 9 8 8 8 5 7 3 0 3 *